SHADOW
OF A BIRD

SHADOW
OF A BIRD

D.M. TOLIVER

COUNCIL OAK BOOKS
T U L S A

Council Oak Books, Tulsa, Oklahoma 74120

© 1988 by D. M. Toliver.
All rights reserved.

Printed in the United States of America.
FIRST EDITION

LC 88-070672
ISBN 0-933031-13-0

Book and cover design by Carol Haralson.

My work during the course of this novel
was endowed by the love of my parents,
Doug and Ina Harvey, and the
encouragement of many friends, notably
Steve Heller, Sallie Gouverneur, Myrna
Daly, Debra Mertz, and Kent Mueller.

D.M.T.

For Shawn, Kevin, Kelly

. . . There's no truth about your childhood,
though there's a story, yours to tend,

like a fire or garden. Make it a good one,
since you'll have to live it out, and all
its revisions, so long as you all shall live, . . .

WILLIAM MATTHEWS

Then, we shall be two and distinct, we shall
have each our separate being.
And that will be pure existence, real liberty.

D. H. LAWRENCE

BABES AND FOOLS

"God takes care of babes and fools. That means Sandra for one, me for the other."

1

Patrick Douglas shifted uncomfortably behind the steering wheel of his truck. His long shanks in grayed blue jeans formed an oversized V on either side of the steering column. As tall as he was, he should have been accustomed to sitting cramped, but the feeling never failed to make him fidget, since it reminded him of the way his knees ached the spring and summer five years before when he was fifteen and had grown four inches in five months, as though some physical mechanism had been triggered because his father had left. His height extracted a toll: people expected more of him simply because there was more of him. Still, it hadn't done him any harm — to grow up fast.

"Come on, will ya? I got things to do." He talked to himself. He was sitting alone.

He looked across the street and between the looping letters of the *Stella Ledger* painted on the front glass of the newspaper office. Between the *d* and the *g* he caught glimpses of Sadie as she turned from one side of her desk to the other. Sometimes the end of the *d* framed her face so that she seemed all face. Her black hair blended with the painted letter and set off her pale complexion, her small features pointed up by high cheekbones. She bent to a lower drawer for her purse, he imagined, and he knew it would be minutes more before she was ready to leave; she still had her camera to load with film. Even so, it didn't

3

mean she had a meeting to cover that night; she took the camera everywhere and sometimes she called out for him to stop the truck so she could clamber out to take a picture of some fool thing she thought would make a front-page photo for the next week's newspaper.

"By God, if you don't have some place to go tonight, we're going to have a driving lesson." He was still looking at her, talking to her, even though she was some distance away. "I'm getting damned tired of hauling you and waiting. Just waiting when I got better things to do."

Things he'd jotted down on his "to-do-before-winter" list: separate mares and foals, organize equipment, cut back the hackberry, paint. They were all there on a slip of paper he had somewhere in his bedroom. And now it was October; summer had slipped past him like a big fish in shallow water — something big enough to get his hands on until it was gone.

The idea of a driving lesson had come to him earlier in the day, and when he left home he'd told Josie, "Don't be in a big toot to start supper tonight. I might take Mom out to Lander's Crossing for a driving lesson." Not that Josie ever got in a toot about much of anything. When he left, she'd been playing her organ and singing, and she still might be doing the same thing when he and Sadie returned.

Patrick pulled off his cap, folded the bill along the worn center crease, and eased forward in the seat enough to slide the bill into his rear pocket. His dark hair fell naturally from a center part into wings across his forehead, then feathered with longer hair over his ears. It curled slightly below the band left by his cap. When he was younger, when things like appearances mattered, he had tried to train one side of his hair to lie down with the other. He would bend toward a mirror, roll his eyes upward to study how his hair swept away from the part. A pale line of scalp started somewhere near his crown and extended straight to the center of his forehead. Undeniably, there was something to prevent his hair from flowing in a sweeping mass to one side of his head. "Whatta you expect?"

4

Gramma Rho would say as she watched him brush with a vengeance. "It's your hair all right. Willful."

Now he hardly took time to comb it. He cut the front himself, simply lifted it a piece at a time and snipped it straight across and let it fall where it would, since it would anyway. Sadie cut the back. In good weather he'd carry a kitchen chair from the oak table out to the backyard, and she'd come with scissors and a mirror. She trimmed the back while he watched; it gave him something to do. When she finished, the wind would have blown the loose hair away, dusted the clippings from his bare back and neck.

Haircut. That was on the list.

And *Finish work on the truck.*

Through the front windshield, he could look straight down into the truck's engine. The hood was gone, the fenders removed, the body dented and in need of paint. The thing was a piece of junk, or so he read in people's faces as they drove past. Kids laughed and pointed in amazement, as though expecting the tires to loosen and roll away in different directions. It didn't bother him. At such times, Patrick lifted his chin and smiled back, with half a mind to call out, "You're looking at the perfect moving parts of the Chevrolet engine." The truck ran like a top, started on the coldest days. He'd seen to that. He knew what was important, and in time, he'd knock out the dents in the hood and fenders, bolt them in place, and on a perfect windless day, he'd paint. Then he and the truck would both be in first-class shape. Until then, he didn't mind driving along, glancing down at the fan whirling in place behind the radiator, the belts keeping time, and every valve in sync — he could see that *something* was working right.

When he looked toward the *Ledger* again, Sadie was coming. Everything about her was swinging — her black hair swinging about her shoulders and against her face, her camera and purse swinging from the same narrow shoulder thrust up and forward, her skirt swishing about angular legs that sent her from the curb as though she were striding through tall grass. She was smiling at him in that sort of pinched way she had, the corners of her mouth tipped up without her lips parting. In a shaft of late afternoon sunlight, Patrick saw her body outlined through her clinging slip, the gauzy fabric of her dress. Brilliant orange and yellow flowers. As she came toward him, the muscles in his neck involuntarily tightened.

"You got no bra on."

"I know," she said mildly. "Thelma Jo back in lay-up turned off the air conditioner, and it got too hot. I took the damn thing off at noon."

"Well, get back in there and put it on."

"For Christ's sake, Patrick. Be reasonable. Let's go home."

"When you're dressed." Patrick's tone was measured, flat, and he bit hard on the rigid flap of skin at the lower inside corner of his mouth that fitted neatly between his eyeteeth. He looked at her evenly, the way a poker player with a full house of aces confidently eyes an opponent. The truck door didn't open on the opposite side. Even the window, rolled up, was lodged there.

"You're forty-two years old. You can't go around town like that." He lowered his eyes briefly.

"But I don't feel it," she countered. "And you know I don't look it." Her hands cinched her waist, and she set her dark curls bouncing with a toss of her head. Her blue eyes matched his in intensity; their cheekbones and jawlines, mildly defined, were similar.

"What about Josie, then? You might give a thought to her."

Sadie's sigh turned into a half smile. "Maybe. And maybe a thought to you, you're saying. Did you ever think of that?" Her eyes lifted to his before she laughed. When she turned and ran back across the street, it was clear he'd played a hand doomed to fail.

God, she could make him mean-dog mad! But at the same time, he knew he shouldn't give a damn. What difference did it make whether she wore a bra? Why was it any concern of his? It was. It just was. And it wasn't only the bra or all those fancy clothes she'd bought or the hair job. It was everything swirling past him, leaving him behind as he tried to hold onto things and catch up at the same time. Like the incessant wind that had been blowing all month. He'd be going to the barn, pushing against the wind until he wanted to stand with his big frame solid against it and his arms outspread and his head pressed back and yell, "Stop, goddamn it! Just hold up a minute."

He blamed his father. And his father's leaving. But even that explanation didn't hold. His father had always been in the process of leaving, hurrying to one construction job or another that kept him on the road and away from home. "Allan, don't worry about that fence," his mother would call out as his father tossed a canvas pack into his truck bed. "The kids and I can finish it up." Allan would leave in a cloud of dust and benign acceptance. If it wasn't the fence, then it was the tractor to keep running or mares to foal out and rebreed or hay to put in the barn. As far as Patrick could tell, his father never earned a living so much as tried to find one. Or find something. When Allan left for good, it was as though all the other times had been practice runs leading up to one "good" leave-taking. Then for a time the three of them — Patrick, his mother, Josie — acted as though nothing fundamental had happened. It was amazing how stubborn they were, pretending, until they finally believed it themselves, that they were going to carry on when little of anything remained of what they had been used to, of what they'd taken for granted would go on. But nothing held. The center gave way like custard. Their lives had changed, that's all, and he recognized it easily at times, like now, waiting for Sadie. Sometimes he thought if he could spread time out, sort through the days the way he would rustle in a coffee can for the right size nut or bolt, then he could put his finger on one time, one place that would give one solid explanation — something he could see, get a grip on, pin down, fit together.

Patrick took a grip on the steering wheel to move his frame forward, then opened the door and stepped into the street. He knew he'd made a poor start toward the driving lesson. Whenever he so much as hinted at going to Lander's Crossing, Sadie stalled either out of simple contrariness or an uneasiness because of the truck's manual transmission. The missing hood and fenders gave her one more excuse — it bothered her, "looking down into all those exposed parts."

Even his father had eventually given up trying to teach her to drive. Sometimes he and Allan waited together in the same place as now. "Comma, Saaaadie," his father would say, drawing out the nickname Patrick knew she disliked. Allan kept the truck idling, occasionally tapping the accelerator to rev up the engine and keep pace with his own overdrive. It seemed that any moment might see him off, leaving her behind. In those days she didn't work every day at the weekly. She was Stella's "country correspondent," and she delivered her column, "Down the Hedgerow," on shopping days in town. People called her at home with their personals, club items, and busybody notes that everybody knew long before they read them in the newspaper. But she took the job seriously, despite Allan's teasing.

When Allan's patience wore ragged from waiting, Patrick, seven or eight at the time, began his game of concentration. Staring across his father's arms braced at the steering wheel and through the swirl of smoke looping from Allan's cigarette, Patrick fixed his gaze on the exact spot he expected his mother to appear. At the point when his concentration was as deep as his breathing was light, when he could no longer hear the truck's idle engine or see his father's sharp profile, she came. The feat was magical and amazing. It was as though something of himself had gone inside, found her, and tapped her on the shoulder, his hand pulling at her skirt, asking her to return.

Well, she'd leave now when she was good and ready. She'd take her time. He turned and rested crossed arms on the truck's cab. He saw Stella's square, the park bordered by shops along the four main streets. The capstone of the square was the pavilion that rose like a crown, its dome-shaped roof lifting up to meet lower branches of walnuts and oaks. It was an airy, open bandstand with a waist-high railing around its six sides; wooden steps at one side led to the floor, and the space beneath was enclosed by latticework. The whole thing was painted an alarming sky blue, repainted, in fact, the same color each spring by women in the Chat and Sew Club. The Stella High School band gave concerts there, the First Methodist Church had ice-cream socials on the steps, and more than one generation of couples had planned summer weddings so vows could be said under the peaked roof.

The pavilion was empty now. Even the park had only a few people taking footpaths to one shop or another. High schoolers, wearing letter jackets of kelly green and white and black, their chests strung with athletic medals jangling like gypsy charms, kicked along through the leaves. A few youngsters had left their mothers' hands and taken to swings, teeter-totters, or spring-mounted plastic horses.

Patrick's eye was caught by one little boy doing a jig step up the pavilion's steps chanting a song, a musical scale up, then down. It eased Patrick to watch him. He saw himself as he would have been at the boy's age, apart yet not really missing anyone. He had an urge to show the boy a secret place beneath the bandstand, to whisper to him, "I know where you can loosen a section of the blue slats. You can hide underneath. You can look out at everyone and no one will know you're there." He'd discovered the hiding place during a wedding reception as he was kicking along, scuffing the new off his shoes. He noticed a loose section of lattice on the bandstand. Lifting it aside, he crawled in and set the section in place again. Squinting through the diamond pattern, he discovered that he recognized most everybody by their feet and legs. Right away, he saw his mother in little flat slippers, standing with the toe of one foot locked at the ankle of the other, taking up as little space as possible. When she began to ask for him — "Have you seen Patrick?" — he crouched down, but he couldn't see her face, only Josie's fat legs astride his mother's hip and swinging fast as

Sadie wheeled about. He scooted in the dust, peeking out here and there, but finally her legs and feet were lost in the crowd. Still he heard her voice calling him. He caught her agitation then, and for an instant he forgot where the opening was. Frantically he pushed against places in the lattice until a section gave way and he crawled free, dodging around legs to reach her. He had never gone beneath the bandstand again after that, though he'd longed to.

Beyond the boy now skipping down the steps, Laurie came from the J & J Cafe on the opposite side of the square. Patrick figured she'd gone straight to work from high school.

She darted into the street, giving a wave to drivers to let them know they could slow for her. She wore a calico apron smoothed over her blouse and blue jeans, but the thin fabric of the apron lay plastered against her, defining her figure as though she had nothing else on. Startled, he realized she wasn't bean-pole thin as he'd always thought. Her clothes usually seemed too big, moving along without her hardly stirring them, all slapping legs of jeans and fluttering little ties under her blouse collars. But now he could see that wasn't entirely true. Furthermore, she wasn't just Rudy's little sister or someone Patrick had casually dated, and this new awareness of her made him turn away.

He took his cap from his pocket, pushed back his hair to square the bill above his eyebrows, and considered a reply to what he thought Laurie was coming to ask.

"Why don't you come in tonight and pick me up?"

It was the very question he expected, but he hadn't anticipated her tossing it out like a wild card. She had surprised him twice in as many minutes.

"Sure. I guess so." He wedged his fingertips into his rear pockets and sauntered to the front of the truck. "You working late tonight?" She was small; even standing on the curb, she barely came to his shoulder.

"You know what Friday nights are like in town. With a game and all." She bobbed her chin over her shoulder toward the

10

J & J. Ash-blond curls formed a circle of ringlets around an earnest face, a pointy little chin. Her neck was long and so slender it was easy to catch the quick beat of her pulse throbbing some inches below one ear. Her eyes were gray; she wore no makeup, and she could have passed unnoticed in a crowd except for a natural buoyancy that would have set her apart.

"There'll be a real crowd tonight," she went on. "It's the alums' game." Suddenly she flung her arms wide and gave a spirited twirl on her toes. "People will come from near and nearer." She wasn't the least self-conscious that she might appear childlike. But that was like her. She took pleasure in being herself, and Patrick found it curiously appealing. A lilt, an easy self-confidence, was hers naturally because she took it for granted. She was like Rudy that way, like all of them in the big galloping family of Kieffers. But then, why wouldn't she be, having grown up in a smothering nest of grandparents, aunts, uncles, cousins, all within a hare's run of each other?

"I think it's supposed to be far and near, isn't it?" Patrick smiled down at her and reset his cap.

"But around here it's all the same. Nobody gets very far from Stella."

"You got me there."

She jammed her fists into the apron pockets, which made little knots over her hip bones that lifted the fabric from her body.

"I can't stay," she said. "People are already milling in. I just noticed you drive up and thought I'd dash over and save you the phone call. In case you were going to call later on, I mean."

"Sure. About what time? Ten, as usual?"

"Or whenever. I'll wait." She gave a skip and started across the park without looking back, but at the door of the cafe, she lifted a wave that nearly picked her up off the ground. He brought his hand from his pocket, but she'd popped inside before he could wave back.

When he faced the newspaper office again, his mother was at the door talking to Lester, his suit jacket draped over his broad back, hanging from the peg of his index finger.

Lester Tessendorf. Making plans. That dandy. He still had his tie nipped up to his chin, as fit looking as a clothing ad. If it had been hot enough for Lester to have shed his jacket, it must have been bad.

"Come on, will ya?" Patrick caught Sadie's eye and gave a curt lift of his chin and then came down hard on the inside corner of his mouth. He tried to think of a way to introduce the driving lesson without raking up one of their scenes.

When he opened the truck door and started to get in, he heard her, a swish of silk and a flounce, behind him.

"Guess what? No meetings to cover tonight." Her sigh drew on happily. "No city commission meeting. No school board." She scooted under the steering column, her camera bumping across the seat beside her.

"That gives you a breather," he said slow and easy.

"I deserve it. It's the first Friday night I've been off in months."

"Well, then, maybe we could work in a driving lesson," he said matter-of-factly, pulling away from the curb.

"God, no, Patrick. Not tonight."

"Good a time as any. Besides, you haven't had a lesson in months."

"To hell with it." She leaned over the dash to peer into the engine. "I get distracted looking down into all those exposed parts. That motor. I forget what to do."

"Engine. It's an engine," he corrected her. "And you don't need to worry about that engine. Just yourself."

He left the square and took the road east of town that led to Lander's Crossing.

"Look at you. You're driving straight on out to the crossing." With a huff, she tucked her legs beneath her. "I'd like to get home. Start supper."

"Josie's doing that." His eyes darted toward her, but she had glanced away so that he couldn't catch her expression. "That's not it," he drew out. "It's Lester. You and Lester got something cooked up."

She snapped her chin defensively. "Lester might come over. Later. That's all. We might run into Chesterfield," she finished in a rush.

He bit down hard on the inside corner of his mouth to hold his silence. Ever since Lester had taken over advertising at the newspaper, not even a year ago, he had been moving in on Sadie. And she should have been able to see through him, see that for all his buttoned-down appearance, his flat belly and hips from working out every day, and hair with the shine of a silver dollar, there was no bone or marrow underneath. He was a grown man, forty-five if he was a day, and carefree as a clown.

Patrick had told her what he thought, explained the obvious in round after round until finally they'd come to the unspoken point beyond which they avoided any mention of Lester — tried to avert scenes which always ended in angry accusations for one, pangs of guilt for the other.

"Besides, you may not be the one to teach me," she spoke up suddenly. "Nothing seems to go right when you do."

"There's hardly anyone else. In my truck." He turned sharply at the dogleg turn, halfway between town and the landing. She swayed against the door and came upright without looking at him. "If you could just get the coordination, you'd have it. Driving a car takes no more know-how than that camera of yours."

"The camera's different. That's part of my job."

"You have to learn to drive too," he spit out. "You can't expect me to . . ." Their eyes locked. The only sound was the whip of road beneath them. She turned abruptly and looked out at the passing scene. Telephone poles cut vertical lines into the even landscape.

Patrick pulled off the highway and onto the flat, hard-packed earth of Lander's Crossing, an open space that ran along Mill Creek. Whipped dry by wind, dust eddied into spirals out of ruts left from treads where high school boys circled their trucks in preparation for drag racing into Stella. No one was there now; they had the area to themselves until after the football game that night.

Patrick put the truck in neutral and the two of them sat quietly, frozen for the instant, as though gathering from the horizon separate measures of restraint. Ahead of them, a line of cottonwoods lifted empty branches, tipping slightly into one another as the wind stirred.

"Come on. Just try," he said. "Raise up and come over me."

Her eyes softened with a smile, and she shuffled her camera and purse to the side. As she raised her hips, he scooted beneath her, and a veil of her dress fell across his face. At the moment he touched her waist, he was conscious of her perfume, something airy that he recognized from times in spring when he rode through the pastures — musk rose, he thought.

She gripped the wheel, set her jaw, and looked down at her feet briefly. The engine hummed.

"Start by going through the gears," he said.

"I know. In the shape of an H. Right?"

"Where's first?"

She started to jam the gearshift to the top of the imaginary H. A squawk filled the cab and her hands flew, clutching the front of her dress.

"Put your foot on the clutch, dammit! The gears won't shift if your foot isn't on the clutch."

"You don't have to yell," she yelled. "I'm trying. Okay?" Her voice softened. "Be quiet and let me think."

Patrick bit on the piece of skin at his lower jaw until he tasted blood. Through the windshield, he watched the fan whirling, the belts lifting in place. Their harmony enclosed him, and he relaxed against the seat an instant before he moved toward her.

"Leave your foot on the clutch and put her into first gear," he began again. "You can do it." The gentle arch of her foot rose above the straps of her high-heeled slippers; the tendons in the back of her ankle flexed as her toe pointed over the clutch.

"Give her a little gas as you release."

But this time Sadie's foot slipped and the truck lurched forward, suddenly throwing him against the dash, Sadie against the steering wheel. The engine died.

"I can't do it." She rubbed her forehead, pale beneath her fingers. "I get so tense. What if I hit something?"

"You can't hit anything out here." Patrick swung his arms in the cramped cab. "Turn the key on. Remember, acceleration, clutch. They work in tandem. Like a teeter-totter." He met the tension with a clenched jaw.

With the next attempt Sadie's foot froze, and the truck went spinning across the open field, jarring into ruts and whipping up dust. Patrick, caught off guard, frantically tried to knock her foot from the accelerator and reach the ignition. For a moment, their arms and legs tangled. Patrick's hands crossed hers; he felt her legs under his as his feet sought the pedal. The heels of her slippers gouged his ankles. Finally, his foot jammed the brake, and the truck stopped with a jolt that threw her against his shoulder as he hit the dash again.

"Goddamn son-of-a-bitch." He craned his neck from one side of the windshield to the other. The metal bar bracing the radiator had jarred loose and now sagged, quivering to one side.

He wasn't conscious of Sadie until her dry-eyed sobs brought him to her. She sat frozen at the wheel, her knuckles protruding across the backs of her hands. Spasms ran through her shoulders and neck, until even her teeth were chattering.

Anger, clearly defined now, welled within him, and he made no attempt to hold it back. "There's no reason you can't learn to drive this truck."

She trembled, breathing in short panting strokes.

His anger mounted, but none of her own surfaced, and he grabbed her shoulders and wrenched her around. "Don't cry. I don't want you crying." His fingers sunk into flesh until he felt bone. "You think I'm going to stay here forever. I'm not." He shook her with each word. "You gotta know I'm not." Her face, turned from him, nodded back and forth without expression.

15

Then rising like a swimmer to the surface of water, she inhaled deeply and pulled away.

"Take your hands off. Don't shake me." Her eyes narrowed, hard as river stone. "If you want to leave, just leave. Pack up your goddamn truck and take off. I never asked you to stay."

"Where was I to go? Where were Josie and I to go?" His voice raised, then imperceptibly softened.

She eased slowly around until her eyes found the cottonwoods again. "You could have gone with him." She slumped her arms across the upper arc of the steering wheel and rested her head; her thick hair fell in tangles about her face.

He leaned against the seat, suddenly tired, all anger drained away. "I couldn't have gone with him. I'd never leave like *that*."

Through the windowpane, the one he had yet to fix, he saw that the golden dusk had been sucked away with the sun. A seam of gray night sky split open before him. How could he hope for her to understand when to fathom it himself seemed impossible?

Silently he watched Ralph Kieffer, Laurie's father, move about near his barn far down the road, a slight dark figure highlighted against the white backdrop of the building. He had begun chores, and from one hand he purposefully swung a bucket back and forth, back and forth. Patrick thought of Josie at home moving about the horses' stalls, tossing hay from the upper loft, filling grain bins. It came to him that probably all of life was beyond comprehension except the accustomed sequence of everyday chores, the reliability of engines. Back and forth. Up and down.

He heaved himself up from the seat. "We've got to fix the post behind the radiator before we can drive home. Move out." His hands brushed the air between them. From a metal box in the truck bed, he lifted wrenches, pliers, a length of baling wire.

"Get the flashlight from the glove box," he told her.

Kneeling on the ground in front of the truck, he lifted the

sagging radiator. She stood beside him with the heels of her slippers slowly sinking into the dirt and her dress dusting against the engine, at times leaning over him, the curve of her body following his shoulders, the single beam of the flashlight she held following his hands.

2

They drove home in a grateful silence. When Patrick reached the county road where gravel kicked up under the rear fenders, he caught a glimmer of kitchen lights through stark-bare tree branches. He turned on the road to home, rumbled across the trestle over Mill Creek, and sped the half mile or so to the house.

The outside pole lamp, as tall as the big frame house itself, suddenly illuminated the yard. Josie had heard the approaching truck; he could see her head framed in the kitchen window. The bay window, protruding from the living room, held flecks of light, and from there, light fell across the awkward old cedars that hung together near the front, with clumpy shrubs extending along the base of the house. Front and back porches seemed to offer some balance to the arrangement. Halfway between the porches, a giant hackberry arched over the roof so closely that the middle branches scraped against Patrick's bedroom window. He had trimmed those limbs any number of times, and still they reached out, scratching a place for themselves against the house.

When he pulled into the driveway, the headlamps pointed up the barn, the fenced paddocks on either side. Needing paint. The barn door was shut and the horses were quiet; Josie had fed and bedded them down for the night. So he took a deep breath and stepped from the truck. It was calm now, in the way the wind had of resting at night, waiting for morning.

Turk was upon him then, curling his body double, whacking his tail against Patrick's knees. Patrick cuffed him gently under the muzzle. "Get on to the barn now," he told him. He grabbed a handful of ruff and noticed how heavy-coated Turk had become. "Ready for winter, aren't you? At least one of us is ready."

Sadie followed Patrick as they went to the house. "Listen," she said and put a hand on his arm. "I'm sorry about the truck. It makes more work for you." He could hear the smile in her voice, and it eased him.

"That's okay. It'll put the move on me to get the hood and fenders on. Before winter."

When they stepped into the kitchen, it was warm with stove heat and food aromas and the bustle of Josie moving about the oak table now set for the meal.

"It's about time," she said. "I've stalled supper about long enough." Her face had its customary gleam as though her cheeks and forehead had been burnished with the purpose of setting off freckles. She flitted from refrigerator to cupboard, but her braid, heavy as rope, remained motionless between her shoulders, straight down her back nearly to her waist.

"Wash up, now. I'm ready for us to sit down."

He and Sadie turned listlessly toward the bathroom, waiting to catch Josie's momentum. Then the phone was ringing — "Oh no," Josie said — and Sadie moved mechanically to answer it, pulling a pad and pencil from a nearby shelf.

In the bathroom, Patrick rolled up his cuffs to the elbow and listened. He could tell within seconds of her conversation how long she was likely to be and if the call meant they'd have to leave again. People called with everything from a pileup at the dogleg turn to the arrival of a new grandchild.

"Just a minute, Annie. Let me get set up here," Sadie said.

He lathered soap up his arms. Nothing pressing. Annie Hibbert with something for the gossip column. Sadie had fallen heir to the column when they'd left Gramma Rho's and

19

settled in Stella thirteen years ago when Josie was a baby. They bought the old Finch place and fifty acres after the old couple retired and moved to Florida. Mrs. Finch was herself a third-in-line country correspondent, and when the Douglases moved in and kept the Finch telephone number, people in Stella kept right on calling in their items for the column. Old Mrs. Manning called every week even if it was nothing more than afternoon tea with Violet Taylor who lived just up the road from her. Women, it was always women who called, began with who, what, and when and stretched it out to a long tale of why and how. Still, Sadie maintained a wry opinion of people's accounts that often wandered into the seamier sides of their lives, and she defended the column. "It's as good a way as I know to put some order into lives," she'd say. "Life is not orderly, but the newspaper is."

Gramma Rho had another explanation: "It's as good a way as any for people to get their names in the paper before they end up in the obituary column."

Josie was leaning against the counter when he returned, with her head cocked for something that sounded like "good-bye." When she decided it was at hand, she took up her dance again in a rhythm that filled the table with fruit salad, buttered peas, and brown bread stacked on a thin white plate. She had quick little movements that seemed to shorten the distance from counter to refrigerator to table. But at times, she could saunter off into her own little world in a way that infuriated Patrick.

"You got chores all done?" he asked.

"All done," Josie said with a nod. "Tugaloo is munching hay in his stall. Chores were easy tonight. Didn't take any time." Her catch phrases came between one turn or another.

In the background, Sadie continued talking and taking notes in her abbreviated style. "Well, no, Annie, I won't put that in," she said.

"What about the horses in the pasture?" Patrick turned back to Josie.

"All there. Fifteen including foals." She leaned toward him

emphatically. "See, I even counted. Now stop worrying and sit down."

"Honestly," Sadie sighed and hung up the phone. "Annie and Fred can't seem to get Betsy clear of the nest. She's never gotten along with that husband of hers — except to have four kids. Everytime they have a spat, here she and the kids come for a visit. 'A visit,' Annie calls it. An extended visit. 'Betsy Palmer and her four children,'" Sadie lifted her voice in modulated tones as though she were reading from a newspaper, "'will be here for an extended visit with her parents, Mr. and Mrs. Fred Hibbert. Unfortunately, Mr. Palmer was unable to come.'" Mischievously, she wagged her shoulders and with a smirky grin slid into her chair beside Patrick.

Josie laughed at her. "But you won't put *that* in. Come on, your supper's getting cold."

"I'm not very hungry." Sadie took only dabs of this and that and then moved them around her plate. "I think I'll just shower and change clothes."

"But you haven't eaten anything," Josie began, "and there's fruit salad here. And chocolate pudding still in the fridge."

Patrick glanced up quickly at Sadie, but she deliberately looked away.

"None for me." Sadie shoved back from the table. "I'm not about to lose twenty pounds and gain it all back."

"Mom, you look terrific." Josie leaned forward as though to add weight to her words. "You don't need to worry about that. You nearly fit in my blue jeans."

"Nearly is not close enough until I lose ten more pounds." She stretched her arms above her head and slowly lowered them until her nails combed her hair back from her temples. Her hair was unnaturally black and he knew she dyed it; the remains of the filmy plastic gloves and the tiny bottles she used were tossed in the wastepaper basket in the bathroom they all shared. Her fingers made wide parts above her ears, and the tiny gold studs, like rounded nailheads, stood out against her lobes. It was all because of Lester, even the earrings. Hadn't the

21

two of them been shopping one day and stopped right there in the middle of the Chesterfield mall, where Lester had coaxed her to have her ears pierced? He recalled the episode as one of their bitterest scenes.

Patrick placed his knife and fork across his plate and snapped his jaw tight with a resolution to remain quiet.

"Guess you'll have to eat two bowls of pudding instead of one, Patrick," Josie said after Sadie left. The sound of bath water running and Sadie's dresser drawer sliding open filtered into the kitchen.

Josie's face was softened by a feathering of red curls never caught with her braid. Her eyes were a deep blue — "Irish blue," Gramma Rho called them.

He shook his head stoically and tilted back on the rear legs of the solid oak chair where he swayed as he braced his feet against the pedestal.

"We'll have pudding tomorrow then. It'll still be good." She picked up a cheery tone, as though she might have been assembling a picnic.

He brought his chair down so that the front legs whacked against the floor. "She won't eat tomorrow either. Won't even be out of bed until noon. And then all she'll want is black coffee. That's what happens every time she has a date with Lester."

"Oh, Patrick, don't be so hard on her." Josie sighed wearily, approaching something better avoided, and began to clear dishes from the table. She eased against the counter, her back to him, her gaze focused on some point of light she might have caught in the darkness beyond the window.

"Hard on her. Jesus God, Josie. You just shut everything out. Even you ought to be able to see that she and Lester . . ."

"Okay," Josie interrupted. "So she and Lester go out once in a while. So she buys a few new clothes. You don't expect her to go around in the old stuff she had, when Lester always looks like he stepped out of a bandbox. Lester's not so bad, if you'd give him half a chance."

"Josie, you're too trusting."

"Trust comes through Jesus, Patrick." She faced him with a hand set resolutely on her hip. "There's a peace with Jesus that you'd do well to find. Talk about shutting out. You're the one who refuses to let Jesus come into your . . ."

"Oh, for God's sake, Josie, hush up that stuff. I don't want to hear one of Old Man Uttermelon's sermons tonight."

A gentle gloom settled about them as Patrick carried dishes to the counter and Josie washed them. The metal hangers scraped along the clothes rod in Sadie's closet.

"Someone's just pulled into the drive," Josie said suddenly. She leaned across the sink of dishes to peer into the night at headlights filling the end of the driveway.

"They aren't driving all the way in." Patrick followed her glance. "I can see someone going to the front door. Coming up on the porch."

Before the stranger could knock, Patrick stepped through the living room and clicked on the outside porch light.

"We was driving along that west county road over there." The man took his hand from his pocket and pointed into the night. "There's a bunch of horses out. Now, I don't know whose horses they are, but one of them is going to get hit."

Behind Patrick, Josie inhaled deeply.

"They're our horses," Patrick said. A cone of light fell across the man's bald crown, the high points of his face and his narrow shoulders.

"I told the wife," he bobbed his head toward his car with the engine still running. "I'm going to stop, I told her. She was all for going on. Wanted to get the kids home, but I said . . ."

"We appreciate your stopping." Patrick turned slightly so that he caught a glimpse of Josie's face, her eyes wide, her fists doubled up at her mouth.

"Somebody's going to come along and hit one of them colts. Valuable animals, I told her." A self-satisfied smile lit his face. "Yours was the first place we seen. I figured they were your horses." The man seemed to recognize then that his speech was taking time, and he made an elaborate gesture with his hand.

"You gotta be off, I know. I'd stay and help you, but Bernice wouldn't hear to it." He laughed self-consciously and dug his hands into his pockets.

"Thanks again," Patrick called after him.

Behind him, Josie stood rooted. "I thought I latched all the gates when I checked the horses. How could I have forgotten?" She wrinkled furrows above her brows.

"You go walking around in a blue fog, that's how come." He took long steps around her. "You can't keep your mind on what's to be done for half a minute. Half the time, you're off at some prayer meeting or playing that organ." His arm swung out to the bay window and Josie's organ in front of it. Sheets of music lay scattered across the top and seat.

"What's the problem?" Sadie ambled from her bedroom wrapped in towels, a terry turban piled about her hair, another snugged across her breasts and knotted beneath one arm. Water beaded over her bare shoulders. "That wasn't Lester, was it?"

"No, not Lester," Patrick said. "Some man to say the horses are out on the far road. Josie's left the gate open."

Sadie puckered her mouth so that her cheeks pushed into plump pink circles. "That's no big deal, Patrick. The horses are tame as sheep dogs." She started back to her bedroom.

He had one arm in a jacket sleeve when he stopped to stare after her. Sometimes he couldn't believe he'd heard her right. As far as she was concerned, horses could run tail-over-hide into the next county.

"We may need your help too," he called after her.

Josie, watching them, gave a jerk to her chin and started through the kitchen. "I'll go by myself."

"No, you're not," Patrick said. "We'll all go."

Sadie fluffed her hair beneath the towel. "I can't go," she said, giving him short shrift. "I'm all wet. You two know what to do as well as I do. Take a little grain and they'll follow like lambs."

He heard Josie take the back steps and realized how little

24

time there was to wait or argue. Even now a foal might be standing stock-still in the middle of the road. He ran from the house after Josie, but as he crossed the driveway, Lester pulled in. For an instant, Patrick stood spraddle-legged in the glare of Lester's car lights as Lester slowed, waved through his window at Patrick, and drove around him. Immediately Patrick thought of his mother, in the house, still wrapped in towels, and he turned in his tracks to go up to Lester, to tell him, "You can't go in yet. She's not dressed. Wait here." But Josie called to him from the barn, and he looked toward her, then back again at Lester, sitting in his red Vega under the dome light. Lester tilted the rearview mirror enough to duck and turn his head to glaze a comb over the neat arrangement of his hair.

When Patrick wheeled around again, the flashlight beam was flaring ahead of Josie's dim figure as she made off around the corner of the barn, and he bolted after her, suddenly conscious of where he was and what he had to do.

He moved ahead of Josie on the path and took the light from her, leaving her carrying the bucket of oats. He ran the light in a great circle around them, in an arc among clumps of buck-brush and low swinging limbs of Russian olive. When they reached the far side of the pasture, he lit the roadside, beyond the fence line, and the beam caught the glistening sway of the horses' rumps as they grazed. The grass was so tall, the horses wrapped their lips around only the seed heads and yanked sideways.

"Hurry, Josie!" Patrick pushed his boot against the bottom strand of barbed wire and pulled against the upper one. Josie slipped through the gap and held the wire for him to follow. Together they eased forward with deliberate care. The horses ate and hardly lifted the lids of their great dark eyes.

"Easy, mare, easy," Patrick said, barely audible. He could smell their sweet hot hides. Behind him Josie rattled oats.

But the mares knew exactly the point to snap up their heads, kick their heels, and spin off down the roadside. They sent the overgrown grass swishing around their flanks like the rush of

25

satin skirts on dancers. The mares bolted so fast their foals hadn't time to bray, only double their legs under them and skitter alongside the necks of their mothers.

"Goddamn 'em," Patrick said. Silently, Josie fell in behind him as they started out again, following the horses, waiting for them to settle again.

Far ahead, twin headlight beams shot down the road, and a truck slowed as it passed the herd.

"It's Caleb," Patrick said, and he felt a slight breeze lift the jacket between his shoulder blades.

"Figured those were your horses," Caleb said as he drew alongside Patrick and Josie. His deep voice was muffled amid an untrimmed beard and mustache. His forehead too was shrouded in near-white hair that gradually darkened as it fell to sideburns and finally diminished to gray strands mixed with the dark gnarled hair of his beard. His eyes held no more color than his faded bib overalls. Beside him on the seat, Sandra reached in front of her father and out the window to Patrick.

"Let me out. I'll help Pat get the horses."

"Sit still for half a second." Caleb put his arm around her and squashed her against his side until Patrick saw only half-moons of light across the milky chocolate of her cheeks.

Caleb and Sandra lived in an A-frame on a wooded acreage bordering the Douglases' horse pasture. They had lived alone for the five years since Natalie, Caleb's black wife, had died during Sandra's birth.

"I've never seen such goddamn stupid animals," Patrick said.

"Well, yes," Caleb drew out. "They're always stupid when they're smart enough to find where to slip out." He nodded with every word or so in emphasis, since his voice labored through a barrel chest and thickset muscles in his neck and shoulders. "Tell you what," Caleb went on, glancing back at the horses. "How'll it be if I drive up where they are and head them back this way easy?"

"It's worth a try. If I can get a halter on Black Judy, the rest will follow."

With a nod, Caleb backed down the road until the beams of his truck lights were narrowed at the horses, yet far enough behind not to startle the animals. In a moment, his silhouette appeared against the lights, square and short, his arms outstretched, relaxed. He might have gathered the herd to him with little trouble. The mares lifted their muzzles, and turning together, they sauntered down the road. Josie kept the grain rattling. Black Judy angled to the bucket as though she had always intended to do so in her own sweet time. Josie held the bucket under Black Judy's nose, and Patrick lifted her head enough to slip on the halter. Then like a caravan, they began the trek home with Josie leading her own mare, Doradella, and the others trailing. Caleb brought up the rear with his truck. The lights flared a long path ahead of them.

When Patrick turned at the crossroads and looked down the stretch of road to the darkened house, only the yard light beckoned. Lester's coupé was gone. Where did they go? The question rose too fast to be shut out. There was nothing to do in Stella, and not that much even in Chesterfield. But Lester had an apartment, and he supposed . . . Black Judy demanded his attention as she snorted and danced sideways, unnerved by the unfamiliar rumble beneath her as she crossed the timbered bridge at Mill Creek.

"Easy, Dory, easy," Josie cautioned her mare.

Looking back, Patrick saw Caleb step from his truck to make sure mare followed mare, a foal beside each. Tugaloo, the stallion stalled in the barn, raised a cry and a chorus of mares answered him. The still night air was split by the ring of their voices, carried back and forth across the open pasture.

As they entered the driveway, Patrick gave the flashlight to Josie. "Give me Dory's lead. You run ahead and check the gates. Check 'em good, now." Her braid kicked up as she ran.

Patrick spanked the last mare's rump to move her through the opening, then he and Caleb rested against the fence, following the pinprick of Josie's flashlight. Sandra pulled herself to the bottom rail and put an arm around Patrick's neck.

"That wasn't so bad," Caleb said. "Sandra and me, we kinda needed a little jollyride tonight."

"We was coming to see Patrick anyways," Sandra said. She smelled of warm milk and apples.

"So we were. I might have forgotten all about it in the excitement. Leave it to Sandra. She keeps me on my toes." Caleb roughed his big paw across her curls. "I'm cutting wood tomorrow. Thought you might want to come along. If you're like me, you could use another load or two before winter sets in."

Patrick studied the mares as they sauntered in single file to the pasture. "I need to separate the weanlings. Get them off those mares. But maybe Sunday would do for that. I know we need the wood."

"I told you Pat would go, Poppy," Sandra said.

"You did at that. Now, hop down off Pat and run get in the truck. If we get an early start in the morning, it means you and me have to get into our beds."

"They won't get out now." Josie rushed up breathless. "I checked gates twice over." She gave a yank to the chain linking post to gate, latched it behind her, and fell in with them as they walked to Caleb's truck.

"Come in for coffee, Caleb?" Josie asked.

"No. Not tonight. Better get home. Put this Sandra gal to bed. She's near asleep now."

"I'm not!" Sandra responded through pouting mouth. "I'm wide awake."

"Like always," Caleb finished, a chuckle and creases pleating the corners of his eyes. "Kinneygarten. Been in kinneygarten two months now, and I'm amazed at how much an old fellow like me has got to learn to keep up with her."

"She's the only little black girl in school," Josie said as they waved them from the drive.

"Well, don't tell her," Patrick said. "Because she thinks color is something you pull from a crayon box. But she'll catch on

28

soon enough now that Caleb can't keep her under his wing."

Once inside, they were met by the left-behind supper dishes still spread across the oak table and the kitchen counter. The sink was full of gray cold water that Josie had pulled away from when she'd seen the stranger drive in. It seemed to Patrick that half a day must have passed since the man — now home with Bernice, his children bathed — had stopped, but when he stooped to glance at the clock on the stove, he was surprised to see it was just past ten.

Josie racked more dishes into the sink, ran fresh water, and Patrick dried as she set them out for him. Sometimes when he glanced at her, he noticed her looking far down the dark road, and he followed her dreamy gaze absentmindedly.

When she finished, Josie dried her hands on the end of his towel. "I'm going up now. You'll turn the lights on for Mama?"

He nodded and looped the towel through the handle of the refrigerator. The stairs creaked under Josie's light step, and the house fell silent. Nothing stirred, not even outside. Turk had gone to his hay burrow in the barn; he rarely barked at anything but coyotes. The horses were quiet; they'd had their exercise. He listened for the whippoorwill that usually started a night song far out in the cottonwoods and moved slowly to the cedars near the house until the melody was clear noted and full. Quiet. The silence seemed deep enough to fall into and to find some cushion of support.

He opened the refrigerator and took a long swig of milk from the jug, balancing the container in his palm. He then wiped his mouth across his sleeve and stared directly at one of Josie's Bible quotations slipped under a magnet on the refrigerator door. New ones appeared every few days. He never read them. He assumed his mother didn't read them either, but Josie stuck them up anyway, as though she might catch one of them unaware. "Food for the spirit," she said, "is as important as storing food for the body." He fancied Josie saw herself as more soul than body and as having more faith than she could see anywhere around her. Innocently, she believed she could take

29

in whatever she experienced and immerse it within, bringing forth something she could live with. He understood why and how she had come to believe that way, yet he sensed the harm of it, though it seemed so harmless. To him, her belief was bottomless as night, as transparent as day. She spent too much time at the Uttermelons', going to church and Sunday school and Bible classes at Stonegate Tabernacle Union. On Sunday mornings — other times too — the union's blue van, the Gospel Chariot, came for her and usually brought her home. She'd been "born again." He hated the expression; it sounded as though she'd left their family to join the Uttermelons. Sometimes it seemed that way, as much time as she spent with them.

At the far wall he flipped off the kitchen light as he turned on the yard light. He passed through the house, dark now with long shadows cast against luminous light that filtered through windows. The square-paned shadow of a bay window lay across Josie's organ. To one side of the living room, the Franklin wood-burner sat where he and Caleb had installed it a year ago. It was an old house, and they had connected the exhaust vents to the flue that traveled up one side of the living room wall, through interior walls upstairs and then out the attic roof. "It's a good thing they left this old flue in for us," Caleb had said. "Makes our job easier. Just goes to show, if you wait long enough, things come back around to where we started." That was like Caleb. He could find a lesson in most anything, and Patrick had learned more from him than from anybody else — even his mother, he thought, or Gramma Rho. Caleb wasn't prone to draw out explanations. What he said came like an afterthought for Patrick to absorb what he could or wanted at the time. Between them there was no tension, no expectations, only acceptance. They could go separate ways for a day or a week, then meet and pick up where they'd left each other with hardly a break in what they wanted to say or do.

Patrick took in the long room, the bookshelves at the end, the low couches smothered in the crocheted pillows Gramma Rho had made that one long spring and summer. Rooms unfolded one into another; the upstairs, even the attic above, made the house seem greater because of its many parts. Still, the house could close in at times, gather itself protectively against the harshest weather. But on sunlit, airy days, with the windows open and screens rattling against a breeze, the house remained serene and cool.

On his way upstairs, the third step creaked beneath his weight, but his secret step, midway between, remained soundless. It did not give him away. The wooden tread on the step lifted to a hideaway beneath. He'd discovered it a week after they'd moved in, and for many years it was his alone, a place to conceal notes and special toys. Eventually, when Josie was older, she found the place, but by then he didn't mind, since he could tell her stories about the house — built when settlers crossed the prairie, he had told her. The step had given them a place to hide valuables against marauders, men traveling west to seek gold, or Indians on the warpath. Crazy . . . crazy, he thought as he ascended to his room, to think that he ever could have believed he could collect things and keep them safe.

In his bedroom, he slipped off his clothes by light coming in the window from the pole lamp. In undershorts, he stretched out with his hands cupped beneath his head, his ankles and feet hanging over the end. He felt chilled but he did not move beneath the covers.

He thought about what his mother had said that evening after the driving lesson. "If you want to leave, just leave. Pack up your truck and go." He didn't want to leave home, couldn't imagine living somewhere else alone. Perhaps she was the one who really wanted to leave. "People change!" she'd yelled at him once during one of their scenes. "Maybe you haven't, but I've changed. I want to do something else with my life." Change, he thought, should be like the seasons, a gradual shading of one into the other. Some things never changed, and he held an allegiance to those things.

There was a time when she never would have forsaken half of Saturday for one long Friday night, but that was before she met Lester. Only last spring, when the mares were foaling, she never left. Late one afternoon, after the three of them had waited all day for rain to slack, he and Sadie had left Josie to feed horses at the barn while they checked mares in the pasture. One mare had been missing.

"She's gone to the back and gotten caught on the other side of the creek," Sadie said. They set out along the bank, searching for a place to cross. The water, channeled between the steep sides of the creek, ran hard and fast. Dead limbs and leaves swirled swiftly in front of the current. When they could find no place to cross, they gripped hands and waded down the incline. Water rushed above Sadie's waist. Patrick struggled ahead, up the opposite bank. When he set his boots into the mire, they held firm. He pulled Sadie up beside him.

They found the mare in a dry grove of Russian olives, the colt beside her and already strong enough to dance around his mother. Patrick slipped a halter on the mare and they started back, Sadie following the colt. When they reached the creek, Patrick plunged ahead without giving the mare time enough for fear. The colt waited on the creek bank pawing the ground, instinctively fearful, but at a touch from Sadie, he bolted. For an instant the water surged over his head. Then he was up, tipping his muzzle above the foam. Sadie was beside him. On the far bank with the mare, Patrick snatched the lead from her halter and returned to the water. With his hands above his head, he made a noose and slipped it over the colt's neck. Then he was out again, slipping back two steps for one, always pulling, keeping the rope taut until he could see Sadie pushing against the colt's rump. His little hooves clawed their way up and out. Through it all, the only sounds had been the rushing water and the shrill screams of the trembling mare. The horses nuzzled each other and bolted toward the barn, casting a shower of mud in their wake.

"Look at you," Patrick pointed to Sadie's bare feet. "You've lost your boots." Her clothes were wet and muddy, and the long switch of her hair hung down her back.

"Boots? What do I care? We got the colt. I stepped right out of the boots and left them in the mud."

"Then they were too big for you," he scolded. "We'll get you new ones."

"Come on, old man," she teased and cuffed his arm. "I'll race you to the barn." She took off running, slipping and sliding along the muddy horses' path. Eventually the rains stopped and the arid wind sucked up the water in the creek. One day Patrick found her mud-caked boots with the soles stuck in the creek bed and the tops crumpled over. But by then, he'd already bought her a new pair.

He pulled the quilt and sheet from the bottom of his bed to his shoulders and turned to his side. Lying awake, he listened for the crunch of tire wheels on the gravel beneath his window, but he heard nothing. He thought sleep was far away, that he would remain awake a long time.

When he awoke later, his room was dark, without light even from the pole lamp. He knew Sadie was home.

What if Lester came in with her? Patrick bolted upright. What if Lester went to her bedroom and folded back the coverlet from her bed? A shaft of anger went through him so fast he tasted a bitter vapor. He felt cold and hot at the same time. The thought had secretly occupied the very front and center of his mind so long now that once asleep, the idea had taken control easily and moved to every part of his body until in one great surge, the thought burst through to him and made it impossible to shut it out. He couldn't stand not knowing, since everything about him now demanded knowing. He lay aside the covers and stood a moment to accustom himself to darkness. His eyes labored to draw in any light as he took the stairs resolutely, trusting his feet to know the feel and sound of each stair tread. What if he found Lester with her? Beside her? He braced his hands along the stairway to keep from shivering. His flesh stood in goose bumps; he was icy cold. If he found Lester, he determined, he would go back upstairs for his rifle. If he found him beside her, he would kill . . . Some light unexpectedly shimmered up to him now near the bottom of the stairs. He avoided the steps he knew would creak, and still feeling his way, he moved quickly through the living room and on to Sadie's bedroom door. He knew what he was going to do now. Moonlight flooded the window and across the easy contours of her body. She was lying on her side, her arm across sheeted mounds beside her. Her leg was drawn up and over something. He was in her room, leaning over her before he recognized the shape of her pillows in the bed beside her. He'd forgotten about her pillows. Within a week after his father had left, she had gone about the house gathering every extra pillow she could find. She piled them in her bed, pushed them under the sheet, fluffed them on either side of her so that no matter how she turned, something met her touch.

Standing over her, Patrick released a sigh from the breath he'd been holding and smoothed his hand along a pillow, pushing it up against her back.

3

The next morning he awoke so suddenly he thought he'd been struck a blow. One minute he was sound asleep, the next he was sitting straight up in bed wide awake.

"Laurie. Laurie. Goddamn."

He spun to the side and jerked his jeans to his waist as though now was not too late to do something. At his dresser, he snatched up his watch. Six o'clock. He remembered drying dishes with Josie and looking at the stove clock. "I should have remembered then. Should have been on my way to town right then." He ran his fingers through his hair and jammed on his cap. "Stupid. Stupid." He'd never completely forgotten about her before.

He took the stairs in three long strides and made a hurried turn around the oak table. It was too early to call her. In fact, any time before Caleb came was out, and once the two of them were buried in Hightowers' hedgerow cutting timber, there'd be no chance.

"Why didn't she call? She could have called me last night." He knew she wouldn't. That wasn't her style. She would have simply found another way home. With Rudy or somebody else.

He'd drive back; from wherever he and Caleb were, he'd come back at midmorning and call her. But on the heels of that resolution came the question of what he'd say. "It doesn't matter what you say. Think of something." And he took

35

another turn around the table. He didn't have much appetite, but without breakfast he'd fade long before noon and never keep up with Caleb. So he buttered slice after slice of toast and alternated bites of bread with slugs of milk.

There was nothing serious between him and Laurie. They'd started dating about two years before, after Rudy's accident. He'd known her forever as Rudy's little sister — not that she was the tagalong kind. She was too busy for anything like that — practicing her clarinet or doing extra assignments for teachers. But when they were at the hospital together to see Rudy, Patrick started taking her home. She was quiet. Not just because of Rudy, although that was most of it. She was never like other girls who had to keep the air blue with giggling, jangling talk. He hadn't realized that about her before they started driving home together, and that fact alone became the trait he most liked. Sometimes he felt she just expected him to read her thoughts as he would fathom the real and hidden meaning of a story from what wasn't written on a page. So he didn't want to drive home from the hospital — she sitting upright in the far corner of the truck looking out at the winking lights of passing homes and shops — and talk about the weather or what she had planned for the next day or even any mention of Rudy. They were both content to listen to the road hum beneath them and say little more than, "Thanks for the ride," or "See you tomorrow, maybe," as she slipped from the truck. They got to know each other through those long silent drives. He always avoided the dogleg turn on their way into Stella and instead took a back road or drove down the main highway a few miles out of his way to get to her house from another direction. Rudy had been in the back end of a truck with five other guys when the driver took the turn at about fifty and snowballed down the embankment. Two jumped clear; two died. Rudy, pinned beneath the truck, remained conscious but unable to move from his waist down. He hadn't broken his neck — just snapped the cable at about the seventh vertebra.

One night Patrick and Laurie were about five miles from

Stella when she broke the silence. "I'd like you to take me by the place."

He looked sharply over at her because he knew immediately where she meant. She sat up away from the seat as though it were too hot to lean against and stared in front of her into the clear night. It was early summer. The windows were rolled down and the breeze kept a constant tug on his hair.

"I don't know, Laurie." The frogs were so loud he could hear them a long way before he reached a pond and for some distance afterwards.

By this time he'd gotten fairly good at scanning the lines of silence between them, and he knew she was thinking that sooner or later she'd have to pass the dogleg turn; she wanted the first time to be with him, not alone or with someone who didn't understand or even with her parents or one of her brothers or sisters who understood too much. That left him. So he drove through Stella and approached the turn just as though he had an errand to run out that way, and he looked straight ahead into the cones of light down the asphalt while keeping an eye on Laurie without turning his head. He knew he could take the turn at thirty-five, no faster than forty; it was nearly a ninety-degree angle in the road. He could just hear that truck-load of damn fools, half tight, their raucous voices bellowing into the night, and see Rudy sitting in the truck bed with his back braced against the rear window. "I thought once about knocking on the window," Rudy had said, "and telling Cal to drop it down a little, but about that time . . ."

Patrick slowed to twenty-five at the turn. Laurie took one deep breath that caught at the end, and then she moved beside him. He put his arm around her, and when he came to Lander's Crossing, some distance beyond and yet not to her house, he pulled the truck in and let it idle. She came to him with a whimper, shivering, trying to choke back the crying. Then she cried. He understood how women cried. He'd been at that point before, and he knew what to do. So he held Laurie and put his face against the top of her head and waited. He did not say anything.

After Rudy came home from the hospital, Patrick and Laurie went out once in a while, or he'd pick her up after her hours at the J & J. There were times, like now, when he wished she'd started dating someone else, as he thought she might by September when she returned for her senior year and he was no longer in school. She hadn't. But then, who could it have been? There wasn't anyone suitable for Laurie, not even him, and he'd thought about breaking it off, but he didn't know how he could do that since she'd think of him as someone to take her to dances, graduation affairs, and he could hardly fade from her picture now. Even so, by this time next year, she would have left Stella for college. She'd probably graduate first in her class, receive any number of awards and scholarships, and eventually move on into the sort of cloudless future he imagined for her.

So he told himself now that Laurie might even laugh when he called to apologize. "That's no excuse," and he washed the words down with milk.

He left Josie and Sadie still asleep and set off for the shed, a lean-to big enough to accommodate the truck in winter with storage besides. Wooden worktables lined one side, heaped with hand tools, machine parts, old carburetors, boxes of nuts and bolts, cans of nails — all covered with a fine film of oil that attracted a moldy blanket of dust. Yet what appeared to be clutter became distinct and singular since within minutes of looking for something, Patrick could put a hand on it. From the tables, all corners were filled with fruit jars, worn tires, garden tools, fence posts, and an accumulation of things it never had occurred to any of them to throw away, since room remained to pile it here or shove it there. Above him, pulleys, rubber belts, lengths of rope, and wire were looped with spiderwebs studded with the white woolly egg sacs and dry bodies of insects. Swept aside countless times, the spiders kept a distance between the length of Patrick's arms and where they began their own housekeeping.

Turk came and poured himself into a soft dirt hole he'd made. His hazel eyes shifted under furrowed brows, his slender muzzle tapered between his paws.

To one side of a table, Patrick noticed the hood and fenders of his truck and almost wished he could stay home and work, but he packed up the saw and a toolbox and set off down the drive to wait for Caleb.

"You can't come, Turk. You might as well stay in your hole."

Without raising his head, Turk lazily waved his tail. Patrick left the shed with a glance to the house. He wondered what time his mother would be up and if perhaps she might start working with the mares and foals, but he erased the thought before it could spin much farther. It had been weeks since she'd even been inside the barn.

Carrying the saw and toolbox, Patrick strolled to the end of the driveway. Far down the road, flannel clouds lay flush with Old Man Prather's barn. He saw Caleb's truck rattle into view before it turned and crossed the bridge at Mill Creek. A hodgepodge from junkers, there was no way of telling what year it might be. Just old. Ageless, Caleb preferred to say, like he was. For all Caleb's wisdom, which seemed to spring unheeded from a mother lode of inherent knowledge, he had a perturbing indifference when it came to his truck and even the equipment from which he made a living. It was what Caleb called a "get-by living for get-by folks." He did odd jobs that other people put off: trimming trees, cutting firewood, yard work, and as little carpentry or plumbing as possible, since he favored the outdoors. He could have farmed the level black soil around his home, and at one time he had. But after he married Natalie, he leased his acreage to his brother Tobias. "Too monotonous for me," was what he said, but there was more to it than that. He and Natalie had married late; they were both in their thirties, and Caleb no longer wanted to be tied to what a season and the land demanded: discing and planting in spring, cultivating and spraying in summer, harvesting in autumn, and overriding all, the ever-present concern of indifferent rain that, once started, seemed unable to stop.

So Tobias took Caleb's ground and never consulted him on anything — just mailed him a check after harvest, which suited Caleb. They had been contentious even as boys, but as farmers assuming rights to their parents' land, they couldn't agree on so much as how a contour should lie across an open field, to say nothing of whether to rotate a plot of ground from beans one year to milo the next. After Caleb married Natalie, Tobias coldly refused any nod Caleb made in his direction. "It ain't 'cause Natalie's black," Patrick had once heard Caleb tell his mother. "It's because she's beautiful. Can't I see what he's married to same as he can? And don't I know what he thinks when he looks at Natalie? What any man thinks?"

Natalie was beautiful. But her beauty didn't count for much in Stella. She was the only black person in town, and Caleb's family tree, with roots back four generations, didn't help her much either. Natalie's friend from the first was Sadie. Sadie taught her how to cook, since she'd never stayed in one place long enough to accumulate a set of dishes or pots and pans. They canned garden produce and made curtains for some of the big front windows of the A-frame, and Caleb offered no objections, even though he said it seemed to him that trees and their leaves ought to be curtains enough. No. There wouldn't have been anything Natalie wanted to do that Caleb would have found fault with, since he clearly worshiped her. She called him "Bear," with a lift of one eyebrow and a lilt in her voice that would have turned the head of any man. Wherever she came from, whatever she'd done, nobody in Stella ever knew, and if Caleb himself knew, he didn't talk about it. Her past became a fiction that Sadie invented and Natalie came to believe. Sometimes the two of them even dreamed up curious little notes to add to the newspaper column: "Mrs. Caleb Burroughs will journey to New York this week to visit her parents, Col. and Mrs. Tyler McGee, who have recently returned from a tour of duty to New Zealand and parts unknown." Sadie was convinced that in time the townspeople would come around, that they would unbend finally, but in the two years Caleb and Natalie were married, few of them had.

Natalie died when Sandra was born, and by the time the baby was three months old, Caleb was carrying her to jobs in the homemade sling that fitted between his broad shoulders. He took only the jobs to which he could take Sandra, and even then he might quit at midday if he felt Sandra needed to go home. People around Stella and Chesterfield considered him unreliable. Still, they put up with the "eccentric old bastard," since no one else could match his superior finish work at a price they never quarreled with. Money meant little to him. He often said it had taken him half a lifetime to "produce a good crop," which he always said with his eyes on Sandra, and he had no time to waste on trifles — making and spending money.

Caleb's truck shimmied to a stop beside Patrick, and he swung his saw and toolbox to the bed.

"I'm going to start fixing up this old clunker of yours," Patrick said as he settled in beside Sandra. "Just as soon as I finish up on mine."

"Whatta ya talking about?" Caleb came back. "An old cur dog like this will last longer than yours, even with all that fancy paint you're planning on."

"At least we're going to drop in a new battery, change the points."

"It gets us from here to there and that's as far as we're going." Caleb's eyes crinkled downward at the corners under gray shaggy brows. He looked out at the world with clear unchanging eyes, and because of his massive beard, he presumed he went along without revealing much of himself. "You start knocking out the rust holding this baby together, and she'd give one big heave and crumple in front of you."

Caleb slowed to rock up over the trestle, and the truck squeaked its resentment; the fenders danced in place. On down the road they passed Redbud Acres. What a hoot! Hardly a redbud remained after Buford Weiscoff and his crew had built homes on five-acre spreads in timbered sections. Weiscoff had bought land from Kenneth Prather that had been thick with redbud and chokecherry — a haven for deer. But the deer scattered as families moved out from Stella, some ten miles east, and Chesterfield, much larger — a city really — thirty-five miles farther still. They called their places "Atlasta Farm" or "Acres A-Plenty," and they traded their station wagons for compacts. They had to have minitractors and riding lawn mowers and posthole diggers and more hours and man power than they had ever anticipated. Patrick could have told them what they were getting into. Any more than an acre meant dawn-to-dark work. His fifty acres took little more time and effort than their five — just more money. But he and Sadie had been able to pick up a little cash as families settled and asssumed rural attitudes. "The kids have been wanting a pony," was what many of them said, and why should he quarrel with that? Sadie had earned grocery money by giving kids riding lessons, and they'd sold a few horses at good prices.

"I know what you're thinking," Caleb said, and his chin whiskers bobbed against the top of his coveralls. "'If you'd take care of your equipment, Caleb, it would take care of you.' I can read it on that serious face of yours."

"That's right. And I've heard you say it a time or two."

"I got no quarrel with that. But the thing is, something is always cropping up."

"And people keep getting in the way," Patrick finished for him. "Like people who have their horses running around on the road in the middle of the night."

"It wasn't that. Wasn't that a-tall."

Sandra took tiny bites of toast and turned first to her father, then Patrick. "Aren't you going to tell him?" she said, her solemn dark eyes on her father.

Patrick glanced over quickly, but Caleb seemed interested in something far down the road.

"Tell me what?" Patrick asked Sandra.

Sandra waited a moment, and when Caleb only began to hum under his breath, she tilted her head up to Patrick. "When

42

we got around this morning, we couldn't find the chain saw anywheres."

"Well, now, we found the chain saw," Caleb finally spoke up. "It's right back there. . ."

"*I* found the chain saw," she said emphatically. She crumpled the last of her toast into her mouth and stuck her little hands into the front of her bib overalls and wiped them across her shirt. "Let me tell it." She leaned sternly toward her father.

"I'm not saying a word." Caleb positioned his hands higher on the steering wheel and looked purposely ahead.

"Underneath the truck," Sandra whispered.

"How in the name of God, Caleb." Patrick whipped his cap from his head and hung it on his knee.

"God takes care of babes and fools. That means Sandra for one, me for the other. When I drove home last night from your place, I never seen it smack dab in the middle of the drive, and I parked right over the top of it." He paused. "Now don't ask me how. I had the damn thing out working on it yesterday, and I must have just sauntered away and it got dark. . ." He nodded along with every other word or so, "And . . . well, you two aren't going to stay sharp as vinegar all your days. Besides, we got a little shower last night and that saw stayed as dry as if it had been put in the shed where it belonged. God takes care of babes and fools. So see there, Sandranna." But his pet name for Sandra had lately begun to stir her to a fury.

"I'm too big for that." She whipped her fists against her father's shoulder, and he cowed behind his arm in mock surprise. "Not Sandy either," she continued. "I'm Sandra, like what Mrs. Dalrumple calls me."

"School makes a body very grown up," Caleb said with a cock of his head.

With that he turned into a dirt road and fell into a pair of ruts with a mane of grass in the center.

"Look there, Sandra." Caleb pointed to a bird perched motionless on a hedge post. Ash colored and small, it could have been an extension of the post itself.

"A chicken hawk," Sandra said, disinterested.

"You better look again. That's a prairie falcon. Smaller than a chicken hawk, much smarter too."

Patrick studied the bird. He could remember Caleb pointing out a kestrel to him years ago. "You won't see them often," Caleb had said. "They can come out of nowhere, snatch up a field mouse, and disappear before you can get your eyes focused." The falcon swiveled its head, cocked a black eye under a white brow, and then rose swiftly, calling once a hoarse *karaka*.

"You didn't look fast enough," Caleb said as the truck slid into a rut, then jarred out and moved down the road.

All morning, as the two men worked, Patrick kept watching the sun, the timepiece he didn't need to wear. He wasn't going to forget Laurie a second time. By midmorning, when he and Caleb stopped to refill saws with gasoline, Patrick said, "I need to borrow your truck, Caleb. Go up to Hightowers' and call Laurie." He gave a yank to the bill of his cap and read Caleb's expression of surprise. "The thing is, I was supposed to pick her up last night after she got off work. With the horses and all . . . I forgot. Didn't think about it until this morning."

Caleb dug into his pocket and tossed a ring of keys in an arch. "You might be in big trouble," he said with a snicker. "And you're worried about my little old chain saw."

"It's not a big deal, Caleb. There were probably ten guys who could have taken her home last night."

"That may be, but if I was you I'd start putting a few nice words together between here and Hightowers' telephone."

Patrick backed the truck; the engine gave a resentful backfire and then settled into its usual moderate pace. He turned a few beginning sentences over in his mind, but no matter what he came up with, nothing felt right. The important thing was to get on with it, and he pressed the accelerator, which only served to jolt the truck into sputtering hops before it slowed again.

At the Hightowers', Mrs. Hightower promptly answered his knock. Slender and dressed in gray tweeds, she matched the cat at her feet. The Hightowers had built a new brick home patterned after those in a suburban tract slowly moving from Stella to the border of their land. Patrick hadn't seen Mrs. Hightower for some time, and now, seeing her dressed like a fashion plate, he couldn't imagine she'd ever spent time in a milking parlor or sat behind the steering wheel of a truck loaded with grain and on its way to town. Her blond hair lay in a cap of soft curls about her face and touches of makeup brightened her lips and cheeks. But then, Patrick knew the Hightowers didn't really farm anymore; they had turned the operation over to a son.

When he stepped inside, his reflection in her tile floor reminded him of his muddy boots, and he back-stepped out again to pull them off. They appeared equally misplaced on her patio, buckled up against her wrought-iron porch furniture.

"The phone's right over there on the desk," she said in answer to his request. "Stay as long as you want. I'm on my way into Chesterfield." She dropped a cape about her shoulders and left with a wave and a swirl of the gray cloth lifting in the breeze on her way to her car.

Patrick tiptoed across the floor, conscious of the silence in the open rooms, stark and orderly. He pushed buttons for Laurie's number and hoped her mother would answer. Laurie's voice was low, unmistakable. He hadn't thought of a thing to say.

"I hope you don't hang up on me," he said abruptly, since it was precisely what he had on his mind. He couldn't hear anything, even her breathing. But he didn't hear the click of the phone either.

"Laurie?"

"I'm here."

"I'm sorry. About last night." Without his boots, he felt

vulnerable as his feet began to chill.

"Okay."

He thought she might have said more. He couldn't tell. Without seeing her, the way she had of lifting her chin or giving a brief jerk to her shoulders, he couldn't decipher what was going through her mind. He realized the silences between them were good only when he could see her.

"After supper the horses got out and" — he paused to consider if he should explain about Josie's leaving the gate open, but discarded the idea when it appeared to imply a shuffling of his own neglect to Josie — "by the time we got them rounded up it was late."

"Too late?"

"What?" He thought it was a question, but what could he make of it?

"It was too late, you said."

"No, it wasn't too late," he drew himself up short when he realized he'd boxed himself into a corner. He hadn't meant to say that, or at least not in quite that way. He fitted the ball of one stockinged foot over the arch of the other. He felt shackled to the phone. "Damn it, Laurie. I just forgot. I was . . ."

"That's more or less what I figured," she interrupted.

"You got every right to be mad."

"It's history." Her tone was cool, hurried, in fact, as though she had other things to do than spend time with him on the telephone.

"I suppose Rudy was there. You went home with him?"

"Rudy? No, I found another way home."

He waited, thinking she might say more, but she only gave an exasperated sigh.

"Well, look, are you working today?"

"Yes. I've got to go now, in fact."

"Maybe I'll see you later on then. Caleb and I are at the Hightowers' cutting wood, and he always likes to break at noon, come to town for dinner."

"Fine. Fine. I'll see you then." The phone clicked. The hum

was deafening. His feet were chilled to the bone.

4

At noon they drove into Stella. Patrick was snared in muddled thoughts of Laurie as Caleb filled the lull with talk of philosophy.

"The thing about cutting wood," Caleb began, "is that it warms you so many times." He gripped the steering wheel near the top, his elbows jutting out, the way a preacher might hold the sides of a pulpit. But his hands gave him away. He had a farmer's rough-cut hands with square hard nails and short stout fingers. "Wood works for you more times than when you burn it, because you work for it. You work to cut it and haul it and . . ."

The shimmy of the truck eased Sandra's head against Patrick's shoulder. When her eyelids fluttered and closed abruptly, he turned her so he could lay her in his lap with his hand cupped at her crown.

"Warms you even before you burn it. We've come full circle on using wood. My granddaddy had an old wood-burner, but not my mother. Had to have gas heat. Frannie too. In that big place she and Tobias have all by themselves. Wood's dirty, Frannie would say. But with propane going up every month, I'll bet she wishes for a wood-burner." Caleb's voice droned on as steady as a fly buzzing in a bottle.

Patrick was hungry, but he wasn't ready for Laurie serving up more than his dinner at the J & J. That cool, detached attitude he'd heard in her voice over the phone wasn't something he wanted to come up against. He didn't know how to react. Laugh it off, maybe? Tease her? "Come on, Laurie, a sweet chick like you shouldn't have any problems getting a ride." God, no. He wasn't about to say that. He had expected her to be a little miffed; she was the sort in which anger seared like flame and then suddenly burned itself out. He could have reckoned with that. But her reserve of indifference — "It's history." — seemed to glaze over a stockpile of undisclosed feelings that weren't indifferent at all. And now he wondered if they hadn't always kept an evenhanded distance, as though sensing the possibility of something stronger which they didn't want to deal with.

He glanced over at Caleb, quiet now. His hair and beard, heavily grayed, took in the high overhead rays of sunlight and caught against wood chips that had been kicked up by the chain saw. *Bear.* Natalie's name for Caleb suited him. Patrick wished he'd been able to see Caleb and Natalie together. Now, not years ago when he'd been too young to know what to look for about the way a man was with a woman. He could have learned that from Caleb, too; just as he'd learned most everything else. Not from his father. He couldn't think of anything he learned from his father — not even how to swim. But the thought of those swimming lessons made him smile now. What he and Caleb had was different — a kinship was born from what they'd worked out for themselves. The feeling was honest and without the obligatory ties of blood.

Sometimes in summer, years before he knew Caleb, he'd come upon him working fields, back when Caleb still farmed, before he had turned the land over to his brother Tobias and long before he married Natalie. Patrick, astride his mare Black Judy, would stay on her back so he could see over Caleb's shoulder as he tinkered with a bolt or checked the hitch between the tractor and whatever he was hooking on behind — disc, planter, spring tooth, mower, wagon — each following in a necessary order demanded by what the earth and the seasons produced. Sometimes Caleb would offer to take him for a round or two inside the tractor cab, and Patrick would tie Black Judy's reins to a tree under shade at the end of the field. "A horse gives a smoother ride," he'd tell Caleb as they bumped over the uneven earth. Far behind them, the white-bellied plovers circled and swooped to the upended soil where earthworms lay exposed and glistening in the sun. Looking ahead over the hood of the tractor, Caleb sometimes caught sight of a killdeer protecting her nest in a shoal. Faster than Patrick could see, Caleb would shove a lever forward and raise the disc or plow just enough to ease over the nest, scattering only a shower of dirt over the dun-speckled eggs. The female would hobble crookedly across the field, dragging a wing — her tactic, Caleb explained, to draw an enemy away.

But it wasn't until Caleb began building his house that Patrick got to know him — really know him. It was the spring Patrick was eight. One day in early spring, he and Black Judy were hardly beyond the barn when he heard the whine of a chain saw. He angled the mare across the creek, rode across the pasture, and went through the back gate that closed off their land. A hay field followed until it was taken over by a grove of walnuts and cottonwoods. The angry *kawazz* of the saw as it cut or the *chur-chur-chur* of its idle lifted among the close-limbed trees. Patrick threaded the mare among a knot of trees and into a narrow clearing where Caleb stomped about, sizing up trees as he talked to himself, his voice and the saw growling in unison. Silently, Patrick surveyed the situation. Caleb moved rapidly, with purpose. Settling on one tree, he'd peer beyond it, sighting the exact place he expected it to fall. Patrick could tell that Caleb was choosy about trees. He didn't want to cut one and take down others as it fell. When he had finished his measurements, he'd cut a wedge low on one side of the trunk and then set the saw blade opposite the cut. Spinning through the bark, the saw sent shivers up the spine of the tree until, quaking, the tree gave way in the direction Caleb had set the notch. Patrick noticed that the wedge determined how the tree would fall — the notch into the tree was like an arrow aimed at where the tree would crack and fall. The trunk became the arrow's shaft. He could see it clearly from Black Judy's back, and he was unexpectedly surprised at the ease of learning on his own, without a word being exchanged between him and Caleb.

Even after Caleb noticed Patrick, he continued to ramble on as though he expected Patrick to understand. "It's never worked," he said. "Oh, I know that's a great big house. Grew up in that house. My dad grew up in it and his dad built it. It should have been big enough for the three of us, but it never was." Gradually, Patrick gathered that Caleb was talking about his life with Tobias and his sister-in-law Frannie. "I used to say I'd move out, get a place of my own just as soon as Frannie started having the babies, but none came and I stayed on. Like a damned fool. Even when Tobias and me was boys that house wasn't big enough. So I should have known. I've always wanted to build a place of my own, right here in these woods. But all I did was talk, talk, talk. I tell you, Patrick, a man can bury what he wants to do in talk. You can feel so damn good just talking about what you want to do that you never do it."

Whatever had happened between Caleb and Tobias and Frannie had been unpleasant enough to finally drive Caleb out. Patrick never knew the particulars and he didn't care. From the time Caleb cut the trees to lay a foundation until long after he moved in and was making cabinets, Patrick was with him. He was unable to stay away. The work itself attracted him — wood and nails, clamps and hammer, dropping a plumb line, eyeing a level. It was the sort of work his father did that he'd rarely been a part of, and now he had a chance to learn simply by watching Caleb. And listening. "The A-frame's the easiest structure in the world to put up, the hardest to take down," Caleb would say. "Nothing stronger than the triangle, one member braced against the other. The shape fits its world, makes itself one with the trees, gives itself up to the wind, and lets the snow slide off its back." The house was a magnification of Caleb, rough-hewn and imperfect in places, yet solid and sensible. In no time, it seemed to Patrick that Caleb had never lived anywhere else, that the house had always been there, its great peaked, cedar-shingled roof tipping up among treetops. It took Caleb nine months, off and on between farming, before he moved in, which prompted him to call the place his "baby." But then he called other possessions "baby" — his truck, and the chain saw, the soulless things he knew he could get his hands on, as though he thought that, as with Tobias and Frannie, a real baby — and for him a wife as well — would never be realities.

"Our little woodchuck's all chucked out," Caleb said with a nod toward Sandra, still asleep in Patrick's lap. Her curls were soft against the palm of his hand. He lifted one until it sprang from his finger and bounced back with the others, all identical.

They were passing fields spread out in the lowlands near Stella. Far beyond the level cropland, the hills sloped to pastures where cattle moved among grass burned dry through August and September. Men in the fields herded combines and grain trucks with the sort of expanded vigor they had not felt since spring, when they were anxious for a growing season to begin. They hurried to finish as though the day — held out as one they had coming, one left over from spring — had to be used now or lost altogether. They were anxious to know how many bushels of grain to the acre they'd got, how the amount compared with last year's or with their neighbor's, and whether to sell or store. "Wait and see," they liked to say, and their deliberations seeped into much of what was left of their lives aside from farming. They hated risks in anything other than what they took as a matter of course: the weather, the fallibility of equipment, insects, and disease.

"Come on, fella," Caleb motioned to a driver waiting at the edge of a field. "Get on out there and get your grain unloaded before rain sets in."

The driver saluted and chugged onto the highway; the grain

whipped up and peppered the windshield in front of Patrick, a hard, bright sound. They had come to the east side of Judge Croft's land where a crew of men combined sorghum and delivered the grain to the Stella Co-op. Far away, the judge's prize purebred Angus looked like dark round stones against the autumn fallow of the hills.

"I'll bet Judge Croft keeps about as many men working as the battery plant," Patrick said with a note of sarcasm not lost on Caleb, who drew his feathered brows together and lowered a scowl from the corner of his eyes.

"The battery plant's not all bad," Caleb said. "Usually closes down to catch up on production about the time hunting season begins. Gives some of the fellas a chance to work their dogs and guns. And their legs." He bobbed his head so that his beard brushed the top of his overalls.

"I knew you'd say that."

As far as Patrick could tell, the battery plant in Chesterfield was like a great maw that took in generation after generation of young men, usually as they graduated from high school, and spit them out when they were ready to retire. If they weren't sucked into the battery plant, they became submissive followers in their dads' boot tracks or they land-squabbled with their brothers as they worked their way into farming operations big enough for only one or two families. As for the girls, most of them married guys they'd dated through high school and then had the babies they'd got started on before they graduated. A few — as Laurie eventually would do — left town for college. Those were the smart ones; they seldom came back. Patrick couldn't see himself in either extreme. He knew he wasn't going to give himself up to the battery plant, and there was no big farm for him to take over — just a fifty-acre horse ranch that he and his mother had never been able to hitch up out of the red. At one time he'd thought about going to the community college in Chesterfield, close enough for him to live at home, but it hadn't worked out; there was too much to do and too little money. Still, that didn't keep Gramma Rho from bringing it up in letter after letter.

Caleb took another grip on the steering wheel and surveyed the judge's barns and outbuildings some distance from the road. "The judge keeps a lot of them in groceries. A herdsman, a barn manager. Big place like that. He even calls me once in a while for odd jobs."

Patrick considered telling Caleb about the judge's sudden interest in one of Tugaloo's colts. He'd been by twice to look over the weanling. He held back; he hadn't even told Sadie yet, since he and the judge were still at what Gramma Rho called "the bridle and fetter stage" — the time when both buyer and seller were too restrained and clannish to give in much to each other. But Patrick had worked enough with the colt to know what he had, and when he'd trotted him out straight legged in front of the judge, he'd glanced over his shoulder to catch a look of admiration on the judge's face. He'd tried to disguise his own expectancy behind a mask of nonchalance and the hedge that he didn't know whether he and Sadie were ready to sell yet. Not that Sadie would care. He bit on the inside corner of his cheek as the thought came like a catch in his side. She really wouldn't care, and he tried to hold the thought long enough to accept it.

They passed the judge's home, where walnuts and hickories arched over the house, a bone-white massive structure studded with stained-glass windows. Twin turrets rose from the roof; the front porch wrapped like a protective arm around one side and across the front. It was the most imposing place in Stella — English Tudor married to prairie homespun. The townspeople regarded it with the same esteem reserved for the park's pavilion — places that set them apart from other small towns that lacked, they thought, a singular air of importance. In the spring, women of the First Methodist Church conducted tours through the home and served spiced tea and lemon wafers on the porch to visitors who came from places even farther away than Chesterfield. They sent all the money they collected to foreign missionaries.

In town, the square was as busy as the grainfield had been. Children played in the park, and women milled about tables full of clothes they had pawed through all summer.

"Sidewalk sale," Caleb said, " I forgot about that."

Racks of dresses and men's shirts hung limp and pale under metal awnings and storefronts. A few stores had retained the same old brick and stone façades they'd been built with. But that was before Semp Davies had discovered he could get federal dollars to spruce up the town. The money was there, he'd said, "and we might as well take our share." Tillie Seymour, who owned the Nook and Cranny her great-grand-father had built, said she wasn't about to do away with the limestone lion's head that dominated her corner. "You just don't cover up something like my gargoyle with pink aluminum." Sadie quoted her in a story she wrote for the newspaper. Semp Davies followed with a letter to the editor pointing out that Roy Yost, who wanted to retain the brick fronts, was hardly impartial, since he owned the newspaper and could print whatever he pleased. Yost replied in an editorial, and for weeks people followed the saga with about as much interest as they gave their soap operas. In the end, nearly half the store owners sided with Davies and covered the brick with shiny pale siding.

Caleb took a parking slot in front of the J & J Cafe, and Sandra bobbed up from Patrick's lap, smiling and blinking.

"Just look at that rag mop." Caleb pulled a wide-toothed comb from a front pocket and smoothed it and his hand through her tight little curls. "What do you suppose your mama would say?" Sandra allowed her head to be pulled toward her father as he combed, and her face spread with a slow smile, since she was only mildly interested in a story too familiar to hold her attention. "Your mama would say, 'Caleb Burroughs, you get that girl's hair combed before you take her in there to eat.'" In a mysterious fashion, Natalie seemed to convey secret messages to Caleb, as though the two of them talked over Sandra's well-being. Sometimes Natalie relayed the message that Sandra should clean up her plate or act a bit more

55

"ladylike," a prospect that sent a pout across Sandra's face.

Caleb tucked the comb back in his pocket and used his fingers to rake sawdust and wood chips from his beard and hair. Untrimmed and unbound, his hair seemed to give shape to his expansive personality.

"And what would she say about your rag mop?" Sandra beamed up at him. His eyes widened in mock surprise.

"She'd say, 'Kinneygarten sure gives some little gals a smart tongue.'" He grabbed her to him and rolled her to his back, and with her arms locked around his woolly neck, they started toward the cafe. Patrick trailed them, thinking they were complete within themselves, a total family. Caleb had become father/mother, and Sandra, not one child but all the children Caleb and Natalie might eventually have had.

"Hey, there." Jock jumped from behind the glass candy case near the cash register. "Am I glad to see you folks. I'd about given up on anyone stopping today." His smile dipped low in his harvest-moon face. A square-cut man, solid as oak through his shoulders, he went limp as bread dough around a midsection that fell over his belt. A thatch of gray hair, as fine and unruly as baby down, sprang in a halo across his crown. In the mirror behind him, his and Jessie's bowling trophies doubled themselves with their own reflection.

"It's okay if nobody wants to stop, Jock," Caleb said. "The three of us are hungry enough to put a big dent in whatever Jessie's cooked up today." Caleb edged around tables spread with calico cloths as he followed Sandra to a booth by windows looking into the street and the square.

Laurie, wrapping silverware in paper napkins, glanced up at the sound of Caleb's voice and then quickly down to the pyramid she was building. Patrick wondered if she'd been waiting near the front, half expecting him, and he started to say something, but she spun around and he thought better of it. He had no sooner folded his legs under the table and eased back against the red leatherette cushion when Laurie was sliding red plastic glasses of ice water across the table.

"The special today is meat loaf," she said. Her eyes followed the trail of water left behind the glasses on the shiny surface. "Of course, there's chicken-fried steak. Like always. Or I can get you menus."

"You just simplified things for me, Laurie," Caleb said. "Make it chicken-fried steak."

"How about Sandra?" Her eyes held to a track between Caleb and her pad.

"Laurie wants to know what you want to eat, babe." Caleb inclined his head over Sandra's shoulder, but he failed to draw her attention from the window.

"I see four kids in my class playing in the park," she said. "Jimmy Hostetter, Charlene Pettijohn . . ."

"Make it chicken fry for her too," Caleb said above Sandra's recitation. "But on the small-fry size."

"How about you, Patrick?" Laurie kept her eyes down as she wrote.

"I'll take about five minutes of your time." He surprised himself, but no more than Laurie when her gaze shifted to his.

"Okay." She slid the pencil into curls above one ear and led the way to the now empty back of the cafe normally reserved for truckers. Patrick scooted into a booth opposite Laurie, but he left his legs stretched out to keep a cramp from starting.

"I never got a chance to say I'm sorry," he began. "About last night."

"It's okay. I understand." She held her face away from him, her hands folded at the edge of the table.

"You said that already. It doesn't come out sounding okay. It comes out sounding like Milquetoast. And you're not."

She snapped around. "Well, dammit, you forgot and I didn't like that. The *forgot* part." She leaned forward so that she seemed to hold onto her words slightly before she said them. "I got to thinking that maybe you were trying to tell me something that you couldn't just come right out and say."

"Like what?"

"Like why don't I start going with somebody else."

"No. It's not like that." But he dropped his eyes defensively and drew in his legs. They were beginning to cramp.

"Come off it, Patrick. You go with me like it was some kind of favor you were doing Rudy or maybe out of habit or something."

"Laurie."

"And sometimes I feel like closing the door on you. That's what." She leaned back into the seat with a sigh. "I wish it were that easy."

They were both quiet, looking in opposite directions. He tried to hold his attention on some antique kitchen tools Jessie had hung on the wall, which spiders had draped webbing from. Women were beyond fathom. Why would they put up junk to attract the insects they didn't really want around?

"But even if I could," Laurie said finally. "Close the door I mean. I'd still see you. Filling up an entire door frame." She smiled, giving her chin a snap.

"Maybe we could try again," he said evenly. "Tonight."

She drew her mouth into a pout. "If you don't think the horses will get out."

"Or some other fool thing."

They exchanged laughter and slid from the booth.

"You still haven't told me what you want to eat." She pulled the pencil from her hair, her pad from her pocket.

"Chicken fry sounds good."

"She's a nice girl," Caleb said when he returned, with a nod toward Laurie. "Do you good to have a little fun."

"I got lots of things on my list ahead of fun, Caleb."

"Revise your list, then."

"You know what it takes to keep a place going. And it could be that this is the year we make it out there. We've always come up short when the payment comes due after the first of the year. The worst time possible. But we got as nice a crop of weanlings to sell as we've ever had. And the market's good for horses right now. They should bring top dollar."

"There's other things to think about, Patrick. Someday

you're going to need somebody to help you run that place."

"Mom and Josie and I have always done it," he said quickly. "Besides, Laurie's not going to stick around Stella." He watched Laurie as she smoothed cloths over tables, set places, dusted the chair seats, moving in an effortless way to make small motions add up to orderliness. "Besides, Laurie's as busy as I am. By this time next year, she'll be in college, and she won't give a thought to Stella. Or anybody around here." She was at the window now — the pass-through where Jessie lined up dinner plates. She brought them platters of beef steak coated in cornflakes and fried honey-brown. Mounds of whipped potatoes, heaped with pepper-flecked gravy, spread in a lake that lapped at the plate rim. She surrounded each platter with bowls of green beans, coleslaw, applesauce, and steaming mugs of coffee.

"Let's see. Milk for Sandra. Right? And rolls. You got rolls coming yet." Her hand lightly brushed Patrick's shoulder. "I'll check back later about pie."

Patrick sliced off a wedge of meat, piled potatoes and gravy on top. "Sometimes I think you're stuck in the same kind of rut with the rest of them around here, Caleb."

"You may be right. But Stella's not such a bad place. Just a little town that never grew up."

"I remember a time when you were going to leave," Patrick said. He glanced out the window. "You were going to take Natalie and leave without even a look back."

"She wouldn't go," Caleb said solemnly. "She wouldn't leave the house. Thought that house was too important to me. But I should have burned the house down and took her and left."

Patrick immediately regretted his contrariness. Caleb didn't like to talk about Natalie in a melancholy way in front of Sandra. But Sandra was unmindful of their conversation. She continued to watch her friends in the park as she took tiny bites of potatoes with the steak her father had cut up. She was pretty like her mother. She'd be a knockout someday, Patrick thought. Her almond-shaped eyes placed above high cheekbones hinted mysteriously of an Oriental heritage. She was the color of her father's coffee lightened with cream.

The first muffled rumble of thunder was so slight that both Caleb and Patrick stopped eating momentarily and cocked their heads.

"You hear it too?" Caleb said. "I figured they were wrong on their forecast this morning. I could smell rain on the wind. Eat up now, Sandra." He tapped his knife to her plate. "No more gawking out the window."

Above the trees in the park, clouds gray as pewter hovered. On the opposite side of the square, Tillie and some of the other shop owners were taking down the sidewalk bazaar, and parents were signaling to their kids in the park. Then he saw Sadie coming across the street into the park. Lester was beside her. Patrick's jaw tightened, and he sat himself firm behind it. He should have known she wouldn't be home working colts. She and Lester seemed caught up in each other, unaware of where they were or of the weather or anything else. Sadie had on jeans so tight Patrick thought they were probably Josie's. A bright red shirt bloused over a snug T-shirt, and the red bandanna, tied midway around her head, allowed curls to bunch at her cheeks and forehead. She was the only spot of color against the dull tree trunks, the gray sky. Lester looked as he always did, starched and crisp in a pastel shirt and tie, clothes that made him look out of place in Stella, as though he were on his way to somewhere else.

When they reached the swings, Lester impulsively pulled Sadie into one of the seats, a black rubber loop that cupped her hips. With his hands at her waist, Lester stepped back holding her poised and kicking until he released her. Repeatedly he caught her, held her, and pushed her off again until her laughter carried beyond the park, through the cafe. Caleb bobbed his head, smiling approvingly.

"You'd think she'd have better sense," Patrick said. "Acting like a teenager." He flattened himself against the seat and took deep swigs of coffee, set the mug down, pushed his hands down his long slender shanks to keep himself in place.

"They're just having a little fun, Patrick."

"I thought it was me you said should be out having fun," he snapped. "She's a grown woman, Caleb. There are things the two of us should be doing right now at home. Colts to work. Stalls. A hundred different things before winter." The ranch, the horses, what they had together — she dismissed it all, just folded up the past into a neat square like a clipping to tuck into an album.

"But look how pretty she is," Caleb went on. "She looks like a young girl."

Sadie's black hair caught about her face as the swing dropped and then lifted into feathery wings when Lester pushed her up again.

"Anybody can see she's pretty, Caleb. But pretty is about all she is. And she used to be something more." Patrick pushed his plate away.

"Could be you don't like Lester," Caleb said evenly.

"He takes up all of her time, that's all. She's never home and she ought to be able to see through Lester. He's nothing but a dandy. Doesn't even belong around here."

"He's just looking out for his interests since he bought a share of the paper from Roy Yost and got that little shopper insert going. He's a businessman. Plenty smart, I suppose."

Sadie and Lester left the park, crossed the street, and came inside the cafe. When she caught sight of Patrick, she gave a wave, and angled around tables holding a few fingers of Lester's hand behind her.

"I thought you two guys would break for lunch." She shrugged off Caleb's offer to move Sandra aside in the booth. "We can't stay. Lester and I are on our way to pick up supplies for the paper before everything closes in Chesterfield. I wanted to catch Patrick before we left."

Sandra crawled over her father's lap and held out her arms to Sadie, who scooped her up. "You're getting too big for me to hold." She kissed Sandra and slipped her to the floor. "Josie needs someone to pick her up at church tonight," she went on. "I thought you could run out to the Uttermelons' for her."

"Caleb and I have wood to get home and stacked before the rain starts." Patrick looked down into his mug of cold coffee.

"It probably won't rain. Only threaten." She bent in front of him to take a look out the window.

"Listen, hon," Lester began. "If Hi-pockets, here, has something else to do, we can take the time. If the stores are closed by the time we make it into Chesterfield, no big deal."

Patrick felt himself getting up then, but he was caught by the look in Caleb's eyes. Usually as pale as his faded denims, Caleb's eyes now narrowed and darkened, as though drawing a bead through the sights of a rifle. Patrick pressed his back into the seat and stiffened his shoulders.

"I think that will work out," Caleb said.

Patrick took a deep breath and held it. He felt he'd been maneuvered into conceding what he would have done freely, and he burned with resentment.

"That's wonderful." Sadie tipped her face to Lester. "Come on, honey. We're free. Let's you and me head out of here." When she reached the door, she turned and called out, "Thanks, Pat. You're one good kid."

His indignation fused with anger. His head was hot as fire. He wanted to run after her, swing her clear of the ground and shake her. She was nothing to him — a tramp that bore no resemblance to his mother. But he pressed against the plastic cushion until he felt the solid wood behind and held his breath. Once she was out of sight, he was shot through with an urge to get outside — to move, to breath again. He jerked up from the booth, leaving Caleb and Sandra, jarring tables in his rush. Laurie was in front of him suddenly, but he didn't stop; he brushed by her. She said something, but he didn't catch it, couldn't wait for her to repeat it. Something about him coming for her later. Later? God, yes, later. And yet he hadn't the least desire to be with her.

62

5

Rain fell flat and hard as silver coins as Patrick and Caleb finished stacking wood under the shed's overhang. It was all child's play for Caleb; he tucked a squealing and kicking Sandra under one arm and logs under the other.

With his shirt cool and damp against his back, Patrick waved Caleb and Sandra on and carried a load of hedge in, anxious to get a fire going in the Franklin. When he passed through the kitchen, his eyes caught a letter from Gramma Rho lying with other mail scattered across the oak table. He hiked the wood enough to snatch the propane bill first. Donny Carroll had filled the tank before winter set in, and his bill was less than they'd ever paid in the past. They hadn't used much propane since he and Caleb had put the Franklin in place. The stove heated most of the downstairs, and a little heat even drifted up to his and Josie's bedrooms. He gave the logs a reassuring pat and exchanged the propane bill for Gramma Rho's letter.

At the stove, he plunked down hedge on top of the letter and newspapers lying about and then, suddenly conscious of time, ran back to the kitchen to check the clock on the stove. It was a little past four, and he figured he had plenty of time to go for Josie and do chores before he went back to town for Laurie. So he laid a fire with care, thinking about each step, even though usually he was too accustomed to the process for it to hold his attention. He nicked the head of a match against the zipper of his fly and dropped the flame inside the stove. As he closed the door a whoosh of air sucked up the flue, and in minutes the first heat snaps of hedge fired against the stove's interior.

He retrieved Gramma Rho's letter, written on parchment-thin paper. Always the same. World War I stationery, he called it. Pale blue, navy-bordered with the red "Air Mail" crossed out. Addressed to "The Douglas Family." Always the same. He slipped a thumbnail under the narrow upper flap and along each side where the paper puckered from the moisture of her tongue. The envelope opened to reveal her letter: a two-in-one package. Across the face of the page, her ballpoint pen had skipped along the slick surface. In places the words faded out, and sentences streamed across the pages like variegated yarn. She hadn't taken the time to rewrite any of it. She was not one to retrace steps. Her *i*s and *t*s were outstanding, though; she had slashed so vigorously with her pen point, the tip broke through the paper. He always read her letters; he couldn't resist the challenge.

Dear Family,

Just got back from carrying a mess of potatoes down to your cousin Della and had to leave them because she wasn't up yet. Can't imagine it. She gets those kids off to school and then goes right back to bed, like as if the day was ending instead of just starting up. I just hollered in her front door, told her she should have been up hours ago and I piled the potatoes all in her sink so they'd be right ready for her when she did get up. I'm finished with digging mine. Now I am set to can the little bitty ones that will shrivel and go to waste unless I do. Sadie and Josie have got yours canned already. That's my guess.

64

He thought about the potatoes. They were still in the ground. The weeds had taken them in July, but some potatoes might have matured. One more thing to add to the list.

Of course, I shouldn't be so hard on Della. She never did much with the opportunities that was handed to her. She got married and started having those babies right out of high school. I am glad Patrick has his sights set on bigger things. College . . .

He glanced up from the page. She had brought herself around to talking about college in her usual crafty manner. She had always been against his delaying college. She had wanted him to enter that fall, and when he didn't, she feared he might not go at all.

College in due time, I suppose. Even if Patrick enrolls late, he will get there one of these fine days. The first in our family to go.

He didn't know why she was so keen on his going, why he had to be the standard-bearer in the family. Nevertheless, he could expect her to reinforce her argument in letter after letter. She reminded him of a willow reed, thin and lithe, slapping against a creek bank until she made a groove deep enough for water to rush through. After Patrick was born, he and his parents lived with Gramma Rho in Somerset, Pennsylvania, where Allan had grown up. It wasn't Sadie's home; she wasn't Sadie's mother, and yet it was strange the way anyone not knowing presumed Sadie to be her natural daughter. Sadie and Gramma Rho were alike in interests, enough unalike in temperament to complement each other. Sadie could be quietly

65

amused by Gramma Rho's authoritarian manner — her "preachy ways" that irritated Allan. At an age and disposition to understand Gramma Rho, Sadie took what advice she fancied and disregarded the rest. They were "born horse people," Gramma Rho would say in a way that implied the characteristic was like being endowed with special grace or genius. Patrick's earliest memories were of sitting astride a horse with his mother's arms around him and Gramma Rho handing up bridle reins to him — expecting him to hold them. In those days, Gramma Rho — along with her five brothers who lived nearby — had a stable of Thoroughbreds. No grandfather. He'd died when Allan was young, Patrick knew. He never thought about him or of anyone living with Gramma Rho. It was natural to assume Gramma Rho had always lived alone, her convictions hoisting her beyond the reach of others.

But even as a child, Patrick had sensed an obscure tension drawn taut between his father and Gramma Rho. Any number of natural barriers seemed to exist between them, which Allan placidly took for granted but which only sharpened Gramma Rho's tactics to dismantle. Allan was always amiable, perfectly polite in the face of her persistence. He smiled and nodded; he seemed in unrivaled accord, but her words passed over him like a summer breeze. "The thing for you to do, Allan," Patrick could remember her saying, "is to put down roots, get yourself a steady job, and settle down with what the Lord intends for you to do with your life." But it wasn't really the Lord's intentions that concerned her so much as her own. She seemed to view Allan's lack of interest in horses, his inability to take the reins of the horse operation she'd built, as a weakness of her own. And she was not one to admit personal frailty.

When Josie was born, Sadie decided they should find a place of their own. Gramma Rho agreed as though she'd been at the point of suggesting it herself, and even Allan took to the idea. "Somewhere west," he had said, and he spread maps across the table and called out names of towns as though their sound alone would indicate a proper choice.

Sadie had saved enough money to buy a truck, and they piled in the furniture Gramma Rho gave them and headed west, purposeless as gypsies. Allan's obvious joy was infectious. The three of them — Josie was only a few months old — sang songs as they drove, camped in parks, and cooked over open fires. Patrick was six, almost seven, and the time remained in his memory as the period when he and his father banded together like thieves, the two of them in an unspoken collusion against Sadie. He and Allan huddled over the road map to consider the direction they might take next, gathered firewood, or bathed naked in the hidden niche of a stream. With the absence of Gramma Rho's overriding presence, Allan governed their lives with an air of expansive resolve. A side of him surfaced that Patrick had never seen before, and Patrick felt suddenly bold in his own right.

By the time they reached Stella, Patrick thought they might travel the byroads forever, and the idea seemed perfect. Sadie, however, was ready for a rest. She was charmed by Stella's square and park. She insisted on buying food to picnic in the pavilion. The town, she said, was like a movie set. After they ate, they left the square and headed into the countryside. It was cattle and cropland. Sadie noticed few horses, and the thought came to her that her own stable would meet with little competition. With Stella located close to cities, Allan could find work easily, she reasoned, and when they happened onto the Finches' old home with fifty acres for sale, her interest quickened. It peaked when she walked through the barn. She strolled about, pointing out how stalls could be made to open into the alleyway and a paddock laid out along one side of the barn for a stallion to exercise in. The loft above would hold more hay than they'd ever need. The pastures beyond opened to meadows that had been ungrazed for years. She walked the fence line, checked the freshwater pond and the creek and came back with her mind made up. Patrick could see it, see it coming as she closed the last gate behind her. "I'm through traveling, Allan," she said, and when Patrick looked to his father, certain his mother would meet resistance, he saw only Allan's neglectful shrug and halfhearted smile. "You've cut your work out," Allan had said. "It's your baby. No more of them kind there," and he pointed to Josie. Patrick caught the resignation in his father, the self-assurance of his mother, and knew their traveling days were over.

Still, the next few years were good ones. Allan seldom left home, which had been his custom during the years they'd lived with Gramma Rho. There he'd found jobs in places too far away to return until weekends. But in Stella, he seemed content with carpentry work he found near town or with repairs and additions Sadie wanted made to the old farmhouse and barn. Patrick was certain their lives would unwind year after year in similar fashion. One day a contractor, passing through, offered to teach Allan welding if he'd sign on with his crew on their way to Texas where "the big money was." And by then they'd come to the place where Sadie didn't have the last word, but the need for money did.

Gramma Rho came every year and stayed a few months. During those times Allan generally found work on the road that paid too much for him to light near home. Other years, Sadie took Patrick and Josie east, sometimes for half a summer. Then Allan would arrive one day, and the next day, he would begin to pack the truck with the boxes of food the women had canned, the school clothes they'd made. But within a few years of their move, Sadie's horse business kept her at home, and Gramma Rho felt less and less like "making the distance."

When Sadie called her to say Allan was gone, "gone for good," Gramma Rho was determined to come immediately. Sadie had held the phone with both hands, pressing it against her ear and cheek. Patrick and Josie stood on either side of her. "Just let me talk some sense into him," Gramma Rho had said with a force that Patrick could hear clearly. But Sadie was equally firm. "No," Sadie had said. "We're okay. We want to keep things like they are. As normal as possible. You never can tell, Rho. He might decide to come back." Josie's eyes met his with a glow he hadn't seen in days. She smiled and he nodded and smiled back. It was the very thing both of them had been thinking, yet feared to say aloud. Come back. Why, of course, he'd come back. He always did, and there was no place for him to go. Where would anybody go once he left home? Home was important. Patrick was fifteen by then, and he barely remembered the lighthearted weeks they'd spent on the road.

"Normal," his mother had said. They would keep things the way they'd always been, Patrick thought, and between them they could build an assurance that Allan would come home. The work of the ranch and the demands of the horses served that purpose, and he fell to it with rock-hard determination. It was late January. Ice in the pond had to be broken so horses could drink, hay had to be thrown from the loft and scattered in paths across the snow, the tractor had to be kept running to clear the roadway. It was important to keep the road open. He kept going to keep up. He resisted sleep, hated to climb the steps to bed at night; there were still things left on the list he'd made, things left from the week before, in fact. Once there, in bed, he didn't sleep; he listened. He knew the sound of his father's truck coming up the road, pulling into the drive.

Allan didn't come back. He called on the telephone. "Your father wants to talk to you." Sadie handed the receiver to him and left the room. He and Josie stared across the oak table at one another. The telephone? What could he say over the telephone? As it turned out, neither he nor his father said much. Patrick nodded while he eyed the toe of his boot. "I'm coming through town," his father had said. "I'll take you and Josie for a visit somewhere." "A visit?" Josie had said. "What could he mean by that?"

One morning Sadie called the two of them to breakfast; the school bus was on its way to Prathers' and would be in their own driveway in minutes. Josie didn't come. Sent to look for her, Patrick couldn't find her. He and Sadie called; outside, their breath froze in front of their lips. When Patrick climbed the loft steps — the last place he could think to look for her —

he found her wide awake, submerged with her pillows and blankets in a hay-nest she'd made with an armload of barn cats. She didn't want to sleep in the house anymore, she said. He asked her why, quite evenly, and as though he didn't know. "There is nothing left of him. He is truly, truly gone. Not even his smell is with us anymore." She was not yet eight years old. Her deep blue eyes glistened without a trace of tears. Her single long braid fell across one shoulder limp and frayed, tangled with hay. He couldn't think of a thing to say to her, and for a full minute they sat with their faces close to each other. But then he lifted a cat by its belly and set it gingerly in the hay, and he scooped Josie up as he would have a sack of grain and hoisted her across one shoulder, his arm locked beneath her rump. She called out. She screamed. Down the steep loft steps, he made his way, with one hand gripping the rail, while the other held Josie. He slipped once, sucked in his breath and steadied himself before he reached cautiously for the next step. Close to the bottom, he lifted her down to Sadie. For some days afterwards, his back and groin ached where her fists and the toes of her boots had beat against him.

It wasn't Josie, however, but Patrick who finally forced Sadie to call Gramma Rho and ask her to come. It was the same unremitting winter, and as it dragged on, he seemed gripped by a strange lethargy that took hold and wore on until he could hardly pull himself from bed to barn. From sleeping intermittently, he went to a state of continuous drowsiness. Once he awoke to find he'd unaccountably gone to sleep in the loft in the midst of tossing down hay bales. He would start to leave his bedroom in the morning and see in the doorway an apparition of the waiting day that assaulted him like a draft. Each day it became more difficult to move through the nameless haze that was stronger than his will. By the middle of February, he was numbering the days until the Easter break at school. One morning he rolled to the edge of his bed, met a wall of ghostly opposition, and turned his face from it. He curled under his blanket and pleaded to stay home. His mother said he was feverish, "probably coming down with something." He slept dreamlessly. When he awoke, he heard a ringing in his ears like a chorus of unfamiliar voices; misty forms stood around his bed. He smiled. They seemed friendly, a fantastic protective clan. He curled into himself, peaceful as a hibernating animal, and slept again. He remained in bed a week, sleeping, trudging heartlessly to the table long enough to eat half a boiled egg and milk toast, then climbed upstairs by bracing his hands on either side of the stairway to steady his shaking knees. Sometimes he could stay awake long enough to watch the snow through his window driving in across the pasture in sudden sweeps of heavy, dewy flakes that formed lace drapery against the window screen. As the snowfall diminished, single flakes blowing into view appeared like seed fluff airborne from cottonwood trees. He'd spring up, imagining he'd slept through winter, holding his hands to either side of his head, light as a balloon, before he realized it was snow. It came to him once that nature had a way of reflecting one season within another. When spring came, when it finally, really came, he'd see cottonwood down and think of airy flakes of snow. He was pleased that such an observation had not escaped him.

One morning he awoke, rolled to his side and looked up at Gramma Rho. Her eyes were darker than he remembered, her red hair lighter, as though some of the fire had been burned out of it and had gathered into her eyes.

"Just as I thought. Peaked. Peaked as a day-old chick standing in the rain. Come on. You're having some breakfast. It's the collywobbles if I know anything, but we're going in to see Doc Brownlee."

He raised to his elbow to protest. There was no money. He was feeling better; he was sure of it.

She put an arm about his shoulders to steady him as he slumped on the side of the bed. "You're feeling better all right. That's plain to see." And she gave a *tuhhh* of air forced between her teeth. She laid clothes across the bed for him. "Now do you think you can get into those things or do you want me to dress you? 'Cause I will, you know. Won't be nothing new to me. I've seen your bottom since the day you was born." She could push her mouth so hard her chin was firm as a peach pit.

He rallied his strength.

Caleb drove them to Stella. That was the same winter Natalie was expecting the baby. Caleb would hardly leave her long enough to walk to their mailbox, but neither Gramma Rho nor Sadie drove, and they considered Patrick too weak, despite his protests. Caleb drove at a speed that challenged himself, the icy roads, and Gramma Rho's declarations to slow down. The truck's bed was weighted with pig iron, and the wheels settled into the worn snow tracks and careened along over ice as though to give a good showing in preparation for Natalie's time.

The only physician in Stella was Myrtle Brownlee. She was seventy, well past retirement — a state of grace that by then she doubted would ever be hers. She had grown up in Stella and had gone east to medical school with every intention of staying. But she met so much opposition in setting up a private practice, which she refused to limit to females and children, and her medical opinions were so colored by what she had "a feeling for" that she found it equally difficult to work in a partnership. When she returned to town, she was greeted warmly. Everybody knew how opinionated she was, and nothing she did surprised anyone. Besides, the town had no physician, and doctors in Chesterfield were considered callous and mercenary. She set up her office on one side of the square and immediately became so busy she never had time, or inclination either, to have her name lettered across the door. Of course, she never married. The men in Stella went to her just as the women did, and they thought of her as a man since she had chosen to do a man's work. When she was sixty-five, she announced her retirement, and the people gave a party for her that spring in the pavilion. Women of the church guild arranged lace-covered tables around the bandstand with gladioluses in wicker baskets on the steps. Everyone came. Three generations of babies she had delivered. But retirement, even for the day, didn't work out. Franklin Detwiler came rushing into town with a hand he'd caught in the hay baler, and they took him to her office. She buttoned on a white smock over her lavender voile dress, and before she had the last suture in place, they brought in Rodney Lucas, who had cut his forehead on a galloping spring horse in the park. She tried gradual retirement after that, opening her office two days a week, but people stopped by her home on the off days because they didn't see any reason "to drive all the way into Chesterfield for this little old thing." By the end of the year, she was practicing as much as she ever had.

Patrick pushed himself to the edge of her examining table and reached behind to hold the muslin gown over his backside. She thumped her fingers across his back and chest, then moved quickly to his face. By pulling down the skin beneath his eyes and peering into his pupils, she could see inside him, he supposed. He studied her at the same time. Her half-moon glasses rested on the nub of a nose pushed squarely in the middle of her face like a ball of putty. He tried to imagine what she might have looked like as a young girl. Cute, he decided. A bow of a mouth tied up a pert round face, dimpling blue eyes, and a general appearance that might have kept people from taking her seriously.

She kneaded her fingers along his neck and under his arms and groin as though looking for lumps in bread dough. She drew blood, took his weight and height, handed him a pint mayonnaise jar and pointed to the bathroom.

"We'll wait for the lab test," she told his mother and grandmother, "but my feeling is he's growing so fast he can't keep up with himself. He's nearly sixteen, and he's six-foot-three with no signs of stopping." She wrote out a prescription to combat his persistent fever and recommended vitamins and a protein supplement, then Caleb drove back into town for them.

After that he made a halfhearted attempt to return to school, but his will to catch up with what he'd missed was as limp as his muscles. When his mother and Gramma Rho suggested he drop out for the remainder of the year and repeat the grade, he could rally little opposition. What did it matter? He had few close friends. Rudy Kieffer, his best friend, was a year ahead of him. The school's top cross-country runner, Rudy had set his sights on the state championship. "You'd never make a runner," he told Patrick. "Too much body interference against the wind." His own body, small and slight, whipped along as though the wind were always at his back. That spring, Patrick would look for Rudy as he put in road miles. When Patrick saw him round the corner and rattle across the bridge, he'd rush out for Black Judy, but almost before he could bridle her, Rudy would be there. "Hurry up, Pat, I'll break my rhythm," Rudy would say, jogging in place. Then they would set off, Patrick astride Black Judy in an easy trot "to set the pace." But the sun sapped Patrick's energy, and he resorted finally to building balsa models or reading, pursuits he would have considered pure idleness at other times. Sometimes Gramma Rho brought her crocheting and sat beside him as he stretched across the couch watching television. She would yank a length of yarn so hard and fast the ball would bounce from the basket. By summer's end her basket was empty, and the couch was piled high with pillow covers made from all her yarn ends.

Sandra was born in late spring. Neither Caleb nor his truck had any trouble getting Natalie to the hospital. The difficulty was the birth itself, but afterwards the doctors, nurses, even Natalie, sent Caleb home. He went reluctantly. She died before he could return. He did not suffer in silence; he was a raging bear. Doctors gave him something meant to quiet him. He slept and woke with renewed anger, revived energy. His brother Tobias came for him and, once home, Caleb took one look at the A-frame and stormed into the woods along Mill Creek.

Sadie sent Patrick to look for Caleb, since Patrick knew all the places he would camp. He was not hard to find, but he remained impossible to reach. When he heard Patrick coming, he'd wait with the burned end of a log from his campfire raised above his head. "Go. Get on back home." His hands were as black as the charred end, his upraised arm as solid as the hedge itself. Once Patrick woke in the middle of the night to the long howl of a coyote coming from the cottonwood grove. He was certain it was Caleb.

Without Caleb, they buried Natalie in the Burroughses' family plot. The town rallied to the event as though Natalie had been one of their own, as though for the two years she'd lived among them, they had not ignored her. Patrick took note of that, the way people put their energies to what showed while they held within an opposing unaltered belief they did not understand.

Sadie brought Sandra home and set up the bassinet in the bedroom she and Gramma Rho shared. One or the other of them got up in the night to heat Sandra's bottle, rock her to sleep again. She was uncommonly good, a balance on the scale of all that had gone wrong that year. She was with them about two weeks when Gramma Rho announced that she and Patrick were taking Sandra home. They packed her few belongings in a brown grocery sack, her bassinet full of clean diapers and her formula in bottles that filled an enamel canning bucket. When they pulled in Caleb's drive, Gramma Rho said, "Now go back off there in the woods wherever it is you find him and tell him we can't take care of his daughter anymore. She's up here in this house of his. Alone."

Patrick found Caleb asleep, sitting upright against a tree too narrow to support his shoulders. Patrick stooped and Caleb's eyes opened directly into Patrick's. He remained motionless. Patrick was very close to him and he met his gaze evenly. "Gramma's putting Sandra to bed in her own room. Right now. And we're leaving her." He waited for Caleb's response. "You understand, don't you?" Caleb's eyes narrowed, he blinked, but he remained silent.

Patrick and Gramma Rho drove home. "It's all I know to do," she repeated. But she had a plan. She intended to return every thirty minutes, hoping that by nightfall, Caleb would have come home. If he didn't, they'd bring Sandra back with them. When they went to check on Sandra the first time, they found Caleb rocking the baby, her dark head bobbing against his ragged shoulder. "You get on in there and clean up," Gramma Rho told him, and she took Sandra from him as he shuffled away.

For the remainder of the summer, Caleb kept the gravel churning on the road between their two homes. Sandra slept too much, he allowed, the entire night. Even if he woke her for a bottle, she dropped off in the midst of it. She had hiccups three times in one day; should he take her in to Doc Brownlee? Once he arrived, terrified, with Sandra screaming. But she was only angry — he'd bundled her so that she couldn't move her arms. Sadie and Gramma Rho gave each other congratulatory pats each time Caleb left with Sandra, as though they were all recipients of some great winnings.

Patrick observed it all, and he came to believe that people were not so much born related as they became related. The accident of birth might have little to do with the bonds people formed for themselves — the daily living connections that hardened by what Gramma Rho called "the rigors." "We've been through the rigors now," she would solemnly intone, as though the six of them had passed together through narrow straits, night shrouded, without stars or moon.

In July, Josie went to Stonegate's church camp for two weeks and returned "born again" after baptism in the Uttermelons' farm pond. "You were baptized when you were born," Gramma Rho scoffed. "Once is enough. About the only thing

76

you got out of that pond was leeches." But Josie was undimmed in her devotion to Stonegate Tabernacle Union, which had its own uncommon beliefs and laws that permeated its members' unusual way of life. Restrictions were severe, but Josie claimed the challenge of limitations forged the spirit. "I'm making a pathway to heaven," she'd say, her face lit like a sunbeam and her voice ready to burst into song. "Our sins are many and we must sacrifice on earth before we see the face of God." Face of her own father, Patrick thought even then. She looked for him all that summer, and he did come some when he wasn't on the road. He took them for visits into Chesterfield, which turned out to be so depressing that even the forced gaiety the three of them mustered could not fill the hollowness of their spirits.

Toward the end of summer, Patrick grew so weary of the women and the piping of their congenial voices that he would saddle his mare and ride to Caleb's. Before he could say two sentences, Caleb suggested they take traps and follow Mill Creek. Bundling Sandra with her gear, they'd leave her with the women while they rode horseback, camped along banks where they could hear water running over rocks and coyotes yipping near their dens, and return with empty traps and new resolutions. When Sandra was a few months old, Caleb began accepting work again, but he took Sandra with him. He bought a sewing machine and made a canvas sling to carry her across his back, and if anyone mentioned the ten days he had lived in the woods, the time he had denied her, he marked the person as unreliable, a fool. He remembered nothing about that time, yet he doted on Sandra as though to make amends for a wrongdoing he could not acknowledge.

By the time school started, Patrick's appetite returned, and when he went to Doc Brownlee for another checkup, he was two inches taller and twenty-five pounds heavier. At school, Coach Hopkins badgered him to join the basketball team. "Hell, Douglas," he'd say, "I can teach you how to hit the basket, but I can't teach anybody how to be six-foot-five." But the ranch, the horses, took his time; he had better things to do than lay up baskets in his free time.

Before Gramma Rho left, she stocked the basement shelves with canned green beans and the freezer with peaches and peas. She made Josie dresses and Patrick shirts that fit to his wrists. Sadie went to work full time at the newspaper office, but people still called at home with messages for the "gossip" column. After all, that was the way they'd always done it.

With mixed feelings, Patrick drove Gramma Rho to the bus station in Chesterfield. He longed for a relief from her persistent convictions held aloft like flags, and yet he sensed that without her, their life together would lose its even pitch. As they drove into Chesterfield, she managed to fill every lull with "her preaching," as his father would have said. In the time it took to drive the distance, she made up for the summers that would pass without her ministering. "Learn to use your height, Patrick," she told him. "You're going to look down on most everybody you meet. You won't have to act big like a lot of men do. You already are. Thing of it is, you may have to act small sometimes, bring yourself down to other people's level. That won't do you any harm." He put her suitcase and her string bags exactly where she wanted them and then stood beneath her window as the bus idled. She shifted a few times in her seat as though to make a nest for herself, and when the bus pulled away, she raised her hand once with a smile that faded in the reflection of the window.

Strangely, he had no desire to go home immediately. Idly, he circled the outskirts of Chesterfield and came upon a carnival preparing to pack up tents. He pulled the truck to the curb and watched the carney men hoof across the barren, trampled earth. Where were they going? What sort of life must it be in which home was always down the road somewhere? They looked like a family; they even resembled one another in dress and manner. But something special held his attention. They seemed to share some inner signal that kept them working together like cogs rotating within the circle of the dismantling carnival. They went about individual tasks, wholly indifferent to each other yet intensely united. Wordlessly, the men took up corners of a tent, and without so much as a glance to one another, they squatted, lifted, pulled, and separated in unison like dancers on a stage. In one gasp, the tent collapsed and lay breathing briefly against the earth. He thought about joining them, going up to them as they took a break — unrolling cigarette packs knotted within the short sleeves of their T-shirts — and asking if they could use him and his truck. He was free. He could go with only the clothes on his back. But it was obvious he wouldn't fit within the machinery of their lives. He could see himself among them, asking senseless questions, stirring their quiet air with waves of motion. He'd never hear the signal that struck simultaneously within them. He pulled away from the curb and and headed home.

He took up Gramma Rho's letter again when he caught something about Ireland.

When my folks came from Ireland, I don't imagine they ever realized that in two generations, the first of our family would be off to college. Patrick will be the first.

She never gave up when she believed in something. Maybe college was the place for him. Not the community college in Chesterfield, but some place far from home. Away from all of them. He pictured himself in a small room in a dormitory with a roommate, someone he didn't know and who didn't know him. There would be all kinds of directions about when meals were served and where and what he could do here and when to go there, and he could lean back and let somebody else do the thinking for a change. Free time. There would be plenty of that. Time that was his own. Would that be free, he thought? The way Josie sometimes talked about feeling free at church? He knew it wasn't and he laughed at himself. He didn't think college was for him, but he lacked the certainty that Gramma Rho had. He wished sometimes he could look straight ahead, as she could do, and see things divide evenly to the right or to the left.

He glanced at the stove clock; it was time to go for Josie. He carried in more wood and stored it in a dry place on the back porch.

Rain was driving home the cold, and it settled into a rhythm to keep pace with the windshield wipers as he drove the pasture road and crossed Mill Creek.

It was some five miles north to Stonegate and the Uttermelons'. Stonegate was a village, set apart from everything else, and the road leading into it was so narrow the county crew never graded it in summer or cleared it in winter. The people of Stonegate took care of their own. Independent and competent, they were wedded to their land, dedicated to each other. They acknowledged Stella only in ways that benefited them: supplies they were unable to provide for themselves or the produce, grain, and pottery they sold. A clay vein surfaced along a gully in a remote area of their land, and from it the women dug earth to mold pots and bowls, which they fired in a kiln. The vegetables they grew were unmatched. The people were uncanny at producing beans, radishes and onions, carrots and peas while everyone else's garden was in the bud stage, and at the end of a growing season, they brought out potatoes, melons and squash, corn and tomatoes blemish free and double normal size. From Memorial Day to Thanksgiving, they hauled their best produce to the square in Stella, but even then they kept to themselves — never went to the J & J to eat and only into Tillie's long enough to leave their pots, red as the women's hands and rough to the touch.

Sometimes when Stonegate's old blue Gospel Chariot was in for repairs and unable to make its rounds, Patrick went for Josie or took her to prayer sessions. He couldn't account for all the members accomplished since they spent so much time on their knees. He'd never paid much attention to the clan until Josie returned from church camp, after her rejuvenation. And then he asked Caleb, the one person who would know. "Stonegate and Stella sorta grew up together," Caleb had said. "When Stella — I mean Stella the saloon keeper — got the town named after herself, there was a certain group of them, the real religious ones, who weren't about to live in a town named after a common . . . named after Stella. So they moved out there right where they are today, bought up the best farm ground in the county, and started their own school, their own church. Their idea was to keep things as much the same as they could, so when rural electricity came through, they passed it up. Telephones too, and as far as I know they still carry in water from wells their great-granddaddies dug. Some of them moved back to Stella in time, but when they left, Stonegaters never condemned them for it. They broke down and bought themselves a bus to bring folks back for church services, and they let them go or come as they please with the notion that sooner or later everybody was going to see things their way, and they had all the time in the world either here or in heaven."

Maybe so, Patrick thought. Maybe they have all the time in the world, but I don't.

He'd forgotten his watch as usual; the sun was cloud shrouded, and he couldn't estimate the exact time. It couldn't be much past four, he thought. Time enough to return home and do chores before going back to town for Laurie.

He turned from the county road onto red clay, solid as old brick, an outcropping of the vein the women used for their pottery. Flint stone pillars flanked the entry. Stretching ahead,

81

close-limbed cedars lined the drive, forming a barrier to the grounds beyond. At the cedars' end, houses and barns spread out in a precise, uncluttered arrangement of narrow brick walkways and glistening white fences. Patrick slowed to admire the order of things, to marvel at the industry.

He left the hardpan and drew up to the Uttermelons' home, one of a number of stone and wood-frame houses that angled in one direction or another around a great wooden barn bordered by catch pens. Stonegaters were practical, Caleb had noted, and they shared equipment, kept their animals together. At the barn, Patrick caught sight of men and boys hustling cows inside to be milked.

There was no porch to the Uttermelons' home, only one narrow entryway. Windows were evenly set, two below, two above, each with heavy stone sills. The windows lacked curtains and in one downstairs room, women moved about, lighting candles or setting lantern wicks to blaze. Tiny points of light flared against the darkness, shimmered across the pale expressionless faces of the women, and were lost in the shadows of the white scarves tied around their heads.

Patrick left the truck and followed a stone walkway to the door, but before he could knock, the door opened, and he faced a young woman with deep-set eyes in a milk-white face. He didn't recognize her, but all the women looked much the same to him.

"I'm Josie's brother. Here to take her home."

He anticipated a glance to meet his own, but the girl held her eyes somewhere near a point at his wrist. She nodded and closed the door gently, so that he took a quick step backwards. Immediately, Josie slipped through, tossing her braid to her back, skipping in front of him.

"Wait for me in the truck. I have something to get in the barn." She loped ahead of him down the path to the barn.

The rain was slight now so that it barely dampened his shoulders. He ducked into the cab and eased the truck forward to meet Josie as she angled her way around cattle. She was

82

clutching something under her jacket; he could tell that much.

"What you got, Josie?" he said after she scooted across the seat and he got in behind the wheel.

"Just close your eyes and hold out your hands."

"Come on, Josie, we need to get home. We haven't time . . ."

"Just do it," she broke in, "and don't be such an old man about it." Impulsively, she pulled the bill of his cap over his eyes. "Come on. Hold out your hands."

He cupped his palms and thrust them toward her.

"Perfect," she said.

He felt warm fur, and when she pushed the cap back from his forehead, he glanced down at a kitten marked in blotches of orange, white, and black. Its fur lifted in a halo around its tiny body, and it settled comfortably in his hands.

"Becky gave her to me. Her name's Freone. She's the prettiest one in the litter."

He handed the kitten to Josie and started down the drive. "She's pretty now, but she'll grow up and be a cat just like the rest of them."

"You know how I can tell she's a girl?" Bemused, Josie stroked along a black blotch of fur and bunched the kitten close in her lap.

"Yes, Josie, I know how."

"Not that way," she shot back, exasperated. "Because she's tricolored. Cats with three colors like this are always female, Becky says."

"Three colors or four, we don't need her. We got cats galore at home."

"One more won't make any difference, will it?"

"That's true. I suppose you're right. One more mouth to feed in the barn."

"She's not wild like barn cats. I wanted to keep her inside, Patrick."

"Not in the house, Josie," he said matter-of-factly. "Animals belong outside."

"But if I leave her in the barn, she'll get wild. Freone is a

83

pet.'

"J　, you know those barn cats are your pets. You're the only one of us who can go out there and pick one up. They see me and run to the four corners."

"Freone wouldn't. In the house, she'd be your pet too."

"I don't want a pet, Josie. I got enough things hanging on." He tightened his mouth.

Josie was quiet. It was nearly dark. The kitten's fur snapped under Josie's hand. An undulating purr like a wavy line stretched between them.

"I'll fix the litter box, take care of her myself. And Mama won't mind. I know."

"When are you going to take care of her?" he shot back. "At school all day, and the rest of the time, you're at the Uttermelons'."

"I'm not."

"Look." He jabbed his chin in her direction. "It's Saturday. Late. And you've been over there," he swung his head over his shoulder, "the livelong day. And tomorrow won't be any different."

"I'll be home right after church services tomorrow. By noon."

"What in Christ's name do you do there to spend so much time?"

"We take Christ's name in prayer and not in vain, for one thing," she snapped.

He drew into himself. The lights from the truck were cone shaped on gravel paths ahead of him. For a time, all he heard was the crackle of electricity passing through the kitten's fur, the snap of gravel in the truck's fender wells.

"It's just another world, Patrick," she said finally. "Another world," she repeated dreamily.

"I can see that."

"When I come down the road between the cedars, I feel myself coming into their world. Stonegate. They're so peaceful among themselves. They never have squabbles, never raise their voices. And there's an order in things. Why, there's never any doubt about what's going to happen. Each day comes regular as the sun and closes the same way."

"But Josie, that's not so different."

"You'd have to come with me, be a part of it all to understand. We honor God. Everything we do honors God. When I'm there at least. And when I'm not there, I'm never really sure. Sometimes I feel like it's sinful to leave."

"Josie, there's nothing you do that could ever be thought of as sinful. Stonegate Tabernacle Union is like a fairyland, a place those people have invented. You mustn't be duped by them. Everybody quarrels. Like we do. We have our spats, but that's because we know and trust each other."

She held the kitten to her. "I don't expect you to understand, Patrick. There's no sense talking about it."

"But don't you see, Josie, you have to live in this world? Maybe it's sinful, but it's the real world."

"I know." She drew out a long sigh. "That's the hard part."

He was momentarily taken aback, and he paused, hoping she'd say more.

"Someday, you know what I'd like to do, Patrick?"

"What's that?"

"I'd like to teach in their school."

He felt a chill as though the dampness of the night clung to his skin. "You mean go there to live?"

"Something like that. It's just something I've thought about. I haven't told anyone. Not Mama. Just you."

"But Josie, there's a whole world out there. And neither of us know anything about it. We've never got beyond Stella. Don't you want to know something about what's out there?"

"No," she said simply. "I'm afraid of what's out there."

"Oh, Josie." Impulsively he reached toward her, and she met his hand with her own. She squeezed his fingers once before he drew back and set his hand firmly on the wheel.

6

"**Y**ou didn't have to come." Laurie's voice was stern, her tone as upright as an obstacle between them. It was dark in the alley behind the J & J where he usually waited for her after the cafe closed. In the darkness, her anger was apparent — he could feel it. In light, he would have focused on her hair or the way she stood, but now he was left with only her brittle voice breaking in front of him.

"Jock and Jessie could have taken me home." He heard her close the back door and walk to the center of the alley and pause. "You didn't have to come," she repeated.

"You knew I'd come." He wished for a shimmer of light, even though he knew exactly where she was standing. He could have moved toward her, found her in a moment, but he waited outside his truck. A mild rain continued; drops were fractured into a fine spray off the bill of his cap.

"We could get in the truck. We're getting wet out here."

"I don't mind the weather. At least I understand that. Wet. Wet." He could hear a whoosh of air, as though she'd flung her arms out or turned on her toes as she'd done earlier in the park. But now she lacked exuberance. "Wet. I can feel it. It feels good."

He opened the truck door, hoping she might take that as an invitation to get in. From the dim cab light, he saw her turn and walk resolutely down the alley into the mist, as unconcerned of puddles as a child, padding through them in soft-soled shoes.

"Hey! Where the hell do you think you're going?" Patrick slammed the truck door and followed.

She wheeled as he rushed up behind her. "I'm going to walk around the square, and I don't even think I want you to come."

"Well, you're going to have a devil of a time keeping me from it."

"You think so, huh?" She crossed her arms and clutched the elbows of her jacket. "All I'd have to do is say 'Boo!'" As streetlights flared from the corner of the square, he could see her as she tilted her head to glare up at him. Her eyes, usually light as mist, were dark with huge pupils. She flung her arms out, snapped around and continued the length of the alley, then turned toward the square.

Patrick thrust his hands into his front pockets, rolled his shoulders in a protective hunch, and followed a few yards behind her. She was angry because of the way he'd brushed her aside as he'd left the cafe that afternoon. Forgotten entirely one night, brushed aside the next day. Naturally, she'd presumed he wouldn't come tonight either. She had a right to be angry. Sometimes he didn't understand himself.

"Sometimes I don't understand you, Patrick." She could have been talking to herself as she read his mind. "I've known you nearly all my life, and I don't know anything about you. The way you act. Why you do certain things. Hardly civil sometimes." Her choppy sentences matched her stride. "Just wheeling on past me like you got better things to do. Well, so do I. I don't need that crap."

Together they stood at the corner of the square and waited as a double line of trucks wheeled past them. Guys in cowboy hats with brims turned up leaned from windows to yell at each other. Girls, wedged in the crook of boys' arms, waved as they passed. Everything was oversized: hats, tires, hood ornaments, square-cut rearview mirrors, dual exhausts, and twin panel decorations. By doubling everything, they had achieved a singleness of purpose. The truckers had gathered at Lander's Crossing after the football game. From there they had driven at a speed to test themselves at the dogleg turn, then sailed into town to rally around the square before zooming back to take the speedway again.

"Just look at them," Laurie said. "Trying to end upside down out there at the turn like Rudy did. Bunch of thunderheads."

He thought she might have meant "dunderheads," but on second thought, he decided she'd said what she meant. "Thunderhead" said it all.

"You may think you're the only guy in this town I'd walk across this street with. And you're absolutely right. That's the damndest thing. You think I'd be fool enough to go with one of them? I mean, even if they wanted to." She swung a hand toward a truck taking the corner on two wheels. "Not on the life of that truck of yours. That's what." Her words were measured with equal parts of scorn and ire.

When the last truck rolled past, Laurie stepped from the curb and across the street. A cone of light fell from a streetlight. He looked into the mist spotlighted within the glow — mist so light he could barely see it, only feel it across his cheeks. Tiny beads of water were already glistening in the web of Laurie's taut curls. Wordlessly, he put his cap on her head so that the bill angled above one eye. She gave him a swift look and then marched ahead like a drill sergeant in front of the darkened stores.

"What's it been now? Two years that we've gone together? Since Rudy's accident. But during all that time, I don't think I've ever got to know you. There's a part of you that's always on reserve. Like you're playing poker and holding your hand close to your chest. Afraid somebody'll get a peek. Maybe even get to know you a little bit." She did not look up.

He hadn't thought of that. She was probably right.

"But lately," she went on, "it's gotten pretty obvious that you don't have time for me. And all I'm saying is that's quite all right. I got things of my own to do, you know."

Another curb. The street lamp shot a path of light through which Laurie forged.

"Besides, you got nothing to worry about. I made up my mind a long time ago that I wasn't going to be like my sisters — one day marching to 'Pomp and Circumstance' and the next day marching to 'The Wedding March.'"

Laurie's three older sisters had been high school cheerleaders, a position of royalty at Stella High School, usually handed down within families. Laurie, however, didn't even try out; she had band practice or extra lab projects in chemistry. She didn't like cheering for anybody but herself.

"Rachel and Jackie were both pregnant before they walked down either aisle," she continued. "God, I think Mom even made Jackie a maternity skirt out of whatever the cheerleaders wore that year. Oh, she went right on. From *rah, rah, rah* to *coo, coo, coo*."

He tried to hold back a smile and brought a hand from his front pocket to brush across his mouth. Without his hat, the mist had gathered in his hair until the water was heavy enough to run down his temples. He ran his fingers through the sweep of hair above his ears.

"That's not for me, I can tell you. I can hardly wait to graduate, and when next fall comes, my bags are going to be ready to move into the first dormitory that will take me."

Another curb. Another street lamp. Patrick stepped across a rain puddle. Laurie marched right through it. He wondered what it would be like to know such certainty, to be so confident about tomorrow that nothing could block the path today.

They were both silent for half a block. Patrick tried to edge her under the aluminum overhangs, but she held her course. They came to the corner where they had begun. The trucks had left; the square was empty except for the two of them. In the drizzle that softened the glare of the streetlights, he felt as though they were somewhere else, an unfamiliar place in which they were the only ones around.

"It's not you. It's me," he said at the end of a deep breath. "It's just the way I am."

"So change a little bit," she replied impatiently, and she struck out again along the same route.

He swung in beside her, his steps reaching beyond hers now, so that she quickened her pace some to keep abreast.

"Change, Laurie, is just another way of saying born again, and I say to hell with being born again. It's all I can do to get through being born the first time. That's enough for me, and I sure as hell don't want to start over. From scratch. It seems to me people give up awful easy on their first life. They get kinda tired of the way things are going and they say, 'Oh hell, I'll do something else.'" He was aware he was talking more than he usually did, but the words seemed to keep pace with his stride. "All the time and money and everything else they've put into their lives don't seem to matter a whit. They say, 'I'll just be born again.' They don't always call it that. Josie does, but most everybody else just says change. 'I've changed,' they say. 'Times change,' they say. I say change isn't all that good." He paused as they crossed a street, turned at the corner and started down another side of the square.

"Whether you like it or not, Patrick, things change," Laurie said quietly.

"I sure as hell know that. Things change faster than I can keep up with. Sometimes I feel like I've been frozen in one spot, able to see everything, everyone moving around and away from me, and me standing stock-still not being able to do a thing about any of it."

"Your mom and Lester, you mean. You don't like the way she's changed. And her going around with Lester."

"No, I don't like that. Lester's a fool, and she ought to be able to see that he's just using her. But it's more than that. I don't like her dumping everything on me. The ranch. The horses."

"So sell the horses." Laurie tossed her arms above her head. "Sell the ranch."

"Just like that, huh? Get myself born again. To do what? Go to college? Hell, I don't know if college is for me. Gramma Rho is the one who knows college is for me, because nobody else in the family ever went, but I don't know that. We've worked out there for thirteen years to get something going, and I'll grant you what we got isn't much. A pretty good stud that throws pretty good colts and a band of brood mares that year in, year out, do their jobs — foal without much trouble. A little land, a little grass." He stopped in front of Classen's leather shop and shoved his fingertips into his rear pockets. "Maybe it's not much of anything to hang onto, but it's what I've known; it's what I've got."

He began again, slower now, thinking as he walked. "It's not the same with you, Laurie. God, sometimes I envy the way you just know what you're going to do with all your life. Your tomorrows are just sitting for you quiet as ducks on a pond, and all you got to do is take aim and squeeze easy on the trigger. You can leave just like you say you're going to and never look back, but it's not that easy for me. I can't be certain of things like you can." He sunk his hands into his pockets and looked at the toes of his boots as he walked. "How can you understand when your life is so different from mine?"

"I'm beginning to." She stopped him with her hand on his arm. "It's the first time you've given me a chance."

He put his arms around her, and she pushed up on her toes, pressing her hands into the center of his back. He took his cap from her head before he kissed her.

"Laurie, this isn't getting us anywhere but wet. I'd better take you home."

"No." She cushioned her head against him. "I've got a key to the cafe. Let's go in. Your stomach's growling at me. I'll bet the last time you ate was when I put that chicken fry in front of you."

"By the time I got Josie home from the Uttermelons' and we finished chores, there wasn't time to eat. I sure as hell wasn't going to cut out on you tonight, and risk being strung up from one of the swings out there." He motioned toward the park. She punched him in the ribs, and they walked the rest of the way to the cafe with their fingers locked.

"Maybe I can find a couple of dry shirts in the back closet," she said. Still holding his hand, she led the way to the kitchen. The streetlights shot through the front windows and cast long shadows in their path.

In the kitchen, she flicked on an overhead fluorescent and, pegging his cap to a chair back, went to the storage closet. When she came out, she had on Jessie's top that dipped off one narrow shoulder exposing the pink elastic strap of her bra. She tossed him Jock's shirt, and he slipped into it; the cuffs ended a few inches below his elbows and the bottom bloused at his belt line. But it was flannel, and he rubbed it against his upper shoulders where his skin was damp.

A long-legged stool sat in front of a counter where Jessie often perched to peel potatoes, and he slid the stool between his legs to watch Laurie as she twirled between stove, refrigerator, cabinets, drawers, gathering material to choreograph a meal. Like his mother, Josie, even Gramma Rho, Laurie resembled all the women he'd watched as they moved about a kitchen with an inherent rhythm. With assured and measured steps, she swung from the freezer, where she broke off brick-hard meat patties, to the grill, and in seconds, sizzling beads of grease ricocheted.

Outside, the roar of trucks blasted the square again.

"You've got more sense in your little finger than any one of them." She swung the spatula like a baton without looking up. "I've known that since fifth grade." Jessie's blouse juggled across her shoulders as she danced between the grill and the deep-fat fryer. "About sixth grade was when you more or less started doing a man's work, taking over for your dad while he'd be away." She shot him a quick glance. "Oh, I noticed. You think I don't understand, but I understand all right. And then after he left for good, I'd see you come to school on Monday mornings, and I'd wonder if you hadn't come back to rest up."

"I never minded the work. It was something we had together after he left. Sometimes the work kept us going. Animals, you know. They don't know you're having a hard time." He brushed through his damp hair, caught beads of water in his palm. "The work. The horses. That kept us together. Yeah." He nodded slowly, his gaze leading off to a quiet point beyond Laurie's activity. "We were still a family. And I thought his leaving wouldn't change that. I mean, a person dies or a kid gets married, goes off to another town — college or a job — the family goes right on. Just like yours will after you leave. You'll come back and find you're the one who's changed. They haven't. A family is permanent, isn't it?" He lowered his eyes to her, and she met them with a glance over her shoulder. "I don't know anymore. Anyway, I handed myself that spiel."

"And now? Now you don't think that's the way it is?"

"Now I sometimes think it's all a trap." He pushed up from the stool and dug his hands into his front pockets.

"You can always leave. Pack your bags, get in your truck, and tell your mom you'll drop her a card when you get to wherever you're going." She pressed down with the spatula on a hamburger and set it sputtering in its own juice.

"There you go again, Laurie, making things sound easy, because they are easy for you. Maybe you're right. Maybe that's what I should do, but that's not something I *can* do."

"Why not?" Laurie brought the plate of food to the counter in front of him. Lettuce leaves fringed outside the buns, and the fries lay crosshatched on the side. He thought he should be hungry, but he wasn't. He waited a long moment, squinting thoughtfully.

"Because that's what he did."

The truckers had made their rounds and had gone. The square was quiet. His words hung like mist in the air between them.

"Just packed his bags, got in his truck, and left," he said.

"But you're not like him. You're entirely different."

"How do I know that?" He picked up a hamburger, set it down again. "Maybe I'm just like him. If I left, just told Mom and Josie I didn't care what they did about the horses and the ranch, that's exactly what he did." Leaning forward, he locked the fingers of one hand in his hair.

"That's not you, Patrick." She rested a hand between his shoulder blades, and the warmth of her fingertips flowed through the shirt.

"Maybe you know that just like Gramma Rho knows I should go to college, but I don't know that." He lifted his head and faced her. "And years from now . . . on down the line from now . . . what if I still haven't figured it out?" She was standing beside him as he sat on the stool, and he tipped his face to her.

"You've done a lot of thinking about this, haven't you?"

He stood and began walking as he talked. "At nights. Nights were worse than the days. Days gave me work that had to be done without thinking. Some nights I'd lie awake, and I'd think, pretty soon, I'd hear him drive in. When he came home from a job, it could be about any time of day or night. But no matter, Mom would fix coffee. They'd sit down at the table and talk for a while. If it was late, I'd hear them and get up and sit at the top of the stairs. I wanted to go down, but you could tell just by listening that they wanted to be alone. After he left, for good, I kept thinking I'd hear them again some night and know he'd come back." He walked the length of the kitchen and then back to Laurie. He tried the stool again. Got up. "I couldn't get it through my thick head how it was all right for them to split, go separate ways, and there was nothing I could do about it."

"Where did he go?"

"I don't know. First one job and then another, just like he'd always done. It finally didn't matter where he went."

"Didn't you ever hear from him? Didn't he send some money for you and Josie?"

"Let me think." But his tone was scornful, and he tilted his head so that the light cast a white hot glare across his face. "I guess the last time he sent any money was Josie's birthday. In April. He's got this thing about sending hundred-dollar bills. On our birthdays or at Christmas here comes a card with a brand-new hundred-dollar bill. Every time. They've never been touched by human hands." He gave a snort that ended in a laugh.

"Didn't he ever come to visit? Take you and Josie with him?"

"We tried that." Patrick nodded seriously. "He'd drive to Chesterfield and call from there. Say he was on his way and could Josie and me get ready. Then he'd come, park out in front of the house like he was selling something. And he'd take us to Chesterfield for the day, go to the show, shop for some new clothes, eat, and talk about nothing." He took the length of the kitchen again with his fingertips in his rear pockets. "We had this little pattern all worked out. It took me five minutes to say yes, I was doing fine, and no, I still wasn't playing basketball, and yes, it might be a cold winter from the looks of the hair-coat on the horses."

"But he was your father," she said in a rush.

"No, he wasn't. All of a sudden, he was this strange man we were supposed to know, and we didn't." He paused. "We had nothing to talk about except things that were safe. If I said something about the farm, what needed to be done, he'd let out a long sigh and wonder if we shouldn't go play miniature golf. Miniature golf, Laurie. I would rather have been mucking stalls. No, we had to keep on the go, running here, there, doing things that would keep us from touching each other.

"One time he took us home, and Josie was really down. She was trying not to cry, because she didn't want Mom to see her. I told her, 'Josie, it's just like dancing around Miss Thompson's maypole.'" He glanced at Laurie. "You remember. Every year, Miss Thompson would take down the tetherball, give us each crepe-paper streamers, and we'd take them around the pole, skipping round and round, wrapping that pole with colored paper."

"I always wanted green," Laurie said.

"You always got whatever you wanted, as I remember. Being teacher's pet and all." His smile puckered the corners of his mouth.

"Anyway, Josie knew what I meant right off, and it made her

95

laugh. But that's what it was like. We each had a little bit of nothing, no past, no future, just that day, and we went dancing around Chesterfield until we'd played ourselves out." His hands flew up as though he were tossing something in the air. "At school, the wind would whip loose all the crepe paper by the end of the day. It was the same with us. Each time we met we had to start over. I'd say to Josie as we walked out to his truck to meet him, 'What color do you want this time?' It was a joke between us. We never told Mom."

"How long was that? Your maypole dance?"

"Maybe the first year off and on after he left. Maybe five times. I was never much for games, and there was too much to do at home to run around Chesterfield. I was sick half the time, too. You remember. It was one thing followed by three. Bad luck comes in threes, Gramma Rho would say. His leaving, me being sick. And Natalie. One time when he called I had a bunch of colts to break, that sorrel of your dad's. I told him I couldn't go. Josie wouldn't go without me, and it was nearly the last time he called. I think he was waiting for me to find a way to break it off, or maybe he found jobs farther and farther away. After that, we got the hundred-dollar bills. If you were to ask me where he is, I couldn't tell you. When his cards come, there's never a return address." He snorted. "But I don't think he ever had a return address in his life — only future ones."

He came back, took the stool, and released a sigh over the hamburgers and fries. "I don't know if I can . . ."

"That's all right," Laurie said briskly, "I'll wrap them up, and you can take them home for your dinner tomorrow."

She made a move to take the plate, but instead, in an altogether natural manner, her hands caressed across his shoulders so that he turned to her without thinking and pulled her against him with his hands moving beneath Jessie's shirt and pressing the small of her back.

"Patrick." She put the side of her face against the top of his head, and he began slowly to move his mouth along her shoulder where Jessie's oversized shirt hung free.

96

"Raise your face," she whispered, and she set her hands on either side of his jaw and kissed him.

He felt himself weaken, losing control. Between them, it hadn't been like this, nothing this strong that he'd had to fight before, and he pulled back.

"Laurie, no." He stood and took her by the shoulders. ". . . take you home."

"Not yet." She came to him again, and he took her head against him some inches below his shoulder. "It's okay, I wanted you to know. I mean, I'm glad you told me."

"I didn't want you . . . It's not you. It's me." Her breath was warm against him.

"It makes me want to be with you." She lifted her face. "Do something."

"There's nothing . . ." It was that baggy shirt of Jessie's. He wanted to put his hands beneath it. "Laurie." Gently he put her away from him. "Laurie. Let's leave. Okay?" He slipped his cap from the chair where Laurie had hung it and pushed his hair back before he set it in place.

They drove toward Laurie's home in silence, with Laurie well centered on her side and Patrick braced against the door frame. It wasn't any good, he thought, getting steamed over Laurie. Or even putting himself in a position where it could happen. There was nothing for them together; all he had to do was to keep things cool for a few more months and she'd be gone. She'd slip this little whore's town, and when she came back, less and less often as the years passed, she'd think of Stella as a nice place to be *from*. He took an undisclosed pleasure from thinking about her as one who had "escaped" Stella. Someday she'd be just a girl he'd once dated, and the only time he'd think about her would be when he caught mention of her in Sadie's column: "Laurie Kieffer is home visiting her parents, Mr. and Mrs. Ralph Kieffer. Laurie makes her home these days in New York (Los Angeles? Santa Fe? Dallas?) but in her business of (interior design? international finance? chemical analyst?) she does a lot of commuting to

97

London and Paris." Maybe that was a little extreme, but probably not for Laurie. Anyone who got away, fled Stella, was destined for something dramatic and exciting. Laurie knew this, which was only one of the reasons she'd been planning a "break" for so long. She was ready to move on and be free; he wanted to leave it that way. For him, though, it was different. Being ready to leave and being free to leave were two different things.

"I know you think that after I graduate, I'll be free to just walk away and never look back." She curled a leg under her to face him. "Just because you've heard me talk about going away to school, about getting away from my family, I know you think I'm going to fly out of Stella and never give anybody another thought." She paused, crossed her arms to clutch her elbows, hugging herself.

He waited. She had more to say.

"And I do want to go. I mean, I've had these plans for years and everything I've done in high school, the courses I've taken, special projects I've worked on, have all been with the idea that I'd go to college." She dropped her hands to her lap and turned into the night with her gaze locked on the spatters of rain peppering her window. "But it's not going to be easy, Patrick." Her voice dropped, then picked up again. "I've got ties here, you know," she said defensively.

He pulled into the circle driveway of her home with the cars and trucks of her family wedged together. Rudy's van filled its customary slot at the ramp leading to the front door. Patrick parked some distance away and switched off the ignition.

"I know," he said, "but I don't want to be one of them. One of those ties."

"Maybe you already are."

"It's not like that. Not yet. It's not going to be."

"But you're certainly not just someone who's going to see me through this last year of school. Someone to take to the senior banquet. Someone to pin a corsage on my dress at the prom."

"I'm not saying that. But there's no sense in making it

difficult. Inside you. We . . . we may feel something, but on the outside where we have to get through one day at a time, it's just not possible."

"You mean just keep things cool. Right? Don't let anything happen."

"I guess that's what I mean. Yeah." He paused, and he knew she was waiting for him to say more. "All my life, it looks to me, things have happened to me without me having a thing to say about any of it. I mean right from the beginning, Laurie. Including birth. And things haven't changed much since then. But sometime in the near future, I'd like to take the reins and set some kind of course of my own. Not just let things come at me from all directions, and whatever gets there first or whatever is strongest takes over whether I like it or not. Anymore, I get uneasy when things are entirely out of my control. God, we have so little control over anything really. Does it just always have to be that way?" He shifted suddenly to face her, but he didn't expect an answer. They sat quietly a few moments, transfixed by the subtle movement of people behind the sheer curtains of the living room.

"Your family in there. Playing cards, ripping it up. Rudy probably brought four girl friends, and they're all crazy about him." He laughed. "Being chairbound never slowed Rudy much."

"I wonder if any of them ever had thoughts like we have. I don't think so. Maybe they didn't want to take the risk. Of leaving Stella."

For an instant he thought of Josie and her desire to live and teach someday at Stonegate, enclosing herself within concentric circles of certainty.

"But they're happy. I never knew a family could be like yours. Whooping it up like a litter of pups. Sometimes I wish like hell that I could be right there in the middle of them without a thought more than what shift I was working the next day at the battery plant. But there's not a chance. I'm not like that. Neither are you. And the thing is . . . we know it."

"Maybe I'm a slow learner," she said lightly.

"Don't give me that crap. You know where you're going. And you're not about to let things get in your way."

"Listen, Patrick, I don't want you thinking you're just some little old thing I'm going to shove out of my way."

"You won't have to. Because I'm not going to be in your way. That's all I'm saying."

He stepped from the truck then, and she slid across the seat, pulling Jessie's blouse as it wrapped her midsection. "How about the family dinners? Our annual holiday extravaganza that goes nonstop from Thanksgiving to New Year's. You haven't forgotten that horse feed from last year, have you?"

"How could I? I usually cart enough chow off to last me most of the year. Matter of fact, I'm running a little low. Time to restock the larder."

She gave him an elbow in his ribs. "I'd kiss you, but in that shirt you smell like Jock's after-shave." She gave a skip and started to the front door.

"And you smell like you've been frying chicken fries all day," he called after her.

She lifted a wave, and Jessie's blouse dropped from one shoulder.

When he pulled from her drive, he noticed the rain had stopped. As he drove, he angled his head one way, then the other to gander through the windshield. Clouds were breaking up; hit-and-miss stars had forced an opening in the sky.

Once home, he started upstairs, but stopped abruptly, wondering if Sadie was home. Her bedroom door was ajar, and he edged in quietly. She was lying among her pillows with her dark hair lapped over one. Home. At least she was home, and he could sleep through the night.

At the upstairs landing, he put his head into Josie's room. She was curled on her side, her long braid twisted across her face and the kitten asleep in the crook of her arm.

He lifted Freone, rubbed one finger between her tiny ears and roused her enough for a yawn. "So you're going to be a house cat, are you?" Her purr drummed against him. At Josie's window, he studied the sky, still dark. But he could feel the day moving in, and it felt good.

7

Bacon. Frying. The aroma was strong enough to wake him. In a muddle of covers, he stared up into dust flecks lazily floating in sunlight. He closed his eyes, inhaled the trail of bacon, and realized, happily for the moment, that he'd overslept. But a portion of the morning, a wedge of daylight, had been cut from beneath him, so he threw off the blanket, swung to the side of the bed, and shoved his feet through rumpled blue jeans, left in a heap the night before.

He should have got up much earlier, when he'd heard Josie leave for church, heard the Gospel Chariot crunch across the gravel and Josie slap, slap, slap down the back steps.

"Are you going to sleep all day?" His mother's voice floated upstairs. He had an arm half through a sleeve, but he stopped and cocked his head when he recognized her teasing tone. Outside his room, he waited at the banister, almost directly above where she stood at the foot of the stairs. She couldn't see him because the stairs turned halfway up at the landing.

"Hey, up there."

"What's the big hurry?" he asked with calculated indifference. "You haven't even started breakfast yet." On tiptoe, he returned to the bed and tugged on socks and boots. "Can't see the hurry. Can't smell the bacon yet."

"I suppose you want coffee in bed."

She was in the kitchen now, standing at the stove, shaking

her head and smiling.

"That'll be great. I'll stay in bed until you have time to run it up here." He pushed up and down until the springs beneath him squeaked. And he waited for her to come to the stairs again.

"Patrick, are you playing games? Are you still in bed?"

He sauntered down the steps and turned at the landing in a loose-limbed skipping fashion as he rolled up his sleeves. "Guess I'll have to get up. I can see I'll get no rest around here."

Near the bottom of the steps, he was greeted by her mock-serious manner and the easy smile she lifted to him. Her face was pale and prominent with her hair drawn back and tied. In one sweep, he took in her sagging blue jeans, her faded flannel shirt, and knew he wouldn't have to risk the question. She was going to stay at home.

He followed her to the stove and leaned over her as she poked the sizzling strips. "God, how long since we've had bacon?" He caught a trace of the smoky aroma clinging to her hair.

"It's going to be even longer if you don't start a fire in the Franklin."

"Fire? Do we need a fire? Just look at the sun." He motioned out the window. "It'll be seventy-five by noon." Sunlight glistened in milky, iridescent patterns over the wet grass. Glassy puddles shimmered in low cups.

"Your Gramma Rho would say, 'This is the day the Lord hath made.'" She gave a slight spin on her toes from the stove to the sink and braced her hands against the counter, leaning into the sunlight. "It is a good day."

She released such a spirit of elation that he felt a sudden quickening of joy and an impulse to lift her up, spin her about the room, swing her kicking and laughing. But he turned abruptly and went to the bathroom, feeling an unaccountable need to hurry now, to take in the day. If he moved fast enough, whittled wasted motion to the core, he could crowd everything in. Nothing would get away from him.

As he ate, he ticked off the things he could remember from his list still in his room. Look over foals, decide which to sell, which to keep. "Keepers" — those they decided against putting through the sale ring — had to be weaned, turned into a separate pasture from their mothers. He disliked the job and had been putting it off. For days after mares and foals were parted, the air was filled with shattering calls: the shrill running whinnies of babies and the plaintive responses of mares as each recognized her own. Months later, when he brought them together again in one pasture, they would nuzzle each other in a casual greeting, but the devotion they had once shared would be severed.

"Slow down," his mother said. "I know you've got lots on your mind, but we'll get it done, and what we don't get done can wait."

"Mom, we've waited long enough. Those colts should bring a good price in the sale ring, and when spring comes, maybe we'll have mares lining up for Tug's service. The sale is . . . when?" He scanned the room for the calendar. "Look there." He pointed with his fork. "Three weeks away."

Sadie stacked dishes in the sink and trailed her fingers through running water. "Well, come on," she lifted brightly. "We'll start now. Dishes can wait."

Outside, a shaft of sunlight narrowed through trees along the east side of the house. Sadie spread her arms to the warmth.

"This may be our last good day, Mom. Before winter."

They walked in step together, covering the short distance to the barn. As Patrick shoved the big door on its metal runners, the barn cats blinked and scuttled to cold corners. The alleyway flooded with light, and in stalls, the horses wheeled and impatiently rumbled for grain. Sadie and Patrick took up tasks in wordless routine; Sadie filled buckets with grain, and Patrick climbed the loft for hay. In the feed room, she turned on the radio and tripped along with a rock tune.

"Tug, Tug, Tug, you're a lu, lu, lu."

On the loft floor above her, Patrick swung hay bales as

though they were bundles of duck down. He lifted them above his head and sailed them to the solid earthen alleyway, where they bounced to a landing or cracked open, spilling hay for Sadie to gather in her arms.

"You know what we're going to do today, Patrick?"

He went to the edge of the loft and peered down. From above, she appeared all face and jutting elbows, with her hands set firmly on her hips.

"Yes," he nodded. "I know what we're going to do today."

She ignored his businesslike tone. "We're going to have a picnic, that's what." She beamed, her cheeks two burnished points at either side of her smiling mouth.

Patrick gave her a shrug and reached for another bale. "We're having no picnic."

"Ah, come on. Down in the cottonwoods. We haven't been back there for months." She paused. "And you don't need to be an old man about it either," she said emphatically.

He hoisted a bale to his shoulders and glanced down. "Move out of the way. This bale's coming down."

She skipped aside. "I know you, Patrick. You're trying to ignore the whole idea. Thinking I'll forget and go on to something else."

He ignored her and tossed the bale.

"But the way you and me work," she continued, "we can get these colts tended to by the time Josie comes home from church. We'll ride the horses out and have dinner. That's all. No big deal. We'll still have the whole afternoon to work."

"We don't have time," he responded stoically and descended the loft ladder. "If we get finished up on colts, I'll work on the truck." He added an emphatic pause. "Maybe we can even get in another driving lesson."

She pushed her mouth into a wrinkle and waved his idea aside. "That can wait." She piled hay so high her face was hidden, and then in a flash, she dropped it all at her feet. "Hey. I just thought of something. Your birthday. It's only a week away. We'll celebrate early."

"Birthdays are no big deal. And will you get with it?" But then he had to laugh when she went at the hay again and came up sputtering with it caught in her mouth and hair.

Together they carried hay out a rear door. He elbowed aside mares and foals to make a way to feeders, and the horses circled them, snatching mouthfuls of hay.

"Besides," Sadie gave him a gentle shove as they hoisted the last of a bundle into a bin, "when Josie gets home, it'll be two against one."

He started to say something, but she anticipated his response and tossed back an answer before he could say anything. "And we're not going without you."

Patrick ran his hand along the neck of a filly. "Then you'd better get in gear. No more dancing around the barn. We need some halters to take out these colts so we can have a look at them."

She let out a childlike whoop of pleasure and made off for the barn. He shook his head. With his arm resting across a filly's back, he felt the warmth of her hair-coat, which already had soaked up a full measure of morning sun.

When Sadie returned with a knot of halters noosed over a shoulder, he pointed to a chestnut colt. "Get that one there. With the blaze. I'll take this filly here." She tossed him a halter. "I got these two pegged as the pick of the lot, but I want to see what you think."

They led the foals through a side gate to a hitching post in front of the barn, where they tied the colt to one side, the filly to the other. Sadie strolled around one, then the other. She ran her hand down the filly's legs, which set the weanling twisting at the end of her halter, her eyes popping as Sadie moved confidently from side to side.

"Easy. Eeeeeesy, girl." She scooped up a front foot, cupped it in her palm and examined it briefly before she set it in place. "You've been working with her, Patrick. She's gentle." She tickled under the filly's chin. "She's nice," she said in mellow, crooning tones.

"What do you think? Which one do you like?"

She took another gander at the chestnut colt, squatted behind him and narrowed her eyes. "Let's see the filly move," she said.

He led the filly directly in front of Sadie. With a click of his tongue and a snap of the lead shank, he brought the filly into a jog. After they'd traveled halfway across the lot, he gave a single downward stroke on the halter and the filly dropped her heels and stood waiting at his elbow.

Sadie chuckled, pleased. "You *have* been working. She moves like a Swiss watch. She's got an eye on you all the time, waiting for your cue."

"She's got a lot of sense between those little sharp ears of hers."

"Okay. Let's see if the colt measures up."

Patrick put the filly back at the rail and worked the colt in the same manner. He considered telling Sadie of the judge's interest in the colt, but decided to wait a little longer.

"Do all of them out there work like these two?" Sadie asked when he trotted back with the colt.

"Not with this kind of class," he said, "but they're broke to halter. They'll lead okay in a sale ring." They walked together to the post, and Patrick looped the colt's rope in place. "But you haven't told me what you think yet."

"I don't know." She gave a dispirited sigh. "I don't think I have the eye for it anymore. Like you do."

"That's no answer. Besides, you'll never lose the knack of recognizing a good horse."

"But I haven't been working with the horses lately, Patrick." She gave a shrug. "What do you think?"

"I know which one I like. I'm just waiting to see if you agree."

She drew out a long sigh that took with it some of her early morning gaiety. "If I have to pick, I'll go with the filly. But the colt is just as nice. Moves just as well. Straight-legged and all."

"That's what I thought you'd say." He paused to lift his cap and reset it across his forehead. "I got a little surprise for you. Judge Croft stopped by a week or so ago to have a look at the weanlings. The colt here just took his eye. He's a picture of old Tug. I think when I finally get through dickering with the judge, he'll pay at least twice what we could get for the colt in a sale ring."

"I'll be damned," she said softly. "You didn't tell me." Her mood flattened. "The judge came to see you."

"I wanted to surprise you. Besides, there's nothing definite about it. I haven't seen any money yet."

"But he came to you. He didn't even stop by the newspaper office to talk to me."

"It doesn't matter. What difference does it make?"

"None, I suppose. Most of the work falls to you anyway." Her words trailed off as though she were thinking of other things. "Sometimes I think these horses, this big place . . ." she swung her arms to take in the pasture, the work arena, the barn behind them. "It just pulls us down into a rut. Keeps us doing things."

"We could live anywhere, even over there in Redbud Acres, and there'd be plenty to keep up." He started back to the paddock with the filly. "But this is our home."

She followed him to the gate and leaned into the fence with a boot braced against the bottom rail. "Hell, home can be anywhere, Patrick. We ought to sell this place," she tossed off. "Move on to something else."

He brought himself up short and leaned across the filly's back. "You sound just like *him*. That's exactly what *he'd* say."

But she ignored the implication. "Be reasonable, Patrick. We might find a buyer now. People are looking for big spreads like this."

He went back to the hitching post for the colt. "Sure. Sure," he said crisp and hard. "Sell every last one of them. Black Judy, Tugaloo, even Simone, that mare of yours we bought in Oklahoma." He pressed his mouth into a frown and gave a contemptuous lift of his chin. "Sure, Mom, and all those mares due to foal and our equipment and every damn thing."

"You don't need to be so sarcastic," she shot back. "It's something to think about."

He swept his cap from his head and slapped it against his thigh. "You think about it all you please. But we're not doing it." He bit down on his inside cheek and stepped away to collect his resolve against quarreling with her. "How long have we been working at this place?" He began evenly. "Thirteen years. And it's just getting to the place where it might pay off. Give it a little time . . ."

"Thirteen years, Patrick, is a hell of a long time."

"Will you just hush and listen a minute?" He shoved his hands into his front pockets and looked far down the road.

What had happened to bring them to this point? Suddenly everything had been whipped out of his hands.

"Tugaloo's foals are coming into their own. This spring, people with horse money are going to come looking at old Tug, and my bet is they'll come back with their mares."

"And then you've really got work," she shot back. "You have no idea what's involved. This place is all right for us, but you start bringing in outside mares, and it's another story. We'd have to rig up more stalls, paint, fix this place up."

"I know. The place needs all that anyway."

"But that's not the half of it. We'd be up every night checking our mares as they foaled and every daylight hour breeding mares."

"We could do it. We've done it before."

Her shoulders slumped as she sauntered away halfheartedly. "I suppose we could, Patrick. That's not the point. I don't much want to do it anymore, and we never seem to give a thought about whether what we're doing is what we really want to do."

"But I thought it was what you'd always wanted. Your own horse operation. You don't just pick up your skirts and go walking away just because it gets a little rough or the mud gets a little deep."

"But maybe we want to do something else." She pressed

down on each word.

"We're not talking about *we*. It's you. That's what you're really driving at."

"So what if it is? You and Josie are growing up, and maybe I don't want to take care of these horses, this place, for the rest of my life." Her voice crackled in the space between them. "I've been stuck out here long enough." With quick steps she started into the barn, but he followed her, dogging her heels.

"You don't do that much anymore. Half the time you're off running around with . . . doing your own thing."

"That's right." She stooped to yank up baling twine they'd left behind, then to hang up lead ropes, halters found beneath hay. "That's what I'm trying to tell you. I got other things I want to do now. I don't want to worry about these horses, worry about you doing all the work. And then someday when you're as sick of it as I am, have you pick up and leave."

A sharp catch in his ribs took his breath momentarily. "I won't pick up and leave. That's not my way. You ought to know it."

His eyes held her briefly, then she spun around, but before she could take a step, he reached her shoulder and with one hand, he twisted her to face him. She raised her hands to cover her face. "Look at me." He shook her gently. "Don't start crying. I don't want you crying." She lowered her hands until they folded like wings in front of her. He could feel her breath at his neck as she leaned back slightly to look at him. "You got no right to say those things." The pain beneath his ribs forced a catch in his voice.

She eased her arms up and around his waist then and sank against him, her head cushioned on his chest. "I know. It was wrong of me." She felt small against him. How could she be so forceful and yet so frail inside her clothes? "But it's for you too, Patrick. If you could only see that. You should have your own life. Outside of me and Josie and this place."

He stroked her back as though in doing that single, simple act, it would ease the pain he felt. "My own life is here." But

110

even as he said it, he gathered a dim understanding of what she meant, of what he hesitated to look full face upon.

In a rush, hay and dust scattered behind him.

"This is the day the Lord hath made." Josie ran to them and wrapped her arms about them. "A perfect day for a picnic."

Sadie stood back from him and took Josie in beside her. "We knew that would be the very thing you'd say."

By midafternoon they left on horses, riding bareback and following paths cupped by the horses through fading autumn pastures. Overhead, a summer sky offered an immense blue, as open and far-reaching as the ocean. Not even threads of white clouds trailed. Ahead of Patrick, Sadie on Simone and Josie on Doradella chattered like schoolgirls. Their hips swayed with the easy rhythm of the horses' movements as they dallied, snatching at low arbors and the swaying seed heads of grass. Pausing occasionally, the mares swung their heads on loose reins to flick at flies along their flanks.

"Look up," Josie called and pointed above her. "The geese are flying south." Sadie cupped a hand above her brow. Patrick looked instead at his mother and sister. He heard the birds' restless voices, a distant gabble drawing closer.

"A perfect V," Sadie called back to him. "You're not looking. They'll be out of sight soon. You won't see them again until spring."

He followed her hand then. Dropping the reins about Black Judy's neck, he placed both palms behind him and leaned back until his loose hair fell to his neck. In flight, the birds appeared as check marks against the great swath of sky beyond. An unconscious efficiency seemed to prompt a lead bird to fall back occasionally and allow another to assume the point position. In the constant weaving and dipping of their ribbon formation, spaces opened between them, yet they remained intense and purposeful in their direction.

When he looked ahead of him, his mother and Josie had ridden to a point near the rear corner of Caleb's land. Sadie turned Simone then and cantered back to him.

"Josie and I are going to ride over to Caleb's. Maybe he and Sandra can come with us."

"Sounds good."

"Wait here if you want. I can carry Caleb behind me on Simone. Josie can bring Sandra." She handed him the saddlebags in which she'd packed a lunch before they'd left. "Hold this. Just don't eat anything." She pulled away. "No peeking either. It's your birthday dinner." She spurted off to where Josie trailed through underbrush.

He didn't have to peek. He could smell fried chicken.

He draped the saddlebags behind the reins over Black Judy's withers and rested back across the mare — back to back. Her black hair-coat had absorbed the sun's rays; she was like a heating pad. As she moved among short clumps of grass, his head nodded with the undulation of her hips. Flies, looking for her flanks, found his face instead. He closed his eyes. Far away, he heard the screech of a bird and thought first of the geese, but the cry was different, yet familiar. *Karaka.* The prairie falcon. Probably the same one he and Caleb and Sandra had seen the day before.

He sat up and looked around him. Shielding his eyes from the intense sunlight, he scanned the sky, but the sun's angle prevented him from catching sight of the bird, of anything. He tried to dodge the glare, but his eyes were filled with light. He glanced down, catching a glimmer of the bird's shadow slicing across the earth in front of him. Descending, the dark form grew larger until each black feather of its spread wings was outlined against the shallow earth. He thought he would see the bird then, that the bird and its shadow would become one as it swooped upon a field mouse, but the silhouette suddenly lifted, ascending until the shadow was a blur. Then nothing. Only seconds had passed since the bird's first cry, yet he felt the time had been much longer. The vision of the bird's shadow remained with him while he waited.

Black Judy brought his attention back as she whinnied to Doradella and Simone, ripping through the pasture. Josie clutched Sandra in front of her, and Sadie rode with Caleb behind.

"God, what a ride, Patrick," Caleb said with a snort. He had both arms wrapped around Sadie's midsection. "I don't think I could have hung on any longer."

"Now, Caleb," Sadie said. "You were ready to race all the way to the cottonwoods."

"I'm getting off and riding with Patrick." Caleb made a move to swing off Simone, but Sadie stalled him.

"Okay. Nice and easy from here on. Simone and I will be good girls."

Patrick watched them angle off ahead of him, their voices growing dim as he lagged behind. The distance grew until they appeared stationary, splendid touches of color dabbed against gray trees, with a blue sky arching overhead. He felt outside of all he had witnessed, yet bound by some invisible thread linking joy, sorrow, and dreams.

They disappeared into the trees, and he was left with the illusion of them that seemed stronger than if he'd been with them. In his mind, he saw them moving about in the coolness under the cottonwoods. Caleb, slipping from Simone's broad back, would lift Sandra from Josie's arms. Josie would scoot, belly down, over Doradella's rump, gripping the mare's tail as she slid. And his mother, dismounting lightly, would lead Simone to the creek to drink. Then turning, she would look back for him.

SON/
HUSBAND

*"The truth is, Patrick, you made a better
husband than your father."*

8

"**I** could use a haircut," he said to Sadie as they drove to Stella one morning. It was mid-November; winter had descended in a cold fury and without snow.

"Too cold to snow," many people said, as they sat over Jessie's warm cinnamon rolls at ten o'clock coffee, which prompted Caleb to declare, "Don't you believe it. Winter's a cheat, the unreasonable season."

"Haircut?" Sadie replied, her voice lifting. "I don't have to cut your hair anymore. You're making money now. You can go to Hank's shop same as the rest of them."

"I'm not spending any more money than I have to. Least-wise, not for any damn haircut. You can cut it like always."

She gave an exasperated sigh and pressed a woolen tam to the side of her head. "Just let me out at the corner." She hiked the straps of her purse and camera to one shoulder. "I gotta catch up with Semp Davies sometime today, and I think I just saw him go into the J & J."

At the square, Sadie hopped out as he slowed. "See you." She had neglected to button her coat, and it fanned out behind her. The air rushed in, brittle, dry, and cold.

"Hey." He leaned across the seat. "What about tonight? Are you going to need a ride home? Or what?"

She brought herself up short, and he gave her a moment to think about appointments she had that day.

117

"Don't think so. I've got school-board meeting to cover tonight. I'll catch a bite in town. Somebody can run me home."

"How late are you going to be?"

But she went right on with only a wave of her hand for reply. Her coat hem rippled at her knees, and her purse and camera swung free as she skipped along, holding her tam in place.

"So much for a haircut."

He left the square for a side street that took him to the Stella Feed and Grain. He had been working about a month for Udall Upshaw, long enough to get his first paycheck, which he'd asked Twila Canfield at the bank to cash. He took the money home and laid it out flat beneath the socks in his top dresser drawer, on top of the envelope containing the birthday card and the hundred-dollar bill from his father. It was the first time he'd been able to get a little money ahead, and he wasn't inclined to hand it over to Twila, see it snap through her fingers and disappear into the drawer in front of her. He wanted a pile of money he could count, not figures to scan in a savings-account book.

Udall Upshaw had asked him if he wanted the job one Saturday morning when Patrick had gone in for horse feed, and he started work the following Monday. Sadie and Josie showed only tepid interest, which cooled even more when they realized Patrick would have the heart sliced out of each day just as they did. But they agreed on an arrangement to divide morning and evening chores; fleetingly, Patrick thought the job might be worth more than money if it meant a return to the partnership they'd once had.

The job had come along when it was too favorable to reject. Work at the ranch idled; there were fewer horses, since many weanlings had been sold at the Chesterfield sale, and months would pass before mares would foal and cycle into season to be rebred. The money from the sale of foals, including the chestnut colt Judge Croft finally had bought, had been deposited in the savings account to collect interest until after the first of the year when the annual farm payment came due.

"Look at that." Patrick had said to Sadie, while he tapped a pencil against the last number in the account book. "And you wanted to sell the horses. We'd have given up too easy if we had."

Sadie, polishing her nails crimson, tipped the corners of her mouth down and waggled her head. She didn't want to hear "I told you so," and he didn't say that or anything else; his pleasure was in the knowledge that the sum, the most they'd ever saved, was largely a result of his efforts.

He left the square for a neighborhood of modest homes kept up well enough to appear luxurious against the little shotgun five-roomers trailing along at the end of the block near a neglected railway spur. Weary clapboards with unsteady front porches, they obviously had become too small for families that lived in them. At one time or another the porches had become spare rooms: overstuffed chairs, freezers, chifforobes, or a mishmash of children's toys had been yanked from inside to the porches for lack of anyplace else, and from there, belongings fell into front and side yards. Sometimes Patrick would drive along and come upon "Hardup" Perry getting ready for school and digging around for a shirt or something in a dresser close to his front door.

At the end of this dismal chain, the feed store blossomed, the one elaborate spot of color, and it would have been out of place anywhere. At one time, it had been merely the last house on the block, the one set closest to the tracks. But some years back, Udall, then in his thirties, decided farming didn't compensate for all he'd put into it, so he sold his land, auctioned off all his equipment, and started the feed store. Selling feed and grain and farm supplies, he reasoned, was the next best thing to actually using them. He was a practical man. He knew that what farmers needed to buy and what they were likely to buy were often two different things, and he stocked both. And while he wrote out a ticket or loaded the back of a truck with seed corn, he could listen to a man talk, adding all the right sounds of consolation — "Hummmmm" or "Ahhh, too bad" or

"Ain't it the way?" — about a hailstorm that had flattened fifty acres of wheat or scours running through spring calves, without putting much of anything into words when there was really nothing to say.

After he bought the little place, he painted it snow-white trimmed in red. He put red-and-white gingham curtains at the two front windows, without his wife's help since she slept days after working night shifts at Saint Theresa's Community Hospital in Chesterfield. He perched red flower boxes on the porch railings and filled them with red and white geraniums. Even the red-and-white checkerboard Purina signs that he stuck in the windows seemed as much decoration as advertisement. One July, the Purina company sent a photographer to take pictures of the store for their magazine, and Sadie got a front-page story and pictures of the man taking pictures of Udall, paintbrush in hand, on the front porch of the feed store. After that, Udall repainted every spring and kept a big stack of the magazines on the front counter with more underneath, but off to the side and not next to his girlie magazines.

Patrick liked working for Udall, which he'd done in the past during fall and spring when farmers bought more supplies than at other times. It was less money and harder work than the battery plant, but he wasn't about to cave in and go to work there. Besides, he thought an outside job would be only temporary, since he'd have to quit when spring came and horse owners started bringing their mares to Tugaloo.

Patrick bumped over the tracks, parked in the rear, and came in through the windowless back storeroom where the cement floor was grain-dusted and crisscrossed with footprints. Light angled back from windows at the front of the store, dimmed in a narrow hallway and fell to gray shadows in the rear. The two areas were like separate worlds — the front bright and cheerful as any kitchen, the back dark and dusty as the inside of a silo.

Patrick walked into the slab of light leading to the front and stuck his coat and cap on a rack.

"Morning."

"Morning." Udall did not look up from his stool behind the counter, where he was peeling one of the two navel oranges he ate for breakfast. He left his wife Judy asleep, and on his way to work, he stopped by Palmer's IGA for his oranges. He cut the hide into neat crescents with his tough, yellowed thumbnail before he folded the sections back into petals and ate the flesh. It was a neat operation; he never needed a napkin. He looked like a man more likely to grow flowers than to follow the dip of a disc through earth or to stack sacks in a dingy room.

"Purina man's coming today." His voice was low and raspy, unaccustomed to much use.

"I'll get a place cleaned out in back. I was mixing grain yesterday and left stuff strung around."

The pungent smell of orange oil lit the air and mingled with the odor of old wood and crimped grain.

"Suits me." Udall fitted the last orange section into his mouth and pressed back a yawn as he stretched up from his stool. He was nearly as tall as Patrick and so slim he looked about the same coming as going. He had the sort of oak-colored hair that assured freckles up his arms, across his forehead, and at the back of his neck.

Patrick made coffee in the kitchen, which Udall had left intact when he'd remodeled the house and had removed most of the partitions to set up bins and display cases. Udall never touched coffee, which included making it. He had no use for cigarettes, beer, hard liquor, or aspirins either, and he tried not to make too much of his girlie magazines, a final concession to an impurity he was unable to either deny or acknowledge. He bought them in Chesterfield or places farther on, and he kept them scattered in with the farm magazines in a corner under the counter where he could reach them easily when things were slow and few farmers stopped. Patrick was aware of the game he played. He'd stick a *Hustler* or a *Penthouse* inside the pages of a *Successful Farming* and begin to look at herbicide ads until, as if by chance, he'd stumble on a posed nude.

121

"It'll be slow today," Udall said. He sauntered to the front windows with his hands plugged into his pockets. He liked to guess what farmers would be doing on given days or at certain times of the year, as though visualizing himself still on the land. "They'll be sitting around their tables on a day like this, trying to figure out whether to sell beans now or hold," he said.

Patrick poured himself a cup of coffee and took it to the front, opposite Udall. The sun was beginning to work its way around clouds, slanting through the panes and sending columns of light to warm the hardwood chairs and tables for the "poker club," as Udall called the old farmers who traipsed into the store each morning well after their wives had given them breakfast and told them to find something to do until dinner. Having retired and given up the land, they had moved to town to die slow deaths in rockers instead of quick ones on tractors. The store — its smell of fresh grain, the loading docks for idling trucks, and the hobnobbing with men who still made a living on the land — kept them in touch with a life that no longer touched them. As for poker — they never played it or anything else for that matter. That was simply Udall's way of saying that farming was as much of a gamble as cards. Patrick had coffee ready by the time the first of the old men shuffled in. They hung up wraps, took their mugs from pegs on the kitchen wall, filled each other's cups, and took their places around the table, as orderly as they'd once been as schoolchildren. After they had convened, they began their recitations: what they thought the weather would likely produce for the day, followed by citings of extreme examples from the past — the deepest snow, the hottest afternoon, the heaviest rain. When talk of weather subsided, they would launch into a litany of farming experiences, which took them to noon. They listened to each other's stories as though for the first time, probably because they'd forgotten much they'd said from the weeks before, or perhaps because they didn't know which stories might not be told the week after. They were tender with each other, especially Mort Brock, who took the rocker to cushion his arthritis. When

122

Patrick announced a low supply of coffee, one of them brought a tin along with sweet rolls his wife had made.

Patrick fitted his mug to a hook and went to the storeroom. It was lit by one high ceiling lamp, but neither he nor Tuffs minded. The yellow tom liked the dark corners, where he prowled behind feed sacks for mice. Patrick swept back his hair and clamped his cap as close to his eyebrows as he could. Even so, in an hour's time, the dust would have stirred and sifted across his clothes and into his nostrils until his throat would taste dry and sour as old mash.

Udall was right. The morning slipped away with little activity. The poker club came and settled into place, and afterwards, only a few others stopped to pick up this or that. When someone entered, Udall shoved his magazines under the counter and picked up work on his account books.

By eleven o'clock, Udall's lanky frame cut across the light into the storeroom.

"Think I'll go to dinner," he told Patrick. It seemed early to Patrick, but probably Judy had the day off. Udall left early on those days and stayed away longer than usual.

Patrick followed Udall to the front, blinking as he went into the sudden flare of light and slapping his dusty cap against his shoulders and thighs. Udall did his best to keep dust in the storeroom and out of the house. He flicked a feather duster about the shelves or handed it to one of the old men, who stirred dust from chair rungs or the lamp hanging above Mort's rocker.

Patrick filled his cup and went to the front windows just as Rudy's van angled to the curb. Rudy was early today. Since Patrick had started working, he and Rudy had begun to eat lunch together at the J & J. Rudy didn't have a job. He'd always assumed he'd go to work at the battery plant, and after the accident, which closed that choice, he was at a loss to think of anything else. He still lived at home and whiled away his time lifting weights or cruising the square picking up loose girls who skipped afternoon classes at the high school. Most everyone considered him well-off, rich even, because of the insurance settlement. Rudy did what he could to elaborate on the idea, often buying drinks for everyone in an easy come, easy go fashion or carting home outlandish presents for his family. Lately, though, he'd discovered books and twice a week he went to Chesterfield's library or snooped in boxes at garage sales for paperbacks. He claimed reading was the fastest way to get wherever he wanted to go, and he read everything — from classics he'd managed to charm his way out of reading in high school to romances that told all the stories they had on their covers.

"That's Rudy already," Mort said, coasting to a stop in his rocker.

"Rudy?"

"Mort says Rudy's here. Early today."

Patrick set aside his cup and met Rudy as he rolled himself up the sidewalk in his wheelchair. When he came to the steps, Patrick tilted the chair back in his arms and lifted Rudy to the porch.

"Put me down now," Rudy said. "I can get this damn door." He swung the door back so hard it stayed in place long enough for him to push through. The old men stirred in their chairs, anxious to greet him.

"What's this? The poker club dozing? And it not dinner time yet?"

They smiled blandly at each other. What could anyone expect from Rudy?

"Enough of this. What we need is something to get your blood heated up." He pushed himself around the table and wagged a finger at Mort. "Aw no, Mort. None of your wild ideas. Nothing strenuous like that." They gave a self-conscious laugh. "Draw up around the table here. I'm going to make honest men of you." He pulled a deck of playing cards from the pocket of his macintosh and tossed them to the center of the table. "Deal the cards, Mort. Little five-card. Jacks or better."

The old men rubbed across the gray stubble of their faces,

jostled in their chairs, gave each other sideward glances of mock surprise.

"I forgot the poker chips, Patrick. See if you can round us up some corn from the storeroom."

Patrick brought out a can of corn and dumped kernels in front of each man, already sorting through his cards. Shortly, they were tapping their fingers against the table to indicate the number of cards they needed and tilting back in their chairs to give each other sidelong glances.

"Come on, boys. Bet with a vengeance," Rudy said. "It's only chicken feed. Plenty more where this came from."

It was well past noon before Udall returned, and the men folded their cards together.

"We'll get in a few hands tomorrow, fellas," Rudy said. They gave lively waves before they buried their hands in their overall pockets, picked their way aross the railroad tracks, and ambled up the sidewalk, breaking away from one another gradually.

"God, aren't you starved?" Rudy asked, heading his van toward the J & J. "I didn't think Udall would ever get back."

"He's always late when he goes home on Judy's day off."

"That's not too surprising when you think about it," Rudy chuckled. "I'd be late too if I had a little dish like Judy sitting beside my corned-beef sandwich."

"Judy Upshaw? I suppose so. She's pretty good-looking."

"Stacked, man. With nice big boobs. No wonder old Udall is late coming back from dinner. I'll bet he doesn't have to look at a *Penthouse* afterwards for three or four hours."

"You and your imagination, Rudy. You work it overtime."

"Imagination, hell, man. When do you suppose Udall gets a piece of tail with her working weekends and nights? That's not imagination, my simple friend. That's good common sexual sense."

"You've been reading too many trashy novels."

"No way. I'm going to ask Udall someday. 'Udall,' I'm going to say, 'what is it you and Judy *do* that takes so long?'" Rudy

125

threw back his head and ripped out a laugh.

Patrick shook his head. "Keep your eyes on the road. See if you can get us to the J & J and something to eat."

"I'll bet Udall would color up like a virgin at a blanket party." Rudy said, still chuckling. "About the way you color up, speaking of virgins." He swung a fist playfully to Patrick's shoulder. "Don't tell *me*, Pat. I can read you like Huck Finn. You're a damn fool for not getting your share. Believe me, it's there for the asking, and the girls would go for you. Big stud like you."

Patrick felt a sudden flush of embarrassment that he countered with a flash of anger.

"My sex life is none of your goddamn business, Rudy." But before Rudy could guffaw at that, he added, "And you don't have to say it. I know. I've got *no* sex life. But it's not as easy for some of us as it is for you." Then he caught himself and clapped his hands at his knees. "Goddamn, Rudy. I'm sorry."

"Hell, that's all right." Rudy reached across the seat to clasp Patrick's shoulder. "You don't need to raise up in all your misguided indignation. I know I get carried away. But it just craps my soul to see you let slip by all that good stuff I can only dream about." Then he let out another of his lumbering laughs. "We're a hell of a pair. One can't do it and the other don't know how." He made an expansive swing of the wheel into a parking space. "Come on. I owe you a chicken fry."

That afternoon after the Purina man left, the day stretched out with Patrick checking feed sacks as he heaved them into lop-ended stacks. The work didn't take much thinking, only muscle. That was one thing he didn't like about the job: it demanded little concentration — didn't rivet his attention the way working with horses did. Horses took everything: muscles, mind, and all his senses to keep from being outsmarted. "Keep a leg on each side and your mind in the middle," Gramma Rho would tell him.

But in the storeroom it was just count, check, and lift, which left him room to think. About Rudy. About his sass and sarcasm. About Rudy's razzing when it came to sex — or the lack of it. So what if I haven't had a girl? Was it written down somewhere that by a guy's twentieth birthday, he had to get laid? It wasn't that easy. Except for guys like Rudy. A guy had to have the "something else." Sex appeal, they called it. Animal magnetism. No, it was much more than that. Hell, Patrick had never seen an animal with animal magnetism. The "something else" was all human, and it didn't have anything to do with how a guy was built or how good-looking he was or even if he could do it, for God's sake. Look at Rudy. He could take Stella's square twice and get four girls on each round. Every girl Rudy picked up had it. Laurie had it . . . in Jessie's blouse. Women like Judy Upshaw were born with it, and by the time they were six, they knew all about using it. But some women, like Sadie, were slow to discover it — that cool, detached sensuousness, sly and foxy. Rudy was a prime example. And Allan. He sure had it. The poor sonofabitch. All he wanted to do that summer was teach me how to swim.

"If there's one thing I'm going to do this week," his father had said, "it's teach you how to swim." The two of them had been on their way to Venerie and his dad's job. It was the summer he was ten, maybe eleven, and he'd finally talked his mother and father into letting him go with Allan. A father-son vacation, he called it. It was July and so hot even the air smelled scorched. Swimming should have sounded like a perfect thing to do. Heat surged up from the asphalt and seeped through the floor of the truck and into the soles of his tennis shoes. But he didn't want to talk about swimming.

"It's hotter than putting up hay," and he laughed louder than he ordinarily would have.

"You ain't going to get homesick, are you?"

"No. No way."

"I'll turn around right now and take you back."

"No. I wanna go on. With you."

"That's the ticket." His father's voice was reassuring, determined.

Allan's fine long hair, faded to a pale palomino, whipped back like a silk fan on the breeze. He was so suntanned he looked muddy, and the long sinewy cords in his upper arms defined his weedy, rawboned body. A near smile always crossed his face whenever he was behind the wheel of the truck, as though he'd found his true center. Sometimes he'd shake loose a cigarette from the pack he kept on the dashboard, light it, and relax until it seemed the cigarette might fall from his mouth. But the paper would stick to his damp lower lip, and the smoke curled up for him to squint through.

They left Stella and Chesterfield behind, seamy withering little towns that looked as though they wouldn't turn anyone's head. Patrick realized they were really on their way, leaving everything behind, when Allan angled onto the interstate, and Patrick felt a sense of exhilaration — the same, he thought, his father must have felt each time he left for a new place, a new job.

They didn't talk anymore about swimming, but the subject was always ready to wash over him in any silence. He was older now, he told himself, he'd be with his father, and he wouldn't be afraid no matter how deep the water. By the time he and his father returned, he would be able to swim anywhere, even Mill Creek — where he'd drowned. Not nearly drowned, as far as he was concerned, but had been swallowed up by the mud of Mill Creek. Four summers before the trip with his father, he and Josie, just a baby then, had gone with their mother to swim at one point along the creek. Bouncing along, watching his mother dip Josie's feet in the water, he had stepped off into nothing. One moment the water was buoying him up, his feet were squishing through mud, and the next, nothing. Nothing to push against. Surprise overtook him first. How could water, so light fingered and weightless, contain the power to pull him, hold him down? He fought with thrashing fury at first. But then, like going to sleep, he simply gave up and eased into the mud as though into the pillow of his bed. In the next instant, at the moment he was content to sleep, he felt himself being lifted up, yanked so hard he thought his mother might be angry with him. For what reason? Oversleeping? Then instantly he realized she was stretching him out along the creek bank and straddling his back, pressing the heels of her hands between his shoulders. With each push, she called his name. He wanted desperately to tell her he was all right, and finally he managed to raise the fingers of one hand. For the next few days, he vomited regularly into the toilet bowl, and as he leaned over, only inches from the curdled mess, he was certain he saw there the tadpoles and leeches and minnows he'd taken in from Mill Creek. After that, he refused to swim in Mill Creek, in any water that came above his knees.

But things were different now, and by the time he returned, he'd be able to swim as well as his father, who could swim anywhere. Even the ocean.

"I've been swimming all up and down the Atlantic coast," his father told him as they drove along. "Your mother and I were married near the ocean. In Charleston, South Carolina."

He was not surprised. He had always pictured his father coming and going from worlds he knew nothing of.

They drove most of the day to reach Venerie. Allan turned down neighborhoods of arching elms to Justine's house. Patrick had never met Justine; she was just someone who owned the rooming house in which Allan stayed when he worked in Venerie. He generally found inexpensive rented rooms whenever a job required him to stay days at a time in one place.

"Besides, Justine's place is only a couple of blocks from the pool. You won't be stuck out in the country with nothing to do while I'm at work."

When they reached Justine's, she was sweeping her porch, slow and easy as though that were all she had to do that day. But when Allan called out, "Hey, Justine!" she straightened up and looked almost pretty. She was a big, horsey woman with blond hair gone to muddy streaks and some years older than his father, Patrick guessed. Her washed-out jeans were cut off at a point that made her thighs appear thick and a sleeveless shirt gapped beneath her arms to show her bra. She rested the broom between her breasts and began smoothing her blouse across her front, sweeping her hair to a knot on top of her head. But nothing stayed. She fell into disarray again as soon as her hands came back to the broom. She was a plain woman, Patrick decided, who had come up against the fact long ago but had never quite given in to it.

She set the broom aside and came down her porch steps to meet Allan. "You're here earlier than I figured. You should have called or something." She lifted her blouse by the shoulders and let it fall back. "Give me time to fix up."

"I made good road time." Allan tilted his head to one side to light a cigarette, squinting at her through the smoke.

"I got your room ready. And waiting. Everything just like you like it."

His smile was thin through a veil of smoke. For a time, it seemed to Patrick that Justine and his father were the only two people standing in the hot sun in the middle of the sidewalk. Their eyes seemed to follow a single track, meet in the center, and stay there. They stood close enough together so that Justine brushed against Allan's arm as she talked. There was something else, something lighter than the still hot air, and it seemed to swallow Patrick's presence in their own sense of each other.

Finally his duffel bag grew heavy, and he set it at his feet. The movement abruptly drew them apart.

"So this is your boy?"

"First time I've taken him with me. I'm teaching him to swim this week."

"Big kid like that, he don't know how to swim?" Her laugh came before she could hold it back. "Are you sure he's your kid?"

130

He and Allan had a room on the second floor with stairs leading from a door and hallway off the porch. One bathroom down the hall from their room was sandwiched between two other bedrooms Justine rented to vacationers, transients.

All that week, he and Allan went swimming in the steamy late afternoons after his father returned from work. Patrick tried to slip into the water without thinking about Mill Creek. How could it be anything like Mill Creek when the pool was all shimmering crystal and turquoise? But as soon as the water reached his chest, his teeth began chattering. With his mouth clenched, a cramp sent a convulsive spasm down his neck and shoulders, and when the water tickled around his neck, he remembered how deceptive water could be, and he lifted himself up to the side.

"Maybe I'll just watch you for a while."

Allan hardly stirred the water. Watching from the side, Patrick could not discern the separateness of his father's body from the rippling water that enveloped him. He could stay so long beneath the surface that Patrick made a game of trying to guess the place Allan would appear. He always surged into the air, casting a shower of bubbles around him that caught light and held it against the bleached downy fuzz of his dark upper body. With one sweep of his head, he tossed back a slick wedge of hair and sailed his arm over his head to signal for Patrick to follow him. "Come on! Don't be a baby!" Allan said, when he could see Patrick had no inclination to enter the water. "Either you get in, or I'm going to get out and throw you in."

Patrick flinched, but he wasn't surprised, really. He had expected the threat to be leveled sooner or later, and he felt a certain relief to have it voiced finally. Strangely enough, the threat forced him from the side of the pool and into the water. It kept him there all week and became, finally, so powerful that it lessened his fear of the water. He actually felt safer in the water than out of it, since the one fear — of the water — was replaced by the greater fear of his father throwing him in unexpectedly. In a disquieting way, he came to think of the water as protection, and when he walked from the locker room or the bathroom back to the pool, he found himself anxiously glancing over his shoulder, sensing his father creeping up behind him.

The lessons did not go well. Allan's natural ability as a swimmer hampered instruction. He was like some schoolteachers Patrick knew, who skipped the basics, assuming them to be too obvious to dwell on. Allan was mystified first, then irritated that his son was so inept in the water, as though Patrick's clumsiness were a shortcoming of Allan's own that he did not want to own up to. Patrick tried, bewildered himself at his inability, since most of his fear had vanished.

"Now swim to me," Allan would say as he backed away, leaving Patrick treading water. But as Patrick started, beating desperately against the water to keep his head free, he knew Allan was continuing to edge backwards, always out of Patrick's reach. Exhausted, he would give himself up to the water just as Allan's hands gripped beneath his elbows.

"You can do better than that. Can't you feel the rhythm?"

"No," he'd retort. "There isn't any rhythm. Not like when I'm on a horse's back."

"Forget about the goddamn horses for once. You're swimming now."

They'd leave the pool cool and silent, and it wasn't until evenings when Justine joined them as they walked down to one of the bars along the main street that Allan began to relax. He was self-assured and aloof with Justine around. Her presence opened a space between him and Patrick that gave some distance to the competition they waged at the swimming pool.

Fresh from a shower, Justine smelled of talcum powder, and she could be pretty with lots of makeup, her lips and nails the same brilliant red. They never talked of anything important: the antics of Justine's cats, around which her life seemed to revolve, or the men Allan worked with whom Justine seemed to know. They smoked cigarettes and drank a few beers and tossed quarters to Patrick for the jukebox. Then they strolled back to Justine's and sat on the steps of her porch, looking for the Big Dipper among the thousands of stars above them, wondering if the heat was ever going to let up or if a rain cloud was ever going to break into that limitless sky. Usually Patrick left them talking and went upstairs to the room, with the air conditioner humming as he dropped off to sleep.

In the morning, Allan left before daybreak to get in as many hours as possible before the day heated up. Patrick, unaccustomed to sleeping late, was up soon after Allan left. In a room beneath him, he could hear Justine's shower running. She worked as a foreman in a canning factory. "Dark as a dungeon," she'd say, "except for all those overheads shining off them metal cans jiggling along the conveyor belt. I come outside, and the biggest surprise I have all day is what the weather's like."

After Justine left, he'd creep down the steps as though someone were still around to hear him. As he went across the porch, Justine's two white cats, perched on the back of her couch, stared with bold blue eyes through the white lace of her curtains. The neighborhood was full of cats and dogs. He'd take off for town to find a little breakfast with money his father had left him, and it seemed the houses along the block belonged to the cats and dogs. Shades were drawn, places were quiet and empty, but the yards were full of cats scurrying under bushes or porches and dogs yapping at the ends of their chains. The dogs made a chorus as he progressed up the street. Still, they didn't seem hostile, only bored, looking for something to do.

He was bored himself, after the first day and the novelty of the city had worn away. He was not one to fool himself, and within a day he realized people in Venerie were doing pretty much the same thing as those in Stella: opening shops, dropping off cleaning, standing on street corners stalling the day. The vacationers were different. Stella had few people passing through, spending money, looking for amusement. The vacationers in Venerie began to crowd the sidewalks by midmorning, intense and hurried. He observed them in wonder. They rushed along in a single lane of sidewalk traffic, coasting around idlers and losing patience with anyone who stopped long enough to cause a traffic jam. He came to the conclusion they'd been traveling so long, cramped together in vehicles, seeing how many inches on a road map they could wear away, that a destination left them unchanged.

Time for Patrick hung as lifeless as heat in the air. The days failed to progress in a steady expected course. Duplicates of one another, they bore nothing to distinguish one from another, and they stretched out indefinably. He caught himself looking for the time and visualizing what his mother and Josie would be doing. Nine-thirty: they'd be mixing grain for the foals. Ten: they'd be hurrying to exercise young horses before the morning grew too hot. Maybe it wasn't so hot there. Maybe it was raining, and it intrigued him to consider where in the distance between them the weather might have changed. But if the weather was different there, then he was unable to correctly gauge what his mother would be doing. The distance grew greater, heavier each day.

As the week drew on, even the swimming lessons were carried out matter-of-factly. Patrick's most accomplished effort was a side crawl that bore no resemblance to his father's effortless stroke. They relaxed in the knowledge that Allan was unable to teach, Patrick unable to learn, and each unconsciously accepted a portion of the blame. Allan never threw Patrick in the pool, and by week's end even that fear, so acute only days before, had evaporated. He was amazed at how things could turn around in such a brief time.

On the night before they left, the three of them cooked steaks on Justine's outdoor grill. She wore a flowered dress with flouncy tiers that emphasized her broad hips, but still she was pretty as she padded barefoot between the kitchen and the patio. She and Allan joked good-naturedly. Allan kidded her about tracking up her kitchen with dusty feet, and she said she'd have tomorrow, the rest of her life, to scrub the floor. She lit cigarettes for both of them, handing one to Allan as he stirred beer into catsup sauce he'd made. Once outside, they forgot whose cigarette had been left cocked over the edge of the picnic table, and they both took drags from it.

Allan fussed over the coals and the meat and the sauce in a way that amazed Patrick. At home, his father never took the least interest in food, but at Justine's, all reticence fell away as he unfurled his hand over particular dishes he concocted. He was lighthearted, almost swaggering. And entirely different. Patrick saw him more as a man than as a father. It was as though a window blind had been raised slowly throughout the week to reveal a hallway with doors left ajar into any number of rooms. It fascinated him to think the rooms always had been there and what each might contain.

When they carried the dishes to the kitchen, Allan stayed to dry as Justine washed. Patrick sauntered into the living room and held the white cats in his lap while he watched television. Justine brought in bowls of popcorn, and Allan followed with a tray of drinks. They could have been a family on vacation, getting ready to start out fresh the next morning.

Sometime during the night, a flare of light woke Patrick. The light came through the open doorway and cut a wedge into the room. Patrick raised himself enough to see his father's empty bed, the sheet and pillow pressed into Allan's angular shape. He smelled cigarette smoke. He was at the point of turning back to sleep, thinking Allan had gotten up for a smoke, perhaps a trip to the bathroom, when above the hum of the air conditioner, he heard Justine's voice. Justine. He was certain of it. He couldn't see the doorway, so he inched down until he saw his father's back, standing in the loose gray shorts he wore to bed. But before Patrick could move, see Justine beyond his father, Allan unexpectedly stepped into the hallway and closed the door.

Patrick began to cry. He had no forewarning of tears at the surface, and it seemed unreasonable to cry. Still, tears brimmed the lower rims of his eyes and ran to the corners of his mouth. He lay back down and cupped his hands beneath his head to force himself to stop crying so he could listen. He heard nothing above the churn of the air conditioner. He tried to pick up Justine's voice again, any voice. He thought about going to her door and swinging it open, surprising them, but he didn't want to see them. He'd seen them all week, touching each other with their eyes, their voices, yet never really touching. He thought of the nights he'd left them sitting on the front steps. He didn't know when his father had come to bed. Or even if he had. Maybe he stayed the night with Justine. Full of remorse, he realized he never should have left them. Or perhaps if he'd taken to swimming better, working harder, his father would have felt less discouraged, less inclined to turn to Justine. He should have known from the beginning . . . . The door opened and closed without a sound. He held his breath and heard only the whisper of his father as he passed between their beds.

Clearly he'd been wrong. His father had gone to smoke a cigarette outside the room. He hadn't been to Justine's bedroom and she had not come to him. She'd never been outside the door. His father was right there; already his breathing was heavy and deep. Justine meant nothing to his father; she was someone easy to know, openhearted and looking for company. His father had stayed in her home any number of times and nothing had happened. Besides, she was much older than his father and not the least bit pretty.

Nevertheless, he kept waking during the night to listen for his father's breathing. The next day, they left Venerie before daybreak and without seeing Justine again. Not even her cats stirred behind the lace curtains.

Patrick slept a good part of the way home. Sleep was the best way to pass the time, and he was anxious to return. Black Judy had had a colt early that spring, and he was certain his mother hadn't had time to work with him. By the time Allan reached Chesterfield, it seemed to Patrick that they never had been away, that perhaps they'd only driven into Stella for supplies and were now hurrying home before supper.

Patrick glanced up from his clipboard to note that it was nearly closing time. Up front, Udall was leaning over the counter with Lester Tessendorf, who was spreading out an advertising layout for Udall's approval. Patrick's view of the two men was confined within the scope of the door frame, with the full glare of the light upon them. Lester, unaware of Patrick in the storeroom, played only to Udall. He gripped Udall's shoulder to bring forth a point, gave out a smile that forced his lips open and exposed a white expanse of teeth. His self-confidence was as starched as his shirt collar. As fresh as new day, he was a picture of vigor and energy set off against Udall's weary appearance, his shuffling, hangdog manner.

Lester began to roll up the layout sheet in preparation for leaving. He still had on his wheat-colored soft outer coat, and he tucked the rolled-up tube under his arm to push his fingers into kid gloves, flexing them to ease them in place. He held his hat, a checkered wool, at the front crease, and he set it with care to one side of his head, over his carefully arranged hair. He stayed a few more moments, still talking, tapping the paper tube against the long side of his overcoat. Lester's swaggering air reminded Patrick suddenly of his father when he had been with Justine, a confident exaggeration beyond anything said or done, a cunning insincerity easily shrouded, nearly impossible to detect in the common light of day. Such people, so easily trusted, were not to be trusted.

It was nearly ten that night before Sadie came home. Treva Whitehair, a member of the school board, dropped her off.

"You still up?" she said as she whisked in the door with her coat unbuttoned and flapping, her cheeks a pink flush from the cold.

"Yes. I thought you might cut my hair. Laurie's family dinner is this weekend."

"Jesus, Patrick. It's pretty late."

"I know."

On tiptoe near his back, she ran her fingers through the back of his hair. "Okay, but let's hurry. I'm tired." She took up the scissors and comb from the oak table while he shucked his shirt.

"I've already cut the top. Just the back and sides."

She set the comb at his forehead and ran it straight back to his nape with her hand following closely. She began clipping over his ears; her fingertips against his neck made him shiver.

"I know, my hands are cold." She stuck the comb in place and briefly tucked her hands between her thighs. Then she placed them on either side of his neck. "That's better, isn't it?" She took up the comb and scissors again, snipping as she ran the comb against the grain of his hair. He held his chin against his chest, his hands folded and his knees bent tight.

When she leaned toward him, he caught a whiff of her breath, sour, crested with the smell of alcohol.

"You've been drinking." He tried to straighten his legs, but he seemed wedged between the chair seat and the light pressure of the scissors against his head.

"It's nothing. The school board didn't meet until seven-thirty. Lester and I went to his place after work for dinner. I had a couple of beers. That's all."

"To his place?" He started to get up.

"Don't move." she said sternly.

"You don't even like beer. You shouldn't drink it when you don't like it."

"I'm a big girl, Patrick. I can take care of myself." She leaned against his shoulder as she cut. Unable to move, his legs ached.

"That's just big-time talk," he snapped out, unable to look up. "And you're small-time, whether you know it or not."

For a moment, the scissors were poised above his head. Then in blunt, precise snips, she began cutting again.

"Hold still. I'm nearly finished."

9

"You kids get to the family room and play. Grandma don't want you underfoot when it's time to take the turkey out."

"Stan, you watch Tammy now. She'll follow 'em down the steps, sure."

"I tell you that English pointer Cruthers bought is a hunting fool. We took her out last weekend and bagged our limit 'fore ten."

"Put them cranberries in the icebox, Jackie. Be a while 'fore the turkey's browned."

"Who we waiting on?"

From where Patrick stood between the living room and kitchen in Laurie's home, he could catch the stream of talk flowing from the men in one room, the women in the other. The house was crowded with family, friendly and full of chatter. Whenever he was among them, he was heartened by the knots of them talking, arguing, joshing each other.

Thanksgiving had come and gone; Christmas was still in the offing, but in Laurie's big overlapping family, holiday dinners were put together at one home or another on weekend after weekend until after New Year's. "One big feed-for-all," Laurie would say with her mouth drawn into a scowl. She grew weary of the annual rite of passage to be endured for the sake of a new year. "I swear, it takes them until Memorial Day to lose all the weight they complain of gaining over Christmas. By then, it's time for family picnics."

No one else in her family seemed to share her views. They loved being together, rehashing stories, tossing cards across a table, leaning over each other to fit puzzle pieces in place. The old people contentedly cuddled the babies, and the parents were relieved to hand them over. And the cousins — a bustling clutch of cousins could take up play at the point when last they had been together, as though the break had been just long enough to renew the novelty of their games, the luster of each other. Or maybe it was the sheer number of them, so many that no one child was left out any longer than it took to find another pack of cards.

For all their unity, there was a certain liberty among them, since no one personality seemed to dominate. Even grand-parents, though esteemed, held no granted position of author-ity. Through countless generations, their dominant genetic trait seemed to be a reciprocal give-and-take. Unconditionally themselves, they assumed that anyone coming within their overlapping folds — as he did or any of Rudy's girl friends or Cathy, the divorcée Laurie's oldest brother Benjamin was to marry — gradually would be absorbed and in time assume familial coloration.

As Patrick stood by the steps leading downstairs into the Kieffer family room, he was unable to distinguish which cous-ins he knew; they grew and changed so fast. They all appeared nearly the same age, all dressed in similar fashion: little soft-haired girls in ruffles and hair bows and little boys in scuffed leather boots and double-kneed jeans. The youngest of the set, Tammy, he supposed, turned at the top step and scooted down on her knees, surveying her course from over her shoulder as her cousins swept around her like a stream that breaks around an impervious rock.

The men waited in the living room for the women to tie up the loose ends of the meal. The women bunched casseroles at one end of a long counter in the kitchen. They fanned bread slices, slivered cakes and pies, and through the long train of food, they left places for the turkey platter and the salads still to come from the refrigerator. Hurried, they spoke in snatches, knowing one would finish what another had begun. "I made Aunt Cleo's . . ." "Oh, that salad of hers would be . . ." "I know, but she always put marshmallows in and . . ." "It'll be just as good." When children darted among them, they swatted bottoms to send kids quickly on, leaving paths clear for the women.

Laurie plugged long-handled spoons into jars of sweet sauce and corn relish and lime pickles. Her cap of curls was caught back from her forehead with a narrow band nearly lost beneath her hair. The effect gave her a crown of ringlets that made her seem taller, more commanding, despite her small-ness. She was waif-like standing next to her pregnant sister Jackie, who occasionally halted long enough to hoist a young-ster to her hip.

Laurie resembled her mother more than any of her sisters did. Watching Mrs. Kieffer bend at the open oven to baste the turkey, Patrick noted the same narrow face softened by lines fanned from her eyes and beneath her cheeks, the same com-pact, useful little body except for the extra flesh folded over her hips and waistline. In Mrs. Kieffer's quick purposeful move-ments, he thought he could detect signs of Laurie years from now. Not that Laurie would agree. He could hear her counter, "Not me. I'm not carrying a baby on my hip, one in my belly, and another dragging on my leg. All I want is that little piece of paper that says I've graduated from college." That's the way she *really* felt, no matter what she had said to him lately to modify those sentiments. Because she *was* different from the others in her family. The last born, she had absorbed all the talent left behind by her brothers and sisters, and now, aware of what she could do, where her ability might take her, she was determined to test the limits her sisters had failed to see. Laurie's combative nature, he knew, was nothing more than makeshift armor against the uphill fight she viewed ahead of

141

her. Even Patrick could feel the shaping influence from one generation to the next. In such a comfortable groove, worn smooth by women in her family, Laurie would find few footholds from which to boost herself. Not that her family would discourage her; they would do what they could to give her a "leg up," but their attitudes would reflect little more than benign tolerance of her energy which, they reasoned, would subside gradually once the idea of marriage and family flowered.

"Ben and Cathy just drove up."

"With her kids or does their daddy get them this weekend?"

"The kids are with them."

"The wheat could use a heavy snow. We had snow by this time last year."

"Christ, I told him. I'm not working overtime on no god-damn assembly line at the opening of quail season."

"Is Cathy and Ben's wedding on or off now?"

"I'm going to tell her, you marry in this family, you marry for keeps."

"Now, Grandma, you stir up the thickening for the gravy."

The front door sucked open to a cold December wind followed by Cathy and Benjamin. He clutched a baby in one arm, a toddler in the other, as though toting feed sacks instead of children. Like all the Kieffer men, he was put together with angles — a square-jawed face with a short, square-shouldered body. The men's ages could be determined by their waist measurements; years and inches increased until the older men resembled hay bales thrust on end.

Cathy wiggled free of her coat while she balanced a platter of cookies at her hip and snatched at her children's caps as they squirmed in Benjamin's arms.

"Somebody help Ben with those babies."

"Trouble with you, Ben, you got too much catching up to do."

"Who we waiting on now?"

"Just Rudy. He'll bring four or five with him."

142

"Not this time. Just Ramona. That little Larkins girl."

"You mean Kyle Larkins' girl? You know, he and I stood there last spring in Halderman's Hardware and talked I bet twenty minutes about the calf loss, and the next day, I tell you, he was gone."

"Now, Patrick, don't go away. I want you to hand me down the gravy boat. You'll save me the time to get out my stool."

Patrick pushed through a current of children to Mrs. Kieffer near the stove.

"Up there. 'Long towards the back. With flowers on it. It looks like a little boat, floating on a China sea." The expression amused him; it was exactly like something Laurie would say. He transferred what he knew of Laurie to Mrs. Kieffer and felt he understood her. When their eyes met, hers were soft as gray flannel, but he could detect glints of steel in them. He sensed that she was a woman who could stand things and was no more likely to tolerate flimsy illusions than cobwebs in corners.

"Now you go on," she said softly. "Look out and tell me when Rudy and Ramona drive up."

Patrick crossed paths with a set of grandmothers, all pastel with light blue hair and pale polyester pantsuits, then bent to whisper to Laurie, "You're going to make someone a great little wife." She flipped a towel and caught him across his butt as he dodged Jackie's belly and came up short in front of Cathy and her plate of cookies. For an instant, the woman halted in place to laugh at him.

"Get this bull out of the china closet."

"Trying for a head start on Aunt Clovia's chocolate brownies."

It was all warm laughter and running voices. A glow of pleasure, even mischievousness, seemed rightfully his, and the feeling sped through him, quick as his laugh.

A volley of voices followed him from the kitchen as he made his way around card tables to the front windows. Cars and trucks edged the big circle driveway, leaving a spot vacant by the front walk for Rudy's van. The Kieffer home was fairly new, built after six children had left for places of their own and only Rudy and Laurie remained. The house was remodeled before they brought Rudy home from the hospital. Patrick remembered coming one weekend to help the men build ramps, widen doorways, install special fixtures in a bathroom. While the men worked, the women set up picnic tables under the elms and carried out food as though another family dinner were in progress. They grieved; yet what Patrick remembered of the day was their laughter — subdued, but still and all, laughter. For them, all things — sorrow, joy, labor — had a time and place, and whichever came could be mounted on their collective shoulders without their staggering under its weight. Never among them did they murmur that Rudy's accident was God's will or a tragedy singled out to them for previous sins. A religious family that seldom passed a church's portal, they would never have considered spiritual intervention for hardships they felt perfectly capable of assuming.

For a time after Rudy came home, his usual high spirits seemed gone for good. He was melancholy and morose. The first time Patrick came to see him, Rudy was lying on his side, away from a bedsore that had oozed open. "I got so little meat across my ass, Pat, my bones poke through." Patrick had been at a loss for words. Complaints were so unlike Rudy. But then something of his old perseverance surfaced, and Patrick was reminded of the summer he'd trotted Black Judy beside Rudy down the road, Rudy's muscle-taut body keeping abreast with the mare's forelegs. "I was laying here thinking about running. And I thought, what the hell. Everything's endurance. You gotta think like a distance runner, Pat. About everything. I used to walk a cross-country course and visualize myself running it, feel my legs pushing up a hill, see my arms working to bring my body along. I knew just how tired I would be at a certain point and where to take the long breaths to ready myself for the final sprint up over a hill and across the finish line. I was pretty damn cocky. I always pictured myself winning; I never ran a race I didn't win before I started. But now I see that just wasn't all ego; that's the way you gotta be in every goddamn thing. As all-powerful as I thought I was, I had the right idea; I knew my legs were nothing without my mind. You know, Patrick," and he pushed up on his elbows to face Patrick, "maybe I been in training for this a long time."

At the front window, with the sheer curtains pulled aside, Patrick watched Rudy angle his van into the slot left for him.

"Rudy's coming now."

"Pat says he sees Rudy, Emma."

"Get the kids washed, Tom. Check Tammy's diaper."

"I ain't changing her if she's got a load. She's just like a damn baler. In one end and out the other."

"Who else we waiting on?"

Ramona, in the bucket seat beside Rudy, kept her eyes fixed on him as he swept the van in place while he maintained his usual high style. With a lift of his chin, an explosion of his fist against the wheel, a spurt of laughter, he appeared as he had all week when he and Patrick had eaten at the J & J. Rudy could talk of nothing but Ramona. He was terribly excited about her, as though she were someone he'd recently met by chance instead of a girl he'd known since childhood. "You mean Ramona Larkins?" Patrick would ask skeptically. "That little washed-out blond? Graduated same year you did? Works at K mart in Chesterfield? *That* Ramona Larkins?" Impossible, he thought. "Rudy, she's not your type. She looks like she's been flatironed from the tip of her head right down to her toes."

But Rudy would hear none of it. "You haven't looked at her lately," he retorted. "She's different. She's not the same as when we were in high school. Anyway," he added with an air of finality, "you're no judge."

Rudy wasn't either in Ramona's case, Patrick decided. Her physical attributes, which Rudy had always noted on other girls, were of no relevance. He wasn't the least concerned about how she dressed or even if she fit in with his friends. The important thing was that she made him "feel terrific." He was adamant about it. He thought "tingling sensations" were returning to his limbs. It was much more than his mind, concoctions of imagination; feeling was returning to his body. She had lit up his mind first, but she had, as well, set off a reciprocal chord in his body. "I can feel, Patrick, and it's more than something going on in my mind. Don't ask me why, but no other girl has been able to do this to me."

She had changed, Patrick thought as he watched Ramona step from the van. She was heavier than he remembered; certainly, she wasn't the slight little thing he recalled from high school. She was plump in the way girls of small stature become when they gain weight with no place for it to go except midsections and hips. Her corduroy jacket failed to zip up the front, and even her blouse gapped around button closures. But the extra weight was becoming; her face was filled with a reassurance that added importance to her small features. She laughed and held out mittened hands to Rudy as he rolled from the van's lift. Impulsively she leaned to kiss him, and he set his hands securely on either side of her ski cap until she fell to his lap. He pushed under her and up the sidewalk. Suddenly serious, Rudy lifted his hands from the wheels and held Ramona, kissed her for a long moment while he stroked her face. But the wheels continued to turn slightly, and his chair inched backwards as they embraced until they ended where they had begun near the van. Patrick turned from the window, conscious of how vulnerable they were, their feelings raw and exposed against the brittle cold breaking all around them.

The door sucked open. "I don't suppose you waited dinner on us."

"Hell, I tried to get your mom to start without you, but she claimed the turkey wasn't browned."

"Saved by the bird, Monie. Come on in now. Don't be bashful. There's a big bunch of them, but it takes two or three before they amount to much."

"Ralph, come on out here and cut this bird."

It was Rudy who remembered that the Island Oasis had a

146

three-piece combo playing, and it was Laurie who jumped at the chance of leaving the dinner early. "Enough of this together-mess, Patrick. Let's go."

He thought briefly of the horses, waiting for fresh hay, even for water now that ice had to be broken. He couldn't count on Sadie; she had taken off with Lester even before he'd left for Laurie's. But Josie, he reasoned, should be home from Saturday evening services at Stonegate; she might have chores done by now.

They were halfway to Chesterfield when a light drizzle gradually built into heavy sleet that ricocheted from the roof of the van and congealed into a lacy fan along wiper blades.

"I dunno, Rudy." Ramona scooted in her seat, swept her hand across haze on the side window and thrust her forehead against the glass. "Look at this stuff." The darkness was lit with flecks of ice, pelted in all directions by the wind.

"Not to worry, doll. Everything's under control. We just slow down and take it easy."

"Mama will be up pacing the floor." She brought an edge to each word as she faced Rudy. "She'll be calling your folks, driving around looking for us. No telling."

"When she calls, Mom will let her know where we've gone and not to worry about us."

"She won't drive into Chesterfield in this stuff," she said thoughtfully. "She hardly leaves Stella since Daddy died. It would be different if I had a big family. But I'm all she's got." Her indecision increased as sleet glazed the highway.

"It's nothing," Rudy joked. "How often do I get a chance to go ice-skating?"

But his humor was lost on Ramona. "Maybe you better take me home. I don't mean to spoil everything. You three could come back after you drop me off."

"No way," Rudy protested almost before she could finish. "I'm not going without you. Besides, we're past the point to turn around."

Laurie leaned from the backseat and put a hand on

Ramona's shoulder. "This van holds the road like a tank, Ramona. And you can call your mom when we get to the Oasis."

"That won't do." Ramona shook her head. "She'd tell me to turn around and come on home."

Rudy edged the van to the shoulder. "Look, Monie." He leaned to her and took her hands. "I'll take you home, here and now. If that's what *you* want. That's not what I want, but that doesn't matter either. What matters is what *you* decide. Then that's what I'll do."

It was dark in the van and Ramona leaned toward Rudy as though attempting to read an answer in his eyes. Whatever she saw brought her to a threshold she seemed to recognize and then cross with confidence, because she took her seat comfortably and folded her hands in her lap.

"All right. We'll go on," she said without hesitation.

Rudy slapped his fist against the steering wheel and coasted onto the highway, taking the icy surface as though the van were fitted with sled runners.

"We're almost there," he said. "You can see the top of the palm tree hanging over that hedgerow."

The Island Oasis, almost halfway between Stella and Chesterfield, was situated some distance from the road in the middle of cropland, making it an island of sorts. A palm tree of iridescent bubbles rose from the roof, an unlikely sight on the flat prairie. When farmers worked the land surrounding the Oasis, often as late into the night as party goers danced, their tractor and combine lights could be seen fanning spotlights around the glowing, luminous tree fronds of the place. And to and fro along the narrow gravel road leading to the Oasis, the sprawling combines and loaded grain trucks choked the cars aside so that, laughing and shouting, the revelers would bump off into the open field, raking milo or wheat aside as they swept past.

Rudy turned from the highway to the gravel road, now open and uncongested. Colorless, rigid stubble stood iced in rows on either side, while ahead, lights from the palm tree quivered eerie and desolate through the sleet.

"This weather didn't scare anybody off," Rudy said as he drove into the parking lot, packed with cars and trucks. Frosted in a solid glaze, their tops and hoods formed backdrops for the multicolored lights. Rudy took a spot some distance from the entrance and hiked his arm to the back of his seat. "Patrick, my good man. It's either take this place while we can and have you carry me to the door, or you drop the three of us off and then park this boat."

Neither choice was to Rudy's liking, Patrick knew. He disliked being dependent on others, and he was pridefully sure of his own ability to take care of himself.

"What the hell. I'm taking this place while I can." He wheeled into the opening.

"Where's your hat?" Patrick said to Laurie as she stood in the shelter of his arm. They were waiting with Ramona for Rudy to come from the van, using his lift to lower his chair to the ground.

"I hardly ever wear one," she said, wrapping her arm about his waist, catching a belt loop to bring herself closer. Icy beads began to lace her crown. He pulled off his cap and cocked it to one side of her head, and when she swung back to him, he knew from her smile that she recalled the night they'd walked the square in a drizzle, with his cap perched to the side of her head. He squeezed her to him, feeling undeniably happy to have the night turning out so well. He felt an honest unrestraint, as he often did, after being in the midst of her boisterous, jubilant family.

"Okay, big guy, let's go." Rudy lifted his arms slightly so Patrick could ease his hands beneath Rudy's legs.

"We'll be there in no time," Patrick said. "If they'd pave these lots, you could sail over them faster than I could run."

"Just don't slip on your ass."

Behind them Laurie and Ramona bumped Rudy's chair over the gravel.

149

Rudy was so close to him, he could smell his after-shave. Solid against his own upper body, Rudy's back and shoulders were muscle packed. But his legs were nothing. Bone, gristle, skin, but hardly anything solid enough to keep Patrick from pressing through flesh until his thumb and fingers met. He was filled with both tenderness and fear for Rudy, as though for all Rudy's crowing, his rooster bravado, little stood between him and what might hurt him. Ramona — her indecisiveness and her waffling between her mother's interests and her own — would lead to nothing but heartache for Rudy. Rudy was serious. Rudy's emotions were direct and strong; hers seemed to flicker, unable to find a point from which to move forward. Rudy, he decided, was better off playing the field, which he'd always done, than settling on one girl — particularly Ramona who promised no more stability than ice underfoot.

"There you go, Rudy." Patrick eased Rudy into his chair and quickly pushed through the doors. Inside, they were met my a heavy warmth and the lilt of music that barely surfaced above murmurous voices and an occasional shrill laugh. Dark figures stood out against amber lights around a stage where two men played guitars and a woman, somewhat apart from the men, sat on a stool with the body of a cello between her legs. She wore a full peasant skirt that looped between her knees and to the back of the cello, where her skirt caught in a drape over her lap.

Patrick glanced around. "Wait here," he told Laurie. "I'll see if I can find a table." He skirted one side of the dance floor until he located a booth and signaled Laurie. She walked ahead of Rudy, waiting until people stepped aside for her. Rudy slowly wheeled himself behind her; Ramona trailed and the crowd closed behind them.

"I'll get the first pitcher," Patrick said.

"Take some money," Rudy called out, but Patrick waved his offer aside and shouldered his way through couples on their way to the dance floor.

He gave his order to a bartender and turned toward the

stage. The men sang a western tune, their bodies inclined toward microphones. They weren't terribly good, but their guitars provided a heavy beat, amplified by their equipment. A sense of rhythm was about all the dancers needed. The girl on the cello seemed to play without noticing them or the couples around the stage. The resonant *thum-thum* of the strings beneath her slim fingers were little more than a harmonic whim against the music, the voices. She lowered her ear near her instrument to catch her own vibrations, and a hank of long pale hair fell loose from the mass gathered across her back and pulled to a switch over one shoulder, a cushion beneath the neck of her cello. Straight fine strands fell in ribbons across her arm and nearly to her hand fingering the strings. She was barefoot — cold as it was — and she tapped the ball of one foot so that her toes struck the pale wooden floor and lifted her heel. Barefoot. He was drawn to her feet — her high white arch and the blue vein that set off her ankle. Her dress, he noted then, was loose and frilly with little cap sleeves and a scooped neck. A nightgown. Not really, but it could have been; it was too light by far for the weather. She could have been in her own bedroom playing for herself. Or herself and one other person. He imagined himself in her room, stretched across her narrow bed, looking not at her but above, to the ceiling, so he could concentrate on the heavy beat of her music.

"Hey, fella, here's your pitcher."

Startled, Patrick shoved the money he had ready into the man's hand and returned to the booth with the beer and iced glasses without looking at the barefoot girl again.

At the table, he filled each glass, and then refilled Rudy's before the foam had settled on his own.

"I never drank beer before Rudy and I started going together," Ramona said. "I used to think it tasted bitter, but," she gave a timid little laugh, "but with Rudy, nothing's bitter." And her cheeks flared with color, suddenly noticeable since she wore no makeup. She had deep-set eyes with lids that half shrouded her pupils and gave her a drowsy appearance.

"Drink up, baby. Rudy'll take care of you." He dropped an arm around her shoulders and pulled her to him. "She still hasn't learned to handle the stuff. More than two glasses and she turns passionate on me." He tipped the pitcher over her glass. "Let's kill this pitcher. Time for me to buy one." He nudged Ramona closer and lifted heavy dark brows in an impish manner. "Tell them how we met, babe."

"Oh, Rudy," Ramona said, embarrassed, "they know we didn't just meet." She fell against him, and her blond hair was set off against the ebony brown of Rudy's hair that lay in a solid wedge to one side of his forehead. She was plain as the tabletop, mild-mannered as a collie pup, and not the least like the host of flirtatious girls, full of guile and mischief, who had attracted Rudy in the past. She didn't seem to have the "something else" that most girls had. But then, maybe it was just as well, since Rudy had enough for both of them.

"Anyway," Ramona continued, "you love to hear the story, so I guess Pat and Laurie won't mind hearing it." She drew in her breath. "Well, it was right here in the Oasis. I had come in with a couple of girl friends I work with at K mart. Nothing else to do that night so I came along for the ride."

"And it's been a roller-coaster ride ever since," Rudy interjected quickly.

"It was just a few weeks ago. Right?" She turned to Rudy.

"Who's counting?" he said.

"My friends found a couple of guys right off, and I was thinking about leaving when in comes Rudy. I saw he was looking at me like he thought he knew me but wasn't real sure. I mean, you know how when you graduate you never see anybody that much anymore. Not regular. And after Daddy died, I started putting on a little more weight than I had in high school. I was nothing but a stick."

"It's what you needed. From a stick to a tender morsel." Rudy gave a growl and moved to bite her neck.

"Rudy!" Ramona dodged, snickering in her hands, then returned to the shelter of his shoulder.

"So in half a minute, he's up beside my table and he goes, 'Hey, Ramona. You must be little Ramona Larkins. What you doing in this dive without somebody to protect you?' I knew he was only kidding, but you know how he is. Anyway, in five minutes, we're talking about everything we've been doing since high school. Not much for me, I can tell you. Five minutes would cover it."

"And since then, we've been making up for it. She could write a book now. All about how she picked me up. How I didn't have a chance."

But Ramona ignored his ribald humor. She gazed thoughtfully into the last inch of beer that she swirled around the sides of her glass. "I don't know. Maybe it was because we were different people. I mean more than different on the inside. We had to *look* different too — me with a little more weight and Rudy, well, Rudy in his chair, before we could see we really *were* different." She paused and put her head briefly against his arm, and he brushed her forehead with his lips. "I used to see Rudy in high school and think how neat it would be to go with him. So much fun like he is."

"And I used to see her and think I was too rowdy for somebody quiet and sweet like Ramona Larkins."

"Rudy, that's not true. They know that's not true," she scolded before she turned back to Laurie and Patrick. "That's why we had to start out brand-new. Like we'd never met before and we had no notions about what we were like. What we *thought* we were like."

"Now, if we could just bring her mom around," Rudy said. "For all my so-called winning ways, I don't seem to be able to win Mrs. Larkins over."

"Oh, Rudy," Ramona said, "give Mom a little time."

"It's tough being the only one," Laurie said. "In our family, there are so many of us, Mom and Dad send up a cheer each time one of us leaves home."

"That must be the reason Mom keeps saying 'Six down, two to go,'" Rudy said with a chuckle. "Pretty soon the folks will have something to cheer about. One more little chicken will leave the nest."

"I know," Laurie nodded. "In about seven months, I'll pack my bags and take off for college."

"I wasn't talking about you, little Laurie," Rudy said with a sly grin. Then he tipped back his head and threw out a laugh. "Fooled you, didn't I?"

"What is this, Rudy?" Laurie leaned toward her brother. "You holding out on us?"

Rudy and Ramona exchanged glances. "The thing is, Laurie," Rudy continued, "I may be gone before you are. I've been looking for a place of my own."

"That's pretty sudden, Rudy," Laurie said. "Do you think you should?"

"I don't know why not. I can have a couple of ramps built on a house, a few changes made inside."

"You mean buy a place?" Patrick asked.

"That's the general idea. I've got the money. And I'm nearly twenty-two. I would have flown the nest a long time ago if it hadn't been for the accident."

"Have you told the folks yet?" Laurie asked.

"No. I'm still looking. But they won't mind. Mom will drag out some old dishes she's been saving, and Dad will be so glad to get my weight-lifting equipment out of the house, he'll probably help me move."

"Sounds like you two have done more than meet and get acquainted," Patrick said. "It sounds pretty serious."

But Rudy and Ramona only laughed and leaned closer together while Rudy handed Patrick a fistful of bills for another pitcher of beer.

"Come on now. Everybody drink up. We got something to celebrate."

When Patrick returned with a fresh pitcher, the girls were gone.

"Took a hike," Rudy explained and nodded toward the restrooms. He filled his glass and took a moment to take down

154

half of it before he pinched a mustache of foam from his upper lip. "Surprised you, didn't I? About finding my own place. I wanted to tell you. Everyday we ate dinner together I thought I'd tell you. I've been so full of it, but the time wasn't right. Monie and I . . ."

Patrick glanced up from his glass to catch the excitement Rudy felt, distilled in the ebony depths of his eyes.

"Dammit, Pat. I know how I feel about her. I got that totally right, man. The *know* first and then the *feel*. The whole time I was screwing girls in high school, getting it every weekend and three nights in between, it was all feel. I never knew a damn thing. I didn't think there was anything to know about it. Knowing, I thought, would just get in the way. I'm convinced I would have gone on like that if I hadn't lost it all. Lost the feeling. Without the accident, I never would have known what it was like to love Ramona. I would have passed her by like the last bus to the museum." He paused to look across the dance floor for Ramona. "So maybe you been right all along. Holding back. Saving it until you know something."

Patrick tapped his glass within the circle of moisture left on the table. "It's going to take me a while to get used to you talking about love."

"For sure, man. Before the accident, love was the farthest thing from my mind. And afterward — well, I figured it was a lost cause."

"Maybe love is always a lost cause, Rudy."

"No. Never. It's the only cause, man."

"But it's not always a two-way street. Maybe Ramona isn't as strong on it as you are."

"You mean what if Ramona doesn't want to stick around. What if Ramona decides she wants the real thing. Right?"

"The risk, Rudy. That's what I mean."

"Sure there's risk. And I'm jumping to take it." He tossed off a laugh. "That's right. Jumping. I can't jump at much else, so why not jump at the chance for Ramona?" Then his usual level of self-confidence returned. "But I tell you, Pat, I don't think

Ramona will move on. Leave me. And if she does, I still won't be a loser. I will have *known* what it was like." Rudy leaned earnestly across the table. "Get me, Pat? To know a feeling and not just feel a feeling."

"Just so long as it's Ramona too. That's all I'm saying."

Rudy tapped his glass against the palm of his hand, all his usual pranks laid aside. "We've come on to each other pretty fast, I know. But I've had a lot of time to think about it. This goddamn chair is like a think tank. One day is like months to me, and in the last couple of weeks, I've spent years thinking about Ramona and me. We've got problems. I know Ramona's mother is not going to want her only baby child to hook up with a cripple who can't give her any kids. And it's hard for Monie to break away. That's one of the reasons I want to find a place of my own, Pat. I think that if I can get Monie to move in with me, it'll be easier for her to make the break."

"Her mother's not likely to take to that idea either."

"I know. And Monie hasn't decided she'll do it yet. It's 'maybe' one day, 'for sure' the next. I can't blame her. Love. Money. I can give her all that, but I can't give her everything. It's a crazy fucked-up world, Pat. Most times when a guy says he can't give his woman everything, he means money, all the stuff money can buy. And I wish like hell that's all it was with me."

Rudy's face brightened, and without looking, Patrick knew Ramona and Laurie were returning.

"Hey." Rudy motioned to Patrick and Laurie. "Can't you two tell when lovers want to be alone? Why don't you try out the dance floor? Report back in about an hour or so."

Patrick took Laurie's hand and threaded a way through the crowd to a spot where he could draw her to him. The tempo was slow; the deep *thum-thum* of the cello filled the shallow places beneath the men's weak voices.

Laurie leaned back enough to look at him. "How about Rudy and Ramona? Were you surprised?"

"It's more serious than I figured. Getting his own place. But

156

why not? I think sometimes about it myself." Over Laurie's head, he caught a glimpse of the girl with the cello. Such long hair, fine as young corn silk. In a sensuous way, she lifted her hands to the neck of the cello to reveal blue-white underarms.

"You do? Really?" Laurie asked, which brought him back to what they'd been talking about. A place of his own.

"It's just a thought." he said. "There's probably no way."

Laurie tucked her head against him and, pressing up on her toes, brought the top of her head beneath his chin. It was good to have her next to him; he felt relaxed and confident, and he fell into the rhythm of the music. He didn't think of himself as "holding back," as Rudy had said, refraining from taking a girl until he knew how he felt about her. He thought sometimes it would be the easiest thing in the world to take a girl to bed. Provided it was someone he *didn't* know — the barefoot girl in the nightgown. The first time, he decided, was going to be with a girl he picked up, not someone he'd known all his life. His eyes continued to follow the girl on the stage. He thought if she looked up, he would try to catch her eye, but she seldom did, and he inclined his head to Laurie's.

He heard Sadie then — heard the high note of her musical laugh — could have recognized it anywhere, even though he never expected to see her. But he did see her, instantly, as he swung around. She was across the floor near the dim amber lights of the stage. She and Lester, not really dancing, only swaying together and caught in an embrace that riveted their attention to each other. In one exaggerated motion, Sadie swung back so that her waist dipped and her hips pushed against Lester. As they took up the beat of the music, her legs doubling the movement of Lester's legs, her arms looped his neck so that her silver bracelets danced with amber lights.

"I'll be goddamned," Patrick said beneath his breath. He had lost the beat of the music and stood awkwardly with his arms slack around Laurie's shoulders.

"You see your mother, don't you?"

"Acting a fool." He bit on the inside corner of his lip.

Sadie brought her elbows to Lester's shoulders, and with her hands locked behind his head, she brought his face to her until her lips caught the corner of his mouth. Lester stopped swaying to hold her and kiss her squarely. After that, they embraced, swaying to the music.

"I saw them earlier," Laurie said. "When I was coming back from the bathroom." She glanced once across the floor.

"She's had too much to drink. It makes me sick to watch her," he said.

"Let's leave then." Laurie spoke abruptly and took his hand to lead him from the floor.

He started to turn back, toward Sadie. She and Lester remained in the same position with her head tucked into the side of Lester's neck, her eyes closed. Lester's face was flush with contentment, and he repeatedly stroked the center of Sadie's back.

"What the hell. Let's go." Patrick followed Laurie back to the table. He had an uncommon urge to be home, to have the house close in around him, to be with Josie, who was home alone. She spent too much time alone or with the Uttermelons. He should have been home himself long ago.

"Rudy, I think we ought to start back," Laurie said and began putting on her coat. "The roads and all."

"Not a bad idea." Rudy checked his watch. "This place closes in another hour or so anyway."

They left quickly. Patrick was barely conscious of retracing his steps to carry Rudy to the van; he failed to notice the sleet had stopped. They drove in near silence; Patrick was conscious of their conversation, of his occasional response, but for the most part, he sat frozen and apart. When they reached Ramona's, her mother started down the steps even before Rudy could stop the van. She was without a coat, and she wrapped the hem of her apron around her lower arms.

Ramona gave Rudy a quick kiss. "Gotta go, honey, before she falls or something."

"See you tomorrow," Rudy said. "I'll call."

She was gone, up the sidewalk and to her mother's side. Rudy drove on, and once at the Kieffers', he gave a quick wave and pushed his chair up the ice-covered walk, his shoulder muscles playing out along his back as he reached behind to stroke forcefully up the ice-glazed ramp to the front door.

Laurie followed Patrick to his truck and stood quietly beside him as he knocked loose the ice frozen around the door frame. Once inside, he rolled down the window. An apology surfaced, but for what? His mother? Himself? Lately, he thought, apologies were about all he had to offer. But she didn't wait for what he might have said, merely reached up and kissed him lightly. "See you, Patrick." She pulled her jacket to her ears and took a few steps backwards, watching as he pulled from the drive. The truck fishtailed a few times when it hit the ice, but he righted it easily and drove on. He was acutely aware of all the reasons to be home: the storm could have brought down power lines; a horse might have slipped and fallen; Josie might have had trouble getting to the pond to break open a watering hole. By the time he crossed the trestle, he had pushed aside the sight of his mother and Lester, pushed aside the disbelief, then anger, he'd felt at seeing them just across the dance floor.

At first he failed to notice that there were no lights, and when he did, he reasoned that Josie had gone to bed and failed to leave any burning. But when he pulled into the drive, the horses set up a shuffling stir, wheeling and nipping at each other, along the paddock fence. In the truck lights, their agitated eyes stared, suddenly night-blind.

"They should be at feed bunks." He ripped from the truck, slipping over the frozen ground. He slammed through the house, without stopping to turn on lights, his hands coasting up either side of the stairway to Josie's room. She wasn't there. Freone, curled on Josie's pillow, stretched up from a sound sleep.

"Goddamn. Josie hasn't even been home. She's staying the night at the Uttermelons'."

He dived back down the steps and out the door, setting his

heels through ice. Branches, heavy with ice, snapped against him and sent a cascade of crystalline shards breaking around him.

"Not a one of them fed." With one heave, he slid the barn door the length of its opening. The squawk sent Tugaloo wheeling in his stall before he lifted a shrill whinny.

"Shut up, stud."

Tugaloo responded with a snappish growl and a crack of his hoof against a wooden panel. The blast reverberated to the beams above.

"You're going to get fed. Hell, yes." Patrick ripped off the jacket that seemed to hold him hot and restricted. Turk poked briefly from his hay burrow. Bemused, he surveyed the situation and tucked himself back inside his den.

"Not a goddamn one of you fed. Or watered. Everything's frozen solid. But do you think either of them cares?"

Tugaloo rumbled an answer.

"Hell, no." Patrick kicked loose hay from his path. "Screwing and praying. Screwing and praying."

The steps to the loft were solid old boards, firm under his grip, but he yanked them as if he might pull them loose and throw them over his head. "Screwing and praying." The words had a rhythm of their own as he took each step.

From the loft floor, Patrick glanced down to the restless stallion as he circled his stall, kicking up urine-heavy hay.

"Shut up, stud. I don't want to hear you."

Startled by a voice above him, Tugaloo halted with ears pricked. Then with an arrogant toss of his foretop, he wheeled. Angry now, the stallion's next call rose like an unbroken scream that brought a chorus of responses from his mares outside. Aroused, other horses in the barn began to set up their own fracas until the sound undulated in a continual lapping noise.

"Shut up. Goddamn it. Quit closing in on me."

At the edge of the loft, Patrick yanked up a bale with a force to pull his arms taut. He stood briefly, as though to gather strength, harden resolve, then with one knee jerk, he brought the bale to his shoulders, up and out with a thrust powerful enough to send it sailing, to carry it far out, slamming against Tugaloo's stall door. Instantly, the stallion dropped his head and smashed his heels into the wall. The crack of splintered wood lifted in a ripple of sound.

"Bitch. You said it, Tug. Bitch. Bitchhhhhh." He leaned as far back as he could, yelled until his throat hurt. "Get the hell out, you motherfucker." The sound, reverberating from the rafters, circled and met an oncoming barrage, a stereophonic roar. He yanked another bale to his chest, braced it, heaved it. Bale after bale. If the twine snapped beneath his hands, he kicked hay aside and grabbed another bale. They sailed into the alleyway, cracking against stalls, bouncing and breaking as they bounded over others already lying like a gigantic comforter on the earthen floor. With each bale, he fired his knee up to add force, propel it in an arch above him. Bales exploded from him. They began to land with only gentle nudges against others below. As twine broke, the hay lay loose and fluffy as eiderdown, and dust rose in a haze. The horses were quiet, frightened, and expectant.

When he was too tired to lift another bale, he pushed his hands into the small of his back and pulled himself upright. "Thank God." He slumped to the side of the loft floor with his lower legs and feet dangling into the opening. He surveyed the mass of hay beneath him and tried to laugh, but his throat was too dry; he couldn't even spit. He was too tired to move. Drained of all anger, he felt weak. Anger was the strongest emotion he felt; it could push him through a day. Now without it, he felt nothing. Nothing. It was good to feel nothing. He thought of Rudy, relieved and jubilant because he could feel again, feel in his body what he knew in his mind. God, no. Feeling nothing was better. He wanted to hold onto that, keep within him a big, empty place that no one could reach, that would never fill up with caring anymore.

His eyes held to one spot in the hay loosely piled into a downy heap. He eased himself to the edge. And lifting his arms, he jumped.

161

10

Down the Hedgerow
The Christmas lesson, "The Meaning Behind the
Coming of the King," was presented by Opal Druckers
on Tuesday in Fellowship Hall of the United Methodist
Church. Fifteen women answered roll call by naming
favorite Christmas toys they had received as children.
The dessert table was laid with a centerpiece of red
poinsettia and white candles in crystal candlesticks.
Charlene Scott provided the candlesticks, adorned with
crystal teardrops, which she had brought back from her
and Mr. Scott's Austrian vacation. Refreshments were
served by the Naomi Circle with LaVern Bethel in
charge. Ester Tunney was named quilting chairperson
to replace Constance Poore, who died last week. Mrs.
Poore had served admirably in this position for 23
years and the women . . .

He scanned his mother's column while he rolled his shoulders to ease the stiffness.

*Mr. and Mrs. Jimmy Wingfield are on their way to
spend Christmas holidays with their son and his
family, Danny and Suzie Wingfield and children,
Debbie, Penny, and Danny Jr., in Denver. They will
motor through the Rocky Mountains and may travel as
far as Las Vegas. En route they plan to stop off to visit
the Casper Williamses, former Stella-ites now living in
Loveland.*

Why did she write such crap, he thought? Not a soul in town
really cared about the church program except the women who
had been there, and why did they want to read it except to see
their names mentioned?

*Cleta Manning and Violet Taylor enjoyed afternoon tea
on Wednesday.*

But then, why did he read it? Stalling. He was stalling, and
he couldn't put off much longer what waited for him in the
barn.

*Mr. and Mrs. Jeff Nelson have recently bought the old
Cartwell home. Mrs. Nelson is the former Rebecca
Cartwell, a 1967 graduate of Stella High School and*

"And the best damn lay in four counties," he finished aloud.
"She will be remembered by the football team of that year as
the only way they ever scored."

He shucked the paper and gave his neck a wrenching twist.
Sometimes he thought he'd like to turn his head off his shoul-

164

ders and set it aside so he could get on with the work at hand and leave his mind to do the thinking someplace else.

"Damn fool thing." Hay curled from the pockets of his shirt, the same he'd worn the night before. "Just makes more work for me." When his fingers combed through his hair, his hands came away gritty. Still, plunging straight down from the loft, landing in the bed of hay, being swallowed up by it, was almost worth a few aching muscles. But now, he had to do something with the mess blocking the alleyway.

"Oh, shit." He nudged back a chair opposite him, drew his feet to the seat, and crossed them at his ankles. His legs formed an angular bridge then, which Freone walked beneath, considering a jump to the span.

"You stay down there, goddamn it." He slouched to one side to scold her. "I'm in no mood to take you on."

She leaped lightly to his knees and tiptoed to his lap where she plied her claws against the rough hide of his jeans before settling into a purring ball in his lap.

"What the hell." He closed his eyes and felt across the table for his coffee mug, but when he put the rim to his lips, the coffee was cold. He plopped the cup on a pile of papers. It tipped and spilled a liquid map across the print.

"Jesus God." He remained in his place and fumbled the papers. "Fucking table is covered with crap. Probably last week's dirty dishes at the bottom." He surveyed the common clutter, absentmindedly folding one paper over another. Josie's library books, her notebook; pencils rolled out onto the floor. "Just a goddamn catchall. They come in the back door and pitch everything. Can't wait to unload." An unopened letter from Gramma Rho surfaced. Sadie's silver bracelets slid from a scarf and clinked against each other. He pushed them aside, and her earrings dropped loose. He lifted an earring above his head until the tiny silver rods, dangling free from the hub, caught the morning light. The hub, he noticed as his interest picked up, was connected to a spike, which in turn, fitted into a receptacle. He pulled the pieces apart. Inserted them again. A male-female connection. Like any number of tools or plugs he used. With a light twist of his wrist, he sent the earring among the papers, scooped Freone to the floor, and came up from his chair. The sudden movement set off the ache idling directly behind his left eye.

"God, it came down a lot faster than it went up. I feel worse than when Caleb and I put the damn hay up there." Last spring — it had been only last spring — they had all worked against encroaching rain. He and Caleb pitched bales to the flatbed wagon behind the tractor Sadie drove. Josie took care of Sandra and carried out iced tea. They said nothing about rain, as though the mention of it — the sound, "rainnnnnn" sailing off into the low-slung horizon — would be enough to bring hot silver streaks in across the pasture.

Idly, he rummaged among the papers until he came up with Gramma Rho's letter. They hadn't sent her Christmas box yet, hadn't even bought her presents or answered her last letter. He knew Gramma Rho and her invincible brand of common sense. She would wonder about them one day and be at the bus station in Chesterfield the next. He didn't need that, didn't need her in the midst of everything else. He slipped his nail along the envelope lip. Her sentences ran perfectly straight across the page, but the words were barely visible, and he held the thin paper against his leg to read it. But that didn't help much either, since her pen had gone skipping along, the words in some places only impressions in the soft skin of the paper.

Dear Family,

I just got back from putting up the Christmas tree at the old folks' home. There was that old Mr. Jacoby with his crooked back . . . set him to stringing cranberries and popcorn . . . so I talked Bertha Mattison into playing the piano. Such a little wart of a thing . . . big enough to go up and down the keyboard the way she does.

166

Who were these people? He didn't know any of them, yet she wrote about them as though they were neighbors, just up the road. And all of them doing senseless, trivial things that could be accounted for in words set down in proper rows, expected and shallow. Like Sadie's column. Yet the true lives of these people could be swirling past them, fraught with any number of unsettling difficulties, even tragedies, but all of that was hidden behind "lovely candlesticks adorned with crystal teardrops," or "afternoon tea," or old man Jacoby "stringing cranberries and popcorn."

I put a box for you in the mail yesterday. A little late, but I don't see why the post office can't get their jobs done same as the rest of us. I know you're busy but . . .

At least she wasn't on her way to Stella. That much was clear. He pushed up from the chair, groaned, and went to the living room and the bay windows by Josie's organ. The sky was dull as bone. A light snow had fallen in the night, and the open fields lay rumpled under a blanket of unmarred white. Open and vast, the pasture and road ran together to the creek where the narrow sides of the bridge cut a wedge into the expanse of white. He shoved his fingertips into his rear pockets and paced the length of the room, glancing at his mother's bedroom door.

"Hell, I'll bet she really tied one on. She won't be up until past noon." He felt anger beginning to surface, and he tried to recapture the emotion he'd felt the night before. No emotion. Nothing. Empty. He had been too tired to feel anything, and he wanted to hold onto that. He wanted to feel himself float down and land into things the same way he'd come into the hay. Effortlessly, no fight left.

"What the hell. Quit stalling. Get on to the barn."

167

He was almost to the back door when the phone rang.

"Goddamn it. She can take her own messages."

He pulled on his jacket and swung to catch the phone in midring.

"Sadie? Is that you? Ted and me are just getting ready to leave . . ."

"Just a minute. This isn't Sadie. I'll get her."

"Pat? You'll do fine. Just take this down. It's only a few lines."

"You'll have to wait." He cocked the receiver across the top of the phone and went to Sadie's bedroom. He shook her shoulder, smothered under blankets and pillows.

"Mrs. McConkey's on the phone. Something for your column."

Sadie groaned and rolled over, her black hair washed across the pillow. Mascara streaked across her cheeks, and he caught a yeasty, sour odor before she buried her face again.

"Take it, will you, Pat?"

He shook her again. "No. You better wake up."

"Jesus. God." She drew the words into long sighs. "Oh, Christ."

"If you want the message, you'll have to get up and take it yourself. I've got work in the barn."

He turned quickly and left, and when he went through the kitchen and closed the back door, he did it firmly enough for her to hear him leave. He moved right on down the back steps and met the cold with a determined edge of his own. He took a swallow of air, so deep it cut into his lungs and set off the pain between his shoulder blades again. But he spread his arms and moved on. It was good to be out, to know the indifference of winter, and he set his heel down hard to crush through the ice hidden beneath the snow.

He had turned Tugaloo into the paddock before he started

clearing hay. By the time the Gospel Chariot made the first tracks up the road with Josie, it was midafternoon, and the stallion and Patrick had stretched out their tight muscles.

Josie came to the barn door with her Bible tucked beneath one arm and her hands knotted into her coat pockets. For moments, she watched her brother with her eyebrows lifted to form wrinkles across her forehead beneath the snug band of a navy ribbed cap she wore that bunched side curls close to her face.

"Why is all the hay down here?"

"I got tired of throwing hay down every night," he said briefly. "Thought I'd toss down a few extra." His words were forced between the rhythm he'd established as he lifted bales and kneed them in place.

"You threw down plenty, I'd say."

"That's right." He stopped after the swing of one bale. "The deal was, you were supposed to do chores last night. I came home and nothing was done. You weren't even here. I had to guess where you might be."

"You knew I'd be at church. With the Uttermelons."

"You could have piled up at the side of the road, for all I knew. In this weather. The Gospel Chariot," he hissed. "God, I suppose you think you'll go skimming across the ice, safe and sound inside that chariot."

"That's not it at all." She gave an emphatic little sigh. "With the ice storm, Father Uttermelon thought we shouldn't start out. That's the reason I didn't come home. If you'd just take time to listen . . ." She paused plaintively.

"And I'm still listening. So why didn't you call me at Laurie's? You knew where I was."

"You keep forgetting, Patrick. There is no phone at our church home."

"That's not your home, Josie," he spit out. "Part of your problem is that you think of that place as your home. Your home is here."

"You're just mad because I wasn't here to do chores," she

169

said defensively and turned quickly enough to send her braid flipping over her back.

"Don't you think I have a right to be?" His words seemed to strike a responsive chord; she squared her shoulders and faced him again.

"We were studying the Book of John, and I forgot altogether about it. You know, Patrick, that John says . . ."

"I don't want to know what John says; I want to know what you say."

"I know I should have been here," she said clipping out each word. "But it just wasn't possible. That's all."

He stood above her on a hay landing with hay stacked to form steps. Beneath him, she seemed small, young and untouched, as though events could simply burn through her, straight through, leaving a clean, edgeless mark that sealed over with one even scar. He jumped down from the hay steps. "It's over and done with now."

He went along kicking through loose hay, wrapping up twine left behind from the broken bales. Josie followed, shifting her Bible from hand to hand.

"It's just that when I'm at Stonegate," she said in her dreamy tone, "I feel Jesus working through me for the good of all of us. It's like I see a special light, and I keep going toward it all the time." Her voice lifted and dropped to form a singsong pattern. "I'm safe there. Coming in out of the storm."

"God, Josie, you sound like some damn hymn." He kept moving and didn't turn to look at her.

"That's right. I hear the music, even though we have no music in church. Still, I feel like I'm playing my organ, hearing voices even."

He twisted twine into a knot and shook his head. "Happy as though you got good sense."

"That's what Gramma Rho would say," Josie said self-consciously.

"And you know what else she'd say, don't you?"

"Oh, yes, she'd want me here, helping you." She paused as

though thinking. "In a way, I am helping you. In the best way I can. Saying prayers for all of us." Her eyes deepened in intensity. She was always radiant when she talked about God, and it was difficult for him to find a point to step in and brush her drifting illusions aside.

"Prayers at the Uttermelons' don't seem to help me one damn bit. Come spring, you know what it's like with mares to foal out and rebreed. And this spring I think we'll have a few outside mares for Tug's service. That means I have to build stalls, more outside runs for them."

She nodded, and he sensed an opportunity to press on. "Seems to me we've been here too long to just give it up now that it might turn into something. You could be working those yearlings, getting them ready for buyers when they come looking this spring." He looped the twine on a nail and took swipes at hay caught on his jacket. "You can say prayers while you're working a colt on a lunge line."

She brightened at the thought. "Oh, Patrick, what you'll think of!"

"I'm thinking of Christmas right now."

"Christmas," she said flatly and waited, as though she were unaware of what might be expected of her on this front.

"We haven't sent our box to Gramma Rho. Haven't ridden out to look for a tree. Nothing."

"It's not too late for all that. We got two weeks, yet, haven't we?"

"Not that long. More like ten days."

She stashed her Bible on a hay bale and began gathering tools and tack, shaking hay loose as she went along. "How about this afternoon? We could run into Stella and get something at Minna's. I'll bet she'll be open late like she was last year." She popped her head from inside the tack room. "How much more have we got to do out here, Patrick? You put Tug up and I'll get Mama. We can go now."

Patrick swung to meet her, but she was out of sight, rustling in the tack room. "Mom may not feel like going," he said. "You and me can go by ourselves."

The noise she was making died away, and when she leaned from the doorway, her eyes caught his briefly before he resumed working. "She'd been out with Lester, I suppose. She wasn't here last night to help you either."

"It doesn't matter. We might just as well go on."

She pressed her lips together until dimples creased her cheeks, and without responding, she marched resolutely toward the house. He followed, walking quickly to keep pace as she stomped past the back doormat, on through the kitchen and around Freone warming herself by the stove.

Sadie's bedroom door was open. She was sitting on the side of her bed, her eyes as dark as water holes against her pale cheekbones. She didn't look up as Josie entered. Patrick met the doorway as though a brick wall had been erected. It was a stranger's room and he couldn't bring himself to enter. Instead, he leaned against the outside wall.

"We want to talk about Christmas," Josie began resolutely.

"God, you too?" Sadie hissed. "Evvvvverybody wants to talk about Christmas. I've been on that damn phone all morning. First one and then another." Something set her coughing so hard she buried the sound, in one of her pillows, he thought. "The entire town of Stella must be leaving for the holidays. The Simmonses are off to her sister's in Dallas, the Chadwicks are going to his mother's in South Bend, as usual. But no, guess what?" She gave a snort and a laugh. "The Yorks have all eighteen grandkids coming and the goddamn john started backing up on her this morning. Fancy that. Hell of a note." She cackled until she had to stop for a breath, which started her coughing again.

She was still drunk, so hung over she couldn't talk straight. He wanted to charge into the room and shake her senseless. He wanted to turn on his heel and leave them both. He pushed himself through the doorway and met Josie's beseeching face. She looked ready to flee. Sadie sat frozen to the side of her bed, her eyes glazed and staring in front of her. She could have been a model in a Sears Roebuck catalogue; the gown was there, but the figure holding it upright was flat and lifeless.

"But about Christmas," Josie began again. "Gramma Rho's present."

"Let me tell you, sweetheart, Christmas is going to come, whether we're ready for it or not." Her voice, edged in scorn, trailed to a whisper. "And I don't feel ready."

"But what about Gramma Rho's present? The Christmas tree?"

"It'll all just happen. As if by magic." She gave a snort and tossed a pillow into the air.

Josie shivered as though to press back a chill.

"Come on, Josie," Patrick said, but Josie turned long enough to put her hand on his arm, as though to tell him she hadn't given up yet.

"Look," Sadie said. "Couldn't all this wait until some other time?" She stumbled up from her bed and halfheartedly cleared clothes from her path. "Better yet. Why don't the two of you go without me this time?"

"But Mama . . ." Josie said.

Sadie gave Josie a watery smile. "I know you've never gone without me," she said wearily, "but there's a first time for everything. I've done that bit, Josie, and frankly, I'm sick of it."

Josie took a step back so quickly that Patrick took her elbow and steered her from the room.

"Go get in the truck, Josie. I've got some money upstairs. I'll be along."

She looked at him as though she were in a trance, and he gave her a slight nudge. "Go on, Josie."

Upstairs in his bedroom, he peeled away some of the folding money he'd saved, and when he came down and through the kitchen, he caught the sound of Sadie's radio playing Christmas carols. He hurried on.

In the truck, Josie seemed to be studying her reflection in the window. For some time, they remained quiet, with only the sound of truck tires mushing through snow. The engine offered

173

its reassuring hum. Some months before, he'd found time to repair the hood and fenders and to fix the passenger door so it opened without a hitch. But he missed being able to look into the engine to watch the precision of its parts. "Its exposed parts," as his mother had said.

"Do you think Mama will marry Lester?" Josie asked, her face still averted.

"I don't know. I suppose she could."

"Sometimes I wish she would. In some ways, it would be easier. But I don't want her to, really. What if Dad came home?" She anticipated Patrick's response and picked up quickly, "It's just a thought, Patrick." She drew within herself for a few moments. "But that's not the real reason. If she married Lester, I know you'd leave."

"I don't think you have to worry," he said, deliberately avoiding her remark. "Lester's not the marrying kind."

"But people get married anyway, don't they." Her tone was flat, unquestioning. "Dad. He wasn't the marrying kind either, was he?"

"No. He's the wandering kind," he answered matter-of-factly.

"I suppose we're all one kind or another," she said and turned back to her reflection. "I wish I knew what sort of person I was." Her gaze was caught on a far point on the horizon. "But how do we know? Who can tell?"

"Usually we don't know, Josie."

"It would certainly help if we did. Just think of all the trouble it would save if we knew what sort of people we were," she said, plopping her hands together in her lap.

"Maybe we're better off not knowing. Maybe we'd just settle back and be whatever we found out about ourselves and never try to be something else."

"No," she said with finality. "I'd like to know. It would keep me from muddling along. We waste a lot of time trying to find out."

"But Josie, you have to discover it on your own for it to be true. You can't have somebody telling you. And you can't come into the world with a note tacked to your bottom that says, 'Josie is the marrying kind.' Or 'Josie is going to be helpful and loving.' Or 'Be sure to buy Josie an organ because she's very musical.'" He knew he'd draw forth a laugh.

"Oh, Patrick. I know what you mean, but it seems we're born with a little tiny bit of something we can't do much to change and it grows inside us like . . . like wisdom teeth that sooner or later have to come through."

"Oh, Josie. The things you come up with."

They fell into silence again. It was late afternoon, but already growing dark, with only hazy outlines of farmsteads set in measured distance from the road, each with great blue silos standing sentinel by the side.

"Do you think he ever married again?" Josie asked finally. "I mean wandering around like he does."

"Who knows?"

"I wish he'd hurry and send our Christmas money. I could use mine right now."

"I got my birthday money. That will see us through. He never sends on time. Christmas money won't arrive until after the first of the year."

"I don't like them, all hard and new like they come. I take mine and wad it up, hard, into a ball, and then smooth it out until it has wrinkles. Softens it up some."

"I'll take mine however it comes."

They drove toward Stella's square, the streets gray and slushy from tracks of vehicles. Even the park was crosshatched with bootprints of people tracing back and forth to shops. But the pavilion stood out in its summer blue, glittering now with tiny white lights strung along the curved roof. A five-pointed star sparkled at its peak. It looked like a jeweled crown, a delicate bauble, that might ascend to its rightful place as a star in the heavens, far removed from the gray and desolate streets of Stella in winter.

"Let's not take too long, Josie." He found a spot some

distance from Minna's Variety Store. "Just pick out something for Gramma Rho so we can get it wrapped and in the mail tomorrow."

Josie gave little tugs to each side of her cap before she climbed from the truck. When they pushed open the door of the store, they set the copper bell jangling — Minna's signal on slow days to come from her back room, where she watched television. But now the store was crowded with last-minute shoppers, and Minna was busy, helping people find things she had forgotten about.

"Minna should have that left over from last year," she was telling Daisy Avey. She usually referred to herself by her name, as though there might be more than one woman inside her clothes. She was a big woman, too big by far to wear most clothes, and her usual attire was what Rudy called her "wrap-around tent."

Patrick went to Minna's glass case at the front of the store. Here she kept jewelry and watches and pen-and-pencil sets, gloves and silverware. Silverware. There was no telling where Minna might decide to put something — usually in whatever cranny she could find, since the store was a haven of miscellany. Committed to a search, one could find anything from buttons to straw hats, overalls to pancake turners. Christmas decorations perched on top of boxes of July sparklers. She had about two of everything, a Noah's ark of soulless stuff.

He went to the back of the case and slid the glass doors along their grooves. At Minna's, people rustled about as they might do in their own closets. She never hired anyone to help, even in busy times such as Christmas, and it wouldn't have done any good anyway. It would have been another person getting in her way; Minna working around Minna was enough. Sometimes if she was chatting with customers or still in her back room — draped off by a faded floral drop — immersed in a "good place" in a soap opera, people in Stella knew to sack up what they wanted and leave change by her cash register. Or they left a note of what they bought and she added the amount to their bills.

Patrick knew what he was going to buy Gramma Rho. He'd thought of it earlier in the day when he'd tried to read her letter. He brought out several boxed pen-and-pencil sets and laid them across the glass top for Josie to consider.

"We got one of her letters at home," he said, "and you can hardly read it for her pen skipping along."

Josie slipped the pen from beneath its elastic holder. "Too nice. She wouldn't use it. She'd save it for good and go right on using the pen that's skipping. Until every drop of ink was gone."

"I suppose. And she probably has four sets she's saving for good."

"But maybe not," Josie offered brightly. "Leave them out and we'll look around." She wandered off, trailing her hand across the counter.

Gloves. He'd come back tomorrow and get Josie gloves. Not that she didn't have gloves, mittens too, but she was forever forgetting them, leaving them at the Uttermelons'.

Glancing into the case again, he caught sight of the pearly surface of a pocketknife. His own knife, the one he always carried, had been Gramma Rho's. She'd given it to him when she'd come the spring he'd been sick. He and Gramma Rho had been mending the fence, he remembered. It was late summer, and by then his strength had returned. "Cut the twine on that spool of wire," she had called out from where she stood down the fence line from him. But he'd had nothing to use, and she had come toward him, drawing a knife from her jeans pocket. "Now you take this one," she'd said. "A body ought not to go any farther than the barn without a pocketknife."

She probably wouldn't have bought another, he decided, turning the knife in his palm. He took it to Josie.

"What about this?" He rolled the knife to his fingertips.

"She'll like that," Josie said instantly. "That looks like Gramma. But what about this scarf?" She held up a square of cloth imprinted with figures of galloping horses. "For Mama or

Gramma Rho?"

For Gramma."

"I suppose so. Mama doesn't wear scarves much anymore."

"Come on. Let's pay Minna while she's not so busy and get on home."

But they couldn't seem to get away. Josie kept seeing someone to talk to, and every time Patrick looked around, Minna was mincing about on her thin legs that appeared far too delicate to support her expansive body. But she could scurry like a pouter pigeon.

"Gadfrey," Minna said when she finally came to the cash register. "All you folks stewing around at the last minute. Sometimes I think Minna could open the week before Christmas and close down the rest of the year." Her voice surfaced labored and heavy through the swell of her bosom. "Just one of those jugs weighs twenty-five pounds," Rudy had once told him. "No shit. My mom told me that Minna got to wondering herself once, and she heaved one up on her canning scales." Minna would do that. She had an uncommon gaiety about most things, including herself, as though she had missed all shades of anxiety and distress.

"This here what you kids want?" Minna said. "Josie, you come around here and pull off a little colored paper and get these wrapped while you're standing here and Minna takes your brother's money." She shifted some to make room for Josie. "Don't you worry, honey. Minna won't squash you." Her laugh came coarse as sandpaper.

"Just look what we got here." She held Patrick's hundred-dollar bill to the light and gave it a snap. "Gadfrey, Patrick, you run this one off on the press out at your place?" She turned a long envelope to a clear spot and tallied the cost of the knife and scarf. She rang up zeros on her register; she seldom bothered to keep daily receipts with anything other than her envelopes.

"How'll it be if Minna keeps your money?" She flipped through currency lying loose beneath the cash drawer. "Since I don't know if I got enough to make change here. You can finish out your shopping with it."

"Better not this time, Minna. Better have my change."

She brought out another laugh and dug around until she had sufficient currency for change. Josie sacked the packages, and when they left, Minna's copper bell jingling behind them, it had begun to snow in the streets. The pavilion floated up through a sweep of snowflakes, outlined with diamond lights.

"The Christmas snow at last," Josie said, and she held her face up to catch flakes, so full and flat that their individual shapes were apparent before they melted against her cheeks.

They drove home in gathering snow that billowed like curtains in front of them. Patrick felt as though they were moving rapidly through space with no road beneath them or open fields on either side. By the time they reached the bridge at Mill Creek, snow muffled the sound of the truck crossing. A point of light glimmered from the kitchen, and the pole lamp cast an eerie circle of illumination that seemed to captivate the swirling snow as it did moths in summer. He slowed long enough for Josie to hop out near the back door, then pulled into the lean-to. It was dark and still in the garage with only the slight noise of the wind whipping snow outside the shelter. He thought of his mother and Josie inside, already talking about what presents they'd bought and why Josie had wrapped them so nobody could see them and who Josie had seen in Minna's. Nothing would be said of the unpleasantness of that morning. Women could do that. They had a collective ability to turn out and turn away from painful, anxious times. They were practical. They knew how to put things away, store baggage on a shelf so they could move freely to the demands of the moment.

He left the garage and pushed through falling snow that defined the shape of the wind as it fell slantwise, only to pick up and wheel in eddies and spin off in all directions. The snow, he thought, studying it closely, was as yielding yet resilient as the tall grass in summer.

"I'm sorry about this morning. I didn't feel well." Sadie

sipped coffee, holding the cup with both hands and staring downward into the steaming liquid. After they'd eaten, Josie had gone to her bedroom with Freone. The table was scattered with dishes, still containing the remains of a meal — cut lettuce wilted under its weight of dressing, grease from a roast congealed into white globs.

He had remained quiet and distant throughout the meal, purposely avoiding comments she tossed in his direction, and after Josie had left, he'd found reason to dally, wondering if she'd approach any mention of last night or that morning.

"You were hung over. Even Josie could tell that much."

"Josie understands. I . . ."

"Josie doesn't understand," he broke in. "There's nothing she can do about it, so she accepts it."

"That's not all bad, Patrick," she picked up quickly. "Accepting." In one swift movement she lifted her eyes, unnaturally dark and without makeup. "Still, I'm just trying to say I'm sorry. I *was* hung over, as you put it."

"Did you tell Josie that?"

"I didn't have to tell Josie. Like I said, she understands. It's you. I knew I'd have to apologize to you."

"Forget it." He tilted to the back legs of his chair to brace his boots against the table's pedestal and give his legs more room. "I don't need it. You pretty much do as you please anymore. Without apologies."

She caught the cutting edge of his voice and gave up a sigh that pulled her from the chair. "Les and I were having a good time. I drank a little too much. I am sorry about this morning. I felt awful. I still felt awful after you left." She swept her fingers straight back through the thickness of her hair.

"But you felt great last night."

"Sure. Les and I had a fun time. That's all."

"I know. I was there. Right across the dance floor from you. You were necking like . . . like you couldn't wait . . ."

"Oh, God." She swung around to face him then. "I didn't know. I didn't see you."

180

"That was obvious." He brought his chair down with a whack against the floor.

The noise gave her a startled jolt, but she quickly regained her composure.

"Perhaps you had better learn to be more like Josie. Accepting. Because Les and I weren't doing anything unlawful. I'm not about to give up seeing Les because of your jealousy. Your unnatural jealousy." She spun back to the window as he pushed out of the chair and paced the few steps on his side of the oak table. "Patrick," she began again when the silence between them had gathered weight. "I don't know if we can talk about this."

"We've always been able to talk about anything."

"That's true. But this isn't about which horses to sell or whether we can afford to lay aside money for Josie's organ."

"I know."

"And it will be putting into words something we both know and can't seem to face very well."

"I guess you'll have to try. You're better with words than I am."

"I don't think I can go back. Back to the way it's always been with you and me. I'm moving forward too fast now. You want the old me back. Baking bread here at home, mucking out stalls with you." With an agitated lift of her hand, she went quickly on. "And it's not all your fault. None of it's your fault. It's mine, but I did it without thinking. Because it was so natural. You were born old and somehow you missed childhood altogether."

He shook his head as though to break in, but she continued before he could speak up.

"No, it's my fault that you never had one. You made it easy, natural for me to lean on you, depend on you."

"We survived. That's the point."

"Like dancers in a walkathon," she said with wry humor. "You've never seen one, but I remember going to them with Polly and Robie McDaniels. You know. That horsey Christmas card we got the other day. They send them every year. From Kentucky. Robie taught me most of what I know about horses, and the rest I learned from Gramma Rho. I started out working with Robie when I was still in high school. He had a little training stable for jumpers outside Lexington. Not big, because he was too particular about his horses to have many hands on them. Polly loved to go to walkathons, and Robie and I went along. They're dumb, walkathons are. Couples take to a dance floor to see which ones can stay upright the longest. We'd bet on a couple and come back every day or so to see if they were still upright. After a day, we'd come back, and dancers would be draped like rag dolls over each other's shoulders, dead weight in each other's arms, hanging on for dear life."

She paused to lean against the chair on her side of the oak table. "That's all I was at first. After your father left. Dead weight. Hanging on to you for dear life. I was such a poor, pressed-flat little thing, I didn't believe I'd ever be able to hold myself upright again. You remember"—she gave an emphatic toss of her hand—"how frightened I was to go to the newspaper office and beg, literally beg, Roy Yost to put me on full time. We sat here at the oak table talking about it. Almost like now. Only then it was you that did all the talking. 'You can do it, Mom,' you said. 'Just march in there like you own the place.' You made me feel like I could. We were like two separate people that purpose had made one. There weren't any guidelines for us to follow." She gave an off-hand shrug. "Not that we looked for any standards. We took what seemed to lie before us and tried to make something of our own. And what we came up with seemed perfectly natural—mother-son, son-husband, mother-wife—I guess that's as good as anything to call what we've had." Her gaze to him was fixed and intent. "The truth is, Patrick, you made a better husband than your father. There was almost a rhythm in his coming and going, like the phases of the moon. But not you. You're as constant as the North Star. But," she paused and turned to the window again where snowflakes had caught to one side of the screen to form a soft drape in the corner, "the thing is I want to be who I am now without you having illusions about what I might have been." Her voice ascended slowly.

"Maybe I don't have any illusions. Maybe most of them are gone."

"No." She shook her head several times. "No. If they were, you wouldn't be so jealous of Lester."

He braced his hand to the chair back, pushed his hair back along one side of his head. "And you want another divorce," he said abruptly. "That seems to be what you're coming around to saying."

"Lester fits my life now," she said simply, crossing her arms so that her hands clutched her elbows.

"I don't want to see you hurt. I'm not much for walkathons," he said.

"I won't be. I'm stronger now."

"There's Josie to think of." He went calmly around the table between them and stood beside her. Together they looked out into the night.

"You know I wouldn't do anything to hurt Josie. Or you." Her gaze seemed caught by certain large flakes drifting into her line of vision.

"Are you in love with Lester?" His shoulder barely touched hers.

"I don't know about love." She gave a hollow laugh. "Talk about illusions!" But then her voice resumed its deliberate edge. "I like to be with Lester. To have fun. For such a long time, I was nothing but a little gray mouse, and it's so damned surprising to see I grew up to be a great big beautiful gazelle." She hesitated moments before she looked up at Patrick. "I know how Lester makes me feel. Whole. A woman. It's something you can't give me."

He left the kitchen then and climbed the stairs to his room. As he lay in bed with his hands pillowing his head, he listened to her move about beneath him. So much of himself was tied to her, and he realized now that he knew little about himself

183

outside of her and what she'd meant to him. He had presumed the same was true for her, but he could see his assumptions were wrong. Illusions, as she called them. She had invented something else for herself. Her life had altered so that what mattered to her was something other than home or family. He was part of the past that she had swept aside. He wondered if he could do the same for himself, but so much of his own happiness had always depended upon the well-being of the family. Home, family — maybe they too were only illusions he carried in his head. He wondered if there was something else waiting for him, a mysterious life that until now had remained hidden, as though there were something unlawful about it.

11

The cold settled like grief. Still and hard and impondera-
ble. Sunless, heavy days alternated with snowfalls until
the frozen strata hardened like tundra.

Patrick hunched his neck and face into the woolen scarf to
meet his ski cap. Only his eyes were visible as he peered out into
the slight hills, rumpled and white. They seemed to absorb the
silvered sky and obscure the horizon. The only warmth he felt
was what he and Black Judy shared as he pressed his thighs
against the fenders of the saddle. Black Judy cracked through
the crest of the snow, chipped it like pottery as she pulled her
foot and leg free. Behind her, Simone, Sadie's heavy-hocked
mare, prudently put a foot into each imprint Black Judy left.
Behind them all, Doradella, with Josie mounted, picked her
way like a reluctant debutant.

"Do you see it, Patrick? Up ahead there," Josie called, and he
heard her even though the wind picked up her words and
carried them off.

He dropped the reins to lower his scarf. "I see it, Josie." A red
ribbon whipped on an outer branch of a cedar, which Josie had
selected and marked a few days earlier. Afterwards, Josie had
begun to prod him and Sadie into riding out for the tree. She
was irritated when other things interfered so that the three of
them couldn't go, and she refused Patrick's suggestion that they
go without Sadie. Still, he didn't argue much, because he was

heartened that the season, secured in traditions too accustomed for Josie to lay aside, had prompted her to spend more time at home, less with the Uttermelons at Stonegate Tabernacle Union. She was busy making banana bread in coffee cans and elaborate Christmas cookies and plump felt animals stuffed with bits of old hosiery Sadie gave her. Sometimes when Patrick came in from the barn to the warm house, the strains of Christmas carols as Josie sang and played at her organ and the aroma of fresh-baked food could throw him back in time. It could have been any Christmas in the past, when everything worked without plans or lists, since the season itself absorbed all time and energy until it was gone in one big swoop.

Now it was three days before Christmas, later than when they usually went for a tree. They might never have found a time to suit Sadie except that she had now decided to invite Lester to dinner, even to help decorate the tree. "It's no big deal," she had said. "I've been wanting to have Lester out, and this is a good time." Josie had tried to catch Patrick's reaction as she said, "Do you think he'll come? He's sort of a dude." Sadie set her mouth in a firm line. "You can both be pleasant. That's not asking too much."

At the tree, Josie swung from Doradella's back and mushed through snow, pumping her arms to pull herself through drifts. The tree branches sagged under the weight of the snow, and as Josie shook the branches clean, the snow tumbled like boulders to all sides of the cedar.

"It's a dandy," Josie said. Her eyes were the brightest thing about the day.

"If we can get it in the house," Patrick said. He dismounted, bringing the saw that he'd held across the saddle. "You know how little they seem out here and how big they get once we set them inside."

"It's not too big." Josie stretched until her fingertips brushed the top of the cedar. "No bigger than last year's."

"Providing you haven't grown any in a year."

Sadie poured a steaming cup of hot milk and coffee from the

thermos she'd filled before they left home. "Hold it near your face for a minute before you drink." Her scarf sagged beneath her mouth, and the vapor from her breath formed a tiny chain of droplets along the scarf edge. Josie held the cup near her cheeks for a moment before she sipped and passed the cup to Patrick. The drink was sweet, the way he remembered it from his childhood.

As though watching an old movie, too familiar to hold her attention, Sadie remained astride Simone and watched Patrick cut the tree. Josie, on the far side, heaved her shoulders against it as it leaned. When the saw bit through, Josie stepped aside and the tree sank with a deep breath to the snow.

"There," Josie said with a toss of her head, "we have a Christmas tree and one less cedar taking space in the pasture."

When she knew they were ready, Sadie passed the thermos of coffee again.

Patrick pulled a rope through lower branches, wrapped the end around his saddle horn, and they started home, with the horses mushing through the snow trail they had made.

The women, ahead of him now, crouched inside their outer wraps as they faced the northwest wind, which had picked up speed and had gathered loose snow into snow devils. Powdery snow dusting around the horses' legs and the ends of the women's scarves whipped free and trailed with the mares' tails. The mares trudged on, with slack reins, their vaporous breath rising like columns of smoke from their nostrils.

When they reached the creek bank, Patrick realized they were more than halfway home, and he lifted his eyes from beneath his scarf long enough to sight the barn roof — a heavy, slate-gray brace against the leaden sky.

Black Judy avoided the creek bank where the other horses had worn a skiddy path and picked her way down an untrodden slope, her hocks dropping under her as she searched for solid earth. The creek bed was dry now, and she gathered herself neatly for a lunge up the far bank. The tree coasted behind. With the final lap at hand, the horses increased their

187

pace. Within minutes, all were inside the barn. Moving quickly, wordlessly, they unsaddled and stalled the mares, bedded them down with fresh straw, clean hay, tepid water, and as though on cue, made a dash for the back door and the Franklin stove, the tree still their caboose as Patrick pulled it over the snow and up the steps to the porch.

"I think I'll go to Caleb's," Patrick said after he had warmed and the women began cleaning house, preparing food for the meal later that evening. The thought of going to see Caleb and Sandra had come to him on the ride home. It had been a week or more since he and Josie had ridden horseback, on a day shot through with unexpected sunshine, to take Josie's banana bread and animal Christmas cookies to Sandra.

He pulled from the driveway in his truck, intentionally fishtailing the bed to vent the elation he felt at getting away from the women. Sometimes they could be as silly as school-girls, teasing and giggling over trifles, stopping in the middle of whatever they were doing to swing into an Irish jig when music from the radio held the beat. At such times, he envied the impetuous spontaneity that seemed inherent to them and left him looking on, bemused and alienated.

He and Sadie hadn't mentioned Lester or their conversation in the kitchen. When they drove to town in the mornings, they spoke to each other with guarded reserve, and the chasm that lay between them seemed entirely unlike the disagreements they'd had in the past when the essential dailiness of their lives and the evenhandedness of the work they shared sealed the rupture seamlessly and made them more united than before. This time was different. They'd had no wrangling dispute, no "scene," and it occurred to him that he and Sadie had been absolutely reasonable, quiet and composed. He supposed that if their lives together had been somewhat like a marriage, their estrangement now was something like a marriage breaking up.

He should move out. It was time for him to leave home, but he couldn't bring himself to say "leave home," not even to himself. Even the sound of the words — leaving home — was unnatural, ominous. Instead, he thought of finding a place of his own. He began a list of the pros and cons of such a venture, noting the things he'd need, how much money the move would take, the furniture he might claim — his bed, perhaps, and his dresser — and the other pieces he would have to buy.

Lately, when he least expected it, he'd dream of Mary Delphinia and of moving in with her. Mary Del, he called her. But that wasn't her name. He knew her no better now than when he'd first seen her at the Island Oasis. In his dreams he'd begun calling her Mary Delphinia — a name as long and beautiful as her silken hair — the girl with the cello. In early mornings, he might wake and be wet from dreaming of her. In his dreams, he couldn't see her face, because she lay with her hair in ribbons across her face and breasts. She held him between her legs as he had seen her hold the instrument she played, with her knees wide and slack, and he came to her alert and searching and complete. He always woke then, sometimes whispering only "Del, Del," and he finished the dream out for himself. It was a nice dream, moving in with Mary Del.

It wasn't Mary Del but Udall who gave him the idea of moving. Mary Del — and the thought of moving in with her — was a fantasy, but he saw Udall as a living, breathing replica of what his life easily might become. It wasn't as much from anything Udall said as from observing him day after day. He'd enter the store, and there would be Udall on his stool peeling an orange. Every morning — two oranges. After he put the last neat section in his mouth, he'd wipe his hands on the insides of his pockets and leave them there while he stood at the front windows. Every morning. He knew Udall was thinking of the men beginning their days in barns, revving up tractors to clear paths for stock or bucking hay bales from barn lofts. Udall missed the dependence of animals and machinery that heightened a man's independence, a feeling less obvious, yet more urgent than making money. Watching Udall with his hands sunk in his pockets, Patrick could see himself in Udall's place, years later, suffocating within the limits of Stella, disturbing dust on chair legs and looking for momentary pleasure in the center of a magazine or taking a wife to bed on schedule. With each new day, Patrick saw his future played out in front of him, and he experienced a fear that reminded him of suffocating in the bottomless muck in the depths of Mill Creek. He could, in fact, see little difference.

One morning in the musty world of the feed room, as he rested from hugging and shouldering full burlap sacks and looking into the other world occupied by Udall and the poker club, he decided to find his own place. He resolved to bring some jarring deviation to his life. His announcement to Sadie and Josie would be simple and unequivocal: "I've found an apartment in Stella, and I plan to move in the next few days." No preamble. No discussion, or at least no more than he could avoid. To their inevitable response, he would reply that yes, he would come back to help when the mares foaled; yes, he would continue to shuttle Sadie to and from town when he could; and yes, he would wait until after Christmas before he moved. But rising as sudden and solid as a stump to trip him was the thought that just after Christmas had been the time of year his father had left, a fact that would badger him and trigger ill feelings for Sadie and Josie. February seemed a more likely time. But by then, mares would be ready to foal, which would mean he'd spend more time on the road than anywhere else. Added to these obstacles was the possibility that outside mares would no doubt begin arriving by late January and February, so perhaps a time in summer would be more practical. And Josie. His leaving at any time would be hard for Josie. Sadie wouldn't honestly mind except for the inconvenience it might cause her, but he sensed that with his leaving, Josie would spend all her time at Stonegate.

Angry and distraught, he went back to bucking burlap

sacks, thinking he was no better than Udall, dreaming of something that was impossible for him to shape into anything other than his fruitless lists. Much as he tried, he could not seem to plan anything that did not include his mother, Josie, the mares, even the land they lived on, and such a chain of interconnectedness was strung before him that he could not seem to break through at any point.

Glancing upward through the windshield, he caught sight of chimney smoke, thin as a pencil stroke, rising amid the trees around Caleb's A-frame. Caleb, he thought, had never let himself be dragged down by cross-purposes. Wholly unlike Udall, Caleb lacked that air of discontent that Udall carried about him like oil of oranges. Yet, Caleb seemed to have no strategy for life; he shambled through each day apparently with little more intention than to keep Sandra sassy fat. He adhered, it seemed to Patrick, to a nameless interior wisdom that he made no attempt to understand, only follow, and such primal instincts, once respected, responded as honorably as intelligence.

He hadn't mentioned to Caleb, to anyone, his intention to find a place of his own, and as he pulled into Caleb's drive, the thought came to him that he might bring it up as he and Caleb talked. Ahead of him, the house sat like a bird ready for flight. Built so that the rear of the A-frame was at ground level, the house extended over the gradually sloping earth until the front deck, supported by cement pillars, rose six feet or more above the ground. The roof line, soaring upward, seemed like the sloping sides of a bird's body with wings tucked, ready to rise in flight.

Caleb stepped to the redwood deck and beckoned as though he'd been waiting for Patrick, tossing his arm up over his bushy head in an exaggerated wave.

"I'll be damned," he said when Patrick reached him. "You've come at the right time. I just got that Sandra to nap. This is the first piece of quiet I've had all day." His arm fell across Patrick's shoulders, and he pushed him into the entry where a collection of Sandra's toys lay amid Caleb's tools, boots, hunting traps — even last summer's fishing poles.

"Just shove aside whatever you can't step over. And take your boots off so you can put those big feet of yours up next to the fire." Caleb padded off into the great open area of the house, centered by the hulking frame of the Franklin stove. He walked stiff-legged, his broad feet turned out in gray woolen socks.

"You look like you're limping some," Patrick said.

"It's not a thing." Caleb swung his arms as though limbering stiff muscles, and his red checkered shirt stretched taut across his meaty shoulders.

"I been sitting around too long. Things are slow over the holidays since everybody's spent their money on presents. I suppose the old arthritis has crept into my knee joints. Eat more honey," he nodded solemnly. "I've been thinking about putting a hive out back. Need to move around some. Make us some coffee." He filled a gray enamel percolator at the sink and set it on the stove burner, squatting to check the flame. "Damn, I'm glad to see you. I'd supposed you were going to let Christmas slide on past without a visit. Now scoot that chair on up close to the fire. Colder that a witch's tit since the snows started."

Patrick smiled. Caleb could speak his mind, be less guarded than when Sandra was with them.

"Caleb, we ought to get away. Set out trapping along the creek or something."

"Now there's an idea," Caleb rubbed his hands together as though eager for the outing. "After the first of the year, we'll set out . . ."

"No. I mean now. Today even."

"Today," Caleb mused. "Today, the boy says," he mumbled to himself. "Just three days before Christmas, and he wants to head out in the worst weather we'll have all winter."

"Hunting, then." Patrick spoke up quickly. "We'd have deer meat to last both of us till spring."

"And you don't think you can wait until after the first of the year?"

Patrick pulled back from the stove, gathered his legs under him, and paced to the far side of the room. "Oh God, Caleb, I suppose." He caught the heavy spice of Caleb and Sandra's Christmas cedar, laced with strings of popcorn and hung with paper decorations Sandra had made in kindergarten. "Wait. Wait. It seems to me we wait half our lives away."

Caleb passed him the handle of a steaming mug. "Take your coffee. And stretch out again."

"Maybe I just needed to get out of the house."

"Just as I thought. I know the feeling. It's hard to live with women — until you live without one." The admission, so unlike Caleb, took Patrick off guard, and for an instant he wondered if Caleb had erotic dreams, as he did of Mary Del, or if he took a woman occasionally to Chesterfield — no, it would have to be much farther.

"Women think different than us men. Don't ask me how, but they do. I can see it in Sandra already. She'll have a little plan to do something and instead of coming right out with it, she'll work me around until I give in on one thing, then another, and before long, it seems like nothing to give her whatever she wants."

"I don't much want to go back tonight, Caleb," Patrick said after thoughtful moments of staring at his stocking feet, braced against the stove rim. "I think I'd like to stay here."

"Suit yourself. You've slept on that old couch before." Caleb indicated the sagging piece of furniture, draped with a faded quilt. "Of course, you don't fit on it too good."

Patrick lifted his gaze to the high beams above him — "the backbone of the house," Caleb called the center ridge from which the vertical members extended. A thin light set a pale glow across the honey-yellow pine, and in the darker elevations a host of spiders had dropped webbing that snagged flies.

"It's good to be here," Patrick repeated. "I don't want to go back tonight."

"I know. I think you said that once."

"I suppose you'll wonder why."

"I suppose I'll wonder, but I won't ask." Caleb replied mildly.

"She's having Lester to dinner," Patrick said without preamble. "Even to decorate the tree. I don't like to be with him. There's nothing to say. Of course, Lester's never short of words. When I'm around him, I have this urge to pick him up by that stiff collar of his and toss him out in the snow."

"Mmmmmmmmmm." Caleb idly tapped his mug against his palm.

"And I don't want you to say one damn word about me being jealous of Lester. I've already heard that. You're damn right I don't like Lester moving in, taking over, taking all her time. But that's not all of it, Caleb. He's no good. And he's no good for her."

"Patrick, they're having a few good times together, a few laughs."

"A few beers," Patrick went on, "a few all-nighters."

"Patrick."

"Yeah, Caleb, I don't think you know the half of it."

"Patrick, I won't . . ."

"No, just wait a minute. I know what you think about her, how there's nothing too good for her because she was Natalie's friend and because of what she did for you after Sandra was born."

"You're damn right," Caleb shot back. "And if you're going to say one word against your mom, you can get up right fast and put your boots and coat on and head out of here. She was Natalie's *only* friend. Not a soul around here, including my own brother, would have anything to do with Natalie. 'Marrying a black woman,' Tobias said. Only he didn't say 'black.' 'Giving our good name to a nigger whore that just straggled into town.' But it didn't matter to your mom what anybody thought. Because she's that kind of woman. And I won't listen to one word, especially from you." Caleb bit down to snap the words off clean and sharp. "Your mom may go out for a few beers with Lester, but she's not going to do anything to hurt you or Josie. I'll grant you, Lester's probably not right for her, but they aren't getting married, Patrick. Only passing a little time. And they got that right without you getting rankled out of shape."

"Look, Caleb, forget it. I should have known what you'd say."

"So she's changed a little," Caleb went on. "She's got a right to a little fun. No matter what she does, or what you *think* she's done, don't you give up on her."

"You make it sound like it's some little stage she's going through. Like Sandra when she gets lippy. Just a stage. And if we all wait long enough, ignore it, it'll pass, and Mom will come around. Come to her senses."

"That's about right."

"She's not a five-year-old, Caleb. But sometimes she acts like it. And it's more than the new looks, the new clothes. It's inside. It's like the somebody she is now has always been waiting around inside to take over, and now that she's in the free and open, she's not about to be smothered back inside again. And this new somebody, whoever she is, doesn't give a damn about anything the other somebody cared about. Horses, the ranch, kids, nothing."

"Now, Patrick."

"So I don't know why I should either. Except that I hate like hell to give up on things. Especially when they're just beginning to pan out. It doesn't make sense."

"You hang on. Sadie's not going to rip off and leave that horse operation. She's worked too hard to get it where it is."

"She doesn't have to walk off and leave it, Caleb. She's got me to run it. She can have it both ways."

"There you go again. You mom's not like that."

"Maybe my mom's not. But Sadie is."

"Just give her a little time. Go on back home. Set the tree up and be nice to Lester. If I can take a guess, Lester won't be around a year from now."

195

Patrick sat motionless for some moments. "Maybe you're right. I can't see Lester sticking around Stella for too long either. And in the meantime, I'm supposed to hang on? Hold things together?"

"You've weathered rougher times."

Patrick went to the stove and refilled his mug, then brought the pot to Caleb's cup. "But sometimes I have half a notion to find a place of my own in Stella. I've been thinking about it more and more."

Caleb squinted his eyes in irritation. "Now that would be foolish. Have you stopped to figure what it would cost to live alone? Pay rent? Buy groceries?"

"I've put a pencil to it," Patrick said defensively.

"Besides the expense, where would you live in Stella?"

"There's that place above the J & J."

"That apartment of Jock and Jessie's is a rat hole. Unless they've fixed it up since Natalie lived there. She stayed there a few months before we were married, but I took her out. I told her, 'You're not staying here. Either you marry me or I'll buy you a bus ticket to wherever you want to go.'" Caleb let out a mild laugh, his eyes caught in the swirl of his coffee splashed with cream. "I was safe. I knew by then she'd marry me. She was no young chick. Neither one of us was. We were both nearing forty, and we figured if we were to have something, we'd better take it and run."

"I didn't know. I always figured she was much younger than you."

"She looked it, all right. Beautiful. Beautiful. Do you remember how beautiful she was? Eyes like a fawn. She'd wrap her hair up into a knot on top of her head, pull it back tight from her brows, and her eyes would lift wide like she could be surprised about most anything."

Patrick looked away, unaccustomed to Caleb sharing such intimate feelings about Natalie.

"In some ways Tobias was right about her. I suppose she'd lived with men. All sorts. I never asked her because I didn't

196

give a damn. We picked up from where we were when we met, and we moved on from there. I knew what I knew from the first night I saw her. When she was left at the J & J by that trucker who drove off while she was in the head. When she found out he'd gone on, she was spitting mad."

"You never told me. As long as we've known each other, I never knew."

"Maybe it's time, then. I don't want you thinking people can't change. Can't be something one day and something entirely different the next. Change, Patrick, being able to, I mean, is what's kept the human race around as long as it has. You wouldn't have known her that night, storming up one side of the cafe and down the other when she knew she'd been left. She started tearing the place up. Jock had to clear everyone out. I sat in one of the booths alone, watching her, and I thought, God, what a hellcat. What a beautiful hellcat. But it looked to me like she was as much scared as anything else. I figured she'd probably worked right hard to get that ride, and she didn't know how long it would be before another one came along. Finally, Jessie calmed her down some, gave her a hot meal, and told her she'd have to move on." Caleb glanced off, his gaze seeking a far corner of the room. "I don't know what possessed me. But I went and sat in the booth with her, and we started talking. And after she finished her meal, I told her I'd take her home. She could stay at my place for the night. She thought she knew what I wanted. She gave a laugh that would have scalded the devil and said however I wanted it, she could deliver. The way she would talk! The sort of language you wouldn't believe. But God, how it did stir me!" He took a heavy breath. "She did. She did."

"But you brought her here?"

"Yes. Right here." He drew his eyes to wrinkled corners and passed his gaze around the room. "By then she was calm as a turtledove, and I was the one all fired up. And scared. She knew that. She knew all about men and what to do for them."

Caleb straightened up from his chair to rub his knee and flex his muscles in a turn around his chair. Patrick waited silently. It was the best way to keep Caleb talking.

"It was late January and cold like it is now, but it was warm in here, and the Franklin was percolating heat to the very peak of the roof. She couldn't get over this house. She walked around running her fingers around the knots in the pine, her hands across this walnut table. Asking how I'd done this. And why. 'Why'd you want to do all this work just to have a place to hang your hat?' And the next thing I knew, I was telling her. Making a big show of telling her what the place meant to me and how long I'd waited to build it and all about how I'd built it. Everything. And pretty soon, out of the clear blue, she said, 'You've never fucked anybody in this house, have you, Bear?' I went weak as a gosling. Couldn't answer her. Not that I needed to, since she knew. But the upshot of it was, I didn't sleep with her. I slept on that old couch there. The next morning I drove her into Chesterfield and gave her money for a bus ticket. And I'll be damned if she didn't hitch a ride back to Stella, talk Jessie into a job at the café, and by the time I came in for my dinner, she was there, bringing out my coffee. I tell you . . . what a delight she was to see! Three months later, we were married. She said, 'I don't know if it's you I want, Bear, or this house.' And I told her, 'It's all one and the same. One and the same.'"

"And you forgot about her past? What she'd been?"

"In the end, the past don't matter much, Patrick. Some days are so good, you forget about what you've left behind. Other days are so dreary, you don't want to pack it along. Besides, Natalie didn't need a past. Your mother invented one for her."

"You mean the stories they made up."

Caleb nodded. "They were a pair. You'd have thought they had grown up together. They had a lark, sitting right here at the table drinking coffee and making up stories. The way your mom told it, that trucker was nothing but a scoundrel who had agreed to take Natalie from New York to California to sell her paintings. He'd driven off with all Natalie's priceless artwork, which, of course, was the reason she was so mad that night he

198

left her at the J & J."

"I sorta remember some of that. The women would call in with stuff for the column, but sooner or later they'd come around to asking about Natalie."

"And your mom gave them enough stories to fill their bonnets. Better than their soap operas. Natalie's father was black, her mother Chinese. Her father had been a colonel and married her mother on a tour of duty in China. Of course, Natalie's eyes, tilted like they were — she got those eyes from her Chinese mother." Caleb shook his head in a mock-serious way. "Her parents had money. They'd sent Natalie to a fancy finishing school in the east and on to art school in Paris, but when she'd gotten mixed up with a hive of Bohemian artists, her parents cut her off without a cent. And when she landed here, in Stella, she'd been trying to get her paintings to the West Coast to sell them. Her parents had a change of heart after we married. At least that's the way your mother told it. Sometimes Sadie would drop tidbits in her column. 'Mrs. Caleb Burroughs has journeyed to New York to act as hostess for the current showing of portraits at the Hyde Park Eastside Gallery.' Course," and Caleb gave a shrug of resignation, "neither one of them knew a thing about any Hyde Park Eastside Gallery." He took his chair and eased his shoulders to the back. "Sadie's stories didn't do much to change attitudes around here, but I think they changed Natalie. She became the woman your mother invented. She took up painting and found she had a real flair for it. People didn't accept her much better at the end than they had in the beginning, but she didn't care. She was someone glamorous and mysterious, and I shouldn't wonder if most of them didn't wonder why she married me."

The bedroom door slammed, and Sandra marched in stiff-legged with her fists thrust on her hips and her mouth in a pink pout. "Why didn't you wake me up soon as Pat got here?" she directed to her father. Then with two leaps and a shout, she was in Patrick's lap, her knees doubled under and her sleep-warm face against his neck.

"God, Patrick, the love affair you two carry on. She don't treat anybody like she does you. Not even me. Gives me the jealous hives."

Patrick scooped Sandra to his shoulder where she teetered, laughing down at him with eyes tipped upward like her mother's. Her hand, clutching his hair, pulled at the roots before she dropped over his head and slid down his back.

"She's a princess," Patrick said. "A princess with a mysterious Chinese grandmother."

Patrick started home late in the afternoon. The thought of staying the night at Caleb's had vanished like smoke up the chimney. Little by little, his uneasiness slipped away in the contented drone of Caleb's voice, which rumbled along of its own momentum like a wagon bumping downhill. As Patrick was leaving, Caleb wrapped Sandra in the quilt from the couch, and they all stepped out the door into the night. Once outside, Caleb gathered Sandra into his arms so that only her face was visible; even that he tucked into the protection of his sidelocks and beard. The night was as snug and quiet as the inside of a cloak with the wind settled into a pocket. Starlight shimmered in the moonless heavens. "Winter solstice," Caleb said, and he pointed to the North Star framed between bare tree branches in a brilliant limbo of its own. "It's winter's turn to do its worst."

Patrick drove home with his thoughts clinging to Caleb's stories of how he'd met and married Natalie. Eased against the seat, he let the truck coast into smooth snow ruts as solid and confining as railroad runners.

"You've never fucked anybody in this house, have you?" Natalie said.

"No. God, no." Caleb turned away from her. She had taken off her clothes in the bathroom and slipped into one of Caleb's

200

checkered shirts she had found there. Standing near the stove to warm herself, she lifted her hands to pull back her hair into a knot. The shirt swung away from her breasts and her stomach, slightly rounded like a partial goblet that tapered to a stem-like narrowness between her legs. "I'll bet you've never screwed a woman anywhere free and open so that you could wallow in the pleasure of it."

Caleb faced away from her, his breathing labored, too tense to give an inch in her direction.

"Hard as you are right now, Bear, you'd be soft by the time you got to me. Here. In your cathedral. Your church home. If it was spring, I'd lead you out to soft matted grass, but it's too damn cold for us to roll in the snow. I want you." Her voice was mellow and mild. "I'd like to fuck. If you think you could."

"Put your clothes on, Natalie."

"I know, Bear. But turn around once and look at me."

Patrick was inside the lean-to garage with the lights of his truck honed upon a tool-laden worktable before he realized he was home. Home. He leaned his head forward until it rested on his arms crossed over the steering wheel. Caleb and Natalie. Caleb would have put clean sheets on his bed for her before he went to the couch for the night.

Inside, his mother and Josie were waiting for him. Josie would have been peering through the bay window for a sign of him. "Go home," Caleb had said. "Put the tree up. Be pleasant with Lester. By my guess, he'll be gone by spring." Yes. Lester would leave. If not by spring, at least by next Christmas. Hang on, he told himself. Out of upheaval, order eventually arose.

Feeling less troubled than he had in days, he knocked snow from between the waffled grids of his boots and went inside.

"Oh, Patrick. Just in time." Flushed and agitated, Sadie spun to meet him. "It's the tree. Josie and I have never put it up, braced it straight." She made a dash for the stove, and her silver bracelets tipped together along her bare, white arms. Her dress was a Christmas red. Thread-thin necklaces swayed and circled her breasts as she dipped from side to side and set in motion the red flounces around her knees.

"Where's my apron? If I get a speck of grease on this dress . . ."

From a chair back, Patrick unhooked her apron and tossed it to her.

"Now go in there," Sadie whispered. "See if you can get the tree in place before supper." She patted his arm as though they were conspirators in a plot.

In the doorway, Patrick surveyed the results of the struggle that had gone on between the tree on one side and Josie and Lester on the other. They failed to notice Patrick. It appeared that the cedar with its thickset spurs had won. Josie's organ had been moved, and one end of the room was filled by the spreading juniper and the fruit of its pine-rich vapor.

"No, Lester," Josie said. "Not like that. Move to the other side."

Lester was clearly out of place no matter where he stood. His hair, usually neatly swept back, had fallen across his face, and like a swaggering young tough, he gave it an occasional toss as though to square off and renew his attack. Tiny cedar sprigs clung to his sweater front as though the juniper had lashed out and caught him a blow.

Patrick glanced back once at Sadie, and she gave him a smile of obvious pleasure.

"Ah, Patrick," Lester said from his position at one side of the tree. "I think you're the one we've been waiting for." He held gingerly to the tip of an outermost branch.

"Finally." Josie stuck her head around the far side of the tree. "Why have you been so long?"

"You need gloves on," Patrick said, and he took a pair from a hip pocket. "For protection. Cedars are the prairie cactus."

"Fine. You've got the gloves." Lester stepped lightly back and began pulling cedar spurs from his sweater.

"Thank goodness. Now we can get the tree up," Josie said.

"Don't you ever buy a tree?" Lester arranged his hair with a few practiced strokes of a comb and pats of his hand.

"Why would we buy a tree," Josie chirped, "when we have them in our own pasture? Taking up room." It was apparent that the two of them had begun the work in a nervous high-strung excitement, which had increased to an irritable tenseness. Patrick tried to catch Josie's eye, to give a reassuring nod, some shade of the security he felt within himself. But with an explosive swing of her braid, she settled opposite him, working intensely to support the tree as he braced the trunk in a galvanized container.

"It's just what most people do, Josie. They pick one up at the Lions Club lot or the grocery store, and their trees are just as important to them as your trip to the back forty for a pasture cedar," Lester persisted.

"We've never bought a tree, Lester, and we never will."

"But Josie, just consider the extra work. Riding out this morning in blizzard conditions, dragging the thing in. And now look. You can't decorate it. You can't even get close to it."

"Here's the wire, Patrick. I'll hold it on this side while you take it around the trunk."

"When I was a boy, I worked at the Lions Club lot. My father was an officer in the organization, and we always had beautiful, soft, long-needled pines in our house at Christmas. My mother ordered special ornaments from . . ."

"But what about when you had a family of your own?"

"A family of my own?"

"Yes. Didn't you ever get married. Have kids?"

"Well, Josie, I was married once, but . . ."

"But what? You never had kids?"

"My former wife and I had no children."

"It must be awful. Growing up without children."

"Josie," Patrick broke in, "stand back and tell me if the tree is straight."

"Oh my, Lester. I don't think you'd better smoke in here. Pasture cedars are dry as dirt, and even a little spark would set them blazing."

"Patrick," Sadie called from the kitchen, "I'm ready for you to carve the turkey. But I haven't sharpened the carving knife."

"I'll do it."

"Tell me when you're ready. I don't want to make the gravy until the last minute."

Standing beside the steaming, browned bird, Patrick drew the long-bladed knife across the textured sharpening rod. "I'm ready."

"Take a look at the sweet potatoes, Josie. In the oven."

"The marshmallows on top are just beginning to brown. I'll set the rolls beside them."

"Put the salads out. The relish tray."

"We have so many bowls, Mama, we almost need the extra leaves in the table."

"There now. Everything's on. Are there chairs enough? Well, come sit down, Lester. We're ready. Where is Lester anyway?"

"I wasn't very nice to Lester." Josie hung on the tree a metallic ornament with its surface chipped and dull in patches.

Sadie and Lester had left for a party in Chesterfield. Josie and Patrick had strung the lights around the cedar and were now slipping decorations on branches.

"I don't think you bothered Lester much. He can handle most things. He's pretty cool."

"I tried to ignore him at first, but he's so full of talk. He fills a room up somehow. His smile is too pleasant, like he knows something the rest of us will find out by misfortune."

Josie wore the gloves now, which made the job awkward. The ornaments dangled at the tip ends of the juniper, and gradually the tree took on the appearance of a child's drawing with pastel balls evenly spaced on the tips of limbs.

"That's just the way he acts."

"And the way he dresses. His hair so slick. And even that little gold chain around his neck — when he moves, it moves like a snake."

"You needn't worry. Lester probably won't stay around Stella."

"Oh, I hope not. I hope he's only passing through, on his way to somewhere else." She hesitated and gave a gasp as though her thoughts had caught her off guard. "But what if Mama wanted to go with him, Patrick? Have you ever thought of that?"

"She wouldn't. I don't think so."

"But we don't know that. If she does, you and I will sit pat where we are. Right here."

They worked in silence after that, without looking at one another, lost in alleyways of their minds that did not bring them out to any clear, true course they could speak of.

Finally Josie came up from the cardboard box with wads of tissue paper. "It's empty. We've used up all the decorations."

"Do you want to string popcorn and cranberries?"

"Oh, I dunno. Do you?"

"It's up to you."

"Let's use the tinsel this year. There's one old bag down here," and she leaned over the box to retrieve limp spangles that fell carelessly to either side of her hand.

They dropped the tinsel along the branch tips, but it failed to swag and cascade in a shimmering replica of icicles. Instead it clung to branches in heaps and lopsided mounds. When they finished, Josie plugged in the colored bulbs, and a pale glow filtered from the branches. In some places, the thickset limbs hung wilted under a mishmash of ornaments and lights; other places were nearly bare. In the process of their work, the juniper had been edged off center so that it leaned with a rakish nod to the right. With an air of unconformity, it had resisted all attempts at domestication, and yet it bore absolutely no resemblance to its straight, defiant stance in the pasture. It was neither here nor there.

They stood back as though distance, a new perspective, might lift the tree beyond their sullen and dispirited feelings.

Later, when Patrick went to his bedroom, he found Josie sitting on the far side of his bed, facing the window. Reflections from the yard light cast up by the snow were caught against the fine loose hairs that sprang from her braid and circled her crown in a filmy halo. Freone, sitting in her lap, spread a pulsating purr around the room.

"Josie, what are you doing? It's cold in here." Patrick lifted a corner of the spread and walked around the foot of the bed to cover her shoulders.

"Freone keeps me warm." Josie stroked the cat, and the fur on Freone's back caught the light as Josie's hair did. "You sit down too. Under the quilt." She patted the place beside her.

Outside the window, the unruly branches of the hackberry poked at the screen. Once when he was very young, he had opened the window as high as it would go, brought the screen inside, and sitting on the windowsill with his legs dangling to the outside and with full confidence that a scheme he had contemplated for weeks would work, he grabbed the limb and swung out. But the instant his butt left the sill, he knew the limb would not hold him. And in the second instant, as he fell, it came to him how ridiculous, how utterly foolhardy his plan had been. The peony bushes, in full bloom, broke his fall, and he jumped up, relieved to swing his arms, turn his head. He ran back to his room and looked in disbelief from the open window to the place directly beneath where the peonies lay flattened and crushed. He was amazed that he could have been so blind to such an obvious reality.

When he glanced over at Josie, she seemed to be looking through the stick fingers of the hackberry and far down the road. The tree's branches were thick with twigs that parted from the main bough. Taken together, they appeared as an oversized road map with veins of insignificant byways breaking away from main arteries.

"Do you think you're going to see him coming up that road?" he said lightly, smiling even.

"That one Christmas I did, didn't I?"

206

"You must have sat here all night. Just staring. It was like if you looked long enough and hard enough . . ."

"And prayed enough," she added with a smile, which he could detect in her voice. Moon glow washed across her forehead and down her nose, the high points of her cheeks, and pointed chin.

No car lights moved along the far road. The driveway glowed beneath them, and the road from the house was lit like a shining path for some distance until it was lost in the night.

"So what would you do if you saw him driving up the road?"

"I was thinking the same thing." She sat calmly, her chin lifted while her gaze remained fixed ahead of her. "I suppose I'd let him in. Out of the cold, you know. But I don't much care anymore. Maybe I've given up. That's the best thing in the end, but it's hard to do. Give up. And I think, where'd that feeling go? The caring. How'd it just melt away like the snow? Gone by spring."

Patrick leaned forward so that his gaze fell beneath the tree limbs. Black shafts of tree trunks were silhouetted against the moonstruck snow, and trivial drifts fell into wells around the bases of trees.

"And you?" Josie turned from the window to face her brother. "What would you do if he drove in the driveway?"

He braced his arms against his knees and did not turn to meet her gaze. "I'd get the rifle out of my closet there, and I'd run him off." The words came in a flat and measured tone.

"No, Patrick, you couldn't do that."

"Yes," he nodded. "I think I could." His voice lacked a trace of rancor. He might have been discussing the time the first mare was due to foal in spring or how much hay might be baled from a field. "But it's nothing to worry about," he continued. "Hartford, Connecticut, is a long way off."

"I know. I looked it up on the map at school."

"You looked it up? Well, what good did that do you?" In surprise, he reared back and came up beside her.

"Just to see," Josie said defensively. "I wanted to see where he lived."

"Josie, that was just where he happened to mail our Christmas cards. That doesn't mean he lives there."

"I know. Sometimes I have a vision of him just winging along the roads, not really living anywhere. I looked at all those little towns around Hartford. Why, there's Blue Hills and Cherry Brook and Pine Meadow and Birchwood, and I could see him stopping off in those little towns to have a cup of coffee or to buy a pack of cigarettes and then driving on. On and on."

"The main thing is not what you imagine, but if he put the hundred-dollar bill inside your card."

"Oh, yes. It was there. Flat and hard as a linen hanky."

"Good. What matters is old Ben Franklin giving you that half-assed smile."

"Did he say the same thing on your card that he did on mine?"

"I suppose."

"'Hope all is well with you at Christmas time,'" Josie intoned in her reading voice. "'I am working on a skyscraper here in Hartford, but we're slowed up some because we're waiting on marble from Verona, Italy. Hope all is well with you in school.'" She sighed. "Imagine. Marble from Verona, Italy."

"There isn't anything special about marble from Verona, Italy. Besides, he probably made that part up."

The ebb and flow of Freone's purr filled the silence that settled around them.

Suddenly Josie brightened. She picked up her shoulders so quickly it brought her up off the bed. "You know what we should do, Patrick?"

"Maybe go to bed." Patrick followed her, spreading the quilt in place.

"No. Let's go back downstairs and make popcorn and string it with cranberries and finish up that tree the way we always do."

She made a dash from the room, but then was back in an instant, pulling sewing thread from a spool. "It's the tinsel that makes the tree look so awful. Tinsel is what Lester would have put on those beautiful long-needled trees his daddy bought at the Lions Club lot. It doesn't belong on a pasture cedar."

Downstairs, they pulled off all the tinsel, first the wads and then the silver strands still clinging to the tree spurs. Patrick piled hedge into the stove until it crackled louder than the corn he popped. They strung the ruby berries and popcorn onto threads until a long red-and-white streamer fell across their laps to the floor, where Freone batted its end. With the streamer looped about her arm, Josie fed the line along the back of the tree and slipped the loops to Patrick, who worked the beading along his side before he returned the ever-decreasing folds to Josie.

He felt joined to her by more than blood or love or a common past. Yet what could it be? A promise of their union seemed to extend beyond all else, a mystery he had no hope of understanding. It was a secret that no amount of study could fathom. Nor could he break it down into a list or take it apart piece by piece and find in the reassembly an answer that had evaded him before. Indefinable, it remained steadfast within its own indistinguishable power.

When they finished, they sipped hot chocolate laced with peppermint sticks, as they'd always done in the past, and sat in the dark with only the tree lights blazing out at them.

12

After the first of the year, any thought Patrick might have had of moving to town exploded in one of his and Sadie's scenes. Lester had nothing to do with this one. She'd been dipping into the savings meant to make the annual payment on the ranch. She began telling him in an offhand way, which immediately aroused his suspicions. "By the way, I was in the bank yesterday" — a seething tightness gripped his chest — "and Ted Pritchard says there's nothing to worry about." He was primed for anger to erupt with her conclusion. "I've had to spend some of that money we saved back from the sale of the horses last fall."

In defense, her anger climbed to meet his. "I bought a few clothes. That's all."

"And jewelry. You must have gone to every goddamn store in the Chesterfield mall."

"I needed a few things." They went back and forth, hardly listening to each other, since it took all their resources to compose the next rebuttal or accusation. They kept the oak table between them, circling it because it had always served as the convenient mediator. Josie came in and listened undismayed for a few minutes. "Pillow shams? What the hell are pillow shams? You don't need to fix up your bedroom." "I didn't expect *you* to understand. That's the reason I haven't told you. Have to keep everything a goddamn secret." "Get the

210

account book. I want to see the figures. Jesus God." Josie edged around them into the living room where she began playing her organ. And singing. Finally Sadie stormed from the kitchen to her bedroom, giving a final declarative scream. "I'm a woman! I need some things! I *want* some things!"

Patrick slammed out the door for Caleb's. His body was scalding with rage, his head bursting, and he met the unmerciful cold with a pang of relief. He whipped the truck along the ice-glazed road, and when he reached the trestle, the truck hit the uneven surface with a force that sent the bed careening to the side, shifting and jarring sideways across the span. He tromped on the accelerator, his hands madly twisting the steering wheel until, in one doubling effort, the truck righted itself and sped on, diving and fishtailing the rest of the way. In Caleb's drive, he rested briefly, taking deep breaths and rubbing his aching knees, until he could face Caleb with composure. This was one time he couldn't confide in Caleb — not that Caleb would have believed Sadie's duplicity.

On that day, the two men left Sandra with Sadie and Josie and set off in Patrick's truck with their chain saws. They had spent most of their spare time cutting wood. Winter bore down like an auger, the cold winds piercing each day. The sun seemed so far away that no single warming ray reached the earth, and the wind sucked heat from the old house so that no matter how much wood Patrick chucked into the Franklin, a drafty chill hovered waist high.

After the men had the bed loaded, Patrick's truck failed to start. Every thought of Sadie — the unfairness of what she'd done, the lack of concern for how they'd meet the payment — leached away in amazement that the truck had failed him.

"You can't count on a goddamn thing anymore," Patrick said, and he wheeled from the cab to throw up the hood, confident that he could find the problem before Caleb could haul his big shoulders out and over the engine. But he couldn't. It wasn't a loose wire or the battery or the alternator, and he ticked off other possibilities as though marking them from a list.

"In the ignition. The ignition froze up on you," Caleb said matter-of-factly.

They hitched a ride to Caleb's, where his truck gave two resentful wangs and shimmied off with a roar. Back at Hightowers' hedgerow, they transferred the wood to Caleb's truck, drove home to stack it, then drove back again with a bar and chain to tow Patrick's vehicle. He insisted on remaining behind the wheel of his truck, connected umbilically by the chain. The warning-light bell sounding *dink, dink, dink,* made him feel a time bomb was ticking away inside his chest. He clenched his jaw and bit on his inside lip to keep from exploding. He took a grip on the wheel and gave it a yank as Caleb turned a corner. His efforts were useless. The truck followed Caleb's without wavering, drawn tight by the constant pull of the chain and wedged in snow ruts with boulders of snow stacked on either side.

"I might as well have stayed at home, racking wood, for all the good I'm going," he said aloud. "For all the good I ever do. Nothing does any good!" he yelled, his voice reverberating in the cab. "Damn, she pulls the rug out from under me every time. I got nothing of my own." His rage burned like rope yanked through his hands.

He took the next day off from the grain store, and he and Caleb worked on the truck in the lean-to garage. Caleb intoned a chorus of "It's just one of them things" to every verse Patrick devised on why the truck should not have broken down.

From Christmas until after the first of the year, letters arrived frequently from Gramma Rho. Her voice — urging him to consider college, that it was not too late to enter at midterm — was so intense he finally wrote to say there was no possibility of his going then, "or probably ever," he added. Her campaign was set aside for one letter, but by mid-January she had renewed the attack. "As I think about it," she wrote, "next September might be the best time for Patrick to start college," as though such a plan had been her original intention. "Laying

out of school a year, as we already know, never hurt anybody."
He pushed her letter aside.

"Rudy's been looking at that little two-bedroom over on Jackson Street," Laurie said, "but he thinks it's too close to Ramona's mom. He'd like to find a little place out in the country."

"He ought to move to Chesterfield. Get clear out of Stella."

"They'd never do that."

"No. Nobody ever does," Patrick said.

"Hasn't he talked to you about it? At dinner when you eat here?" They were sitting on the same side of a booth in the J & J. Laurie was working, but things were at a lull, since everybody in Stella was still at the basketball game.

"We don't meet much anymore. I've been working through my lunch hour, picking up the overtime, and Rudy drives to K mart to meet Ramona."

The cafe was full of the aroma of cinnamon and apples. Jessie had set out a crock of steaming spiced cider and doughnuts, her custom on game nights with people coming and going. As they arrived, they took what they wanted and deposited change in a dish at the end of the table.

Laurie brought her legs up under her in the booth and pulled her calico apron around her ankles. She wore a plaid woolen skirt and a navy sweater that made her skin pale and translucent. She had kicked off her pumps beneath the table, and she curled her toes inside navy hose.

"You're pretty quiet tonight." She dropped a hand to his upper leg, and he glanced down at it, her fingers so thin her knuckles stood out and the white half-moon of her thumbnail rising into the shell pink of the tip.

"It's nothing."

"It's something."

213

He looked beyond her to the square, quiet, steeped in snow with shadows from the streetlights casting their elongated bodies over stacked snow.

"You're pretty dressed up," he came around to saying, "for slinging chicken fries. What's the occasion?"

"I'm meeting somebody special," she came back quickly, yet softly.

"He'd better be special. For you."

"He is." She ducked her head to his shoulder and instinctively his arm went around her. But it made him sad to hold her, to feel a sort of melting weakness overcome him, that he was unable to fend off. Lately he had begun to feel they had dropped into a lull, a tread-water place in time, where the future seemed far away while their emotions moved in double time. He felt them being drawn to some inevitable conclusion he had thought to avoid because of their strength and convictions. If not his own definite plans, then certainly Laurie's would have deflected the unforeseen. But Laurie seldom spoke of her college plans, which racked him with anxiety and made it apparent he would have to check his own emotions as a safeguard for them both. Yet the thought of her leaving often cut him with remorse and left him with a keen-edged knowledge that, in fairness, he could do nothing to hold her or be the cause of relinquished plans.

"Have you sent in all the registration forms you're supposed to?" He gently took his arm away, but still she edged against his shoulder.

"Yes."

"And your dorm room?"

"It's too early for a reply on that."

"What about grants and scholarships?"

"Let's walk around the square." She nudged him in the ribs. "There's nobody in here. Won't be for hours."

"It's pretty cold out there."

She was already lifting her apron over her head. "Come on. You've got your down coat I made you at Christmas. And I

214

have a hat, at last." Her voice lifted with laughter. "I won't have to wear your cap." She left to get her wraps, angling around tables to the rear of the café.

From his rear pocket, he brought out his limp cap, ran the fingers of one hand through the wings of his hair, and set the cap on to hold his hair in place. He had folded the coat Laurie had made him into a neat billowy square and placed it in the opposite seat. He'd been amazed when he'd unwrapped it, lifted it, a deep forest green, from snowy tissue paper, mystified that she could make it — stuffed with goose down, light as a vapor, warm as a fever.

"This is the first coat I've ever had that really fits," he said as Laurie met him at the door. "Long enough in the sleeves. Long enough all over." He smoothed the front of it so the pockets of goose down rose and fell under his hand. "It breaths," he said, "on its own."

"I got a good do on it." She smiled.

"But you never measured me. To get the fit."

"I measured you." She gave a shy smile and enclosed her crown of curls with a woolly tam, placed to one side of her head. Then she doubled a matching scarf around her neck. They were a deep burgundy color that marked a contrast with Laurie's light hair and eyes and transferred a glow of color to her cheeks. He and Minna had discovered the set when he'd gone back looking for gloves for Josie's Christmas present. While Minna had brought out boxes of flannel pajamas and stacks of muslin tea towels, he'd uncovered the scarf-and-hat sets under a counter. "Gadfrey, those have been in here for three Christmases," she said. He perched the hat on his fist and brushed across the fluff, sending a halo of fur to meet his hand. The hat was Laurie's, he decided immediately. "Genuine angora." Minna said. "Can't get them this year at all. I saved these for you, Patrick." And a laugh boiled up from the depths of her great round stomach.

Outside the J & J, currents of cold air caught the soft strands of Laurie's hat and lifted them to the light. He grinned and playfully tightened the scarf about her neck.

"Do you think I'm pretty?" she said impulsively.

The question was unlike her, and for a moment Patrick was taken off guard. "Maybe." He gave a flick of a smile. "You're a sorta washed-out little dab."

He was prepared for her to come back with a teasing remark, but she dropped her eyes and tucked her gloved hand into the pocket of his jacket, a way she had lately of slowing his stride and keeping abreast.

"I know. I always wanted to be pretty. Stunning, really. With lots of soft, curly black hair and a figure with all the right bumps and lumps."

"I was only kidding. You are pretty. Especially in your own hat." He glanced down, still hoping to raise her spirits. He joined his hand with hers inside the pocket, and immediately her fingers laced his. "Besides, what's pretty? Lots of girls can be pretty. They buy it at the drugstore. You got something else."

"Like brains, you mean." She tipped her chin, and the streetlights set off candle flames in her pupils that had expanded until only a border of gray surrounded them.

"Brains, yes. And more. Perseverance, I guess they call it. You may be little, but you'll push on through life like it was a swinging door."

"Maybe not. Maybe I'll never get out of Stella."

"Sure you will. Come fall." He hesitated. Took a breath. "And college."

"I don't want to talk about college, Patrick. Not tonight."

"You'll feel different when the time comes. The closer it comes, the . . ."

"Oh, Patrick, do you have to bring it up?" Her voice fell.

They walked on past the window of Classen's leather goods, past a hand-tooled saddle that at any other time might have caught Patrick's eye. He slowed his pace and tried halfheartedly to release her hand, but she renewed her grip.

"Don't pull away, Patrick," she said evenly. "You don't want to any more than I do. You're just being . . . you're trying to be sensible."

He stopped abruptly at Tillie's corner. "One of us has to be, it looks like."

"Why don't we just forget about being sensible?" She kept her hand holding his in the pocket and brought the other to his waist. "Just to see what would happen."

"Oh, Laurie girl." He put his arms around her, and she came to him, laying her head against his jacket as though coming to rest on a pillow. His skin, suddenly sensitive, attracted the fur of her hat so that it rose, brushed, caressed the underside of his chin and his neck.

"You've talked about college for as long as I can remember. Have you forgotten how you used to make fun of everybody around here? Your own sisters? Giving up a chance to do something before they caved in to 'the family formula,' you called it?"

"Self-satisfied little bitch, wasn't I?"

"No. You don't talk like that. You knew what was important and how to get it."

"Maybe something else is important."

"You won't feel that way once you get away. Hell, if you don't go, you'll look back and say, 'I had a chance once, but I passed it up . . .'"

"For something better." She pressed her hands into the small of his back and lifted her hips against him.

He brought his hands to her shoulders and stepped back enough to study her face. "Laurie. You and me . . . it would be different if . . ." Her eyes were trained on him. A slight frown formed a crease between her brows. "I got nothing, Laurie. Nothing. I don't even know why you . . ." He turned away. Nervously, he lifted his gaze and caught a full-face view of Tillie's gargoyle, the stone lion's head protruding from the corner of the shop. The streetlight set off the detailed carving of the stone in sharp and dramatic relief. The lion's great ruff curled and waved about his heavy lifted brows and eyes, smooth and round as river stones. The mouth was open, lips drawn back — in something like a sneer, Patrick decided.

"If what?" Laurie asked. "It would be different if you had money? Some kind of high-paying job? A hundred acres of pasture? Is that what's keeping you from saying how you feel?"

"I don't know how I feel," he came back quickly, without thinking. "I only know part of it. The sex part. Hell, yes. You were standing close enough to me to know that. And I know what you want me to say. But I can't do it. It's not right for me yet. Not for you either." He had to keep moving, so he paced to the corner and turned near Tillie's gargoyle. Laughing, he thought; the damn thing's tongue was lolling out with laughter.

When he looked back at Laurie, she hadn't moved from the spot where he'd left her. She looked cold. Hurriedly, he stepped to her and crossed his arms over her shoulders.

"Goddamn, my legs ache, Laurie. My knees."

"Let's walk again."

"You're cold. Shivering."

"We'll walk fast."

Now Laurie took big steps, two to his one, with her hands in her own pockets. Their concentration seemed riveted on one spot in the cleared walkway where they were about to step.

"I think you want me to leave, go to college, as much for you as for me."

"I don't get you."

"You don't think you can leave, but you want to see me go. It's like I take a little piece of you with me."

"Yeah. I'll watch you go and shout" — he lifted his head — "'There goes Laurie Kieffer. She's going to make it. Move over, Stella. She's coming through.'" His voice echoed out across the square, still empty except for the two of them. But Laurie didn't laugh.

"But you could do that too, if you could only see that."

"No, I couldn't, because I've no place to go. You got something waiting for you. College. A dorm room. And you're leaving free and clear. That's the only way it can work, Laurie.

218

Free and clear. Some place to go and with nothing dragging behind. That's the way it is for you, and I want it to stay that way."

She turned abruptly at the corner, crossed the street, and entered the park. Aimlessly he followed. She reached the pavilion, where lights were only dim reflections and strange exaggerated shadows loomed across the snow. She started up the bandstand steps, he behind her; but when she turned, a few steps above him, she faced him evenly, and he kissed her. Met her mouth squarely with his own and put his hands to either side of her face and kissed her. She pressed down, her head now leaning over his, and while she kissed him, she took his cap and tossed it to the snow behind them. His hair fell back; she spread it back between her fingers. He dropped his mouth along her neck and found the woolly depths of her scarf. Immensely warm, his breath came hot against the scarf and returned damp against his cheek.

"I want to touch you," she said.

He could feel her hands smoothing the outer fabric of his jacket, seeking a place to go beneath. He recognized a quick, hard urge to pick her up, carry her someplace. A place of his own. He thought instantly of the soft bed of earth beneath the bandstand, and he bent to take her up.

Her scarf. He was breathing so rapidly, he couldn't take a breath. But then he caught himself and pulled away, his mouth wet with saliva. He smeared his jacket sleeve across his lips, stumbled at the step, and trudged the distance to the floor of the bandstand.

"Patrick." She followed and leaned heavily against one of the upright posts. He bent over the railing, drawing in the cold night air until he felt his breath returning, his strength ebbing back.

"Just tonight, Patrick. I want to be with you."

He raised his head slightly, not looking at her, but to the stars beyond. "Just tonight." He said it to himself. "One time. Hell, one time won't do it. And where?" He straightened until he

219

swung one arm into the night as though to take in all of Stella's square. "Where, in God's name? Here?" he shouted. Then lowered his voice. "On the wooden floor here? Christ, I haven't even got a blanket for you." He took a few steps; his fingers trailed along the railing. "Where else? The front seat of my truck maybe?" He brushed long side hair from his face. "In your dad's barn? My hayloft?" He seemed to be numbering off the places. "Behind the cottonwoods at Lander's Crossing? Everybody goes there. What the hell." He chucked his arm in a circle over his head.

"Patrick, it's not like that."

"It's not, is it? Well, then, it must be like this." He set up a pace again. "We get married. Right here." In one sweep of his arm, he indicated the pavilion. "Have one of those great big affairs, and then I go to work at the battery plant and you stay right on at the J & J. But not for long, because the babies start coming. We know the formula. We got the family formula down pat." His legs ached. He kept moving. "Why in hell is it that life turns us around so that we end up doing the very damn thing we said we'd never do? To take us down, that's why. Bring us down and sit on us until we got no will or strength."

"You make it sound so awful."

"It is awful, goddamn it!" He wheeled toward her. He heard the echo of his voice, a high-pitched roar, before he lowered it. "There's no place for us. You can't give up everything for one good fuck."

She reared upward, as though pushed, then as quickly, fell back against the support, which seemed to propel her forward. With a burst of energy, she spun across the space between them and grabbed the front of his jacket. But her fingers only clutched the airy, downy interior.

"You can't say things like that! Not about us!"

She grappled with the jacket, trying for a hold on him, and in her struggle, her hat lifted and floated, feather light, to the bandstand floor. He seemed to see them in slow motion, her intense little face, clenched into knots to hold back tears, her body swaying back and forth as she yanked at his coat. And he, motionless and untouched by anything she did.

He pulled her to him, hating the vision. "I didn't mean it like that," he said. "You know what I mean."

"Sometimes I don't." Her voice, nearly inaudible, caught in her throat. "You have so much anger in you."

"Not for you. Never. It's so heavy, what I feel for you. So damn heavy in me. But when it leaves, when it just goes up like smoke, then you got nothing."

"It won't be that way."

He held her protectively, one hand at the back of her neck. "I don't want you to want me, Laurie. That's all. I don't want it to happen. Because nothing will work out of it. From it." His voice was thick. He kept his head up, away from her face, her neck, the pulse he could see throbbing just above the edge of her scarf. "I don't want to hold onto you. I don't want nothing holding me."

From far away, the first sounds of the people returning from the basketball game floated in on the cold night air. Truckers arrived, squealing tires at each corner of the square. The townspeople had left their cars at the school parking lot and were walking briskly now the few blocks to the J & J, anxious for hot cider and doughnuts. Laurie shivered, her teeth chattered, and he loosened his arms around her to open his jacket and take her inside. They stood that way a few moments, watching the flashlights of the walking people coming toward the square, a bobbing white necklace beneath voices raised in cheers and chants.

13

"You're on a roll." Sadie handed the phone to Patrick and snickered. "Tug's going to have a full court this spring. But they're going to be fussier about those mares than they are who their daughters marry."

It was late January, and now when the phone rang it was often horse owners with inquiries about Tugaloo. With his colts and fillies making a favorable showing on tracks and in show rings, horse owners wanted to consider the big chestnut stallion as an appropriate mate for mares, soon to cycle into the breeding season.

Judge Croft, whose discernment for superior horseflesh equaled his shrewdness about people and who frequently said he used what he'd learned in dealing with one to handle the other, had passed word along that the Douglas stallion was one to consider. Callers frequently began by saying, "Judge Croft thought I ought to give you a call."

Patrick could barely disguise his pleasure. He was confident that by summer, he and Tugaloo would have earned enough money to offset the shortage Sadie had incurred on the ranch's annual payment.

"You and Tug have your work cut out for you," Sadie said. "But I'll take time off. Later on."

Patrick knew exactly what lay ahead; they'd had a few outside mares in the past, but special provisions had never been necessary. Most of the mares brought to Tugaloo were neigh-bors' horses, close enough for Patrick to ride to the ranch, keep the few days it took Tug to breed them, then return them. It was a crude sort of beginning, but he, Sadie, and Tugaloo had learned enough to bring them to the present opportunity and a chance for something that could honestly be called a business.

Horse owners calling now lived some distance from Stella, and they were "stud shopping." Not only Tugaloo but the ranch itself would be weighed against other stud farms. A stallion's bloodlines, the performance records of his offspring, were only part of their concerns. The barns, paddocks, and stalls had to be immaculate, every board in place, and without a nailhead protruding to catch the soft underbelly of a foal. In many cases, owners hauled in mares with newborn foals, a pair considered far too valuable to take chances with. If outside pens appeared thrown up in makeshift fashion, owners wouldn't even turn off their trucks long enough to look at a stud. A pile of day-old manure in a far corner, a stall lacking fresh bedding, grain working with weevils were all indications to check their lists for locations of other farms.

Then there was the stallion himself. Mare owners wanted to see him fiery and feisty when released in a paddock, but once haltered, they expected a model of contained, mannered strength. They wanted their mares covered and settled by a prepotent sire and not some overzealous cat, mounting with his hooves clawing, his teeth ripping.

Patrick wasn't worried about Tugaloo; the stallion was keenly aware of what was expected of him on all fronts. He could be downright embarrassing cavorting before strangers scrutinizing him from the paddock fence. He seemed to sense that his performance might determine an increase in his harem, and he could stand — swan-necked and tossing his foretop — for a moment of admiration before breaking into a fluid pulsat-ing run around his enclosure. Merely to enter his stall with certain equipment was clue enough to relay what was expected of him. His show halter set him gandering over Patrick's shoulder to see whom he could impress and the workaday halter aroused him no more than a currycomb. But his heavy leather breeding halter rendered him such a quivering bundle of anticipation, he would be stiff and ready to mount before he reached a mare. He responded with the most natural joy, however, to the bridle and bit. When Patrick slipped a bit across the bars of his mouth, he knew a holiday was at hand; he was free from performing. The two of them would set out, Patrick often riding bareback with a light rein and their linking intuition directing them into the hills, jumping natural barriers as they swallowed the ground ahead.

After the phone calls from horse owners started arriving and appointments were made for people to see Tugaloo, Patrick told Udall he needed some time off from the grain store, at least until summer when he had "foals on the ground and mares settled." Udall wasn't pleased. "It's my busy season too," he said, "and if I get somebody in here to take your place, I can't lay him off when you get ready to come back." Patrick agreed, and he quit altogether at the grain store. The poker club had a party for him with punch and cookies their wives had made, and they played cards, with Rudy joining, until the store closed. Patrick didn't regret his decision; the ranch, still risky as a business, was worth the gamble. He felt that all of them — his mother and sister, the horses, and mostly himself — had reached a watershed that, with a final driving effort, would break in their favor.

He set up a card table in his bedroom for keeping records — breeding dates of mares, when foals were born, inoculations given. He made lists — added four things before he had crossed off two. Even before his alarm went off, he awoke from a fitful sleep and began immediately to estimate the number of plywood sheets he'd need to divide large stalls. Some nights he'd call Josie or Sadie, whoever was home, to the barn long enough to hold one end of a plywood panel while he set nails in opposite corners. Then he'd send them back inside. "No, I can manage now. I'll call you when I need you." He had little time to spend with Laurie. "Wait. Wait," he told her, "until I have everything finished." He needed no one; fired by an internal flame, he burned through January as if it were dry newsprint and lit the corner of February. Events, unfurling faster than he could keep up with them, only whetted his curiosity to see if he could measure up to what he believed fate had handed him and what he expected of himself. He was no longer a mere reflection of all that had happened to him; he had his own purpose, as defined as Tugaloo's, and the feeling went through him straight as a plumb line.

He glanced back through the rear window of the cab at the plywood he'd bought. He'd spent most of the day in town, picking up supplies, finishing up odd jobs for Udall, eating the noon meal with Rudy. It was late now and he was in a rush to complete the stalls in the barn.

He rumbled across the trestle at Mill Creek, the sound of the truck's crossing no longer muffled in snow. Mounds of snow, now gray-streaked with road dust, had sunk into themselves, and patchy places appeared in the pasture where horses pawed through to reach incipient grass. He welcomed every positive indication of spring; he needed longer days, more daylight.

He pulled the truck as close as possible to the barn door, hopped out, and began lifting plywood when he realized he had on the jacket Laurie had made for him. So he took a slushy path to the house deciding to change clothes and grab something to eat, leaving the remainder of the day and evening uncluttered.

In the kitchen he dropped his jacket to a chair back and with some surprise noticed his mother sitting at the oak table. She remained motionless as he walked around her. He noted her wan appearance, her head bowed sluggishly, with only her satin wrapper reflecting the amber, shimmering tones of late afternoon light.

"Did you come home sick today?" he asked.

She continued to stare at some point in the palms of her

hands, pink cupped as shells one inside the other. Her breathing was so slight, he could detect no movement about her at all.

Curious, he glanced at the clock. Just after four. Normally she would still be at work; Josie should be the one home, delivered by the school bus by this hour.

"Why didn't you call me, if you were sick? I was at Udall's part of the day. I would have come, brought you home."

But the work awaiting him compelled him to move quickly around her to the refrigerator where he pulled out the jug of milk, cheese, and lunch meat. From the kitchen window, he noted the day receding, sliding away with the long rays of sun. So he hurried, cracked open the plastic package of meat, and sloshed milk in a glass. Then an odd suspicion, like an unexpected stench on the wind, hit him.

"How come you're home?" He faced her.

She heaved a sigh so forced it brought her hands to her face. Glancing in amazement about her, she slumped in her chair, crossed her arms on the table, and laid her head in the crook of her elbow. It appeared she had suddenly awakened to something she could not fathom, and she wanted only to resume sleeping.

The room, set in sepia tones, cast amber reflections across her narrow back, shimmered down her satin wrapper. The tiny knots of her backbone rose like pearl buttons. Even her dark head held a golden tint.

Without thinking, he stooped, and with his head near her shoulders, enclosed her with one arm.

"What is it?"

She failed to respond, and he shook her gently as he might had he been rousing her from sleep.

"What is it? Josie? Is it Josie?"

Deliberately, she brought herself up and faced him. Her eyes glistened, and her cheeks were wet. Yet she wasn't crying. The wrapper fell away from her knees and revealed skin that was pale and golden. He pulled her to him until she leaned into his arms with a sob breaking through. Her pulse, strong and fast, throbbed through his shirt.

Tight with apprehension, he said, "Where's Josie?"

"Josie." It was the first word she'd spoken, and she drew the name into a hesitant recollection. She pushed away to regard the depths of his eyes. But she seemed to find no message there and she turned away. Yet unable to leave him entirely, she smoothed his cheek with her fingertips, idly lifted a lock of his hair.

"Oh, God." With an agitated heave, she shoved him aside then. Her shoulders trembled; she drew in repeated sobbing breaths, as though fighting for air. He stood up and braced himself against the counter.

"Goddamn it, where the hell is Josie?" He made a dart around the table and to the doorway leading upstairs.

"Gone."

He leaned across the table, leaned as close to her as he could. "You tell me where she's gone. And why."

But he knew, really. He took in the satin wrapper as she turned away, and he calculated the panic in her voice, coupled with the remorse in her face. He fell back against the door frame, dizzy with a nausea that linked him to some old feeling from the past.

Sadie pulled herself upright, the wrapper a motionless streamer down her back to the floor. "Josie came home from school early today. I don't know why. Lester and I were here. Together. She found us. She ran. I couldn't stop her."

"Jesus god." He lifted his chin to halt the tremble in his voice. "You're no better than he was. Josie and I wanted you to be. But you're not. You're no different." It was a revelation, from which he felt suddenly wiser.

"You make me sick." He rested his head against the door frame, turning away, miserable and distraught.

"I'm trying to say I'm sorry." She glanced over her shoulder. "If you could only . . ."

"Understand? No. Never." He shoved away from his brace

and paced the length of the room. "Sadie this. Sadie that." He remained on his side of the table. "Whatever Sadie wants Sadie gets, and this time, what Sadie wanted was . . ."

"Patrick, please." She started around the table.

"Don't come over here." He swung around but she was beside him, her hand reaching his arm. "Don't!" Without thinking he lifted his arm, merely to push her aside. But it was a blow, unintentional — still a blow — and it spun her halfway around the table. His fingers caught near the neck of her satin wrapper. As she pulled away, the garment slipped from her as easily as a ribbon from a package, and the filmy thing was in his hand.

She backed away, facing him, her legs slightly parted as though bracing herself for another assault. She was breathing so heavily the cords in her neck stood out as long runners to the dark points of her body: her nipples, the dark hair at the joining of her legs. In the dim light, her body appeared silken, as though the wrapper had left a satin residue across her skin.

"Go. Get Out." He hardly heard the words himself.

Her eyes widened in surprise, then narrowed, as though she'd beheld a side of him unknown before. She fled.

He slouched against the table, realized he'd bitten into the side of his lip, and spit a long trail of mucus that hung from his mouth until he coughed and wiped it back with his sleeve. Deliberately he pulled himself up. Dregs of sunlight still lit the pasture. Without faltering he went to her bedroom and confronted her in front of her dresser as she tossed lingerie in a drawer. She yanked up panties and faced him to step into the legs that melted over her like liquid satin. She slipped her arms into bra staps and leaned forward until her breasts met the suspended cups.

"You give me no chance. No quarter. Nothing." She spun about the room, gathering clothes, avoiding him, her manner defensive, yet watchful, as though she was somewhat fearful of him and of what he might do next. "I'm not saying it was right, Patrick. I know it wasn't. It was a dumb thing to do, but sometimes things just happen. I mean, surely you and Josie know that Lester and I . . ." She tossed her hands above her head, "But I never meant for anything like this to happen."

He listened, aloof, emotionless.

"I don't expect you to understand," she hurried on. "Things never get taken out of your hands. Always in perfect control. Christ, how was I to know the school would send Josie home early today. Just as soon as we find her . . ." Her voice was muffled through the sweater she pulled over her head. "She can't have gone far."

"Get out."

"Go to hell."

"I want you out of here."

"This is my house." She wheeled, her eyes dry, her voice as firm as parched earth.

"This is not your house. It was our home. Now get out."

"You can't make me do anything like that." Her defiant eyes glinted like mica chips.

"I can. Get." He shoved her toward the door. "Before I hurt you."

"No, Patrick, don't do this."

He shoved her again. Quite calmly, resolutely, as though driving a hesitant mare toward a narrow opening. Little by little, with his eyes never leaving hers, he nudged and pushed her through the living room and into the kitchen. She took halting steps, tried to speak, stopped once to grip his hand, which he shrugged aside.

"Go." His voice was a blade cutting the path between them. "I don't want to see you."

At the back door, she snatched his jacket from the chair and ran. The jarring slam of the door jolted him upright. He felt as though he'd been moving through a dream, but now, in one blast, everything that had happened fell away. He stepped toward the door, to call after her. But her wrapper in a satin puddle caught at his feet. He picked it up, and its aroma, strong as the musk of pasture rose, came to him. He wondered how anything so slight, a second skin really, could have concealed so much. At the kitchen window, he saw no sign of her. She seemed to have vanished, lifted up on the last amber rays of light.

He folded the gown carefully, walking slowly, unaware of where he was going until he met her dresser drawer still open as she'd left it. He let the wrapper slip from his hand and melt into the satin undergarments. Idly he trailed his fingers through them, and the clotted sweet smell that assailed him was stronger than anything he felt. He thought he should feel something — passion, anger, guilt, loneliness — but if present at all, they faded in authority and he was left with only the aroma that rose from the drawer.

He could see clearly that all his life — his father's leaving, Sadie's loneliness, Josie's search, his own shabby pursuits — had led to this inevitable point and that nothing he had ever done could have avoided such adversity. With nothing else to lose now, he would remain untouched by whatever happened to him. Steel-hardened by this reality, he folded the satin garments within the drawer as he closed it and left her room, glancing once at the bed where blankets lay frumped at the foot and her pillows shrugged to the corner.

WINTER
INTO
SPRING

"A horseman dies only in the dead of winter, never spring when he has everything to live for."

14

Patrick was frantically awake, kicking free from a snake-coil of sheets that bound his legs. Doradella. Check her. He had to check her. And three other mares he'd been watching. But it was Dory's first foal, and she could easily have trouble delivering. Had he failed to set the alarm when he was up last, three hours ago? Or had he in a stupor slammed the thing off as it rang and gone back to sleep? But he was awake now and with a lunge to the side of his bed, he thrust his feet into the relaxed tubes of his jeans, left as he'd dropped them when he'd stumbled back to bed after checking mares. In two quick strokes, he meshed the zipper over the fly, cinched the belt at his waist.

"Move out of the way, Freone." He brushed the cat from his shirt, flung her to blankets piled one by one to the floor as nights in early spring had warmed. Feather-light, she was on the bed again caressing his back as he sat to pull on his boots. As a last resort, she had taken to sleeping with him, or at least as close as he would permit, usually in the heap of covers at the foot of his bed.

Or Coca-Cora, he thought, and took the stairs. She might have delivered by now. She was as ready as Dory, heavy-bagged with a skim of yellow wax over the teats, waiting for the lips of a newborn to break the seal and take the first milk. Cora, though, had been as good-natured as she always was, and it was Doradella, usually an even-tempered mare, who had swung to nip him as he'd bent at her belly. But Cora was an old hand at birthing; she'd slip this one as easily as the previous five, and it was Doradella, Josie's mare, who worried him. Still, any number of things could go wrong, and he couldn't take the chance of losing any. Not a single one.

At the kitchen window, he stretched out a yawn and surveyed the day. Still dark, and a heavy fog boiled up from the earth and swelled around trees; the barn's roof rose above the cloud cover and hung suspended from its perpendicular sides. Even the road was only a gray line that dissolved into mist. Out the back door, a mantle of fog dropped over him, and his warm body absorbed the moisture. He looked to the east and detected the first glimmer of morning light breaking through. It would be daybreak soon; the heat of the sun would burn away the fog.

He took the path to the barn and went straight to the grain room for the bucket of oats he'd left earlier. Tugaloo began a rumble that set off the mares in other stalls, but Patrick ignored them and swung out with a halter and lead rope hiked to one shoulder.

"Turk, better stay here," he told the collie at his heels. "A mare's not likely to want you around." The dog turned on the path and trotted back, his heavy pelt parting down his back and falling to either side as he ran.

Patrick fell into the horses' path, the silent, heavy fog swirling up at his feet. "Probably nothing," he said aloud. "Dory's probably standing out there with the other mares like she was the last time. Big as the barn door, determined to have that baby in her own sweet time. Nothing so stubborn as a mare due to foal." With a start, he broke his stride and picked up his head as though he'd heard a voice. "Nothing so stubborn as a mare due to foal," she used to say. Always anxious to see a newborn, Sadie normally would have been directly behind him. As fast as he walked, she could keep up. Involuntarily he glanced over his shoulder. She wasn't there. No one was near. But lately he'd recognized Sadie's favorite expressions coming through his own speech as though he were filling in for her since she wasn't at home, but living with . . . Lester? God knows where. And Josie. Still with the Uttermelons.

He quickened his pace, consuming the path ahead. In the open, level stretches, the fog had been brushed thin by a slight wind, and the first light of day cast slender rays that slanted like gray rods through the mist. Patrick squinted and began to search out the point where he'd last seen the mares, moving his line of vision along the margin of light. He caught sight of them — like distant hillocks, their bodies rose against the ashen horizon with the easy slope of their withers melting into their rumps. They were grazing; their heads and necks dipped beneath the line of light.

"Eight, nine, ten." He nodded with each count. "One's missing, I think." He moved closer. Instantly, a head, ears pricked, stood silhouetted against the skyline. Then every head emerged. The mares gave a startled jump followed immediately by a snort of recognition, as though mildly annoyed at themselves for being surprised. Uninterested, they fell to grazing again.

Patrick moved easily among them, running his hand along the undulating swells of their bodies and gently nudging aside their muzzles when they reached for a dip into the grain bucket. They were so familiar to him, he knew one from another as much by personality as by coloring and markings.

"Don't lay your ears back, Calabana. The grain's not for you." He snapped two fingers across her insistent muzzle. "Cora. There you are. No baby yet?" He dropped his hand along her rib-sprung barrel and held it low, waiting for a kick of the foal, but he could detect no movement. The foal, resting, hoarded energy. Black Judy sidled up to him and laid her chin across his shoulder, waiting for the slip of the halter over her head. "Not this time, Old Jude." The long stiff hairs around her muzzle caught in his beard and sidelocks, now heavy with moisture. Her breath was herbal with meadow grass. But Doradella wasn't among the mares; he was certain.

235

"You're one shy, Jude. She's given you the slip and gone to the back to have her baby." He hiked the halter up his shoulder and cut off the path into open pasture where the dew, gathered in new grass, pressed through his boots. In the valley, the fog trailed gauzy scarves across the creek. Hesitating long enough to sight a crossing, he dropped down through the fog and sank his heels into the soft earth of the creek bank. He took the momentum from the downhill slope to leap the span of water and bound halfway up the opposite side, still holding the grain bucket upright and in front. His long hair parted into strands and ran in ribbons over his ears. He seldom wore his billed cap now, and his hair, untrimmed for weeks, had length and weight to fall without disturbing him; he swept it behind his ears and to his neck.

At a knoll, he scanned about and chose a section of pasture overrun with low-lying brush. Through mist, the pointed tops of cedars stood above amethyst haze. For a while, there was no sound except his own walking through the gray-green light. He expected Doradella to sense his approach long before he could see her. He would more likely hear her or her foal, so he stopped occasionally, head tilted, for a sound of brush stirring, a croon from the mare. The cowbirds had begun their early morning *chirr;* in a bevy they stirred from tree to tree as though checking on one another. But beneath their sudden commotion, he thought he'd heard the guttural hum of a mare.

"Dory?"

The mare answered, and he moved steadily forward, repeating her name, swishing oats in the bucket as he parted bud-knotted branches of Russian olive trees.

"What you got there, lady?" The mare's dark form was bathed in shadow. "Just look at that. Four white ankles. I can catch that much. Brand spanking new socks on that baby."

As though to acknowledge praise, Doradella arched her neck and kissed along the foal's hips. In answer, the foal flicked its tail like a handkerchief and dipped its head to the mare's underbelly, feeling, smelling for one of the two nipples extended with milk.

"You ready to take this baby home, Dory?" He turned oats in the bucket, and instinctively the mare took a step toward him before she caught herself, wheeled, and nudged her foal to the side.

Patrick hunkered close to the ground and remained quiet, trusting the music of the oats to attract the mare. And she cocked her head to the soft sound of hard kernels. Sidestepping toward Patrick, keeping herself between him and her foal, she came to the bucket and buried her muzzle deep into the grain.

"Thatagirl, Dory," he crooned. "Let's see this baby. Nice baby. You and Tug did all right." His lullaby drew the foal toward him. "A filly, Dory. A spring bonus."

There it was again. His mother's voice, and he gave a sigh of annoyance with himself. Spring alone, she would say, was the gift that offered warm days and sweet pasture grass and time, finally, after an interminable winter's wait, for a mare to foal. If the foal was a filly, she was the bonus, the bribe that whetted a horseman's expectations for future springs. The immature slope of a shoulder, the length of bone in legs nearly as long as a mare's, the daring lift of a head, all set a horseman pondering what this filly, only hours old, might produce one day when mated with a particular stallion. "A horseman dies only in the dead of winter," she would say, tossing off a laugh. "Never spring when he has everything to live for."

Patrick crouched at Doradella's head until she lifted it enough so he could ease the halter over her ears. She gave up a deep sigh, as though comforted by its familiar weight.

"Josie will be proud of you, Dory. I'll tell her you've got a real beauty. She'll have to take some time coming up with a name half as pretty as this filly."

But he didn't know when he'd see Josie to tell her about the filly. Couldn't even gauge what Josie's reaction would be. Normally she would have been elated, but now — now, he didn't know. She lived in another world — only miles from him.

He doubted he'd see her this week, since it was crowded with care of mares and newborns, checking and rebreeding mares. Then wasn't it today — yes, this afternoon — when Judge Croft was hauling in his young stallion for Patrick to begin training? He brought his head up sharply as though to jog his memory. He had lost all track of time. The first week of March, and still Josie lived with the Uttermelons; he hadn't been able to bring her home as he had thought he would. All he could do was visit. Couldn't even telephone.

"It's like a monastery, Dory. A goddamn monastery." He dropped an arm across the mare's withers as she ate.

Sometimes when he got to Stonegate and the Uttermelons', no one answered his knock. Not a sound came from the tomblike house; even the animals in the barnyard were silent — having their own prayer meeting, he supposed, since Josie had told him no one could be disturbed when they were in meditation in the prayer room. "We don't even hear you, Patrick," Josie had said. "You'll have to leave. You know I'm all right, so go home." It made him furious; he wanted to beat down the door. But she was all right. She was probably better off there than at home. To protect her, to leave her in the sort of peaceful limbo she seemed to need now, he hadn't even told her that he had forced their mother to leave, had pushed Sadie out of the house. He couldn't bring himself to tell Josie any of that.

Josie had been the one on his mind that day after Sadie had left. He knew where Josie would go, and he didn't even stop to look for her in the hayloft. Without knowing how much time had passed since Josie had discovered Sadie and Lester, he sensed he had to hurry. It was important to intercept her before she reached Stonegate. He had the ominous feeling that once Josie was enclosed inside the dark folds of the Uttermelons' home, he might lose her altogether.

He took off in his truck, the slush of snow beating into the fender wells and holding him back. He floored it, fishtailed the turns and looked for Josie as he drove, but he didn't see her. It was nearly dark by the time he reached Stonegate, darker still when he turned into the close-limbed cedars that funneled him down the hardpan and into the stretch of grounds at the house and barns.

He made a dash for the back door, but as had often happened before, a woman seemed aware of his presence before he knocked. This time the door opened and Mrs. Uttermelon met his eyes unflinchingly. Momentarily, he felt disarmed before her. Yet she was nothing but a dry wisp — lank gray hair drawn back so tight it pulled her gray mouth and eyes in the same severe angle.

"I'm here for Josie." He stood his ground.

"I know." She tucked her arms beneath her apron, girding herself. "Josie wants to stay with us for a time."

Their gazes held them to each other like steel rods for a moment, and then he pushed around her small frame and burst immediately into a kitchen dimly lit by oil lamps. Several girls, some young women, stood frozen on the far side of a long trestle table. Their figures were so dark they melted into the shadows of themselves cast on the far wall. Two or three held babies straddling their waists, gripping the full sleeves of their gray dresses. And the babies, little bald-headed things, stared at him as unblinking as their mothers — expressionless as cattle at a gate.

"Josie." His voice bounded along the narrow walls and filled the room. Still the women didn't move or acknowledge him in any way.

"Josie." Louder still and unconcerned about the noise he made. "Josie! I'm here for you."

"She can't come down," Mrs. Uttermelon said behind him. He glanced briefly at her over his shoulder, struck incredulous by her boldness and the unlikeliness of her comment.

Saying nothing, he left the kitchen through an archway that appeared to lead upstairs. The persistent spat of Mrs. Uttermelon's firm feet followed.

"Reverend Father, he's a-coming up." Mrs. Uttermelon's voice echoed ahead of him.

It was pitch-black. Lamplight from the kitchen failed to illuminate his way, and he felt along the walls, searching for a banister. The toe of his boot kicked against a wooden riser, and with his hands on either side of a narrow staircase, he started up steps. A flickering candle, its shadow tulip shaped against an upper wall, caught his attention. Helmut Uttermelon's face was suspended above its light. The man was as tall as Patrick with a great shock of white hair cast back from his forehead as though he were standing in a wind. With calculated steps, he advanced with candlelight sailing up over him. His deep-socketed eyes were hidden under the shade of heavy brows. He could have been put together by plan: his arm muscling blended into heavy shoulders, his neck almost as wide as his broad-cheeked face.

"You can't go up." His voice, deep and resonant, filled the narrow staircase. "Go back down." He met Patrick midway on the steps.

"Tell Josie to come down here or I'm going up after her."

"She won't come down. And I won't move. You can't go up." The undeniable truth of his statement, flat and emotionless, enraged Patrick.

"You bastard. Get the hell out . . ." He shoved Uttermelon, but the man didn't give even a quarter turn; his shoulders were as broad and meaty as Caleb's.

"Josie," Patrick shouted. "I won't leave until you come down."

Uttermelon set his jaw, clean shaven, with jowls molded like congealed lard. Standing beneath him, Patrick hated his impassive face, his unblinking stare, and in one swift movement, he reached up and pinched through the flame of Uttermelon's candle. Swallowed in darkness again, Patrick tried to heave the big man's solid bulk aside, but he made no headway. It was like pushing and shoving an unwieldy, yet docile, punching bag that gave neither to the right nor left.

Slowly Uttermelon pressed down with his musky breath, heavy as the smell of wet cowhide.

"Fuckin' bastard," Patrick said. "You let my sister go or I'll tear your goddamn place up."

Uttermelon said nothing. Patrick clenched his jaw and struck the palm of his hand. Thinking. Thinking of what to do next. Uttermelon had backed him to the landing, and in the kitchen, the women were transfixed, still gaping at him.

"Josie, I'm still here. I won't leave."

The stairs behind Uttermelon creaked, and Patrick sensed Josie's presence. "Josie. Come on. We're going home."

"It's no use, Father," Josie said. "He won't leave. I knew he wouldn't."

"Evil leaves when we refuse to give in to it, Josie," Uttermelon said.

"You don't know him, Father. He never gives up on things. He doesn't mean anything by it."

Infuriated, Patrick listened. Their talk seemed to assume he wasn't near or that what they had to say concerned only themselves.

"Josie, get your coat. We're going home."

"Father, it would be easier if I talked to him. He'd understand then."

"The easy way is not God's way."

"Josie, I said come on."

"But Father, you know the penance I've already paid."

As though weighing the pros and cons of a decision only he could make, Uttermelon hesitated long enough for Patrick to shove around him, but Josie's hand came up to stop him.

"Wait, Patrick. I'm coming."

Relieved, Patrick fell back only to have Uttermelon take the lamp from his wife and indicate to Josie that she could move on.

"Let's get the hell out of here, Josie." Patrick moved to take her arm, but she shook him off.

"No, Patrick, Father Uttermelon says we can go to the prayer room."

She went ahead of him then, the lamp lighting her way. In

241

the candle glow, he noticed her closely drawn head. No wispy curls sprang up from her crown. He stepped quickly behind her. "Josie," he whispered, his voice drained to a whisper. "Your hair."

She didn't respond and continued to a room at the end of a hall, where she led the way inside and closed the door behind them.

"My God, Josie." He took her shoulders and turned her slowly while she bowed her head to allow him a full view of her head and neck. Her braid was gone, her head a clipped smooth cap; not a wisp remained of the curls that normally clung to her forehead and neck. He placed his hand protectively over her crown, covering the tiny hair swirl. All the hair she had left circled out from one point.

"Jesus, what have they done to you?" He ran his hands down either side of her face. Her head appeared narrow and small, the skin of her forehead drawn back to her nape.

"It feels funny without my hair." She tried a light, mirthless laugh. "I wanted to save my braid at first, but Father Uttermelon said it would be better if I gave the entire thing up. It didn't matter, really." She went about the room lighting candles from the flame she carried, not the least uneasy.

"You mustn't blame anyone. It was my decision. Father Uttermelon and I talked about it. He said my penance must be something dear to me, something I would never give up in the outside world. So it had to be my braid."

"You haven't done anything to pay a penance for."

"Oh, yes. We're none of us free from guilt."

"You couldn't help what you saw, Josie. You can't pay for something she did."

"It's more than that. For the sins in all our lives. If I don't, there will be no rewards, no way to heaven."

"What if there is no heaven? Nothing but this life? What if this is it, and we have to make do with the here and now?"

She shook her head, refusing to look at him.

"Let's go home. Did you bring a hat? You'll need one."

242

"No, I want to stay for a while."

"Josie," he said patiently. "You can't stay here."

"Just for a time," she spoke up quickly. "Father Uttermelon says I'm welcome. I do my part. I'd like to learn how to be more like them. They are so at peace with themselves. And the outside. What goes on out there" — she gave a sweep with her arm to indicate the world beyond Stonegate — " doesn't come in at them."

"No, Josie. I want you home."

"I want to live here for a time. In Christ. You don't need me. Mama doesn't either." He was surprised at how soft her voice was, yet firm. "That's how it is with me, and I don't want you to try to talk me out of it. It won't do any good. My place is here."

"This is a nightmare," he snapped. "You can't be serious. In this dark place? Saying prayers like a monk?"

With a sigh, Josie dropped to the floor and sat cross-legged with the candle in front of her. It was a big drafty room, void of furniture, he noticed, except for a wood-burner in a corner. A slight draft stirred the flame so that the light faded at times and her features were lost. She could have been any one of the women in the kitchen. Looking down at her frail head, the thin covering of hair against her scalp, he sensed how useless it seemed for him to stay since the sister he had come for was so distant. Still, she radiated a confidence to indicate she already had absorbed some of the security and peace she spoke of.

"Besides, Patrick, God wants me to stay here. I know that now." A smile bloomed across her face as she looked up at him. "He came to me in a strange way while Father Uttermelon was cutting my hair. I was sitting on a high stool with my chin against my neck. He didn't unbraid my hair, but just cut the whole thing off. Sawed back and forth with his old scissors. Then he tossed it to the floor near my feet. I sat there looking at it while he cut the rest of my hair. I thought I would cry. About my hair. About it being gone. But all of a sudden, Dad came to me."

243

Patrick turned away and took a few steps from her, but listened closely.

"I remembered how he used to pull my braid over the top of my head and tickle my nose with the end of it. Remember?" He glanced over his shoulder and mustered a smile. "Or how he'd pick up the end and go galloping behind me, pretending I was the horse and he held a rope. I hadn't thought about those things since he left. Oh, my mind had tried to think about them, but there was always another part that wouldn't let them in. But here, I could think about him without hurting at the same time. Do you understand, Patrick?"

He returned to where she sat and folded his legs under him to sit opposite her. The candle between them flickered, so aware of her voice that it stirred almost imperceptibly as she spoke.

"Caring started coming back. I thought I didn't care about him, where he was, what he was doing." She waited for a moment to catch her breath. "But that's foolish because I always have. And I could see that here. The pain was gone. I could even say to myself that I missed him, really missed him, Patrick, and I could let that feeling come to me. Then, just as clear, I knew there were lots of times when it was the same with him. That he'd never stopped missing us, wondering about how we were doing. I could hear his voice, 'Josie, you look like a little pixie without your hair. I kinda like it.' I had gotten a message from him that he really did love us, had always loved us. He just couldn't live with us anymore."

Patrick shook his head. "That makes no sense. You don't leave somebody because you love them."

"I think you can. Right now I think the only way I can love you and Mama is here. Away from you. I still love you, but sometimes you both make it so hard. You and Mama are so strong and I'm not that way. I think if I could just go somewhere, a quiet, peaceful place, and let my own strength get a good head start, then I could come back and hold my own."

"Maybe things will be different now."

"They're different already. Don't you see that?"

She moved the candle aside and took his hands. "I swept my hair up with the dust on the floor and it meant nothing to me. It was hair — only hair — not *my* hair, not *my* braid. I'm where I want to be right now. I want to find out more about me."

"You almost sound as though today, seeing them, had nothing to do with your running away."

"I guess maybe that's right," she said thoughtfully. "But I feel bad about Mama. I don't want to go back and see her just yet. Tell her not to come see me for a while either, Patrick."

For an instant, he thought of telling Josie their mother wasn't at home, but he held back.

"I was scared." Her hands were in her lap now, fitted inside each other and held between her knees. "I thought he was hurting her at first. When I came in I thought I heard a noise, so I picked up Freone to keep us both quiet. Burglars, I thought, maybe. I crept around through the living room. A huffing rustling sort of noise. At Mama's door. Open some. He had her across the bed. Pushing. I thought he must be hurting her. I screamed at him and ran in." Her voice had become quieter and quieter. "He came back from her. So quick. And without his clothes on. Mama too. She looked like she didn't know who I was. After that I just turned and ran. I still had Freone, but I ran as hard as I could."

"Jesus God." Patrick reared back on his haunches, unable to look into her face.

"But it's not like with animals, Patrick. So I didn't know at first."

"Jesus Christ." He pushed himself up from the floor.

"If that's a prayer, Patrick, it's all right to say in here, but not a curse."

On the far side of the room, he tucked his fingertips into his rear pockets. "It's a prayer, Josie," he said, quietly.

"There's one thing more. Before I forget. It's Freone." She stood up and began walking about the room whiffing out candles she had lighted earlier. "I've left her in the woods at the far end of Mill Creek. I didn't remember bringing her with me.

I just ran and kept going until I was here. I knew I couldn't bring Freone inside. She'd have to stay in the barn with the other animals, and she's never lived outside, never learned to defend herself. So I put her in a tree and told her you'd come for her."

"I've come for you, Josie." He faced her, standing close.

"I know." She placed her hand at his wrist. "I knew you'd come. But take Freone home."

"I can't leave without you."

Her face was clear and clean without curls around it. "Yes you can, Patrick. And I can't go."

Without saying more she led the way from the room, her shoulders a black wedge against the light she held aloft. They walked wordlessly past the silent women and to the back door where Helmut Uttermelon himself stood unsmiling and confident. Josie held the candle high above her head to light Patrick's way to the truck. He couldn't imagine himself leaving without her, and yet he was. He had the sensation that whatever contest he'd been engaged in, he'd lost. But when he turned to Josie, her smile to him was radiant and expectant.

For a fleeting second, he thought of snatching her up, holding her across his shoulder and running with her, screaming and kicking, until he had her in the truck with the doors locked behind them. But there was something about her that made him know she wouldn't resist, but she wouldn't stay either. "I want to find a little peace," she'd said as though the discovery, fragile and rare, would unquestionably be her own someday.

The light from her candle lit his way halfway to the truck. With his hand resting on the door handle, he looked back from the dark to where she stood with light falling across her bare head. He knew she was waiting for the hood light to come on when he opened the door. He got in and drove off quickly, and when he glanced back before he entered the tunnel of cedars, the doorway was dark.

He found Freone easily. She came scampering to him as soon as he called. She nuzzled his face and rode in his lap as he drove home. Her purr trembled through her throat, down her stomach, and finally he felt it against his legs. He took some comfort in that.

15

He had thought his mother might return on her own. The whole awful episode might, within a few days, a week at the most, turn out to be another one of their stormy scenes. Each time the phone rang and he ran to answer it — thinking she was calling to say, "Why don't you pick me up tonight?"— it would be some woman calling in a social item for Sadie's column. He took the messages carefully, writing quickly to keep up with their clipped phrases.

In fact, the day after she left, he thought Sadie had returned. When he entered the kitchen late that afternoon, he spotted the green jacket she'd taken, now neatly folded on the oak table. He presumed she was home. "Mom?" Relieved, he listened for her voice, even though he sensed she wasn't there. He had always been able to come into the house, though silent, and know instantly that she was somewhere in it. He tiptoed through the living room to her bedroom. The door was closed as he'd left it. Inside everything was the same; her bed covers ruffled, her pillows stacked. He pulled open the drawer in which he'd folded the satin wrapper with her underclothes. Empty. With one step, he snatched open the closet door. Everything was gone, even the hangers. In despair, he leaned wearily against the door as it closed behind him and at the same time caught a reflection of himself in the triple mirror above Sadie's antique dressing table. Two vertical morrors were hinged on either side of a center mirror, each attached to the back of the dresser. He could recall the way she would sit at the bench facing the center and adjust the mirrors on either side to catch a view of herself from different angles. By tilting the mirrors just so, three separate reflections stared back. He'd done it himself as a child, playing at the the dressing table. Three different boys. One day — perhaps he'd been four and still living with Gramma Rho — he had scratched "Pat" with a straight pin in the top of the dressing table near the back. When his mother discovered it, she took him by his upper arm, rushing along so fast his feet barely touched the floor. Confronted with the wrong, undeniably his doing, he claimed it wasn't him, Patrick. It was the other boy. "It was the bad Pat," he had told her.

He ran his hand across the vanity top, gathering dust in his palm. Where her perfume bottles had marred the dark varnish, their pale circles stood out as rings within rings. Behind them, he traced his etched name. Her room was bleak and desolate; he left quickly and resumed work outside. He found he couldn't bring himself to enter the house until very late at night. He tried to recall if there wasn't an old cot in the attic that he could set up in the barn.

But later, days later, he thought he should have gone for her then. Immediately. Even if it meant going to Lester's apartment where he presumed she lived. Yet when that idea came to him, he turned it aside; he didn't know how to approach her, what to say once he got there, how he would confront Lester. Coupled with these thoughts were others of himself. The revulsion he had originally felt for her and what she'd done was wedded now with something equally repulsive he felt for himself. "Be honest. You threw her out," he told himself. In a morass of indecision, he followed the work of the horses and the ranch like a beaten path.

He went to town no more often than necessary and stayed no longer than it took to pick up supplies. While there, if he caught sight of a woman resembling Sadie, he was wedged between conflicting urges to see if it truly was she or to turn and flee. What could they say to each other, meeting unexpectedly? Nothing. He knew both of them would stammer, look in opposite directions, perhaps mention the weather now that weather was so unimportant to their lives. It might not have been so, he thought, except that they knew each other so well.

He presumed she came and went to Stella with Lester. But she was secretive about it. The townspeople didn't seem to know she wasn't at home; the women called regularly, and conscientiously he recorded all their messages and took them weekly to her office. But he went only in early morning, before she had arrived, and he scooted the envelopes under the crack beneath the door. He looked for a response from her, a message she might have left for him, but none ever awaited him. Still, it seemed like a conspiracy they shared — the only thing that linked them — and he took it as a favorable sign that when Josie and Sadie returned, which he was confident would happen in time, few people would be the wiser.

Of course, Caleb knew. And Laurie and Rudy, whom he'd told when they came insisting they all to the Island Oasis. He couldn't take the chance of encountering Sadie there, but he didn't tell them that. "There's too much to do right here. Why don't you just go on and leave me to my work?" Rudy left, took him at his word, but Laurie, undeterred by anything he said or did, continued to come occasionally with a meal that she kept warm and waiting for him until it was too dark for him to work longer outside.

Caleb came two days after Sadie left. His arrival didn't surprise Patrick, since he knew Sadie must have gone directly to Caleb's the day she left. Patrick knew Caleb would never reverse his loyalty to Sadie, and so he had anticipated Caleb's reaction as he came flying into the driveway that day. The old truck sputtered to a stop near the barn, and Caleb burst from the side as if there were no door and came quickly to what he'd been brooding about. "By god, you go get her. You get in your truck there and you drive till you find her." His eyes were

250

squinted, nearly lost between his unruly beard and eyebrows. Sandra, for once speechless, knelt in the seat, waiting for Patrick to answer. But Patrick remained silent. "You shouldn't have given up on her. You don't give up on somebody you love." Patrick said nothing to prolong the meeting, and he was relieved finally when Caleb gave a futile wave of his arms and turned on his heel. But as he started to climb in the cab, his bristly head appeared over the top, and he called out, "Don't you believe in love?"

Patrick thought about that. When he went to bed tired, still unable to sleep, listening to the hackberry limbs scratch his window screen, he wondered about love. Love, he had always thought, was as commonplace as an instinct, uncomplicated and useful. Was there really any difference between love and simple endurance? The two seemed mutually sustaining, as wedded as the timeless rhythms of the seasons. He knew he loved his mother and that nothing she had done could destroy what he felt. Their arguments, even her being in bed with Lester, faded into foggy mist — heavy, dirty weather. What had survived was something else, love, he supposed, fragile and permanent. Yet it disturbed him to think he might have given up on her, on himself, on what they'd had. No, he decided when he probed the idea, he wouldn't quit until somehow he had found a way to bring them back together again.

He missed them. He longed to hear Josie's organ music thundering through the thin walls of the old house so melodic he could hear it sometimes as he drove the road home. He missed her brook-babble croon to Freone, her ever ready hand when he needed a hand, and the meals she fixed on schedule. Or it would have been a comfort to have been able to talk with Caleb, hold Sandra in his lap, but he knew Caleb wouldn't see him until he'd made peace with Sadie, and anything Patrick would have said would have been viewed by Caleb as limp-limbed alibis.

He missed Sadie. He didn't understand why that should be.

Why once gone, she didn't go. A vision of her remained that caused him to remember clearly the way she'd looked in the half-light without her clothes. He'd seen her nude before — surprised, inevitable glimpses that occurred as he stumbled upon her in the bathroom or she upon him. But he never imagined her body to be so vivid, yet at the same time so natural and unaffected. In the veiled light of the kitchen, she could have turned in any direction and revealed herself to be authentic and virginal. No symbol, no illusion. Woman. It aroused him to think of her as a woman, making love to Lester. He pictured them as Josie must have found them with Sadie holding Lester in a grip of arms and legs and Lester's body crouched and drumming. He remembered the summer he'd gone to Venerie with his father. He was certain now, when he thought of it, that Allan had gone to Justine's bed. He could see Allan then as a man as well as a father. How strange, he thought, lying in bed, that his parents' sexuality was established for him when he thought of them as making love with another man, another woman, and not with each other.

Surprised, he even found himself much more conscious of women than he'd ever been before. He'd pass a girl on the street and unfailingly drop his eyes to her breasts, curious, hopeful that she wore no underclothing. He often dreamed of Mary Del in more erotic ways than ever before. She came to him in all manner of elaborate dress which strangely allowed a vision of her body beneath the massive folds and flounces. She called to him to rip off the clothing, to hurry; she tore at seams herself. "I'll bet you've never fucked anyone in this house," she'd scream at him. He tried, but he couldn't take her — except awake. Once jolted from sleep, he finished out the dream to suit himself.

Once when he had gone to Chesterfield, he saw Mary Del standing on a street corner. She took his breath with unbidden desire. It had been one of those unseasonably warm days, a harbinger of summer, and she held a swath of her long blond hair to the top of her head as she stood talking to a man. Wisps of child-fine hair hung below her hand, around her ears. She had on a perfectly plain summer dress of soft cotton paisley held to her breasts by narrow straps tied behind her neck. Patrick followed the line of her upraised arm to the hollow of her armpit, so smooth it could have been scooped out with a spoon. Her breasts swung loose inside her dress. He imagined himself untying the straps, letting her dress fall to her waist, and ignoring everyone, coming around to sip from her ample nipples as casually as if he might have stopped for coffee. He never dreamed of Laurie. When she came, she set about directly to arrange a meal, clear a path through the kitchen. She remained only long enough for him to finish eating, then she left quickly. They parted, hardly kissing, barely touching.

From a sound sleep, he would awaken in sudden fits at the slightest noise. At first it was hard for him to distinguish whether he was asleep or dreaming. He'd lean toward the window to peer through the hackberry in full leaf, thinking he had heard a car pass over gravel. But there was no car, and he'd take to his pillow again with his hands behind his head to keep from falling directly into sleep. He thought of all the times he'd yearned to be by himself, when the chattering voices of women had sent him off astride a horse to the cottonwood grove or trudging with Caleb along creek banks.

When he knew he'd bypassed sleep altogether, he went downstairs to the dark kitchen with Freone padding behind him. The moon's luminous glow across the counter and the bare oak table was light enough. He'd pour milk in Freone's saucer, a glass for himself, but he couldn't drink it. Freone finished it, which was just as well, he figured, since she was pregnant. "What's Josie going to think of you?" he scolded her. "Whoring around in the woods." The next morning he would start work groggily, the routine of it holding him to course.

"Four white socks and a star to boot," Patrick told Josie. "You couldn't ask for anything nicer." Big ruffly New Hampshire Red hens pecked along near Josie's feet as she gathered eggs in the Uttermelons' hen house. He'd been anxious to tell her about Doradella and her filly, so after he'd stalled the pair, he made a trip to Stonegate, figuring he'd still have time to return home before Judge Croft arrived with his young stallion.

"I'm not surprised. I knew Dory would have a filly." She scooped a hand in each straw nest, admired the egg if she found one, or dipped a second time if there was none.

"I bet you've already got a name picked out, then," Patrick said.

"No. I thought Mama could. She's so good with names."

"Mom's not naming her." He was at the point of blurting out that Sadie knew nothing of the filly, but he caught himself. He had come to serve as a liaison between Josie and Sadie, whom Josie still refused to see.

"The filly's yours," he went on, "and you can come up with a name good as anybody. I'll have to send in her registration papers soon."

"Then you name her this time, Patrick. It wouldn't be right to put a name to her without ever seeing her."

"You can see her any day you want."

She offered a complacent smile and continued her work, mincing about the hens scratching at her feet.

"Have you got enough clothes, Josie?" he began again after a pause. "Do you need me to bring some things from home?"

"No," she answered brightly. "What you've brought me already is enough. If I run short, I borrow from Betsy."

"And school? Are you getting back and forth?"

"That's no problem. The women take me in with them in the Chariot as they haul in pottery and garden stuff. Now we have radishes and peas and green beans. All sorts of things. Goat cheese and milk too for Palmer's. Every morning they drop me off at school. In the afternoon, the school bus brings me here."

"And school? What do they say at school?"

"About me?" she asked as though questions would have been irrelevant. "Oh, I simply tell them I am visiting with the

254

Uttermelons. Because our family is going through a . . . a . . ." She drew her lips into a tight knot, creased her forehead in thought. "A period of transition — that's what you call it — and I am staying with the Uttermelons while things work out."

"I suppose that was something Old Man Uttermelon told you to say."

"No, but Mother Uttermelon suggested it. She says transitions are common in the outside world, but Stonegate doesn't have them. She says no one will ask 'unseemly questions' — by that she means they won't be nosy. Transitions happen to everyone and can be about anything — divorce, death. Even a new baby. A new job. And she's right. No one cared the slightest about our transition."

"And your hair? That's part of the transition?"

"My hair? Everybody liked it. Said I was right in style. Lots of girls wear their hair short like this. But I told them I didn't do it for style; I did it for Jesus, which is altogether a better reason for doing anything." She fingered the fine strands at her temple. "But it's coming in curly. And the same color."

"Did you think it would be different?"

"Oh yes. I feel so different everywhere else, I thought it was bound to show up in my hair. Like your beard." She dropped her hand to one side of her face as though she might be touching him. "So much red in it. And your hair just as dark."

She placed her egg bucket on a shelf and went outside carrying empty buckets to a pump. Patrick followed and gave the pump handle a few limp strokes before water spilled from the spout into Josie's waiting bucket. Sloshing water beyond the bucket rims, he carried both into the hen house and filled galvanized containers as she lifted their lids. The hens stood with expectant beaks ready to bob into the first ripple of water, their pulpy red combs lopping to the side, watching him with dark, defiant eyes.

"I'd better go, Josie," he said when they finished. "Judge Croft is bringing a two-year-old over this afternoon."

"A filly? To be bred?"

"No, no," he said quickly. "A young stallion he wants me to start. Tell you the truth, I was surprised when he called and asked me about it. He's got plenty of handlers at his own place, but he says they're all busy now, and he wants someone to take some time with this horse. Start him right."

"Then you're the one."

"I guess, but I'm pretty busy myself right now."

Josie nodded and dropped her eyes to the path in front of them. "I know. I know you and Mama want me to come home, but tell her I just can't yet. I know once I come home I won't see Dad anymore. He's not there. He's never been there. But here he's with me a lot."

On other visits she'd told him of visions she'd had in which Allan came and talked to her, usually from whatever building he was working on.

"It's just a dream, Josie."

"No. Because I'm awake when I see him. I know just exactly what he looks like, how his voice sounds. I bet you don't remember a thing about him."

"That's right. I wouldn't know him if I passed him on Main Street in Chesterfield. And if I did recognize him, I wouldn't stop."

She passed over his sullen attitude with hearty indifference. "Just yesterday I saw him up on this big tall skyscraper, and he said, 'Josie, being up here lets you know how important people are. That's right, important. Someday I'm going to bring you up here right alongside me so you can see what I mean.' But I told him, 'You go ahead and tell me.' And he went on." She paused to moisten her lips. She had devised separate tones to distinguish Allan's voice from her own. Sometimes it took her moments to produce the effect she desired. Patrick waited. "'From way up here, it looks like every person is the same,'" she continued in Allan's tone, "'but when you really get a bead on one person and begin to follow that person down the sidewalk, you can see that person is like none of the others. She swings her arms entirely different, carries her head like nobody else.

Right then, Josie, I have a little game I play.'"

"I'll bet," Patrick interrupted. "Games were about all he was good at."

"Now Patrick just hear me out." She gave up a sigh. "Then he said, 'I think, why, that gal could be Josie. That one there in the blue blouse and her gray work pants. That's Josie all right. I'm following Josie, walking off there fast like she does, going to meet Patrick.'"

"Josie," he broke in, "that's nothing but a story you tell yourself. You spend too much time mooning around."

"'Why if I hurry up and climb down off this building,'" Josie continued, "'I'll catch up with Josie and we'll go off together to . . .'"

"Josie, stop it," Patrick snapped. It irritated him to see her falling deeper and deeper into a fantasy.

"Just you wait. Someday he's going to come back. He's going to take me with him."

"He's not coming back. He's still out there looking for whatever he left looking for. He didn't know then what it was, and he still doesn't. He's still out there, winging his way from one place to another. A bird's got more sense. Even the damn barn swallows come back to the same nest year after year."

She lifted her face to him in a gesture of frustrated tenderness. "But he wasn't like us. Wasn't like you or Mama at all. And he got tired of pretending, of trying to be like us when all along he never cared a switch for any of it — the ranch, the horses. Maybe he couldn't even be a father like he thought we wanted. So he had to go away from us to be our father. And you don't know. Maybe he has found whatever it was he was looking for, and now he's just waiting for us to come find him."

"I wouldn't walk from here to the road for him."

"He knows that. I'm afraid he won't come back with you feeling like you do. Maybe someday you and me could pack up your truck and drive till we find him."

For an instant he was caught in the recollection that Caleb had said the same about Sadie — "Get in your truck and drive till you find her."

He slipped behind the wheel of his truck. "I got better things to do, Josie. And so do you. When he left, in case you've forgotten, he told us he had to go. Had to find something on his own. As if we were the ones holding him back and he had to get us out of his way before he could find it. Well, I don't intend to get in his way again. And I don't want him in mine."

Josie's eyes glistened with moisture. "But he'd like to say something else now. Something he couldn't say back then because of how bad we all felt. Another chance."

Nothing Patrick said penetrated Josie's beliefs and visions. No mirror he held up to her reflected anything but her own wistful innocence and nothing of the long, harsh past behind her. Despite his own negative feelings, he was often bemused, enchanted by her convictions that allowed her to say easily whatever came to mind. Amazed, he often left feeling better, less lonely, than when he had arrived. Perhaps he and Sadie had thwarted Josie, and for a time at least, she was better off at Stonegate than at home. He was relieved to think of her swathed in a silken cocoon, private and aloof, biding time for her own metamorphosis.

Patrick kicked fresh straw to the four corners of a stall in preparation for Judge Croft's young stallion. When the judge had called to ask if Patrick would like to handle the two-year-old, he'd been unable to decide the reason. The judge had trainers and handlers of his own. Even Jimmie Jettison, who would come with the judge, was considered reliable with horses, a reputation that had survived despite his short temper and wandering ways. It was Tugaloo's colt, which the judge had bought last fall, that had influenced him. "I like that youngster I bought from you," he'd said over the phone. "I could tell he'd been handled right from the day he was born and it shows on him now."

And the colt *was* promising. One of Tugaloo's best offspring. With a disposition like a kitten, the weanling had been both playful and gentle, yet curious, eager to learn.

But the stallion the judge was bringing was a two-year-old. For good or bad, he'd already have many habits that might be far removed from what could have been developed with proper handling from the beginning.

"I'd like for you to take a look at him, start him under saddle, anything you see fit to teach him some manners," the judge had said. The horse wasn't going to be easy, Patrick thought. He'd take time — a commodity in short supply. Another time, when Sadie and Josie would have been at home to help, would have been more suitable. Then he could have devoted most of his time to training the stallion. But now — still, he wasn't going to turn the judge down, lose the opportunity. The judge's request was another indication the business was taking off, gathering momentum, and in a year or two, their horse business might be well on its way.

A rattling squawk of metal abusing metal brought Patrick to the barn door. Jimmie Jettison, with the judge seated beside him in the truck cab, made a wide arch into the driveway to accommodate the judge's four-wheel-drive and two-stall horse trailer. It was one of two or three matching rigs the judge owned, painted in his colors of dubonnet and silver with *The Croft Farms* lettered on side panels. It was an enviable place to be, Patrick thought, owning more farms, more horses, more cattle, more of everything than one could keep track of. There was no telling how many farms the judge had. He was more aware than most of foreclosure sales, and he had bought more than one piece of ground by sending one of his men to make the final bid from the courthouse steps. But then, the judge set great store by the size of things — including his own girth.

"Told Jimmie you'd be in the barn." Judge Croft waved from the window with the crook end of his cane. "'It's spring, Jimmie,' I said, 'and that boy won't get to the house even to sleep.'"

"You're close to right, Judge. I've been thinking of putting a cot up in the barn." Patrick took a swipe at the perspiration gathered across his forehead. The sky was cloudless, and the sun poured down an unremitting stroke of heat. His early morning search for Doradella and her filly in the cool foggy haze seemed days earlier.

Judge Croft swung open the door until it caught at its zenith and was well out of his way. With a hand beneath his girth, he lifted his weight from his groin to swing his legs around and edge off the seat. Once on the ground, using his cane as a third leg, he moved with ease, with quick little steps, as though he'd learned early to conserve energy for the business of getting from one place to the other. He wore a lop-eared cotton hat with a loose brim ruffled at his forehead and ears — his spring head covering. Seasons were forecast by one of four hats the judge wore unfailingly unless he was in court: soft suede announced winter's arrival, cotton for spring, a straw panama came along at the onset of summer, and a light woolen fedora in autumn.

"Bring him out, Jimmie. Let's see if Patrick wants to stay up nights with this youngster." He adjusted the floppy hat brim over his eyes and pulled the back even with a fringe of gray hair resembling lamb's wool.

Without speaking, Jimmie Jettison gave a curt lift of his predominant chin and went to the side of the horse trailer. He held the tail of a cigarette to one side of his mouth and squinted into the smoke that caught beneath the brim of his cowboy hat. The band sunk into a groove it had worn into his forehead. He spent summers at racetracks burning for mounts and winters in Stella settling for barn work. He had never married, as far as Patrick knew, but he always had a woman. He moved from one to the other like he did horses. But he had a way with women.

Patrick waited at the back of the trailer while Jimmie unlatched the side window and untied the stallion. A steel-gray muzzle thrust forward, knocking Jimmie's hand aside. Retaliation was swift. Jimmie lashed out with an arm, as quick as a snake's strike, and rapped the stallion's nose so hard he thrashed his hindquarters against the trailer sides.

"Goddamn sonofabitch." Jimmie curled his lip to one side of his mouth with the cigarette licked to the other. "Open up the back end and let the motherfucker out."

Patrick dropped the bar across the rear of the trailer and gave the door a heave. In a rush the stallion backed, trailing the lead rope attached to his halter. He stood quivering an instant to survey his surroundings, then wheeled and tightened his leg muscles to lunge. But in the flick of a second the stallion was still, Patrick grabbed his head by the halter, spun him around, and nabbed the lead rope. Taken off guard, the stallion locked his knees, passed a disdainful gaze over Patrick, and arched his neck to yank free.

"Look there, Jimmie," Judge Croft bellowed, "see what a little size can do for you? When you stand so tall you look them square in the eye, they have one hell of a time pulling the wool over you."

Sparse as a weed, Jimmie squared his narrow shoulders. "You'll need more than that." He released smoke from his mouth with a hiss. "You'll need a two-by-four to back him up against the side of the barn and knock the shit out of him."

Patrick wasn't listening to either of them; his attention was on the gray. Although young and not yet fully developed, he already showed growth and stamina along his shoulders and back. Even so, he was fine-boned and slender through the neck. When he tossed his head, testing Patrick's grip, a smoky gray mane rippled and fell in a thin wash, fine as child's hair, across his forehead and eyes. Pewter bands ran the length of his face and ended at a snip of white between his nostrils, as though he'd dipped his nose in cream. A trickster already, the gray quickly managed to steal a few inches of lead rope from Patrick's hand by repeatedly snapping his head upward. He used the advantage to circle Patrick while he studied his chances to pull away. His legs sprang piston-like and balanced under the long muscles of his belly. Attentively, Patrick watched the flick of the horse's ears, the toss of his head, even his tail switching irritably. Friends first, Patrick thought, and then we'll begin teaching you a little respect for someone other than yourself. With each small circle the horse made, Patrick allowed him a few inches of lead rope until the gray had edged five feet or so from Patrick. Finally, Patrick nipped the lead rope just enough to pull the stallion in line yet never enough to entirely discourage him.

The air was filled with the heavy bray of Tugaloo in his stall. From the pasture, a band of mares rushed in to crowd the fence line where they pranced and squealed like cheerleaders. The gray jolted to a stop and lifted his head to answer, and his voice quivered down the long reach of his throat.

"We can put this fella up now, Judge," Patrick said. "I'll keep him and see how the two of us get along."

"Fine. Fine. He'll test you every chance he gets, but you're up to it." The judge hitched his cane in step with Patrick as he led the gray to the barn. They left Jimmie rolling a cigarette, his knee braced against the side of the truck to hold the parchment while he sprinkled loose tobacco in a paper crease. "Just between the two of us, Patrick, I don't think Jimmie's the man for this horse. Sometimes Jimmie does all right with a horse that doesn't cross him too much, but this gray is headstrong. Over the years I've found the best thing you can do for a young horse is to match him up with a handler who understands his language. That trick alone usually makes the difference between a winner and a loser."

"It might take us a week or so, Judge, before we're talking the same language."

As they passed the stall enclosing Doradella and her filly, the judge stopped and braced himself on his cane while he peered inside. "Now that's a sight."

Excitedly the mare circled the filly and whimpered. The foal, in response, hovered close to the mare's shoulder, her wide-set eyes alert beneath long lashes still dewy.

"Is Tug the sire?" the judge asked, moving just enough to keep his eyes on the agitated pair.

"He sure is."

"I'll be damned. Flashy little bitch. And size, too. She could be three months."

"Born early this morning," Patrick said, trying to keep excessive pleasure from entering his voice.

As he led the gray stallion down the alleyway, horses inside stalls raised a ruckus, gandering at the newcomer. Like eager and expectant show-offs, they snorted greetings, pranced, and swaggered about their stalls. Finally they came to press their noses against the wire enclosures, reaching through with flexible upper lips. Tugaloo, with the composure of authority, stood stiff-legged and leveled an insolent gaze as the gray passed him. For his own part, the young stallion made a show of himself as best he could under Patrick's hand. He managed a few wild tosses of his head, sending his foretop and mane in ribbons and twisting his hindquarters under dancing rear feet.

The judge followed slowly, tossing loose hay from his path with his cane. "It's a good thing I bought Tug's colt last fall. You should come take a look at him someday. A yearling now, you know, and in another year, he may be tough to beat."

"If he takes after his old man," Patrick said, opening the door to an empty stall.

"I suppose I should have brought that yearling over along with this one," the judge said. "You're probably the logical person to finish up his training."

"I've got about all I can do right now, but I don't want to turn work down."

"In that case, it's something we can talk about." He stopped again in front of Tugaloo's stall. "Now here's the Tug." Bracing a hand on his cane and his belly against his hand, the judge leaned forward until he could get a full view of the chestnut stallion. "Ah," he nodded in admiration. "Marvelous. Marvelous," he mused. "One looks at him and knows all things are possible." He turned then and started again down the alleyway. "Perhaps one of these days I'll offer you a price for old Tug that you can't refuse."

"No. I don't think so. Tug's been a part of our family for a long time. He goes back to a foundation sire my grandparents brought from Ireland, you know."

"What sire would that be?"

"Bonnie Blue Scot of Byerly Scot."

"Well then, he has the blood, doesn't he?"

"He's been a good horse for us," Patrick said.

"This greenhorn you have here," the judge pointed with his cane, "is virgin, you know. We haven't used him on mares."

"Just as well," Patrick replied. "By all rights a stallion should be trained before he stands. Otherwise, he can't think of a thing but covering mares. Can't keep his mind on business." He nudged the horse until his rump was wedged into a corner. "A horse is real good at only one thing at a time." Patrick gave the stallion his full attention, but he continued to direct his conversation to the judge. "Whatta you call this fella? Something besides Gray Boy, I hope."

"Not much better. His dam was Twilight's Glitter, an old mare you may remember, but I lost her when this upstart was born. His sire is our good stud Lastarondo. So he's registered under Twilight's Last Gleaming. The name was a natural for him, but a nickname never seemed to surface, so we just call him Gray Son around the barns."

Patrick rubbed his hand along the horse's neck, easing toward his withers. "Right out of 'The Star-Spangled Banner,' are you? Easy boy, easy. A patriotic sonofagun, all right. You've got the spirit." His croon brought the stallion's ears forward. "A real patriot." Irritated that he had been made to stand so long, the gray scuffed through his straw bedding. "Settle down, Patriot. Easy, big boy. Come now, Patriot."

"That's a name to suit him." The judge chuckled and tapped a tattoo with his cane. "It was worth the trip over just for a proper name."

Patrick slipped the halter from the stallion's head and for an instant, Patriot stood as if in a trance, unaware his head was free. Then with a snort, he wheeled and circled his stall.

264

"He's got class," Patrick said and closed the stall door behind him. "But sense too. He'll learn quickly." He measured his stride to match the judge's mincing steps as they left the barn.

"I'll be waiting to hear how you get along." The judge hoisted himself to the truck seat and reached over to grab Jimmie's waiting hand before swinging his legs up. "If he gives you any trouble, call Jimmie here and he'll come for him."

"I'll come all right," Jimmie said. "With a rifle. It's the only thing that spoiled sonofabitch understands."

"By the way." The judge lifted his cane to indicate he wasn't ready to leave. "We didn't talk about your fee, Patrick, but you set it and I'll pay it. That's what I told Sadie the other day when I was in the newspaper office."

"You've talked to her?"

"About other matters, really. But I told her I planned to come over today with the stallion. She said there was no one any better with horses as far as she was concerned. That's saying quite a lot, even allowing for her partiality. She said I was to work out all arrangements with you. You pretty much handle the business anymore, so let me know. Either a flat fee or so much a week will suit me." The judge's upraised cane was enough signal for Jimmie to drop into gear and leave in a churn of dust down the road.

For some moments, Patrick stood pondering what the judge had said. Apparently Sadie hadn't disclosed or indicated in the slightest that she no longer lived at home or that any rift divided them. Likewise, it appeared she held no ill feelings. She might return any day, he thought. At least a crack had parted in the door between them; she might be waiting for him to nudge the door open. Distracted, he sauntered to the house, and in the kitchen, he tried to prepare a meal while he debated going into town to look for her. He would simply go into the newspaper office and up to her desk. He imagined the surprise that would cross her face, her hands hesitating over her typewriter. "Look," he'd begin. "Don't you think it's time for you to come home?" Lester would be around, of course, standing protectively at Sadie's side. "I think you'd better leave," he'd say. "Your mother's living with me now, Hi-pockets. Why don't you go home and grow up?"

He'd kill him. Patrick slammed the refrigerator door with a jar that knocked Josie's Bible quotations to the floor. He couldn't face Lester without snatching up the closest club and slamming into him. Patrick paced the kitchen, tried to eat, chucked the remains in the garbage, and went outside again. He'd gain nothing by seeing her, and he stood to lose everything in a confrontation.

Nothing he had planned seemed to fall in place so he pulled the truck under the hackberry. Scooting his body along on top of gunny sacks, he slid under the chassis, and within the manifold intricacies of cables and linkages and mountings, he tinkered. Grease ran in rivulets down his arms until lost in the creases of his sleeves; oil dribbled and caught in his beard. Unconcerned, he continued working, squinting muck back from his eyes, pursing his mouth in concentration. Grease, velvet smooth, oiled his way as he slid along the wires, pressed his fingers around metal protrusions. He came up finally like a diver surfacing water, suddenly aware of the natural world instead of the inky depths where he had cruised for hours. The quandary of whether to confront Sadie and Lester seemed remote now. He'd been unaware of time or weather change. The sun was gone, and when he scanned the northwest horizon, heavy clouds hung drooping bellies full of rain. Thunder rumbled like hooves across dry ground. He hurried now to feed horses in the barn. In a rush, he loped across the pasture to check mares due to foal, decided to bring inside those closest to birthing, and ran back to the barn for halters and leads. In the tack room, he grabbed up what he needed and slipped into a rubber slicker before making off through the paddock again, still eyeing the distant clouds and the angling gray bars of rain.

The band of mares was huddled along a west bank of Russian olives, sensing rain and looking out together. He pressed among them, pushed rumps aside to check bellies and

266

udders, slipped halters over the heads of some. The lead ropes hung like signals from beneath their chins so that when he went back through them, he snagged the ropes, two or three to a hand, and led the mares out from the band. He picked up a trot, and the mares fanned out around him, making room for each other so that the ones farthest from him quickstepped along, their belly muscles groaning against the effort.

The rain began in a chill drizzle, but he pushed into it, his long hair and beard protecting his face from the mist. He swung the mares into the barn where the warmth hit their sides and made them tremble and hunch into themselves. He stalled each amid the snorty bugle calls of other horses, then filled their bunks with fresh hay, their buckets with water. The animals grew quiet as he moved among them, his voice and hands as soothing as the sound of rain tripping across the barn roof.

When he finished, he stood a moment at the front, watching rain fall in slanting parallel bars. Darkness had begun to close in, and the house, bathed in shadows, loomed vacant. The panes in the windows appeared as black reflections, hollow as caverns. The wind that had carried the rain clouds whipped through the upper branches of the hackberry until the tree hung over the attic, its limbs spread out across the roof and against his bedroom window. He turned back once toward the horses. There was nothing else to do, no other place to go, so he ducked his head and bounded across the open space between the barn and the house.

In the kitchen, Freone pranced around her empty bowl, snapping the end of her tail.

"I hear you, Freone." He poured milk for her, and as he stooped, he noticed Josie's magnetic holders scattered where they'd fallen when he'd slammed the door in anger earlier that day. He retrieved them, along with the slips of paper containing her Bible verses, and he placed them in a row across the front of the refrigerator. He peered inside among the little cans and jars of food he'd shoved to racks. A half can of peas gone white with mold — perhaps it was corn — there was no way of telling. He lifted three hot dogs, slick and rancid, then chucked them to the back. From a lower cupboard, he brought out a can of pork and beans, opened it, and sat at the oak table with the can, a fork, a loaf of bread, and the jug of milk. At the table, he forked through the cold beans, pushed among the newspapers until he found the most recent copy of the *Ledger.* At one time he'd hardly given the paper a glance, but now he read it from front to back, beginning in the middle with his mother's column. Some of the messages were ones he'd written himself now. After he had begun taking the notes the women gave him, he was at first at a loss as to what to do with them. It would arouse the women's suspicions if their messages didn't appear in the column and delivering the scribbles he took over the phone would be insufficient for Sadie to write them up herself. He decided he'd have to do it, and he took to studying back issues of Sadie's column to determine how she gathered the loose bits and pieces into some sort of readable form. Names and dates, places and events followed in a logical order, he could see. So he began preparing his own column on ruled notebook paper, pleased with his writing ability and his editorial skills. The first time he delivered it, he could barely wait for the next issue of the newspaper. On the following Wednesday when he picked up a copy at Udall's, he turned immediately to the column. It was exactly as he'd written it. He was shot full of surprise, then elation. He began to embellish on his writing, to add contrast. "The Stella Garden Club took to the open road last Tuesday to gather debris around the square in preparation for their annual spring fling. It is a well-known fact that each year club members plant lovely spring blossoms in Stella Square for the enjoyment of all." Sadie used it as he had written it — even "took to the open road."

Now he raked among the papers until he found the notes he'd taken from Ida Markum when she called the day before. When he found them, he read what he had scribbled as Mrs. Markum had talked. "Birthday club. Wednesday. Thelma Clothier's. 4 birthdays. lilacs, green mints, nuts, lime sherbert, cake, roll call, favorite spring flower, next month, Katherine Pickett's."

Mrs. Markum had almost forgotten to give him the names of the birthday girls. "Oh, yes, Patrick," she offered. "It's a good thing you remembered. We can't leave them out. It was Betty and Zelda Knapp. They're first cousins, not sisters, you know. And Frances Gains and Eunice Cox. Eunice has got to be eighty-five, and if I didn't go by and get her, help her . . ." But he interrupted. "Would you spell those names for me?"

He put the can of pork and beans on the floor for Freone and studied his notes. He thought he had a lead.

"The windy month blew in four birthdays for the Stella Birthday Club. Birthday gals were cousins Betty and Zelda Knapp and Frances Gains and Eunice Cox." He hesitated, glancing back at his note. "The club met Wednesday at the home of Thelma Clothier and everyone answered roll call by telling about a favorite spring flower. Mrs. Clothier's table was decorated with lilacs, green mints, nuts, and lime sherbert. Of course, they all had cake. Next month the club will meet at the home of Katherine Pickett. Mrs. Markum will go by for Mrs. Cox as usual."

When he finished, he looked around to see if he'd taken any other messages, but he could find none. He ran the blunt end of the pencil through his beard where it still itched sometimes. Then he put four black circles under the birthday club as he usually did to separate one item from another. And he wrote: "The Douglas Horse Ranch had the first foal born Monday morning. A filly. A spring bonus. The mare, Doradella, did a fine job on her own even though it was her first foal. The filly, a deep red chestnut, has four white ankles and a star. She's doing fine."

Then he folded the paper and slipped it in an envelope, and on the outside, he wrote Sadie's name.

16

Patrick idled the truck at the mailbox and retrieved an envelope from Judge Croft — a check, he supposed — and a letter from Gramma Rho. He put the judge's envelope aside and anxiously slipped his thumbnail along the narrow upper flap of Gramma Rho's letter. To ward off suspicions, he had taken to writing to her himself, making excuses for Josie and Sadie. In the past he'd seldom written; he considered letter writing akin to going to church — something to do at Christmas and Easter, gratefully, to relieve himself of the chore the rest of the year. But now he didn't object to writing Gramma Rho, since it meant receiving replies, which sounded so much like her own voice that she could have been in the same room. Even her sermonettes he read word for word: "Just remember, next fall when you start college, you'll thank me for persisting the way I have." Or "Work hard now. Your best friends are your two strong arms." And another time: "Cling to your flying hours, Patrick, and let each day bring out your best." Her sentiments, abundant and well aged, carried a maudlin ripeness he had once mocked but now found curiously comforting.

Dear Family,
Another letter from you, Patrick. I can almost see how busy you are these days with extra mares there for

Tug's service. Didn't I tell you, Sadie, he was the pick
of the crop that year? I knew, as soon as he got four
legs under him, that we had the makings of a good
sire. Papa always said I was the one with an eye for
horses. In case you've forgotten, Tugaloo was born right
here, and his lineage goes back to the thoroughbreds
my parents brought from Ireland. One Irish stud and
two mares. All around me are Douglas land and
Douglas horses, but most of it belongs to my brothers
now. Not a stallion on my brothers' land can measure
up to Tug and I'm glad you've got him.

Although Patrick could barely remember the circumstances,
he knew they had gotten Tugaloo and Black Judy from
Gramma Rho at a time when she'd sold out to her brothers.
Most of her horses, her training equipment, even some of the
land that had been deeded to her by her parents had been lost.
It was a difficult time. Even as a child, he sensed nothing was
happening the way Gramma Rho intended, and his father
seemed in some way to be responsible. Gramma Rho's eyes
would follow Allan like she was waiting for him to sit still long
enough for her to pounce on him, but he was too agile; he was
always just out of reach. Everything else was, too. Things
were snatched from her grasp, a condition she was unaccustomed to accepting. She held onto what she wanted the way
she held onto a horse's reins — with a light touch yet undeniably firm. A silent fury burned through her, and from the tone
of her letter Patrick gathered that the source of the flame
remained.

He began reading again.

Most of the colts are on the ground here. I walk down
the road and back along the wooden fences to get a
look at the mares and their foals, but it's not the same

*as when I had a hand in it. I have to tell you that I
miss my own. Spring never comes if you haven't a
mare due to foal. Some of these babies could use old
Tug's genes, I can tell you. Davey, my brother, insists
on using this weak-legged stud that invariably produces
weak-legged foals. I tell him, Davey, how many times
have you heard Papa say faults breed through. But he
can't see it. It's a fact. Faults breed through. For both
horses and men. Well, I had better sign off before I
stew myself into getting on the bus and heading your
way. I'm not much for that long bus ride, and I hate
sitting with a bunch of busybodies who know nothing
but what happened on the soap operas. The truth is,
I've been thinking about a trip. I'd love to see you all,
see those new baby colts you tell me about in your
letters, Patrick. You and me could walk among them,
and I could take a wet muzzle in my hands, smooth
their unruly hedge of mane. Don't forget a touch of
molasses in their feed for their hair-coat and a handful
of dry milk powder for stamina. It will soon be Josie's
birthday. Barely a month away. Time goes. Why is it
we let time outmaneuver us?*

She sounded sentimental, he decided, unlike the woman he
remembered. In a weak moment she might be tempted to make
the journey and he didn't want Gramma Rho flying around
setting everything straight according to her eye, blaming him
for what had gone wrong. He was certain she would side with
Sadie as much as Caleb had. She wouldn't believe Josie had
stumbled upon Lester and Sadie in the bedroom. "Josie's mis-
taken," she'd say, biting off the words like a piece of thread.
"That much I know."

Patrick glanced to the end of her letter and read quickly. She
hadn't decided on the trip yet, but once the idea arrived, she
wouldn't stew over it long. She wasn't one to muddle in a

hornet's nest of conflicting notions when a course of action was little more than striking out in one direction. But she hated the bus ride, and the thought of the journey would put her off, he decided.

He mushed up the driveway to the barn, the truck tires spinning in mud. Lately, it had rained so much the ground was spongy, and he wished for some of the red hardpan that lined roads at Stonegate. The paddocks and grounds around the barns were a mire. Places where the horses had sunk hock-deep filled with water and remained like miniature ponds pockmarked across the paddock. All week, the mares had stood with heads lowered, their rumps rounded against the pelting rain, their tails plastered between their flanks. Foals huddled, copied the stance of their mothers, and waited until the rain stopped long enough for them to tip their muzzles to nurse. If rain slackened by afternoon, the mares took their foals to rest under low branches of Russian olives — leaving them as if at a nursery — while they went about the business of filling their bellies with grass, their udders with milk. Without knowing they waited, they waited for sunshine, for days to warm through their wet hides, for the earth to dry in places where they stood sociably together.

Sometimes he worked Patriot in the rain. The horse loved it. The chill invigorated him, lifted his spirits, and sent him snorting at the end of a lead shank or sputtering mud over his hocks and over Patrick. Patriot took every chance of catching Patrick off guard long enough to pull away and run tail-over-hide around the arena. But Patrick was on guard, always aware of the gray's games. The stallion had been such a challenge, Patrick had taken to reading Sadie's old training manuals and books. As he looked through them, he found the places she'd underlined, the commands she had barked at him when she had sat atop a fence line coaching his training methods. "You never use that whip like a whip," she'd say. "It's nothing but an extension of your arm and hand. Reach down with it and tickle that colt's hocks." He could hear her voice, see her as she'd been then. But he tried not to think of her now, where she was, what she was doing.

At the barn he unloaded grain and supplies purchased in town before deciding to work Patriot. The stallion had conserved a morning's worth of energy in the stall and was ready to romp.

"Settle down, big guy."

Patriot cavorted at the end of his lead, grabbed a length of rope, and playfully tossed it over his nose. He was fresh and full of fire. When he picked up the smell of the mares, he sidestepped beside Patrick, arching his neck and preparing himself to cover.

"None of that good stuff for you." Patrick snapped the knot end of the rope across the stallion's belly. "You got too much to learn yet."

Patriot snorted a spray across Patrick's shoulder.

In the training arena, Patrick allowed the stallion to move out to the length of the lunge line attached to his halter. With Patrick standing in one spot, Patriot trotted the circumference of the circle as Patrick slowly turned. Patriot was animated, tingling with a desire to run. He pointed little fox ears at any movement that caught his attention and picked up his heels in spirited fashion. But by the fifth circle, the stallion was growing bored with a familiar routine.

"I know you're ready to move on. By next week I think I can start you under saddle."

Patriot flicked his ears, listened briefly, and moved out in long, fluid strides, his forelegs snapping up the ground his rear legs had thrust his body forward to receive. As his muscles and tendons loosened, he settled into a beat as regulated as a military march, and Patrick relaxed. The rope, slack now, was nothing more than the link to send messages. A snap or two along the line and the stallion increased his pace; drawn taut, Patriot dropped his heels instantly. They moved together, though apart, their thoughts humming along the length of rope, their minds as one, and the symmetry of their union was as consistent and balanced as the circular pattern around which they worked. When once Patrick sat astride the horse, the same symbiotic association would serve as a bond between them.

It was nearly dusk by the time Patrick prepared the last mare for Tugaloo's service. In the barn he dropped a lead rope over his shoulder, shoved fetlock hobbles and an elastic bandage into a rear pocket, and went outside to metal panel pens he had erected to confine visiting mares. Inside one, he snapped the lead rope onto the halter of Julie Prescott's sorrel and led the mare to a paddock, near the barn. Tugaloo caught the mare's scent and offered her a throaty rumble. The mare, a virgin, replied with an excited whinny and pulled against Patrick's hold.

"No, lady, this way." Patrick renewed his grip and led her into the paddock and up to a solid plywood panel placed upright between two posts — a breeding stanchion he and Sadie had built some years before. Here he tied the mare so short she was unable to turn her head, but still her eyes rolled back as she watched him work. Her excitement bordered fear and he attempted to calm her by stroking her hot neck. An old mare, Black Judy for instance, would have stood expectant, waiting for the feel of the stallion across her back, but the virgin mare remained fractious and wary.

From his rear pocket, Patrick flipped out the leather hobbles and squatted at the mare's heels to fit the bracelets around her ankles. She lifted her feet repeatedly to avoid him and irritably swatted her tail, catching him on either side of his face.

"I know, lady, it's not the best way, but it's faster and easier. I can't take the chance of you kicking Tug's balls off."

His last maneuver was to wrap the elastic bandage around the mare's upper tail and pull the end to meet her mane where he then tied strands of coarse tail and mane hair together. Her tail now lay to one side of her body, and the mare's vulva, relaxed and moist, lay exposed.

He stood back. "It's crude, lady, but it's the best I can do single-handed."

As he started back to the barn, he could hear Sadie grumbling beside him. "It's rape. That's all. Rape of the mare." She hated hand-breeding done in its practical manner to protect mares and stallions. "A stallion should have his little band in the open field," she would say. "Then every day or two, in their own good time, when the grass has greened and the days have warmed just so, he can check his mares and bring them around when they're ready."

"I know. I know," he said aloud. "But it's the only way for now."

In Tugaloo's stall, Patrick offered the stallion his leather breeding halter, sweat-stained a brittle black. "Come on, big fella, let's finish up. You must be more tired than I am."

Tug growled, tossed his mahogany foretop from between his eyes, and nudged his nose into the halter. "I could take this lead rope off and you'd know where to go, wouldn't you, Tug?" The stallion's pace quickened and at the sight of the mare, he raised his voice. The mare answered and attempted to greet him, but her rear feet were locked in place and in front she met the solid resistance of the plywood breeding stanchion. Frustrated, her hide shimmered across her body like a heat wave.

As Tugaloo approached the mare, Patrick relaxed his grip on the lead rope, and the stallion circled the mare's head. Growling and grunting, he caressed her side and along her neck, gently nipping her withers, running his lips to her ears. Then he remained near enough to receive the bite she gave him along his jaw, and he lifted his head for her lips to glide over his neck. Though aroused, he was tired. His penis was flaccid, loose as a sleeve. For an instant Patrick considered freeing the mare and letting the two run loose in the paddock. But Tugaloo began working again, moving around the mare, nibbling under her belly and at her hindquarters. The mare waited, her eyes and nostrils flared. At her side, Tugaloo reared slightly as though ready to mount. The maneuver stiffened his penis, and it glided unprotected from the sheath. He snapped it against his underside, stepped to her rear, mounted, and efficiently placed himself over her. She squatted slightly to receive him, and with one direct thrust, his mouth braced at her neck, he penetrated, pumped, relaxed. For an instant his front legs dangled awkwardly, while he rested over her withers. Then he raised himself, stepping back until his penis fell loosely from her, then he dropped to the ground. With one long heaving sigh, the stallion turned uninterested, covered himself and started toward the barn.

It was nearly dark when Patrick started to the house. He was dead tired. All desire to eat had left hours ago, and the only thing he wanted was a hot shower and bed. But before he reached the back porch, he noticed the headlamps of Ralph Kieffer's truck as it crossed the trestle. Laurie was coming with his supper, he imagined, and he slumped to the steps.

"I've brought spaghetti and meatballs." She came from the truck as though arriving for a church supper. "Have you got the table set?"

"You betcha. With the fish forks, cloth napkins and the wine glasses. Oh, hell, I forgot to pick up the wine." He snapped his fingers and opened the back door to follow her inside.

"Go back and look in the truck. See if I didn't leave the wine in the seat." And she kissed him when she reached a step that put her even with his mouth.

He retrieved the wine and when he came inside she was clearing the table of accumulated debris, stacked there during the week or so since she'd last been there.

"I see you've fired the maid. I presume it's the same problem. She can't keep away from you, and she's been chasing you around the barn loft again."

"Something like that."

"You have time, sir, for a shower before dinner." She waved him aside with elaborate pretension. "I've laid out your tux."

He laughed and made a grab for her, she shied and then came instantly to him. "Better yet," she leaned back to look into his face. "I'll give in gracefully and let you anoint me with horse

277

perfume."

"Don't say anything." He moved his hands up and down her back, across her shoulders. "Let me just feel what you're like." At the smallness of her waist, his hands crossed, and he pressed her against his body with a force that brought her feet off the ground.

"You've been around the horses too long." She pulled away.

"That's for sure. Tie 'em up, mount, hit with what you got, get 'em settled."

"Go." She waved him away. "Go take your shower."

When he came from the bathroom in clean clothes he caught the smell of tomatoes mixed with beef, and the first hunger pangs gripped the base of his stomach. The kitchen was dark except for a candle that bloomed in the center of the oak table, now covered with a cloth.

"Hey, Laurie girl."

She had set the table with china and silver from his own kitchen, yet none of it looked familiar in candlelight. Tiny flames danced multiple reflections off everything — the slim plates, clear goblets, silver spoons, Laurie's eyes. The spaghetti nested in a white tureen, now amber, which his mother stored on a back shelf and seldom used.

"I'll sit down. You pour the wine," she told him as she took a chair, folding her hands in her lap.

He did as she said, needing direction, feeling disoriented, as though he'd rushed too quickly from one place and time to another. She was right, he decided. The constant company of animals, his occasional monotone to them, or his increasingly trivial thoughts had left him ill-prepared to join a party.

They ate with lapses of silence, Laurie leading conversation. He was hungry, the food was good, and he wanted to eat quickly. Instead he tried to handle his fork the way Laurie did when she placed it in a mound of spaghetti and turned the fork until it gradually pulled up a nest of spaghetti. Then she raised it to her mouth without a single tomato tail flipping against her chin. His efforts were unsuccessful, and he resorted to cutting through the heap with his knife and fork.

"Haven't you seen Rudy lately?" she asked midway through the meal.

"Not for a week."   "Things are moving along pretty fast. He hasn't found a house yet, but he told the folks he plans to move out."

"What did they say?"

"Pretty much what you'd expect. They'd like for him to wait until summer when we can all help get a place fixed up, make curtains, paint, pour cement for the ramps he'll need."

"Sounds good. And Ramona? He's bringing her around?" Quickly he caught himself. The expression was one he and his mother used when they talked about a stallion and mare. But he knew Laurie was unaware of the lingo, and an explanation seemed inappropriate.

"I think she's ready to move in with Rudy," she rushed on. "But her mother's still a problem. She tells Ramona she can't have babies if she marries Rudy. They can't have normal sex."

Patrick gave a laugh that resembled a snort. "Maybe there is no normal." Briefly he thought of the hobbled mares he had prepared for the stallion.

"You know Mrs. Larkins wouldn't say 'sex.' Rudy says she tells Ramona, 'The marriage can never be consummated.'" She lifted her chin as though delivering a sermon.

"I think she's wrong about that."

"Rudy says she is. But you know how Rudy talks. You can't tell."

The candle was half gone. Still its single flame glowed as brightly as when their meal had begun.

"I think they've worked out something for themselves," he said finally.

"Maybe that's what it's all about. Love and sex. And working out something for yourself."

Later they washed and dried the dishes with the light from the ceiling lamp. "Too bad you fired the maid," Laurie had quipped and snuffed the the candle flame with her thumb and finger, dampened with the dregs of wine from her glass.

"Have you seen your mom?" Laurie asked with subtle casualness, her eyes on the plate she was washing.

"No. I saw Josie last week and told her about Doradella's filly."

"I'd think you'd run into your mom in town."

"I don't go often. And when I do, I'm there and gone." He thought about his early morning jaunts to the doorway of the newspaper with the messages he had written for the column, but he saw no need to mention that.

"And she doesn't call? Or anything?"

"No. I've decided it's better this way. Maybe we need a little time. A little space."

"It's a damn funny thing to me." She lifted her head and looked thoughtfully into the night. It was black beyond the windows, the moon too slight to afford even shadowy light. "I mean the way parents can up and leave. Call it quits. But kids can't. Kids have to stay, no matter how bad the parents are. Too bad kids can't divorce parents sometimes."

"Aren't you forgetting something? She didn't leave. You know why she's gone."

"She could have come back by now. She knows what it's like with these mares."

"It'll come together in time. She and Josie will both come home. I can't see the when or the how yet, but this is where they belong."

"In the meantime, you'll stay, holding it all together. I think you grew up to be the person you wished your father had been." Her smile was whimsical, full of sly good humor.

Wearily, he watched her fitting together the dishes she'd brought. He hated for her to leave, but he was too tired to talk longer.

"Patrick," she said suddenly, "I could stay tonight."

She slid the dishes to the counter and came to him. He held her briefly, his chin resting against the top of her head.

"What I need is sleep. In about three hours from now I have to start getting up to check Simone. I mean, it's not . . ."

"I know. The party's over." She tried to sound lighthearted, but she kissed him good-bye with a smile more constricted than gentle, and he was filled with remorse as he watched her drive away. Rejected again, she probably thought. God, could he never say anything, do anything with Laurie that it didn't sound wrong? She had every right if she never came again.

The rear lights of the truck flared as she braked at the trestle. Momentarily, he thought she might be stopping, that she might turn, and he longed for her to come back. The truck lights jerked up as she bumped over the trestle, dimmed after she crossed, and disappeared altogether when she rounded the corner.

17

Two days later Laurie was back.

It was dusk when Patrick looked from the interior of the barn and noticed the lights of Rudy's van in the driveway. He assumed that Laurie was bringing supper and that Rudy came with her, intending to stay the evening. He was in the midst of stalling Simone, his mother's chestnut mare. The previous year, the mare had foaled in the pasture, but the colt had been stillborn. To avoid a similar mishap, Patrick had decided to keep an eye on her as her time approached.

He was surprised when he came from the barn to see that Rudy was leaving and Laurie, her silhouette caught in the van lights, stood in the middle of the driveway, watching her brother pull away.

She gripped a suitcase in one hand and clothes were draped over her other arm. As Patrick approached, she dropped the suitcase, an anchor at her feet, and hiked the clothes a notch up her arm.

"What's the deal?" Patrick said, coming up to her.

"I'm moving in," she said without ceremony. She made a dive for the suitcase and hiked toward the back steps.

Thunderstruck, he stood staring after her — the suitcase knocking against her calf, her jeans flapping beneath her flowered blouses, still on hangers. Without a pause, she took the back steps, jiggled the case around to grasp the door handle, and in one freewheeling motion, swung open the door and stepped inside.

She was out of sight before he could gather his wits. "What the hell . . ." In three enormous strides, he was up the steps and into the kitchen where he caught up with her and spun her around so fast the suitcase struck him on the knee.

"What the hell do you think you're doing?"

"I told you, Patrick. I'm moving in. I've brought my things." She trembled slightly, as though she felt a chill, but with one deep breath, she squared her shoulders until she seemed to reach his level. He noticed little flecks of gunmetal gray among the soft flannel of her eyes.

"I can see that. But you can turn back around and take them out to the truck. You're going back home."

Ignoring him, she placed her belongings on a chair and glanced around the kitchen as if the room were unfamiliar, and she wondered where she might go next.

"Laurie, would you make sense?"

The question seemed to clarify any indecision she felt, and she gathered her belongings and left in a huff, taking off through the kitchen and into the living room.

He circled the oak table twice, pushed his hair back behind his ears, and shoved his fingertips into his rear pockets. When he paused, he heard the unmistakable sound of metal hangers sliding across the rod in Sadie's closet and the twin snap of suitcase catches. He whipped around to his mother's room.

"You can't stay here."

Preoccupied, she lifted clothes from her suitcase and refolded them neatly into Sadie's dresser drawers. For an instant, he had the feeling he was the one out of place and that he'd barged unwelcome into Laurie's own bedroom.

"I don't know why not." She glanced up briefly. "There's nobody else here." She made a circular motion with her hand.

"Jesus God, Laurie."

"Look at these drawers. The closet. All empty."

In disgust, he gave a half turn away and caught her reflection in the triple mirror of his mother's vanity. Laurie's image moved purposely from mirror to mirror as she continued to unpack.

"You can't stay. I don't want you here."

"Maybe you don't, but you need me, whether you want to say it or not." She snapped the lid of her suitcase closed and slid it to the back of the closet. Idly she spaced her blouses on the clothes bar, her eyes following her hand's precision. "I drove home from here the other night thinking I should have stayed then. Wanting to stay. I could tell it was the same with you, but you'd never just up and say it. I must have stopped beside the road five times between here and home. But I couldn't bring myself to come back. Not then. But the next day I decided I wasn't going to pay any attention to what you *say*, because what you say is not what you *mean* to say." She picked up the rumpled spread at the foot of the bed, stacking Sadie's pillows in the corner. "But it's more than that. I hate the thought of you locked away here. Alone. With no one. So when I got home the other night, I talked it over with Rudy."

"You don't have to tell me what Rudy said. I can guess." He pulled his hands from his hip pockets and gave a halfhearted toss as though throwing confetti.

"Yeah," she nodded and smiled. "That's what he said all right."

"And your folks?"

"My folks know I'm here."

"And they said, 'That's fine if you want to go over there and live with Patrick.'"

"Not exactly." She paused, her arms crossed beneath her breasts, her back to him. "Mom wanted to know if she needed to make me any maternity clothes."

"Get your suitcase." He shoved her aside to reach the closet. "I'm packing every goddamn thing up and . . ."

"And what?" she shot back and wheeled in his face. "Throw me out?"

She could have struck him, he slumped so fast. "No. No. I'm

284

not going to do that."

"I'm sorry, Patrick." She came to him quickly. "That was my ace in the hole. I didn't want to use it."

"It felt more like hitting below the belt."

"Probably. But I mean to stay. You don't eat. You sleep in the same clothes you work in. Most of the time you're out there in the barn with the horses." She tilted her head to him, her voice brightened. "What difference will it make if I'm sleeping in the house?"

They walked together to the kitchen, and she began poking around in the refrigerator.

"You won't find much in there," he said.

"Except spoiled food." She lifted out jars sprouting spongy mold.

"What if Sadie decides to come home?" he shot out as though thinking aloud.

"I might tell her she can go back and live with Lester."

He shook his head, smoothed his hair back from his forehead. "Laurie, I don't think I can handle your smart-ass remarks."

"Then don't ask dumb questions."

"They're not dumb. What will people think, your living here?"

"Who's going to know? Stuck out here. Don't make such a big deal out of this, Patrick. Men and women do this sort of thing all the time. And for a lot less reason." Then she tossed up her hands abruptly. "I know. I know. But I don't want to hear how you're not like everybody else."

"And neither are you," he retorted.

"I don't care what people think. Or say. But I do care about you."

He felt he was no match for her; his arguments seemed commonplace, even old-fashioned and ridiculous. He watched her across the space of the oak table and recalled how often he and Sadie had worked out their differences, the table serving as a buffer. Now Laurie. He felt, as usual, on the losing side, and he wondered if all such exchanges with women were destined to leave him feeling depleted and inadequate.

"Your folks shouldn't have let you come," he said lamely.

"Actually, Mom and I talked about it quite a while ago. When your mom and Josie left. I told her then I should be here, helping you. She wondered if you couldn't stay with us, but Dad — I have to hand it to him — he said right off you'd never leave as long as you had mares to foal out. And that's when Mom asked if she needed to make any maternity tops like she had for Debbie and Jackie. Anyway, they didn't act too surprised. As it turns out, she and Dad lived together before they were married. So she never felt she could come down too hard on us kids. What's good for the goose is good for the goslings."

"It won't work, Laurie."

"Look. I'm not going to sleep with you. It's not going to happen by default." She looked down, then glanced quickly up again. "I'm here to fix meals and wash clothes and work in the barn. Oh, I can learn about horses. And I'll keep right on going to school, and studying like I always have, and after the mares are foaled out, I'll pack up my things and go back home and that will be the end of it."

Said in her clear unmistakable way, it sounded as though it might work.

She made things easier and she made things harder, and Patrick wondered if that wasn't always the way with a woman.

The next morning Patrick drove Laurie to school feeling drowsy from a breakfast much bigger then he normally fixed for himself. He was unaccustomed to starting the day lulled by a full stomach and a trip to town that would temporarily sidetrack him.

"This won't work," Laurie said, catching his thoughts. "I'm not going to be much help if you have to stop everything and

286

bring me to town. I'll ride back home on the bus today and see if I can use Mom's old clunker."

"That's not necessary. Your mom may . . ."

"I've got to get a couple more things anyway. So don't pick me up today." She was out and gone as he pulled into the school parking lot.

That afternoon he heard her mother's car before he caught sight of it — an oversized tub of a station wagon that popped and roared like a thrashing machine.

"I'll put a new muffler on that thing this weekend," he said as he met her in the driveway.

"No. Forget it. Mom just drives it around town."

"And change the oil," he went on. "Probably needs a new filter."

"She's driven it this way for years. You're not going to do one lick to it. You've got enough to do."

"I'll do what needs to be done." He paused and leaned toward her. "And if you don't like it, you can pack up your things and go back home. Where you belong."

Her face fell, and he felt instant remorse. She so seldom accepted defeat that she didn't know how to mask it. But she could shrug a grudge faster than he could lift his hands as a sign of apology, and she came back, "You're pretty good at hitting below the belt yourself."

In the next few days, he spent more time than ever in the barn. His body was there, at any rate, even though his thoughts, beyond all reason, would rush back to where he knew she would be sitting at the oak table with her books scattered about, her mouth pressed down in concentration, the eraser nub of a pencil lost among a clutch of curls. He found himself leaning on the hayfork, glancing toward the barn door to see if she might enter with a mug of hot coffee in her cool hands. When she arrived, as she often did in late evening when the northwest wind sailed in damp and chilly, he would appear surprised. He tried not to look as though he'd been ready long before he'd heard the slam of the back door. He hated himself

287

that he was so ready.

When he got up near midnight or one o'clock to check the mares and Simone in her stall, he would be halfway down the steps and half asleep, wondering why he'd left lights burning in the kitchen. And there she'd be, padding about stocking footed, pressing clothes or making pies.

"Making pies? My god, why are you still up?"

"I'm always up until now. Or later."

He'd groan, comb back his hair, and sit in an oak chair, sluggishly feeling for his boots beneath it.

"Is it all right if I come with you?" she asked on the second morning.

"There's nothing you can do. Probably nothing I can do either. I just check."

"Then I'll come."

They set out, he following the path by rote and she behind him, walking into the beam of the flashlight he held for her. Only the sound of their boots sucking in and out of mud, and the persistent drone of the frogs from the creek bank filled the silence around them. Suddenly he coudn't imagine having left without her. Her presence was so vivid that it brought him full knowledge of how truly alone and lonely he had been. He stopped on the path, his mind so full of thoughts of her, he'd forgotten entirely his reason for being there. She came up behind him and put one hand lightly at his waist. "What is it, Patrick?" He hastened on. "Nothing. Nothing," he lied.

The next morning, he had to wake her, tapping on the bedroom door.

"Laurie? Do you have class this morning?"

"Oh god."

"I've left eggs in the skillet."

"Eggs? No eggs. Put the kettle on. I'll just drink tea."

She never ate breakfast. Only tea and toast. She always showered in the morning, rushing out the back door with her hair still wet, driving off with one hand while she fluffed curls dry with the other. She could do four things at once while he

288

was thinking about where to begin. He was amazed at how much he'd learned about her in two days when he had known her nearly all his life. By the third day, any high-minded convictions he might have had about taking her back to her own home washed away. Fleetingly he wondered about what others might think or about what he would do if Sadie or Josie returned. He brushed aside such thoughts as though sweeping scattered straw from a fresh path.

On Saturday morning, it was nearly ten before she was dressed and outside where she found him stretched out beneath her mother's car.

"Hey, you down there." She squatted beside his feet with a cup of steaming tea perched on her knee. An assortment of wrenches, hammers, and muffler clamps was laid out in a row.

"It's only — what? Noon? And you up already?" His voice, muffled from beneath the chassis, sounded droll. Tools clanked as he dropped them to the ground. "Do you see that half-inch wrench out there?"

"Where?"

"Near your feet."

She glanced to either side, selected a long-handled tool, and stretched it under the chassis to meet his hand.

"No, that's not it." He wiggled out, hunching up his knees until his shoulders were free.

"How do you know so much about . . . about most everything?"

"From doing it wrong so many times." He slumped back with the wrench and scooted under the car again.

"But you must have learned somehow."

"Caleb, usually. I'd ask him a couple of questions, and the next thing, he'd be doing it all." He tightened clamps as he talked, his words arriving haltingly, as though muscled out around the work itself. "Then I'd tell him, 'Caleb, just show me. Don't do it. I can't learn like that. I have to be able to see it with my hands.' Sometimes we'd go round and round, but I could say about anything to Caleb."

"How much longer are you going to be?"

"I'm nearly finished. Tightening the last muffler clamp. I've already changed the oil."

"Maybe I'll start dinner. We can eat early and have the afternoon free to work in the barn."

"Give me about an hour." He drew himself out again. "Tug's got a mare to breed. I want to corral some of the colts and get halters on them. Otherwise they'll be wild as guineas."

"Maybe I'll plant the early garden," she said, looking off to the far side of the house where the soil was heaved into ridges. "I found seed potatoes on the back porch. I can plant other things next week when I'm off for spring break."

"That's right," he said thoughtfully. "You'll be home." Smiling, he wiped each finger of grease and glanced up to meet her beaming expression.

It was late afternoon when they took Simone from her stall so Laurie could brush her while Patrick removed old bedding.

"Look under her and see if her teats are waxed. But be careful. Watch her rear feet. She's cranky."

"She's got yellow wax on the tips," Laurie said as she stooped at the mare's side. "And she's leaking milk. Is that a good sign?"

"It was a good sign a week ago when she was due. She's holding off because she doesn't want to foal in the barn. She prefers the pasture, but I don't want to take any chances. That baby she's carrying should be one of our best."

They bedded Simone in fresh straw and filled her hay manger, but the mare, her head lowered, eyes half closed, was indifferent. She backed into a corner, eased up a rear foot and lifted a sigh that rattled her sprung rib cage.

"She's not going to eat. That's even a better sign than her full bag. I think I'll sleep out here tonight."

"You might as well. It'll be easier than getting up every hour to check on her."

"Maybe you can do it," he said lightly. "You're up half the night anyway."

"Silly." She bobbed her head against his shoulder, in an easy, affectionate manner, and he put his arm around her. He wanted to touch her, to tell her something. Words wouldn't do. But he checked himself and took up the wheelbarrow load of soggy straw and started from the barn.

"I'm going in and set out leftovers for supper," she said. "You come when you can."

He looked after her, the nearly imperceptible sway of her hips in loose jeans, her arms swinging as though to rush herself along, and the points of the scarf tied about her head, bobbing in beat with each decisive step. Spring break, she'd be at home with him every day, the whole day through. The elation he felt cut away any thought he might have had of asking her to leave. Without glancing back at him, she went up the back-porch steps with the assurance of one belonging there.

Later when he went inside, she was slicing ham on a wooden cutting board. The house was always clean now, newspapers folded and stacked in a corner, the stove and counters uncluttered, a laundry basket full of clean clothes often waiting for him to take upstairs.

"Your girl friends have been calling," she said with a wry smile. She had taken to calling them his "girl friends" — the women with messages for the column — and she found it hilarious when he told her he'd written a good part of what made up the column. She had no reservations about answering the phone, offered no excuses if anyone seemed surprised. "I have half a mind to tell them you can't be disturbed."

"Be nice to them, Laurie. Think how lonely my life would be without them."

"Yeah. Well, one of them is hot for you, because the phone has been ringing off and on since I got in."

"Probably something important. Like the Stitch and Sew Club drove to Chesterfield to buy Easter dresses."

"She'll call back. She's in need, I tell you."

The phone rang and he shrugged. "Sorry about that, but . . ." He locked the receiver at his shoulder and fumbled about for a pencil and paper.

"Okay. I'm ready, Mrs. Shepard. If you are." He glanced up at Laurie, amused and crafty. "Just a minute, Mrs. Shepard. Guess I need a pencil."

Beguilingly Laurie wrinkled her nose and wagged a pencil in his direction.

He reached for it, but with a spin Laurie shoved the pencil into curls above her ear. Humming and jazz-stepping to the other side of the table, she ignored his advances.

Patrick pressed the receiver against his knee. "What is this? Games?"

She shrugged. "I don't like your girl friends." She was a nymph, her head cocked, her hands defining her tight little waist.

"But you know I love you." He had meant to make a joke of it, to say it in a chiding, offhand way, but he didn't. His voice, without him being aware of it, became soft and serious. All pretentiousness dissolved; she came naturally to him. He felt such a release, such a surge of pure joy that he hung up the phone without even looking at how he placed the thing in its cradle and took her to him. He did it so fast, he snapped the breath right out of her as though his own life depended upon what she could give him. Without her, without her mouth inside his own, her hands pressing life into him, he would suffocate. She seemed to hold the source of oxygen, of life itself. For an instant, he thought he would lower her to the floor, but he didn't. Without a wasted motion, he led her to the bedroom. Fleetingly, he feared he would hurt her, that he would surge right through her, pinion her to the bed. Yet how could he? He was suddenly weightless, and now he no longer needed the oxygen he had craved moments ago. He soared above her, lifted into space and the exhilarating places even his dreams had never dreamed.

They slept forgetting themselves, soundly, as though they

292

had postponed love and sleep for urgent things now immaterial. He awoke first and knew instantly he was in his mother's bed with Laurie's head buried in his shoulder. Her curls were tangled with his beard; her arm lay loosely over him. His hand still cupped one cheek of her backside. Blessed with rest, he remained perfectly quiet, not even moving his eyes.

The room was dark except for a metallic quivering of light across the sheet at the foot of the bed and along the ridge of her body against his. She drew one knee slowly up his leg, tucked her face deeper into his neck.

"Are you worried about Simone?" Her breath fanned out warm against his shoulder.

"I don't give a damn about Simone."

"Patrick, I didn't . . ."

"Don't say it."

"All right."

"Did I hurt you?"

"I can't remember. It was so fast."

"Too damn fast."

"Was it like you thought it would be?"

"I hadn't thought about it like that. No. What about you?"

"Something took over. I didn't even think about what to do. My body knew it already."

"I felt like I was drowning at first. I couldn't get a breath. I hadn't felt like that since I was a kid, trying to swim in Mill Creek. A long time ago."

She woke him shortly later. "We have to check Simone." Rolling to the side of the bed, she sat a moment with moon glow from the window forming a river of light down her back. They dressed in darkness, picking up clothes as they found them and passing them to one another. They left the house, holding hands, touching, free finally of the tyranny they had imposed on themselves.

As soon as Patrick clicked on the barn light, Tugaloo shuffled and snorted in his stall. Farther down the alleyway, Patriot set up a chorus and other horses joined. Simone remained quiet, slumped, yet upright, in the same spot Patrick and Laurie had left her. Perplexed, irritated, Patrick slapped a fist against his palm.

"She's got to have that colt, Laurie. Otherwise, we'll lose them both."

He thought once of calling Sadie, but he discarded the idea merely because he hadn't the time to find Lester's number in the phone book. This was his colt; they'd manage on their own.

"What about Doc Willey?" Laurie asked.

"He's no good unless you get him before five. He starts drinking after that, and by now he's dead to the world." He studied the mare. "I'm taking her out and walking her around. Let's get her moving."

But Simone barely lifted her feet as she trudged behind him. Her head appeared too heavy to hold upright; her shoulders were hunched within herself. Occasionally she stopped altogether, despite Laurie's urging at her hindquarters.

"Come on, girl, one more time."

When he returned Simone to the stall, she gave an extended sigh and circled the bedding. She made an effort to paw through straw and then with a heave, she sank to her side, her belly protruding like a whale. She let forth a long low growl and rubbed the side of her head and neck back and forth in the straw. Her side heaved and with a lunge, far faster than she appeared able, she snapped forward so that her forelegs were rigid and ready to spring up.

"Get at her head, Laurie. Pull her back down and see if you can hold her there."

Patrick squatted at the mare's hindquarters. "That colt ought to be far enough down so that I can feel him." He rolled his sleeve to his upper arm, and gently using his fingers to open the mare, he eased his hand into the mare's vulva. He sup-

294

ported himself against her flank and looked above, concentrating on the loopy strands of cobwebs in the corner of the stall. He closed his eyes to let his fingers see. His hand was enclosed now in a velvet channel, warm as blood. Within the passageway, he felt solid knuckles. Knees. He ran his fingers down a bony foreleg, gently eased it forward. Then the other leg. He kept his eyes in one place, his mind in another. The foal's hooves, spongy as gristle, were now forward in the birth canal. His arm slid out easily, and he stood back from the mare, his eyes fixed on her hindquarters, waiting for the first contractions to complete the job he had begun.

"Little fella had his legs turned back." He gave Laurie a triumphant smile.

Laurie squatted at the mare's head. "Good girl. Easy does it, Simone. Just a little while longer," she crooned.

As though set upon by a strange affliction, the mare rocked her head in the straw, first stiffening her legs, then jerking them under her in an effort to rise. Laurie held the mare's head, rubbed her jawline and outstretched neck. Spasms reverberated the length of the mare's body. Laurie kept up her singsong. Patrick paced the stall, took up a post finally near the mare's flanks. Simone moaned and two tiny hooves, one slightly above the other, appeared and hung lifelessly at the opening. The mare rested; Laurie took a breath.

"Come on." Patrick stood briefly, then squatted again, clenching his fists between open knees.

A second contraction brought the foal's head lolling to the straw. Patrick put his hand beneath the dark wet jaw, supporting the foal against the weight to come.

"She's okay, Laurie. One more time."

The mare groaned, quivered, and the foal slipped from her, black and lathered with mucous, eyes sealed, its rib-sprung sides already beginning to heave.

"Goddamn, Laurie." His eyes were smarting as though he'd been through fire. "Goddamn, Laurie girl."

"Is he okay?"

"Christ, Laurie. It's a filly. We got a filly."

The days melted into one another as they did into themselves in early mornings. Nights were taken up with the care of mares as they foaled, their rebreeding, and Patriot's consistent schooling. Sometimes they went to bed too exhausted to do anything but hold each other and fall asleep almost before Laurie could turn to her side and he could cup her to him.

Mornings were different. He awoke ready, she waiting.

On the Saturday morning a week after Simone's filly was born, they lay in bed — Patrick propped against the headboard and Laurie's head in the hollow of his stomach. They had gathered Sadie's pillows from the corner to place under Laurie's hips and fill the depression in the mattress. Now the pillows were pushed about them in every direction; a sweet metallic odor rose from the bed.

"What is it that's supposed to be the great common denominator?" Laurie asked in a musing tone. She held a pillow to her breasts as though holding a coverlet.

"I don't know. I think it's sex."

"That's right. Brings you right down to the basics, doesn't it?"

She moved her head enough to glance up at him. "Remember how uppity I was? Debbie used to tell me. Jackie too. 'Just wait, little smarty. Someday you'll have the hots for somebody. You'll ache so bad.' 'Stupid,' I told them. And they said, 'There's only one thing to cure an ache like that. You'll see.'"

He cupped his hands behind his head. Beyond the window, the peach trees were frilled with blossoms, in a rush to fruit.

"I thought they were crazy," Laurie continued. "Screw. Get pregnant. Then married. Like A follows B." She laughed at the quizzical expression he cast. "Oh well, in our family, the women always got thing backwards. It'll never happen to me, I told them." She pushed the pillow from her breasts and rolled to her side. Her cheek was as smooth as the inside of a shell. "But I know exactly how they felt. What they meant. All I want are mornings."

Her breath was warm; his own breath began to shorten. He reached down and pulled her beside him, but he only held her. His hands did not move across her body. A wave of sadness passed through him. Why was it, he wondered, that every joy carried its own flaw, a blemish maturing with the fruit?

"Every morning has a noon," he said with a dreary edge. "It will soon be noon today. What about then? Or three o'clock next week? A year from now?"

"I don't want to talk about that." She turned him, swaddled him with a leg.

"Sooner or later we have to talk about what happens after the basics."

"But not now." She rubbed her knee to the inside of his thigh, trailed her finger along the dark line of hair beneath his navel. He brought her hand up and held it near his chin.

"Look out there." He motioned toward the peach trees and the level dark earth beyond. "At your garden."

"Garden?" She raised on one elbow. "What's the garden got to do with anything?"

"Nobody plants a garden who believes only in the mornings."

She nudged him in the ribs playfully. "That sounds like something your Gramma Rho would say."

"I suppose. It's just that sex makes you feel that's all there is. You think you're so goddamn powerful, nothing can touch you."

"Listen. That's the way I want to feel. I've paid my dues, bided my time, and taken too much crap from you. Waiting for you to . . ."

"Grow up?"

"I wouldn't say that." She nestled down into the pillows next to him.

297

"Well, I'm all grown up now, teacher, and there's something I think we'd better talk about. You know that as well as I do. A year from now we could have a baby. Christ, for all we know you could be pregnant right now."

"That wouldn't be so bad, would it?"

He rolled to the side of the bed and sat up. "I don't know." His fingers combed through his long side hair. "I just started thinking about it." He paused as though waiting for a solution to surface. Then he stood up and began searching for his clothes. He slid into his shorts, hoisted his jeans to his hips. "Yes," he said, "Yes, it would, really. Everything would be taken out of our hands. Our whole future dictated by one natural act. And it doesn't have to be that way." He slipped into his shirt.

"Where are you going?" She sat up quickly, doubling her knees and wrapping her arms around them.

"To town. To get something to use. I sure as hell know we're not going to quit having sex. But we're not taking any more chances either."

"I'll not have a goddamn rubber. Besides," her voice suddenly softened, "if anybody's going to do anything, I'll do it."

"One of us does something or I'm going back upstairs to sleep."

"And I'll follow you up there. I can fuck in that bed as easily as this one."

"Then what do you suggest?"

"I don't think I'll get pregnant." She put her chin on her knees, her eyes following him as he moved about the room.

"You don't know."

"I won't."

"Laurie." He studied her narrowly. "Laurie. Why can't you get pregnant?"

She tilted her head, twisted her mouth into a tight little bow. "Because I've been on the pill for two months."

"Jesus God, Laurie." He jerked his head to one side. "You knew. You knew the day you moved in that we were going to end up screwing."

"I didn't. I didn't mean for it to happen. I just thought to be on the safe side . . ."

"You little twist. I ought to screw the hell out of you."

"Try it. Just try it." She threw her legs in the air and made a lunge from the room. At the door, she turned back. "You think you're such a stud. Just try it."

She took off up the steps, in and out of the bedrooms, her voice sailing behind her in peels of laughter. As he ran after her, he shed his shirt. His pants he dropped at the top of the stairs.

18

The next day, Laurie drove home to see her folks; Patrick went to see Caleb. He didn't realize he was going until he was almost there. He'd taken the truck to check the westbound fence line, but after he'd crossed Mill Creek and turned south on the county road, he sighted Caleb's truck ahead. The thought of mending the fence slipped from his mind, and he followed Caleb as though that had been his intention all along. Caleb, lifting seed potatoes from the truck, let the sack drop in surprise and bobbed his head as though agreeing with himself about something.

Sandra jumped from the truck seat and ran to Patrick with her arms outstretched, the metal buckles on her rubber boots snapping at each other. Patrick scooped her up. She twisted from side to side, as limber as a little fish, as she tried to keep both her father and Patrick in her sight.

"By God . . ." Creases fanned at the corners of Caleb's eyes from a grin hidden beneath his moustache. "You're a sight." He started to say something else, but instead, stirred the air between them with a hand that finally came to rest on Patrick's shoulder. "By God, you *are* a sight." He gave such a tug to Patrick's beard that it brought laughter from the three of them. "Sandra, how'd you recognize him with a face like that?"

"He's rough and soft like you." She clutched him at the neck, her fingers lost in his beard.

"Well now. I don't know what we're standing here for." Caleb scooped his arm up in an elaborate wave. "Come on in, now. Sandra, aren't you getting too big for Patrick to carry?"

Sandra coasted down the outside of his leg, and she and her father followed Patrick up the steps to the deck as though welcoming him back from a long journey.

"Just step over this trash," Caleb said, moving ahead to clear the entry. "Watch out for the poles. The hooks there." He held them back like tree branches and then scooted aside the chain saws — their blades in metal puddles — and oilcans and a fitted box of tools with wrenches and pliers erect as old maids in church pews.

When Patrick took a chair at the table, Sandra hiked herself to one leg and began to play with yellow seed packages fanned across the table. Her palms were pale and fine as chalk dust.

"Looks like you're ready to plant a garden," Patrick said.

"Popcorn. See there. Sandra wants to plant popcorn and peanuts this year. Won't grow in this soil, I told her. Not sandy enough for peanuts." Caleb sloshed water into his gray enamel coffeepot.

"Worth a try, isn't it, Sandra?" Patrick said.

"You could stay and help us plant." Her voice was shy, but her eyes, tilted slightly, gave her a daring pixie expression.

"I don't think Patrick has the time for that," Caleb interjected, still behind them, mussing about in cabinets. "He's too busy with mares to think about a garden."

A smile spread slowly across Patrick's face as he thought of Laurie's garden. He wanted to tell Caleb about Laurie, of him and Laurie, but Caleb spoke up again.

"Have you got foals on the ground by now?"

"Most of them. I had no problems. Except with Simone."

"I wanna go see the babies." Sandra interrupted. "Poppy, let's go right now."

"Sandra," Caleb turned from ladling coffee and lowered his brows to a solid bushy hedge. "You get down from Patrick's lap and go play. Go out and start hoeing in the garden."

301

"I won't go." Sandra arched her back and shoved her hands into the loose top of her bib overalls.

Caleb resigned himself with a sigh. "I guess it's all right. Truth is, Patrick, she's waited long enough to see you. She's missed you up a storm." He set the pot over a burner and joined Patrick at the table. "Now what were we talking about before we were so rudely interrupted?" Sandra, in studied preoccupation, maneuvered seed packs into an even row.

"Simone was the only one that gave me any trouble," Patrick said.

"Simone? Your mom's mare?" The chair creaked against Caleb's weight as he pressed back and rocked the front legs off the floor.

"She had problems last year, so I stalled her. A good thing too. The filly's legs were turned, but once I got them straight, she came along fine."

"A filly. Your mom will be pleased about that."

"Yes. I suppose she will. At one time you couldn't have kept her away after she'd waited all winter for a foal." He paused, and then without thinking too much about it, he said, "About Mom, Caleb. I thought I'd look her up. Let her know her mare is all right. And about the filly."

"I'd say so. She'll want to know."

"You've seen her?" Patrick set Sandra aside and went to a window overlooking a spot outside where Caleb had prepared a seedbed. A string drawn taut between two upright sticks marked a row.

"I see her every day or so. I go to the newspaper office sometimes. Or we go to the J & J for coffee."

"So how is she?" Patrick asked matter-of-factly.

"Okay, I guess. It's hard to tell about women. They can put on two shades of rouge and a little lipstick and be damned if you know."

"She still living with Lester?" He held his gaze to Sandra's tire swing, idly spinning as the wind picked up. Behind him he heard Caleb tap his mug against the table.

302

"She never lived with Lester."

Involuntarily he jerked to face Caleb. "I just supposed when she left . . ."

"You supposed wrong. She took that little apartment above the J & J. The one Natalie lived in before we were married."

"Then she won't be hard to find."

"She never would have been hard to find. All you had to do was . . ."

"I know, Caleb."

"No more talking." With the brush of her hand, Sandra scattered paper packets across the table. The hard kernels rattled with a hollow sound. "You've talked long enough, Poppy."

"Young lady, I'm going outside right now and get me a pear limb." Caleb pushed back from the table. Slowly. "I'm going right now."

Sandra watched his placid movements and, undeterred, went to Patrick and lifted her arms. He swung her to his shoulder. "Take a look out there at your tire swing." She tilted her chin as though to see a long distance. "Go on out and before I leave, pretty soon now, I'll give you a big swing."

She wiggled down and ran for the door as Caleb, finally upright, sauntered after her. "Your jacket. Get your jacket. There's still a nip in the air." She nabbed her coat on the run.

Patrick dropped a corner of his mouth, a sidewards grimace. "How much longer do you think you're going to get by with that old pear-limb gimmick?"

"Guess I've taken it about as far as I can, but I haven't come up with anything any better." His pale eyes deepened, flicked with mirth.

The two men finished their coffee and prepared to follow Sandra outside. Distracted, Patrick hardly followed Caleb's talk; he was thinking of his mother, about her living alone, and of Caleb meeting her for coffee, listening to her side of the story, always understanding. Abruptly he turned back at the doorway. "How come you two never married?"

"Who? Your mom and me?" With his hand holding the bill of his cap, Caleb hesitated, taken aback. "That's a hell of a thing to ask."

"No it's not. I never thought of it before, but I don't know why not. You should have married her a long time ago."

"Should have," Caleb mumbled, as though to himself. "You're thinking of the movies. Life is never that tidy. Should have. People don't fall in love because they should. Sometimes they shouldn't fall in love at all, but can't help themselves. Other times I think it has to be earned. That's the way it was with Natalie and me." Patrick watched Caleb closely, but with the mention of his wife's name, Caleb seemed to drift, his eyes playing across the upper beams where the pine absorbed the mellow hues of sunlight. "I was ignorant, foolish, still simmering in Burrough juice passed down to me like the land. I had to get away, get out from under Tobias and Frannie, build this house. Start over. When Natalie came along, I had stripped myself clean. It was the same with her. From the first night we spent together, we seemed to understand that we'd earned another shot at something good." His eyes scanned the far corners of the high beams. "Maybe it was the house. She loved this house. A cathedral, she called it." He caught himself, aware of Patrick's intense expression, his own words spilling over each other. "Go on, now." His hand brushed Patrick's shoulder, and he set his cap low across his forehead. "Your mother's a fine woman. But you know that."

They went down the steps, Caleb trailing.

"That's one funny smirk you got on your face," Caleb said, and he turned Patrick by the shoulder to study him closely.

"There's something I haven't told you, Caleb," Patrick began. "Laurie moved in with me a week or so ago." He paused. "One night she brought her clothes, and I never took her back home."

"Son-of-a-gun," Caleb lifted his cap, reset it purposefully. "I should have known." He tossed his hands to his shoulders. "I should have guessed right off."

Sandra waited, her legs dangling through the rubber tire, her hands gripping the rope overhead. The swing hung from the outstretched arm of a great oak, one that had held seniority and had determined the site where Caleb would build his house. Sandra called out, rocking back and forth, tipping and twirling, setting the lacework of leaves above her whispering against each other. He took up the sides of the swing and lifted it above his head to rush beneath her. Screaming and kicking, she ascended into the arms of the oak, its leaves quivering to accept her. He seemed possessed of a power he had failed to recognize before, a fantastic elation coursing through his body. The swing, descending, met his outstretched hands, and he rushed again, giving a great leap that lifted him off the ground, ready himself to soar upward.

He had planned to go home after he left Caleb and Sandra; instead he drove toward Stella, as though from habit, too long overlooked. He thought of Caleb with Natalie the first night they were together. "From the first night we spent together," Caleb had said. Patrick smiled. Of course, they'd been together, had made love, from the first, even though Caleb had told him differently months earlier. "She took my bed and I slept on the couch here," Caleb had said then. It didn't matter. Patrick could imagine how it might have been.

"You've never fucked anybody in this house, have you?"
"No. God, no."
"I can see why. The place is like a church. A cathedral. I suppose it wouldn't seem right."
She left the warmth of the stove, and as she walked slowly

305

about the open room, she ran her hands along the sloping walls, up the heavy vertical beams as far as she could reach. She had shed her clothes and put on one of his old checkered work shirts that struck her leg at midthigh. Relaxed, casual, she made no effort to close the front; a path of dark skin lay open between her breasts and over her stomach.

"I can feel you. In the wood." She spread her fingers, caressing knots in the pine. "You're here, all right. Powerful."

Her hands circled above her head, and the shirt dipped and lifted to expose the half-moon of a single naked hip. "Under my hands." One foot was cocked behind her, and its color, a perfect shell pink, matched the palms of her hands.

"The wood here is smooth as skin, even warm." Her fingers traced a whorl left in the pine. "Hard right here. Little grooved and splinters." She could have been talking to herself, her voice barely discernible. But his body responded as though her hands had found a way beneath his clothes.

"I can feel you strong in me, Bear." She remained with her back to him, her hands braced against the side of the wall.

He came to her so swiftly she was at first unaware of his presence. He wrapped his arms to her front, taking her breasts, pressing himself into her backside. She relaxed immediately, tipped her head back until it rested against his beard. His hands circled her stomach in the same way her hands had caressed the wood. Lower still, he lifted her slightly between her legs.

"The Lord is my shepherd, Bear . . . I shall not want . . . Makes me to lie down . . . Bear . . . I shall dwell in your house."

He took her up into his arms and carried her to his bed.

He was in town. Without realizing it, he'd covered the distance between Caleb's and the square. He glanced out the truck window. The common fabric of the town was spread out around the pavilion, which glowed a stunning blue against a dirty fleece of clouds. Voices of the children in the park lifted clear as bells. A few people rushed around in midweek shopping before places closed, and merchants dawdled in doorways, jangling rings of keys in expectant hands. Couples ambled to the J & J, the men walking together and the women walking together, as though they belonged that way. Casper Reinhardt scooted around two couples and made an elaborate gesture of opening the door of the cafe. The women laughed, and Elsa Connard tapped his arm in a flirting way as she passed in front of him. Patrick glanced up then, directly above the doorway to the apartment's double windows, shrouded by thin curtains that billowed out against screens. She would be fixing supper, he supposed. Alone. He drove slowly past the J & J, and his eyes dropped to the line of vehicles parked curbside. Yes, alone. Lester's Vega wasn't around. Maybe she wasn't even seeing Lester anymore; Caleb hadn't said, and he hadn't thought to ask. It didn't matter. He drove the square, hanging back, glancing often at the windows, the twin squares of filtered light shining in the gradually descending darkness. He thought he might see her shadowy form, but none appeared. It occurred to him that even when he'd driven around the square in early morning to leave the envelopes with the messages — those foolish messages — she could have been at the upper windows with the curtains parted, looking down at him. And if he'd caught a glimpse of her or even had known precisely where she was, he wouldn't have gone for her. A certain time, a necessary space between them had been essential before he could feel as confident and unrestrained as he did now.

He left the square and started home. To Laurie. She would be home by now, waiting for him. He wanted to tell Laurie that he knew where his mother was and that he meant to go for her. Go for Josie too. It was time, past time.

Lightning ripped a white-hot seam across the leaden sky,

and instantly, as though waiting for a signal, raindrops struck the windshield and shattered like glass before they fell into the sweep of the wipers.

"Not tonight," he said aloud. "I'm not going to say anything tonight." Rain fell in a gray sheet, so heavy the hood of the truck parted a wave of water as he passed through. "Goddamn rain."

He slogged through mud to the house. Drenched, he stepped inside dripping and Laurie met him with a quilt.

Later when the telephone rang, he padded barefoot and naked to answer it. Without hesitation, without even listening to the first word of the message, he said, "Just wait up a minute, Mrs. Tyler. You'll have to call Sadie at the newspaper office. That's right. That's too damn bad, but I don't take the messages here at home anymore."

From the bedroom, Laurie cheered.

The next morning he was awake with the first gray light, the first bird call. But he made no move to leave Laurie's side or to rouse her for lovemaking. Always he woke first and began their love pattern, still fresh and flawless. He was always amazed at how little teasing it took for him to arouse her. Kisses and nips at the throbbing point in her neck, licks along the rounded slope of her breast before he took her nipple. Stroking, murmuring. "Comma, Laurie girl. Comma." Still half asleep, her arms and thighs would part, her desire swelling to match his. "There. There. Now." He could slip in hardly moving, roll her to his stomach, and hold her low while they rocked together, locked in place, soaring beyond their own vaulting emotion. God. Sex was all relief and release. He ached now, his penis throbbing and hard; but he cushioned himself against her soft backside, put his arm lightly over her to cup a breast, and remained suspended in the heady sensation of wanting her, knowing he could have her in a second, yet restraining himself. The imposed constraint seemed to divert his emotion and send it coursing through other parts of his body. Fired with all sorts of conflicting thoughts, he visualized his mother and Josie returning, finding Laurie with him, in bed together. This fucking bed, he thought.

He welcomed the light cover of cool sheets against his hot skin and burrowed into the hollow of the mattress. It occurred to him that his backside lay in a sling his father had prepared. Night after night with Laurie, he had eased himself into the shallow place his father had once slept in. It was an old bed. They had brought the walnut headboard, the frame, even the mattress with them when they moved from Gramma Rho's. He remembered helping his father slip sheets of plywood under the springs to lend support. At other times he'd taken one end, with his mother at the other, as they'd flipped the mattress foot to head. But nothing altered the imprints worn by bodies other than his own. Even his grandfather's. As impossible as it was to imagine Gramma Rho sleeping beside a man, she had. Then the bed had come under the lovemaking of his mother and father. Now it was his and Laurie's turn. And perhaps there had been others. Others besides Lester. He conjured up a fantastic picture of the lovemaking, even the conception of children, that had happened in this one historic bed. Remove the sheets and he might trace his own bloodline on the stains to be found on the mattress. He pressed back a laugh. What stories the bed could tell — this three generation fucking bed.

Laurie stirred against his confined laughter. She moaned and began to turn to him. "No, Laurie girl. Not yet. Go back to sleep." He cupped her to him, easing her head to his upper arm.

Nestled in that congenial groove, he seemed catapulted back in time, an observer in a familial process that coupled men and women not only in sex but in everything that could happen, from abundant happiness to wild despair. A thousand silent faces, all blank, of uncles and aunts, cousins, his mother's parents whom she seldom spoke of, danced a vaudevillian act before him. Some were the relatives that Gramma Rho mentioned in her letters. "Your Uncle Davey" who was unable to recognize a crooked-legged stallion or "your cousin Della" who slept the morning away. They seemed to hold a place open, welcoming him. He sensed that he belonged, yet he was unable to slip among them since he knew so little about them. What he did know was insignificant, like the bits and pieces that made up his mother's columns — "Mrs. Viola Welch enjoyed afternoon tea with Mrs. Edwina Crabb last Tuesday." Stale and hollow platitudes that might trick you into believing you actually knew about people. Even what he and Laurie had experienced could be reduced to an item that could appear in the column. "Patrick Douglas and Laurie Kieffer have been busy this past week with work at the Douglas Ranch. Patrick's mother and sister have been away on an extended visit." There was more to know than minor reports, and he experienced an uncommon desire to know something about the lives of people he sensed gave significance to his own.

He eased up from the hammock he rested in and rolled to the side of the bed. "No. Not yet," he answered Laurie's murmurs. "I'll come back." Slipping into his clothes, he left the house for the barn. He found himself moving faster and faster as he worked. Like pistons, his hands pulled twine from bales and cracked the solid mass across his knee. He took to the pasture in even, swinging strides to check mares and foals. The sun was out now and lay shimmering across the mares' flanks, sleek as women's hips. Like women with long hair, the mares tossed luxuriant tails to their shoulders. He looked them over quickly and then backtracked in his own footprints left in mud. Far ahead, the paddocks and barn, the work arena to the side, were squared off and skirted by pastures stocked with ankle-high grass. Soon now it would be time to cut and bale hay, store it in the loft, repair machinery, prepare for the onslaught of winter. He knew the routine by heart.

Walking swiftly, his jeans brushing a subtle rhythm, he thought about what he had to do next — bring home his mother and Josie. It was clear that first he'd have to explain his plans to Laurie — now that he knew what they were. They'd be apart for a while. At least until they married.

"Marry Laurie?" He halted in the path, and his gaze went beyond everything else to the road at Mill Creek.

Naturally, he'd marry Laurie. Their time together had been no casual live-in affair. She'd made it clear she was ready to give up college, all her plans, for marriage. Besides, was there really any other choice?

He could see the house, positioned well in front of the barns. It was a big house. Big enough for the four of them. "With one lousy bathroom?" No. He didn't want to live in the house with Sadie and Josie once he and Laurie were married.

Then a house trailer. They could set one up in the pasture. Over there. That way he and Laurie would be close by. He'd be there to manage the ranch, see that everything was running smoothly. Of course the ranch wouldn't provide enough money for all of them, and he'd have to find a job and Laurie could work. No babies right away. "Jesus God."

Without realizing it, he had passed beyond the barns. He was half running now, panting, down the drive and along the pasture road before he checked himself. Ahead, the road ran unbounded straight across the bridge at Mill Creek, then divided into three directions that went on and on as limitless as the sky above.

Like a child rising from a long nap, Laurie came to the kitchen still pale from sleep, her gray eyes wide with light.

"Jeez, what time is it?" She bounced curls about her head. "Why didn't you get me up?" She pulled out a chair at the oak table and slouched to the seat. She had on one of Patrick's T-shirts that hung shapeless to her knees.

Patrick glanced at her and quickly back to eggs he was

beating to a froth. "The day's half gone."

"I thought you were coming back to bed. We could have had breakfast there." It was her foxy tone. He kept his back to her.

"There's too much to do, Laurie. I've let it slide as it is."

"My God." Close to laughter, her voiced edged toward seriousness. "Does this mean the honeymoon's over?"

He poured eggs sputtering into hot bacon fat and stirred the bubbling liquid as if the skillet had no edges. "Goddamn it, Laurie, it's not funny."

"I'm beginning to see that." She doubled her legs up, her heels braced at the chair edge, and pulled the shirt to her toes. She watched him narrowly.

"I've got to work Patriot today. If I don't get the saddle on him and out on some trails, he's going to be rank enough to pitch me."

Her gaze was intense as heat.

"Training a horse is not something you do whenever the spirit moves you." He sat the jam jar on the table with a thud, laid out silverware that scattered in a riot. "Especially a horse as smart as Patriot. He's always testing me. He should be worked every day, even if it's nothing but the basics." He was aware of words doubling back on themselves. "And the mares and foals." He ladled eggs beside bacon, roofed them with buttered toast. "The foals need hooves trimmed and a . . ." When he brought their plates to the table, he could no longer avoid her dove-gray eyes, now hardened to burnished steel.

"And what, Patrick?"

He set the plates down carefully and took a chair across from her. "Let's eat breakfast first. Then we'll talk."

"To hell with breakfast." She gave her plate a shove. "We'll talk now."

"You're right. Now."

"And we won't talk about the horses. Since the horses have nothing to do with it."

"Right. We'll talk about . . ." He rubbed his hands down the long muscles of his legs. He thought they had begun to ache, but he felt no pain at all. "I have to bring Sadie and Josie home," he said moderately. "She isn't living with Lester like I thought. She's in that apartment above the J & J."

"You've already seen her?"

"No. But I went to see Caleb yesterday. While you were gone. He told me. Then I drove into town and saw a light on in the apartment. I know she's there. It's time to get things settled."

"I guess that pretty much wraps it up, doesn't it? Knocks down all the blocks around our never-never land."

"You knew we couldn't go on like this. Playing house here." He took their plates back to the sink.

"But spring break. I've got all next week off. I wanted it to last at least until after then."

"It wouldn't be any easier. Maybe harder." He remained with his back to her. "And I can't wait any longer. I've got to get things settled."

"What's another week? You can go for them the next week, the week after."

"No. I know what to do now, and I don't want to put it off."

"It's your mother." Her voice was flat. "I used to hate her. I thought that if she was just some other girl, some ordinary girl, why then I could handle it. I could come on to you, not strong, but easy. Be the kind of girl I knew you'd go for. But your mom is no ordinary girl." She lifted a mirthless laugh. "Or mother either."

"We had a partnership more than anything else." He pushed back from the table giving his legs stretching room.

"No, it's more than that. It's like you've already been married."

He turned to face her. "Sometimes it felt like that, a marriage. The responsibility of it. I know for sure that marriage is hard. Not like sex. Making love is easy, natural. It's all instinct. What you and I had. Perfect, Laurie. And I'd like for it to go on and on like that — waking up with a fresh fuck every day."

"It's more than that, Patrick." With a thud, her feet slammed to the floor, and she was out of the chair before she could stop herself.

He took her hands when she reached him. "I don't mean it was wrong. It was like we were making a discovery." She took her chair again, quiet now, but he stood and went to stand in front of the window. "Sex was always such a mystery to me. It still is in some ways. You can lose yourself in that white-hot thrill. Forget everything. But it's not like marriage, I can tell you." He smiled over his shoulder at her briefly, then turned back. "There's no mystery about marriage. It's complicated. Hard. Sorrowful sometimes. It weighs you down. It's every day, and every day is lined out for you as regular as that calendar up there." He lifted his hand in a sluggish wave to a point above the refrigerator, but his gaze remained ahead, down the road. "There's a kind of sadness in that. To have your future so mapped out." He paused. "Just before you got up, I was coming in from checking mares. I was thinking about you and me getting married. I didn't see anything else open to us. I thought about living in this house, but canceled that idea. Then I figured I'd bring a house trailer in and set it up out there in the pasture. Things flooded my mind. You working at the J & J and me trying to get on at the battery plant. Doing every damn thing we always said we'd never do. The babies coming when we weren't really ready, and your trading recipes with your sisters, and us going to your family to-dos. Then years from now you've got a baby on each hip and we pass each other without hardly knowing who we are. Sex is still the only mystery. Everything else is cold, stone facts. I tell you, Laurie, the next thing I knew, I took off running down the road."

"I don't believe it."

"I did, I tell you." He came quickly round to face her. "Left you here. I was on the way to Mill Creek before I turned back. And I got to thinking. Is that what I'd do? Sometime? Sometime when I couldn't handle things, would I just leave? Like he did?"

"You wouldn't. In a hundred years, you wouldn't."

"Maybe not. But I did it then. And I didn't understand that either."

She sat quietly, studying her palms. "You only talk about sex and marriage. What's to become of what I feel for you? Don't you believe in love?" Her eyes were misty. She blinked back tears.

It was what Caleb had said once, he remembered instantly.

"I don't know yet. Not like you do. I'd like to plunge in with that what-the-hell attitude like you and Rudy go at most everything. But that takes faith, a kind of trust. I'd never have asked you to live with me. But you came, believing something great was going to happen, that you could make things work. 'I'm moving in,' you said. Remember?" They faced each other with smiles. It seemed months ago, months that had passed like seconds.

"Love takes faith, trust, and maybe you even have to earn it in order to believe in it. I remember something Caleb said yesterday when he was talking about Natalie. When he fell in love with Natalie. He said he had to strip himself clean to be ready for love. He had to start fresh, build his own place, leave everything behind."

She shook her head, resigned and sluggish. "It's not something you can take apart like you do your truck engine out there. And it's not just sex like bringing a mare and a stallion together."

"I know that."

"But maybe it's not getting married either. At least not now." She came around the oak table and put her arms around him. He held her, her face against his chest.

"I think you should go work Patriot now," she said after several moments. She began raking up the dishes, scraping out the congealed mass of eggs still on the plates. "Training horses, you know, is not a sometime thing. And if you don't get out there on that stud, he'll pitch you sure." Her voice picked up. "He's probably a hell of a lot smarter than you are."

"Laurie girl."

"Go on, now. Will you just go on?"

Riding Patriot in an easy lope across the back pasture, Patrick sighted the clothesline full of sheets and pillow slips. He gave the stallion a heel and lifted his hips enough to take a canter into the paddock. He swung down, tossed bridle reins around a post and ran without thinking until he heard the back door slam behind him. But he knew she was gone, even before he saw her note, neat as a napkin, folded in the center of his plate, and smelled his supper warming in the oven.

He snatched at the phone. "That's the way I wanted it, Patrick," she said. "It's no big deal. I'll see you tomorrow or the next day."

Sooner than sunset, loneliness returned and reclaimed its territory. He returned to his room, an alien in his own bed. He traveled the stairs or sat in the kitchen with Freone. The next morning he woke in a fit of desperate desire for her and cursed himself first for ever having taken her to bed and then for giving her up. He went about his work with a separate melancholy awareness as though some part of him had moved aside to watch and sneer.

The next day as he was making up his mother's bed with sheets Laurie had laundered, he heard Rudy at the bottom of the back-porch steps.

"Hey, are you in there? I need a hand," Rudy said when Patrick came to the door. "A couple of legs would be better, but I'll take a hand right now." He gave his boyish, exuberant grin.

Patrick lifted Rudy from his wheelchair and carried him to an oak chair in the kitchen.

"Why didn't you bring Laurie?"

"She says you need a few days apart. Besides, if she was here, you two would head for the sack. We couldn't talk, and that's what I came for."

"About me and Laurie?" Patrick asked warily.

"Hey, big guy. Take it easy. I'm not here as a representative of the family. Dad's not loading his shotgun or anything. In our family, they think there's something wrong with the females if they don't stake their claims early."

"But it's a little different with Laurie and me. She's not pregnant and we aren't making wedding plans."

"I know. Laurie explained it all. To the folks too. She told them you and her had plenty of time. You wanted to wait a while, and she wanted to start college like she'd always planned." He shrugged. "It sounded straight to me."

"I miss her."

"Hey. I know what you miss, man."

"Oh hell, Rudy. Shut up, will you? Laurie and I did more together than roll in the sack. I don't think I could have saved Simone's filly if Laurie hadn't been here."

"At least you found out what you've been missing all these years."

Patrick stretched his legs until he could brace the toes of his boots against the pedestal of the table. "So how is it with you and Ramona? I bet you came over here to tell me something I can guess."

Rudy grinning. "I'm going to need a best man to get me up the pavilion steps."

"You sonofagun. I suppose I'll have to wear a tux. The whole nine yards."

"If they make them long enough you will. We're having a big formal affair. A garden-party reception in the park. The end of August. Ramona has to check and see which date we can reserve the bandstand."

"Have you found a place yet?"

"We're going to have a house built. The folks are going to give us a couple of acres. We're going to have the basement dug, the frame put up, and Dad says the family can pitch in and get it finished. Mom and the girls are already haggling over wallpaper and paint."

"I suppose you brought Ramona's mother around?"

"Hell. I'm thinking about a one-bedroom house. Otherwise she's liable to move in with us."

"That's great. Just great, Rudy."

"So how about you?"

"I'm going to bring my mom and Josie home. Tomorrow. Friday night. We'll have the weekend then to get straightened around. Put things back together. After that I'm moving out. Maybe I'll take that place she'd been living in, above the J & J. Or maybe I'll move to Chesterfield."

"You mom might object to that."

"I'm going anyhow. My mind's pretty well made up."

"Laurie will like that."

"Yeah. Maybe Laurie and I can live together for the rest of the summer. I don't know. She should leave Stella. Go to school in the fall like she's planned. And hell, I haven't thought far enough ahead to know how I'm going to swing it financially."

"Laurie didn't mention any of this."

"That's because I haven't talked to her about it. I just made the decision today."

"I won't say anything to her."

"No, don't. I want to pull it off first."

"Well, you never know how things will change for you from one day to the next," Rudy said in a rare philosophical mood. "Hell, by August, you might be ready for a double wedding."

318

19

He drove into Stella knowing precisely what he was going to say — until he got there. During morning chores, he'd worked out several beginnings, then eliminated most. Get to the point, he told himself. She'll know why you've come. Stalling will be useless. Sadie's responses, which he played out too, all came to the same end. They would simply load up her belongings and drive home. From there, the two of them would go for Josie. He felt entirely confident, nearly smug.

It wasn't until he approached the square that doubt accosted him. It was late in the day, and the sun had left the air close and steamy. Sadie's windows were open, and the thin curtains riffled to the screens. The park and the streets bordering it were filled with people, spilling out in all directions, crisscrossing on the paths, angling about like fish in a tank. The pavilion, lifted above all the activity, seemed set apart and protected, as though cupped under glass.

Patrick drove slowly and leaned over the wheel to watch for children as they darted from between parked cars. Unrestrained, they seemed exempt from caution. It wasn't until he saw high schoolers wearing band uniforms and toting instruments that he realized the final spring recital was set for that evening. Too hot for woolen jackets, the band members had left the fronts flapping, their tall fringed hats pushed to the back of their heads. The horn players blasted out greetings to one another and as they lifted instruments, rippled reflections from overhead lamps swam along the length of gold and silver metal.

He looked for Laurie. Every covey of girls attracted him, but he didn't see her. When he sighted her sisters, trailing their kids, and then Rudy and Ramona, he searched for her familiar face, her body he knew so well now. She wasn't among them. She hadn't come. If she'd been anywhere on the square, he would have seen her instantly. She would loom into his vision, something bright and unmistakable. The snap of a snare drum brought him around. "Don't think. Move."

From the square, he pulled into the alleyway behind the cafe. Stairs began at one corner of the building and ascended diagonally along the weathered frame. A handrail ran the length of open steps and along two sides of a landing outside a door painted a startling yellow. He held his line of vision to the vertical splash of color and started up the steps. Blue lard canisters, boxes tipped inside each other, trash overflowing barrels that Jock and Jessie pitched from the back door filled the space beneath the steps. Inside Jessie was frying chicken, and the aroma trailed him, grew stronger as he climbed. His fingers slid weightlessly along the handrail, and he thought again of something he might say as soon as she opened the door. Mechanically he lifted his hand to rap, but before he could knock, as though Sadie had been waiting for him, the door opened and they stood facing each other, his hand only inches from her face. He forgot entirely what he had been about to say.

Startled, Sadie gave a slight jump back. "Patrick. Well, Pat." She clipped the words nervously and shifted her gaze to a point beyond him. "I wasn't expecting you." With an abrupt turn, she crossed the bedroom, a small dark room without a window.

When he waited at the threshold to scuff dirt from his boots, she turned back to him. "Never mind. You can't hurt anything," she said.

320

When he closed the door, the room seemed as narrow and dark as a cave. Ahead of him, the other room, where he followed her, was equally small and dingy with only the two front windows open to sunlight and a view of the square below. Here the ceiling was so low he had to stoop to keep from bumping his head. He felt constricted, as though he'd tried to wedge his oversized frame into a child's playhouse. Everything was in miniature. Even the makeshift kitchen, jammed into one corner and containing an enamel-topped table flanked by chrome-legged chairs.

"Better sit down." She gave a brittle wave of her hand. "You'll get a crick in your neck standing up in here." A smile barely tipped the corners of her mouth, but it offered relief enough for him to nod and ease into a chair. But as he scooted under the table and tried to adjust his knees, he jarred the edge so that crystal salt and pepper shakers danced across the top and before he could reach for them, Sadie rushed to scoop them up.

"I'll take these. Out of your way." She idled about the stove, pushed the shakers to the back, draped a towel across a glass rod and finally gave him one long studied look.

"Your beard." She brought both hands together near her mouth. "I noticed it right off. It makes you look older. I'm surprised though. So much auburn in it."

"Something of Josie, I guess. And Gramma Rho." It was a beginning, he thought, but hardly one he'd rehearsed.

"Well. Coffee. Why don't I make a pot?"

"Fine. Sounds fine."

Her dark hair, tied back with a red rubber band, sharpened her features and pointed up the plainness of her face. She wore no makeup, no earrings; above her ears, identical wings of gray hair branched off from her temples. She was thinner, and yet her quick movements brought life to what she wore. Stooping now to strike a kitchen match against a burner, the long muscles of her arm defined the soft folds in a blouse as vivid as marigolds.

"I didn't know this place was so small." To allow himself more space, he tilted back on the chrome legs until they set neatly into dimples in the linoleum. The room looked as though Jessie and Jock had tried to remodel in an afternoon between the dinner and supper crowds. Slapped-up paneling buckled in places from the wall. The room was bare of pictures, ornaments, even furniture. One corner was filled with a burly brown chair crowned with a white crocheted doily. In front, a table had been placed to hold Sadie's hulking old black Remington that he recognized; he had often lugged it from the newspaper office to the truck and home when she was behind in work. Yellow "roughs" lay scattered across the card table or in wads where she'd kicked them beneath. His gaze lingered on the familiar.

"It's not so bad. Easy to care for. But I don't suppose you came when Natalie lived here."

"No." At the table's edge, his fingers traced the dark outline where enamel had chipped away. "I didn't think she stayed here long."

"No. I think Caleb knew from the first night he met her he was going to marry her." She breathed a slight chuckle that seemed to relax her. "Only a few months. They couldn't stay apart once they'd found each other."

It struck him that they'd hardly ever talked in such an easy bantering way about trifling things. Their voices were so soft and low they hardly stirred lint. The scent of Jessie's cooking was the heaviest thing between them.

"I went to see Caleb yesterday. The first time since . . . in quite a spell." He paused. "He told me you were here."

"You didn't know?" She swung around to him and then quickly back to what she was doing at the stove. "No. I guess you wouldn't." Then, quietly. "You thought I'd be with Lester."

"It doesn't matter." He started to get up but remembered the ceiling and remained where he was, pressed in place.

"I'm not with Lester." She hugged her arms to herself and ambled to the front windows to push aside the curtains and take in the street below. "I live by myself." She wheeled around as though to catch his thoughts in midair. "I don't even see him anymore." She went back to the window. "Still, you might as well know, Patrick. I'm not sorry about Lester. Lester and me. Just sorry it happened. With Josie. I know it didn't do her any good. God, she scared me so bad that day that whatever I felt for Lester was gone." She submerged a hollow laugh. "All the time your father and I were together, I was always afraid one of you kids would walk in on us, but . . . Jesus, there's a bunch of people in town today."

"Band day in the park."

"Yes. I remember now writing the story for last week's paper." Idly she picked up wadded papers from beneath the table and pressed them between her palms. "I haven't seen Josie. But then, you know that. At first, I couldn't bring myself to it. I wasn't about to come out home. I didn't even want to go down to the school — just two blocks away." She tossed her hands above her in a gesture of futility. "Sure I was ashamed. I couldn't bear the thought of Josie's righteous eyes." She made a defensive stab with her hand. "You know how she can look at you. With the eyes of an angel and hard as the devil."

He realized then that Sadie presumed Josie was at home with him. But before he could say anything, Sadie began again. "Terrible, I suppose, but the longer I waited the harder it got. And the easier it was to hole myself away here. I couldn't even answer the notes you wrote. I tried. I must have written a hundred replies, put them in envelopes with your name on the outside, but I couldn't leave them under the door for you." She shoved her hands into the side pockets of her slacks and paced the few steps in front of the windows. "The thing is, I knew you and Josie were all right. At home together. Doing just fine without me. Josie's strong. You know someday Josie's going to wake up and say, 'Move over, World. Make room for me.' And you, Patrick. You're like those hills beyond Stella." She jerked one hand toward the window. "All easy slopes with flint underneath. No. It was me I didn't know about. Maybe I wanted to see if I could live without you." She lifted her eyes to meet his. "Maybe Lester was a way to break away. Coming here," her eyes scanned the low ceiling, "was my final chance." She smiled at some indeterminate point. "I think I made it. I came out okay."

The room was bathed in heat and the tallowy smell of Jessie's cooking. From the street and park below, voices filtered in through the windows like murmurs of a distracted audience. The coffee on the stove began to perk and spew over the lid; Sadie dashed across the room to flick off the burner.

"I don't want any coffee," Patrick said. "Don't pour it. It's too damn hot in here." He brushed his hands through his hair, started to get up but he remembered the ceiling and pushed himself back into the chair. "This place is like a hole. A hovel. I don't know how you stand it." He rubbed his knees, expecting to find them aching; they weren't.

"It's not so bad. The boundaries are prescribed, the rules easily learned." She smiled with evident pleasure and poured herself a cup of coffee. "I take my showers in the mornings because I know Jessie will need all the hot water at night. And I walk everywhere. I don't need to learn anything about shifting gears." She inclined her head as though thinking aloud. "So simple. I could tie up the four corners of my life as neatly as a head scarf. Sometimes I stay here most of the day, writing. Mondays I take off and drive into Chesterfield with Jessie when she goes for supplies. One day I took a story I'd written into the *Chesterfield Daily*. About old man Dinsmore and those wood carvings he does. I took pictures of him working. And I thought why not try for something bigger than the *Ledger*. I did the story on my own time. Free-lance. And Jessie encouraged me to sell it. 'Take it in to Web Olin at the *Daily*,' she said. 'What've you got to lose?' So I said why not?" She took up her pace again, firm and self-assured. "I took my copy and my photographs into Mr. Olin. Scared. Scared just like I was when I first went in to Roy Yost to see about working at the *Ledger*. Only then it was you telling me I could do it. I thought, 'God,

324

am I always going to need someone to urge me on?' I don't think I drew a complete breath until after I left. He took my story. Didn't say much more than that he'd look at it, and I thought that was the end of it. Then on Sunday, the next thing I knew people were saying they'd seen my story in the *Daily*. When I went out and bought a paper, there it was. My story. My pictures. My byline. I couldn't believe it. A few days later I got a check for thirty dollars in the mail. I've been writing a story every week since then."

He caught the sounds of the band, the sliding wail of a trombone, the blast from a trumpet; in an off-key rhythm each tested melodic limits. Then, lifted above the sound of the instruments, a sputtering squawk erupted. Someone — probably Emmett Fairchild, the band instructor — was hooking up the microphone. Fairchild's voice sounded harsh and grating. "Testing, one, two." The heat was oppressive; the food aroma, heavy and rank.

"What about now?" he said. "It will be Josie's birthday in a few days."

"I know. I hadn't forgotten. I even half expected you'd come. I hoped you would anyway. To make it a little easier for me." She came to him, slowly lowering her eyes to meet his. "But I don't want to look at you and see there what you expect me to do, what you hope I will be."

"Or what," he said with care, "you hope I will be. Or Josie either. Maybe you haven't had time to think much about it, but none of us — not me, not Josie — has come to the other side the same."

"No," she shook her head resolutely. "I can't imagine you ever changing, Patrick."

He remembered the ceiling as he got up, and he held his head to one side until he could step into the archway between the two rooms. "I can't talk in here. It's hot as Hades. The whole goddamn town is walking around underneath me. I'm going home." He started toward the back door, painted yellow even on the inside, and the only spot of color in the room. With his hand on the doorknob, he faced her. "You can come or you can stay. Whatever." He swung the door open, anxious for a breath of air.

"Patrick. Just hold up a minute."

He glanced back to her silhouette framed in the doorway against the front windows.

"Ladies and gentlemen, for our first number tonight . . ."

Fairchild's voice sailed through the open windows, but whatever it was the band was going to play was lost beneath Sadie's jubilant voice. "Patrick. Here. Wait. I'm taking my typewriter."

It must have been a march, Patrick thought later, something with *ump-pa-pa* that set the tempo for him and Sadie as they filled the boxes they collected from beneath the steps. The band was still playing as they started home.

Patrick rolled down the window and set his elbow on the edge to let the breeze whip his hair. Caught up in the free open spirit of the wind, he guided the truck down the road, barely touching his fingertips to the wheel. The road was free of traffic, and ponds and low-lying marshes, the rasp of frogs rose and diminished as he drew near, then passed. In the late evening the landscape melted into a gray haze. Farmhouses and their outbuildings, set some distance from the road, blended together and appeared like gray ships afloat in the mist.

It was good to be leaving Stella, bringing Sadie home. Before the night was out, he'd have Josie home too, and he felt the sort of robust pleasure and expectancy of one returning from a long journey. Of course, he'd have to tell Sadie why Josie wasn't at home, why they were going to Stonegate for her.

Sadie wedged herself in the crack between the truck's door and the seat as though tucking into her own thoughts. Her belongings were between them, her typewriter on the floor at her feet.

"I don't know what I'll say to Josie right off," she said as much to herself as to Patrick.

"Josie's not there, Mom. We'll have to go . . ."

"I know. She's probably at a prayer meeting or something at the Uttermelons'. But I mean when she comes home."

"We'll have to go for her." He realized that didn't explain anything either. "What I mean is, she hasn't been at home since the day you left. She went to the Uttermelons' that day, and she's been living there."

"With the Uttermelons? How could that be?"

"I went for her that day, but I couldn't bring her home. She wouldn't come. She was rock firm about it." He darted his eyes from the road to Sadie. "She wanted to live there for a while. And as it turned out, it was probably for the best."

"Oh God." She pulled a towel from one of the boxes and pressed it against her face, rocking back and forth.

"This isn't going to be easy." He reached across and laid a hand briefly on her shoulder. "Remember what I said back there. None of us is the same."

She looked up quickly, her glistening eyes holding points of light. Then she pressed the towel against her mouth, smothering a sob.

"Don't start crying."

"I won't. I'm okay."

"I don't think we'll have too bad a time with Josie," he went on rapidly. "She's ready to come home. It's her birthday."

Sadie gave a determined heave away from the seat. "She's not staying there any longer. We're going for her tonight, Patrick."

He kept his eyes focused on the cones of light on the road in front of him. "Another thing. It's her hair. She had all her hair cut off. For some kind of penance."

"Damn. Damn." Her voice came strained through clenched teeth.

"But lots of it has grown back now."

"You've gone to see her then? She hasn't been alone."

"As often as I can. Not much the last week or so."

"Don't stop at home. Drive right on to the Uttermelons'."

"No, we'll have to go by home. There's no room for her until we unload some of your things. But we won't stop any longer than it takes to set your stuff out."

"Good. Just hurry."

He took a deep breath and began again. "There's something else."

"That means you've been alone, too," Sadie spoke up quickly. "Foaling out the mares, up half the nights. I thought Josie was there to help. You can hardly do it all alone. Caleb? Caleb came?"

It wasn't going to be the least bit difficult after all. "No. Caleb didn't come." He waited a long moment and then faced her, searching for her eyes in the dark. "Laurie's been with me."

Sadie fell back against the seat. "Laurie?"

"About two weeks ago, she moved in." He smiled, his head turned toward the passing darkness, and visualized the way she'd looked the night she'd come with her suitcase and clothes, staring after Rudy.

"You mean you lived together?"

People had the damnedest way of talking about sex, he thought. Lived together. Slept together. Fuck. Screw. All of them fell far short of what he and Laurie had. Making love. Making *a* love. Making *the* love. That was closer. Assaulted by desire for her, he had a sudden urge to turn the truck around in the middle of the road and find her.

"Lived together?" He tipped his head into the breeze to catch its coolness. "I dunno. That seems more like what you and I have had. Laurie and I had something else."

"I'll be damned." Nervously she patted her knees, then hid a laugh behind her hands. "Right there at home?"

"That's right." He gave a great snort of a laugh. "In your bedroom. In that fucking bed."

As though to cover embarrassment, she snapped her hands across her face, but then burst out laughing. They laughed together.

"Oh, Patrick. That beats all."

Even before he turned the corner toward home, he thought he saw lights shimmering through budding tree branches. Once he had a clear view of the house, he could see it was ablaze with light. The yard light. A beam shot out from the barn and fanned out into the driveway. He thought first of Laurie. Would she have come back? No. No. Gramma Rho? God, who could tell? Then Josie.

"Josie." He jammed his foot against the accelerator, knocked across the trestle. "It's got to be Josie."

When he wheeled into the driveway, Sadie already had her hand on the door, ready to push out. "Wait." He grabbed her shoulder. "She doesn't know. I never told her either — that you haven't been home."

Sadie started to say something, but the whack of the back door forced her to turn, peering frantically into the glare of lights. "Mama?" Josie's voice was shrill as a scream. "Mama?" She stood spotlighted, and Sadie, without a word, as though a single word would have slowed her, jumped from the truck and ran to her daughter.

Patrick thought they looked like joyous schoolgirls sharing secrets. They fell together as though they ached for the touch of one another. Then they stood back at arm's length to determine if any changes had come about in the faces they had held in memory.

Patrick put his arms across the steering wheel and lightly placed his forehead against his wrist. "Jesus God."

He couldn't get the two of them to stop talking. Each time he shoved away from the oak table with, "Tomorrow's another

329

day. It might be a good idea if we . . ." one or the other would begin again. They were like music boxes, gradually winding down, but ready to tune up again with the slightest turn. Of course, he could have gone upstairs to bed at any point, but each time he made the effort, Josie or Sadie would say something to keep him lingering.

"Every time I thought about my birthday, I thought of home. Both of you. I couldn't stay away. Father Uttermelon brought me home in the bus, and I looked everywhere for you. I kept telling myself, they're here, they're here. In the barn or on the horses. Then I knew you had to be in town. I remembered the band concert. Of course, they're at the band concert."

Sadie and Patrick exchanged glances, and it was Sadie who told her.

"You mean . . ." Josie gave them a long puzzled look, "And neither of us knew about the other? How silly."

"If you hadn't come home, we were going after you," Patrick said.

"Just burst into prayer meeting?" Josie's eyes glowed.

"That's right. Bash the doors down. Carry you off." He tried to hide a grin.

And it was at the point when they had finally begun to say, "Maybe we'd better . . ." and "I'm getting pretty tired . . ." that the phone rang.

Sadie swung to the clock. "It's after midnight."

"It can't be the women calling at this hour. Besides, I've been telling them . . ." Patrick lifted the receiver, but even before he could say a word. . . "I'm in Chesterfield, Patrick. Now you come get me."

"Gramma Rho?"

"How long will it take you, Patrick? Can you be here in ten minutes?"

"It takes a good forty-five to get to Chesterfield, Gramma."

"Then I'll start out walking."

"You can't walk on the highway. Just sit there in the bus

330

station, and I'll be along quick as I can. I'm leaving now."

"I'm not at the bus station, Patrick. I'm afraid to tell you where I am."

"Then how'd you get here?"

"That's another story. But never in my life . . ."

"Where are you, Gramma?"

"At this place they call the Island Oasis."

"I know where it is. Just sit tight and I'll be there as fast as I can."

"I'm not staying inside. It's a disgrace. Now hurry along, Patrick."

He replaced the phone. "She's at the Oasis, and God knows how she got there."

"Just hold up. Don't break your neck," Sadie said. "She'll be all right. She's never met anything she couldn't handle."

"But if she takes a notion to start out walking, she will. Carrying her suitcase right down the highway."

Sadie poured him a cup of coffee, and he set out for Chesterfield with a feeling he didn't quite understand. He marked his lack of enthusiasm to being tired, the excitement of having his mother and Josie home, but the prospect of a summer ahead with Gramma Rho laying a hand to everything was more than he wanted to think about. It wasn't that he didn't . . . *respect* came to mind. Love, too, but respect seemed to fall in front and crowd love aside. Love. Respect. They were like twins, weren't they? Conceived and born together, bearing likenesses, the one — respect in Gramma Rho's case — gradually overshadowed the other. No. It was just a notion, rising from the way he remembered how she carried herself, ramrod straight with an upward tilt of her chin as though posing a challenge and daring anyone to meet her head-on. People had their appointed places in life, and they should set about with purpose, she thought. If one rose early and worked late, accomplishment soared, obliterating worthless distractions. "Nothing's so hard as getting started," she'd tell Patrick as they left the house before dawn to mend fence, a job he detested. "Come

331

along now. Think of the joy you'll feel to look back along a fence line and know it's as straight and tight as you can make it."

The only tailspin she seemed to meet was Allan. When he came to take Patrick and Josie for a visit, he'd park his truck at the end of the driveway and wait for them. "You children stay here," Gramma Rho said once and started on ahead of them with, "Now see here, Allan," booming out even before she reached him. Without waiting, Allan ripped off, billowing dust into her face. She returned, quivering with rage. "I'll have nothing more to do with him. Nothing. I tell you, faults breed through. Faults breed through," she'd mutter, leaving Patrick and Josie confounded. Nevertheless, they needed her then. Her self-assured, determined attitude had given them direction, and they had followed her like a compass point. But now. No. Not now. He sensed each of them — Josie, his mother, certainly he himself — had gained a measure of self-reliance; fortification from Gramma Rho was unnecessary.

The hood of the truck sliced through heavy mist swirling across the road. The stuff was thick enough to slice and serve on a plate. Surely she wouldn't take off walking, but he looked for her unmistakable form as he held to a course near the yellow seam running down the center of the highway.

When the Chesterfield turnoff lifted through fog, he angled off the highway and began looking for the bubbling spike of colored lights at the Oasis. The fields he passed now swayed with an ocean of yellowing wheat only weeks away from falling under the combine. He slowed at the gravel road leading into the Oasis and drew into the parking lot. Almost immediately, he saw her long black coat, the hem flopping about her knees, her stride so brisk, the mist swirled up enclosing her face.

"Right here, Patrick," she called before he could stop. With one swift motion, she unlatched the door, swung her suitcase to the floor, and brought herself to the seat beside him.

"Well now, aren't I the one glad to see you?" He waited for what he believed would be an inevitable comment about his beard and untrimmed hair, but she only gathered her satchel purse into the pocket of her lap and leaned to him with a kiss on his cheek just below his eye. When she drew back, the pulsating neon light from the Oasis fell across her forehead, but even that strange appearance failed to change her face, composed of straight lines with pale translucent skin stretched over narrow bones. Perhaps only her hair, the color of old brick, was dusted with more gray.

"Is that the only suitcase you brought, Gramma?" Patrick motioned to the one at her feet.

"No. There's one in that blue van over there." She pointed through the windshield, and as Patrick drew beside it, she was out in a flash and back again with another bag, which she heaved to the truck bed before she took her seat again.

"Well, Patrick, I have learned my lesson. Learned my lesson, I can tell you."

She hadn't changed. Not a bit, he thought. They might have been returning home after buying a week's supply of groceries.

"I suppose you met someone coming in K mart, and when you found out they were coming this way, you just asked them for a ride." He smiled over at her sitting away from the seat as though something pinched between her shoulder blades.

"Not that a-tall. I didn't ask a-tall." She gathered herself upright. "Can you see this road, Patrick?" She pitched forward to stare into the fog. "Is that the center line you're on?" She angled her shoulders first one way and then the other.

"I got here in one piece," he said mildly. "I think I can get us back home."

"Of course, Patrick." She relaxed slightly against the seat. "It's just that I've had such a ride, such an experience. I can't tell you . . ."

But he knew she would.

"Well, I went to this wedding, an older couple right there in town. She's a widow lady. I've known her for years. Her daughter, by her first marriage you understand, was the bridesmaid. Such a sweet, beautiful little thing, I thought. All in pink organdy. The daughter, Roxanne, had these two little girls. Flower girls they were. And Roxanne told me she and her husband and the little girls were leaving the next day, coming right this way. When she found out I was planning on taking the bus, she insisted I ride with them. They'd bring me right to the door, she said. She had a cousin she could visit here in Chesterfield." She shuffled her purse closer to her stomach and inclined her shoulder to him. "You can't believe a word people tell you anymore."

"So you left with them?"

"That's right, Roxanne and that so-called husband Tommy Jay. And those two adorable little girls."

"But they weren't married? Right?"

"It didn't take me long to see that." She straightened up, waiting for his reaction. "I knew, Patrick, because married folks don't act like that."

"Like what, Gramma?"

"Married people don't carry on. Just carry on over each other. One time she leaned back to me, back there in the back with those two little girls, reading stories and coloring pictures, and she says, 'Too bad you don't drive, Mrs. Douglas. Tommy Jay and me'd take the back and put you and the kids up front for a while.'" She paused to gather her thoughts as though they might have scattered to all sorts of unseemly regions. "Can you imagine? Imagine that. Just as though I didn't know perfectly well what she was talking about. And those little girls. Right there in front of those children."

"But you got here, Gramma."

"It's a wonder. We'd stop at a shopping center to eat, and the two of them would go running off. Leave those little girls and me, one clutching a hand on either side, for two, three hours. Oh, it didn't take me long to figure out what they were up to. What I was along for. One time I said right out, 'I don't care to stop anymore. These children need to get on home where they belong.' Sometimes I thought about going to the nearest bus stop, but then I wondered what would happen to those children. Would they leave those babies alone in that van while they went off somewhere?" An answer seemed unnecessary. "They certainly would. Just leave those babies."

"So where are the kids now, Gramma?"

"At the cousin's. They left them off there. They was to bring me out home, but they pulled into that bar without so much as a by-your-leave. That's when I called you."

"It worked out fine. We happened to be up late."

"With the colts, I bet. Well, I'm here now to lend a hand." She paused a moment before she cast a long sideways glance in his direction. "Now, about your beard, Patrick. I presume that's some passing fancy, a whim."

He rubbed his fingers across his jaw. "I dunno, Gramma. The girls kinda like it."

"Patrick Douglas. Have you got yourself a girl friend?"

"Looking them over, Gramma. Trying to find one like you."

"One like your mother is what I'd say. And you'll do well to find one like her. Tried and true."

He smiled into the fog, rising like smoke around the hood of the truck as he drove on.

20

The envelope addressed to Josie arrived a few days before her birthday. Gramma Rho and Sadie stood on either side of Patrick for a look.

"It's from him all right. His handwriting," Patrick said. "But no return address, just like always."

"He sent her card early this time. That must be a first," Sadie said and returned to a sink full of dishes.

"Just put it up and let it be. It's a good thing Josie's not home from school yet. The way you two carry on." Gramma Rho moved away, too busy with matters at hand to linger over the day's mail.

"The postmark is Charleston, South Carolina." Patrick held the envelope to the light, but the paper was too heavy to see if money was inside. "That's pretty far south for him, isn't it?"

"Who's to know where he's been?" Gramma Rho knotted a scarf to the back of her head tight enough to pull her forehead smooth. "A man like that."

"Charleston?" Sadie swung him a backwards glance, her hands suspended in the water. "Is that where it's from?" Thoughtfully she twirled her hands in the water, catching soap bubbles between her fingers. "Charleston's a beautiful city. Right on the ocean."

"That's right." Gramma Rho said. "That's the place you married him, isn't it? Foolish, foolish girl." Then she seemed to catch herself, aware she was being detained. "Enough of this. Just standing in one place jumping up and down. I'm going to the garden to plant the rest of the beans. I can't imagine why you're so late with everything this year. Seems to me you should have had most everything in the ground by now."

Sadie gave Patrick a sidelong glance — one conspirer to another. There seemed little need of telling her they had lived apart; they had quickly returned to a way of life reminiscent of the years when Gramma Rho had lived with them. Sadie took a vacation from the newspaper after Gramma Rho arrived, and the two women picked up from the precise point when last they'd been together. They took up planting in the garden where Laurie had left off; they halterbroke the spring foals and picked up on the breeding records Patrick had kept. He felt out of place with them, found no consolation with Caleb, and in evenings with Laurie, he encountered frustration of a different sort. He still hadn't mentioned his intention, stronger than ever, to find a place of his own. He had thought he'd move above the J & J, but one look at that cramped hole had changed his mind. The only practical measure, he told himself, was to locate a job first and then a place to live. After that maybe he and Laurie . . .

"I'll be along in a minute," Sadie said to Gramma Rho at the door.

Patrick tapped the envelope against his palm and glanced again at the postmark. Charleston, South Carolina. "I remember him saying something about the ocean. Swimming in the ocean."

"He did a lot of that just before we were married," Sadie said thoughtfully. "It was summer — the water so warm, we lived on the beach most of the time in a tent. Just kids — vagabonds — the way he always wanted to live."

"How come Charleston? Neither of you were from there."

"That's where he wanted to go. The ocean attracted him like a magnet." Her gaze held to the scene out the double windows. "I didn't know him very long before we married."

"How come?"

"He came to Lexington to pick up a string of ponies for Gramma Rho. Robie McDaniels had Thoroughbreds he took off the tracks and sold for jumpers or polo ponies. I was just out of high school, living with Polly and Robie."

"Your folks had died by then, hadn't they?"

"Yes. That summer, your dad came down with a truck and a horse trailer to buy a few head from Robie, but the truck gave him trouble on the way. After he got there, he had to stay a month or more, first to overhaul the engine, then because one of the mares took sick."

"And when he left, you went with him."

"That's about it. I told myself — told Robie and Polly too — I was going along to take care of the horses. Especially that sick mare. But that wasn't it. I wanted a home of my own. Something of my own. And I couldn't bear his driving off without me when I knew he wouldn't come back. In the month we'd been together I thought we'd gotten pretty serious, but when he got ready to go, he didn't seem to care if I stayed or went. 'Suit yourself,' he said. He had a way about him, like he was pushing you away so you'd be sure to stay."

She shook her hands above the sink and dried them along the seam of her jeans. "After we were married, he couldn't wait to get home. To Gramma Rho's. 'I can hardly wait to see her face when you walk in,' he said, like all he wanted to do was to stand on the sidelines and watch her reaction. But if she was surprised, she never showed it. She just scooped me up like a lost chick, and when she found out I knew just about as much about horses as she did, I was the same as her own. So she had the last laugh. They were always practicing one-upmanship on each other, one trying to get the best over the other. They used that skill just often enough to keep an edge to it."

"He never cared anything about horses, did he?"

"Not that I could tell. We lived with Gramma Rho, and he took jobs working on cars, overhauling horse trailers, and then construction, metalwork — about anything that kept him on the road. I got so I could tell when he was ready to leave. He used to provoke an argument so that once he was gone, you could almost be glad of it. Sometimes I wondered if he'd married me so I could take his place with Rho and leave him free."

"What about his dad? Was it the same with him?"

"Grady? Grady Douglas? I never knew him. He died when Allan was about eight or so."

"Died? Just died?"

"Not exactly." She gave a cynical half smile. "Rho used to say there were two things the Irish knew more about than anybody else — good whiskey and blooded horses. Grady, I guess, was an expert on one, she on the other. He came home drunk one night. Nothing unusual from what she's told me, and she locked him out. He went to the barns. Maybe he was smoking. Maybe he had nothing to do with it, but the barns caught on fire. She and her brothers lost everything except for a few horses they had at other tracks and some of their foundation stock they got out of the fire. 'The screaming of those horses caught in flames,' she once told me, 'tore my insides out.' I don't think she was ever the same. Grady died in the barn. They didn't even know he was in there until it was over. In all the years after, her fury never cooled, and I suppose your father felt the heat of it."

Sadie clutched her hair to the nape of her neck and twisted a rubber band around it. "But Charleston's a lovely city. And the ocean. The ocean is like our pastures. The waves lap into shore like the grass falls under the wind. Sometimes when I've watched you on the tractor plow a furrow across an open field, the cowbirds following, swooping down for worms unearthed, it reminds me of the gulls dipping to the ocean waves."

After that Patrick thought often of his father. Working Patriot in the arena, he would look beyond to the pasture along the road and the grass, knee-high now and ready soon to be leveled by the cutting blade. As the wind worked through the grass and the sunlight set it amber, he could see, as his mother had said, that it must resemble the ocean. But then, how could he know? He recalled the way his father would come up through the water in the swimming pool in Venerie, giving his head one great toss so that his hair fanned out to spin a crystal shower. He imagined his father swimming in the ocean, letting himself be taken in the surf only to rise in one great leap beyond the waves. Thoughts of his father and of the past were somehow comforting now since he seemed disengaged from so much of what he confronted daily. For all his determination to cut his father from his life, Allan had probably always been with him, he decided, an unbidden presence. Still, he would entertain no false notions about him, nothing like the air-built illusions Josie constructed. "I don't care if he sends a birthday card or not, Patrick," she had told him, unaware that the card had already arrived. "I can feel him thinking of me. 'Josie,' he says, 'maybe I won't send a card this time. I'll buy new tires for my truck and come see you instead.'"

"That's crazy, Josie," he had told her. "He'll never come."

"Laurie, it's crazy, but Josie somehow believes he's going to show up for her birthday tomorrow. And he's not. He's already sent her card."

"What if he did? What a surprise that would be for everyone."

"For Josie's sake, maybe we wouldn't run him off. But we wouldn't set a place for him at the table either. Gramma Rho wouldn't hear of it."

"South Carolina is far away. I wouldn't think he'd come. Not after all these years."

"Yeah. I wonder if he ever married again. There was a woman. Justine. In Venerie. Pretty nice. He could have gone back for her."

Laurie lay back against his chest as they sat in the truck

340

parked in her drive. They hadn't seen much of each other, hadn't made love, which they accepted with philosophical resignation. Since they had known the best, the comfort of a home, the ease of bed and pillows, they were unwilling to belittle the memory for something less. They kissed, took the breath from one another kissing, until he would take her hands away and draw himself to the open window. What they'd done wasn't wrong, but still they suffered for it.

Now she caressed his arm as it lay beneath her breasts.

"Did Rudy tell you? They've set the date. They can get the bandstand on the tenth. August 10." She giggled and tilted her head, snagging her curls in the bristles of his beard. "Ramona went to see Doc Brownlee yesterday. She couldn't figure out why she was tired all the time. And sick."

"God. You mean . . ." He raised his shoulders, looking for her smile in the dark.

"Pregnant. Yes. Mom's going to make a maternity wedding dress. She told Mrs. Larkins she'd do it. She's had so much practice."

"Rudy. I'll bet Rudy is feeling like a king."

"He went right out and bought everything. Trains, dolls. All sorts of books."

For a time they were quiet, their gazes held trancelike by the night sky flecked with stars.

"I suppose your folks think we should make it a double wedding."

"They mentioned it."

"And you said?"

"That we weren't ready for the big step. We wanted to save up a little money. And that I might as well start college, since I've made plans and all."

He had a fleeting impulse to tell her he thought they could be together again before she left Stella. In a place of his own. But he held back. Wait, he told himself, until it's something more than words.

"The folks thought that sounded like a perfectly logical thing to do," she went on. "But . . ."

"But what?"

"I think I was making it up as I said it. Just something to say. I don't know if that's what we'll do at all. I don't know what we'll do. We sit here, talking about something that isn't anything you can talk about unless you're watching it slip away."

Freone had her kittens in Josie's closet the next morning on Josie's thirteenth birthday. Three sightless, rat-tailed babies too weak to mew, they expressed pleas in pantomime, all gaping soundless mouths and plying claws. Josie determined the father to be the Uttermelons' renegade tom since two kits were covered with a carroty down resembling the orange commando of the woods near Stonegate. The third was a calico like Freone and therefore female, Josie announced. "You don't even have to look."

Sadie and Gramma Rho were already preparing Josie's birthday dinner by the time Patrick was up for breakfast. They had moved the oak table from the kitchen to the living room where it sat in front of the bay window, spread open, waiting for leaves to be brought from the attic.

"I'll fix a breakfast sandwich," Gramma Rho said to Patrick. "You can eat on your way to the barn, and then I don't want to see you the rest of the day."

"Suits me."

"Caleb and Sandra will be here by three. I presume you'll have Laurie here by then." She stirred about the kitchen, talking, yet never raising her eyes from her quick-fingered hands.

"I'll go by for her later this afternoon."

"Now don't be late. Don't stop somewhere along the way."

"Have you got that ready yet, Gramma?"

"Because I know you young people. You don't want to get

too serious when you've got college facing you."

"I don't give much thought to college," Patrick said mildly.

"You could take a few courses at the community college in Chesterfield and stay right here at home. For a start, I mean."

"I'll take the sandwich and get out of your way."

It was a hard fried egg and ham on toast, and he wrapped a napkin around the lower half of it and ducked out the back door.

He stowed the sandwich and Gramma Rho's advice in about the same time, no more than it took him to reach the barn. He bridled Patriot and lunged to his bare back on the move, unmindful of direction. With the reins lightly fed through two fingers of his hand, he cushioned his backside into the congenial sway of the stallion, shaded his eyes for a moment, and smiled. Suddenly he was unteathered, beyond the territory of events that had held dominion. The sun was like a yellow machine manufacturing heat and light into a blinding clear fluid, so distant that no shadow appeared to fall to either side of him or the horse. Random clumps of pink pasture rose fanned out their smooth petals, and other wild flowers — haughty lupine, stately branches of Queen Anne's Lace — were scattered among the common daisies.

Patriot felt the light rein and extended his trot to reach the mares grazing and the foals stretched out full length to soak up sun. The mares gave the stallion one cool glance and dipped their muzzles into grass again.

"Trot on, Patriot. The mares aren't interested in your sexy ways."

Tugaloo had bred the mares by now; they were settled, sedate and queenly matrons.

When Patriot reached the creek, Patrick lifted the reins enough to check the stallion. At the bank, the horse tucked his head and moved light-footed down the slope. Once in the water, running strongly from March rains, he pawed a roiling spray until Patrick ducked, laughed, and gave him the heel up the opposite side. Then the two of them cut a path toward the grove of cottonwoods. Marking the breeze, snowy cottonwood seeds drifted aimlessly to meet him.

He recalled the unseasonably warm day, near his birthday in October, when he and Josie and their mother had ridden out to picnic in the grove. Lying across Black Judy's hot back, feeling the bite of flies, smelling the aroma of fried chicken his mother had left while she and Josie rode on for Caleb and Sandra, he had been lifted up by the call of the prairie falcon. But he never saw the bird — only its shadow, first distinct and disengaged, then suddenly a blur that dissolved as the bird soared upward, no longer tethered to its shadow. The recollection left him with the feeling that both past and present were doubling under him. The only key to life — past, present, even future — was the unaccountable mystery of it.

Patrick stepped to the ground from the truck seat and reached back for Laurie's hand.

"Wait," she said. "My present for Josie," and she stretched to the far side of the seat for a box with curly ribbons. "I got her combs and barrettes and different-colored ribbons for her hair. Minna just got them in."

He looked at the ribbons in Laurie's hair, a lavender of satin sheen that held curls from her face and was lost in places where her hair rose over it. Her dress was light, scattered with lavender flowers and scooped enough in front so that light caught the high fine bones of her neck and shoulders.

"You look so pretty," he said suddenly. They kissed, she sitting in the open doorway of the truck and he standing in front of her. The box she held lay between them, yet her other hand came light and warm to his upper arm. He bent and kissed the pulse he saw throbbing in her neck and caught her body scent of baby talc and lavender.

"I should think you'd know we're a-waiting on you,"

344

Gramma Rho called from the back steps. "You two come along now with a quick step. We want to eat before Josie opens presents. Caleb and Sandra are already here."

Gramma Rho shooed them on through the kitchen, steamy with food aromas, and into the living room. Sandra in extravagant pink ruffles came demurely toward him.

"Do you like me?" She tilted her chin and offered a flirting dark gaze from the corners of her wide-set eyes.

Patrick took her offered hand and turned her on toes of patent-leather shoes. "You're beautiful. Cotton candy from the carnival. Throw away your overalls."

She took his hand and wedged herself neatly between Patrick and Laurie.

"Don't tell her that," Caleb said. "I'm not about to iron all the flounces and laces they put on little girls' dresses." He had already loosened his tie and unbuttoned his top shirt button.

The expanded table had been covered with a cloth and laid with the best china. In the center a white pitcher held yellow iris picked from wild beds along the fence row and stalks of lavender lupine gathered from the pasture.

He felt singular and apart from them and the scene around him, an impersonal observer who might be reading the account in Sadie's column: "The Douglas family celebrated Josie's thirteenth birthday on Saturday. The birthday girl, dressed in blue gingham and white lace fashioned by her grandmother, sat at the head of the table covered with an Irish linen cloth, an heirloom of the Douglas family. A lovely bouquet of yellow iris had been gathered by Josie's mother. Those attending this special occasion were . . ." Yet he felt blessed by what he truly knew of them: his mother's smiling eyes seeking assurance, Josie's nervous glance as though expecting someone, Gramma Rho as upright as though little steel pins might be holding her backbone rigid, Caleb's deep emotion hidden behind his beard, Sandra's flirting warmth. And Laurie — her reservoir of energy and buoyancy.

"Now the birthday girl, our teenager, goes at the end,"

Gramma Rho began, "then Laurie and Patrick. Next Caleb and Sandra . . ."

"I'll sit by Patrick," Sandra said.

"All right, little miss, you by Patrick and then Caleb." She turned back to the kitchen, passing Sadie in the doorway carrying relish trays and salads.

They took their seats self-consciously and unfolded cloth napkins over their knees.

"Everyone join hands," Gramma Rho directed, "and I'll say grace."

Patrick caught Josie's glance through the bay window and down the road before she bowed her head. Her wish that Allan would appear was useless, he knew.

Above their bowed heads, Gramma Rho's voice lifted to the "Amen," followed by relaxed laughter as they began passing dishes and platters of food. When they finished eating, Gramma Rho cleared the table and carried in the cake with candles tossing flames. Little points of light caught in her eyes and jumped to Josie's glowing face once Gramma Rho set the cake in front of her.

"Make a wish," Gramma Rho and Sandra said together with locked hands and tight lips, as though their own efforts would aid Josie. With a quick glance down the road, Josie closed her eyes, drew her breath into her cheeks, and puffed a running circle above the candles, which winked flames and went out.

"You get your wish," Sandra shouted.

"Here, young lady, remember your manners," Caleb cautioned and patted ruffles smooth across Sandra's shoulders.

"Your presents next," Gramma Rho said, and she took the cake to the kitchen to cut it.

Beneath the table, Laurie's hand found his upper thigh and he covered her hand with his own.

Josie turned to a pyramid of gifts and Allan's card beside them. She reached for the card first, hesitated, then put it aside. She unwrapped packages, admired the gifts, and then sitting in a nest of crimped paper wrappings, she took up the

346

card.

"Charleston, South Carolina," she said without expression. "He's far away, isn't he?" She lifted her eyes to Patrick as if he alone might understand what she felt. He smiled at her and nodded for her to go ahead. It was just the usual card and a hundred-dollar bill, he wanted to tell her. Then she brightened. "Of course, we can't tell. He could be on his way."

"You got your family all around you, Josie," Gramma Rho said. "Everyone is here."

"Hey. I'm here," Sandra called out.

"I just thought . . . I've had this feeling all along."

"Go ahead, honey," Sadie said. "Open it."

Josie fitted a fingernail under the seal, drew out the card, and from its interior, the stiff new bill.

She shoved the currency aside. "Here's what he says: 'Hope all is well with you on your 13th birthday. The big one-three. You're growing up beautiful and it wouldn't surprise me if you cut your hair now that you're a teenager.'" She fluttered her hand above her brow and took a quick look down the road. "It's like he can see me. Knows my hair is short." A smile spread slowly across her face and settled in her eyes. "There's more. 'I am here near the ocean and it is a beautiful sight. It is still too cold to go swimming, but I have tested the water and found it invigorating.'" With a squint, she glanced quickly at Patrick. "What does he mean by that, Patrick? 'I have tested the water and found it invigorating.'"

Patrick shook his head, puzzled. It was an uncommon expression, unlike anything he might have expected Allan to say. He recalled other notes with equally mysterious messages. "I'm waiting for marble from Verona, Italy," Allan had written once. And now, "tested the water and found it invigorating." The simple words seemed to contain an uncanny meaning trapped within the sentence. Bemused, he said them over to himself.

"Who's to know what he means, since he doesn't know himself," Gramma Rho said.

"Now, Rho," Sadie scolded, then turned again to Josie. "Don't get your hopes up. He's not anywhere near here."

"You shouldn't say that. We don't know. Why, I feel that if we drove as far as Stella, we might find him waiting for us."

They sat dazed, momentarily taken back by Josie's innocence.

"Maybe I should go look him up," Patrick said, half in earnest. But once said, the words seemed to take shape and form a logic of their own.

They blinked, turned astonished expressions from Josie to Patrick, and fell back against their chairs. Laurie's hand left his leg.

"You can't be serious," his mother said.

"It's ridiculous," Gramma Rho said.

"Sure," Caleb said with a smile hidden behind his beard. "We'll roll out the red carpet when you turn up with him."

Patrick said nothing; he gave the idea no more than a second thought. "Why not? I can find him. I'll just drive till I find him."

"We can," Josie said and jumped up, scattering tissue paper. "We'll go together."

"No," Patrick returned thoughtfully, raking his fingertips through his beard. "No, Josie. I'll go alone."

"But I always wanted to go. Even when I lived with the Uttermelons."

"Uttermelons?" Gramma Rho said and stood to look at each of them in turn.

"You haven't thought this through, Patrick," Caleb said. "You won't get far in that old truck."

"Take the truck?" Sadie spoke up. "Leave us?"

"Yes. I'll take the truck." He pushed back from the table, gathering his thoughts, his mind leaping ahead. "And take my tools. Might have to work on it along the way."

"He's not leaving. That's final."

"Is this your idea of getting even?" Sadie yanked up and came around the table. "Because of me and Lester?"

"Who's Lester? Do I know Lester?"

"You and Lester have nothing to do with it," Patrick said mildly. "Maybe it's something I want to do for myself."

"Patrick, there's not a thing in God's world . . ."

"You won't find him," Sadie said. "By now he's moved on."

"That's possible."

"And even if you do, I don't want him here. I don't want to see him."

"I understand." Patrick stood unflinchingly under the weight of her stare.

"But I should go with you," Josie said again.

He looked around and noticed Laurie was gone. Hurriedly, he left and caught up with her as she entered the barn.

"Jesus, you believe in dropping bombshells." She gave him a lame smile.

"Honest to God, I never gave the idea a thought until just now. I knew how Josie felt, thinking sure he'd come. I kinda thought he might myself. But then I thought, what the hell? Why don't I go?"

"And it's not because of us? Running away, like that morning when you took off and left me in bed?"

"No, I don't think that has anything to do with it." Their shoulders brushed as they strolled near the stalls, empty now except for Tugaloo and Patriot. "But I want to put a little space between us. And the time we had together." He paused. She waited, aware that he had more to say. "I was going to move out. Get a place in Chesterfield so we could live together for a while before you left Stella. But the more I thought about it, the less it seemed like a good idea."

"I know. Maybe it would just box us in."

"I've got to get out. On my own. Make the break. And maybe this is one way to do it."

She put her arms around his waist, snagged her fingers in his back belt loops. "Why don't you leave tomorrow?"

"I think I will. The sooner the better."

"And the sooner you'll be back."

"Just give me a little rope, Laurie. No promises. But I'll be back before Rudy's wedding."

She loosened her hold and took a few steps back. "But what if you keep on going? And don't come back?"

"How will we know if I'll come back or not, Laurie girl, if I don't go away?"

Later that night he was stuffing shirts in a duffel when Josie came to his bedroom.

"I made something for him. While I was living with the Uttermelons. A clay pot. I was thinking about him while I turned it."

"I'll tell him that."

"I think you'll find him. Straight off."

"He won't be hard to find."

"When you look for him, go to all the places they're building skyscrapers. And when I see him in my mind, he has a beard now. You know, if I were to go with you, Patrick, I would recognize him right off."

"I'll know him. It hasn't been that long." Patrick put aside his packing and took her hands. "Josie. You won't run away to Stonegate anymore?"

"No. I'll be fine. With Gramma here. And Mama."

"When I find him, Josie, I'll call on the phone, and you can talk to him."

"Yes." Her eyes glistened with surprise. "We could do that, couldn't we?"

"You really are going, aren't you?"

Stretched out fully clothed on his bed, he had his hands

braced behind his head, listening through the open window to the hackberry branches poking at the screen.

"It's not such a big deal. I probably should have done it years ago." He looked up at Sadie as she stood with her arms locked beneath her breasts.

"It's just so useless."

"I don't see it that way."

"And what if you do find him? You'll have nothing in common. Nothing to say to each other."

"No, I don't believe that. We'll probably have lots to talk about. He'll have his own story to tell. If nothing else, I'll see how he lives, what he does. I can tell him about Josie."

She wrenched her shoulder up, lifted a heavy sigh. "It's so unfair."

"I guess fairness isn't something that gets measured out in equal portions."

"I can't drive," she hurried on. "I'll be stranded here. We won't even have a vehicle."

He brought himself up from the bed, only mildly annoyed. "I'm not going to argue about it, Sadie. You can sell a few horses and buy something cheap with an automatic transmission. You can take driving lessons from the high school."

She started toward the door, then turned back. "The horses. You were just getting the business started."

"The mares are all bred. The business can wait. Or if you want, you can sell the whole damn thing."

"I suppose you'd like that. Then you wouldn't have to come back at all. You could keep right on going, following in his footsteps."

"Yes. There's that risk."

A quiet rage mounted within her. "Like Rho always said. Faults breed through."

"No. I'm not the least like him. Or anybody else either."

She clenched her jaw. "It's like he won. In the end, he won after all."

"No, he didn't. Because I wasn't the prize."

He was up before dawn, working on the truck, packing his tools. When he came inside, the women moved quietly about. They ate breakfast together and said very little.

"I have a road map for you." His mother placed the folded map by his plate. "And Robie and Polly's telephone number in Lexington."

"Yes. I might stop there."

"About your hair. Do you want me to cut it before you leave?"

"No. I don't know that I want it cut yet."

"Just be in your way," Gramma Rho said. "Driving and blowing in your face."

"Where do you think you'll stop tonight?" Josie asked.

"I don't know. I don't really have any plans." He pushed back from the oak table and swung his duffel to his shoulder. "I want to get started before the sun gets too high."

The women followed him to the truck. Gramma Rho, packing a grocery sack, went around him when they reached the truck and opened the door to stow the sack on the floor. "There's fried chicken in the bottom. And you'd probably better stop and eat 'long about noon because it won't keep." She stood back. "Lots of fruit. A body should eat fruit while traveling. And don't forget . . ." but she seemed to lose track of what she meant to say, and she shoved her hands into the side pockets of her jeans. "Well, what's keeping you?"

"Not a thing, Gramma." He drew her to him, and she placed a dry kiss on his cheek. He held Josie, kissed his mother. She put her hands on either side of his face, and through his beard, the warmth of her skin came to him.

"You'll be all right," she said with a secure nod of her head.

"And so will you." She reached up and kissed him lightly.

He turned once to look back at them as he pulled from the drive. Gramma Rho stood resolutely between Sadie and Josie. Josie sailed her hands above her head as though waving pennants; his mother lifted her arm once and then let it fall gently to her hair that fluttered about her face in the clear morning air. Her long satin wrapper whipped in waves about her slender legs.

He thought of Laurie still asleep, and he held that vision of her.

He drove down the road and glanced toward the pasture where the mares were leading spring foals to graze in dewy grass. The foals darted ahead and circled a challenge to one another until the long shrill whinnies of the mares called them back.

He rattled across the trestle and turned the corner and thought once of looking back. He knew precisely the place to see first the barn and pastures, then the house framed within tree boughs now fat with buds. Instead, he unfolded the map. With his knee braced against the base of the steering wheel, he used both hands to spread the map across the seat and follow the line that led to Lexington and from there to Charleston. He thought he might not stop at Lexington after all, but drive on, resting some, and then on through the night until sometime in early morning, he would hear the ocean.